Praise for Ted Dekker's Novels

"Dekker delivers his signature exploration of good and evil in the context of a genuine thriller that could further enlarge his already sizable audience."

— *Publishers Weekly*

"[Showdown] strips the veneer of civilization to the darkness of the soul, revealing the motivations and intents of the heart. This is a difficult book to read and definitely not for the squeamish. It brings home the horror of sin and the depth of sacrifice in a way another book would not—could not."

— *Author's Choice Reviews*

"Calling [Showdown] unique is an understatement. Ted Dekker has successfully laced a contemporary thriller with searing spiritual principles."

— *In the Library Reviews*

"Toss away all your expectations, because *Showdown* is one of the most original, most thoughtful, and most gripping reads I've been through in ages . . . Breaking all established story patterns or plot formulas, you'll find yourself repeatedly feeling that there's no way of predicting what will happen next . . . The pacing is dead-on, the flow is tight, and the epic story is downright sneaky in how it unfolds. Dekker excels at crafting stories that are hard to put down, and *Showdown* is the hardest yet."

— *infuzemag.com*

"The prose is smooth and tight, the message on target, and the ideas daring. This is one showdown you won't want to miss."

— ERIC WILSON,
focusonfiction.net

"Showdown is a well-written and suspenseful novel that can and will give Stephen King and Dean Koontz a run for their money."

— *www.1340mag.com*

"[In *Obsessed*] an inventive plot and fast-paced action put Dekker at the top of his game."

— *Library Journal*

"[In *Obsessed*] Ted Dekker brilliantly weaves two years—1994 and 1973—and two locations—the United States and Germany—into an exhilarating thriller of passion and hope."

— *Christian Retailing*

"With the release of *White,* and the culmination of the Circle Trilogy, Dekker has placed himself at the fore of Christian fiction. His tale is absolutely riveting, and the redemptive value at the heart of the series only makes it all the more remarkable."

— MICHAEL JANKE,
CM Central

"One of the highlights of the year in religious fiction has been Ted Dekker's striking color-coded spiritual trilogy. Exciting, well written, and resonant with meaning, *Black, Red,* and now *White* have won over both critics and genre readers . . . An epic journey completed with grace."

— Editors, BARNES AND NOBLE

"Dekker is a master of suspense and even makes room for romance."

— *Library Journal*

"Full of heroic action, deep meaning, and suspense so palpable your fingers will dig grooves into the book's outer cover, *Red* magnifies the story of *Black* times ten, raising the stakes to epic proportions. But Ted Dekker's biggest ace in the hole is that he understands what so many others never realize: substance and meaning *can* go hand-in-hand with exciting, cinematic storytelling. *Red* is a thrilling, daring work of fiction that not only entertains—it inspires. Why aren't there more stories like this?"

— ROBIN PARRISH, editor,
Fuse Magazine, www.FuseMagazine.net

"*Black* has to be the read of the year! A powerful, thought-provoking, edge-of-your-seat thriller of epic proportions that offers great depth and insight into the forces around us."

— JOE GOODMAN, film producer,
Namesake Entertainment

"Ted Dekker's novels deliver big with mind-blowing, plot-twisting page turners. Fair warning—this trilogy will draw you in at a breakneck pace and never let up. Cancel all plans before you start because you won't be able to stop once you enter *Black*."

— RALPH WINTER,
Producer—*X-Men, X2: X-Men United, Planet of the Apes,*
Executive Producer—*StarTrek V: Final Frontier*

"Put simply: it's a brilliant, dangerous idea. And we need more dangerous ideas . . . Dekker's trilogy is a mythical epic, with a vast, predetermined plot and a scope of staggering proportions . . . *Black* is one of those books that will make you thankful that you know how to read. If you love a good story, and don't mind suspending a little healthy disbelief, *Black* will keep you utterly enthralled from beginning to . . . well, cliffhanger. *Red* can't get here fast enough."

— *FuseMagazine.net*

"Just when I think I have Ted Dekker figured out, he hits me with the unexpected. With teasing wit, ever-lurking surprises, and adventurous new concepts, this guy could become a real vanguard in fiction."

— FRANK PERETTI

"[With THR3E] Dekker delivers another page-turner . . . masterfully takes readers on a ride full of plot twists and turns . . . a compelling tale of cat and mouse . . . an almost perfect blend of suspense, mystery, and horror."

— *Publishers Weekly*

"Ted Dekker is clearly one of the most gripping storytellers alive today. He creates plots that keep your heart pounding and palms sweating even after you've finished his books."

— JEREMY REYNALDS,
Syndicated Columnist

"Ted Dekker is the most exciting writer I've read in a very long time. *Blink* will expand his fan base tremendously. Wonderful reading . . . powerful insights. Bravo!"

— TED BAEHR, President,
MOVIEGUIDE Magazine

"What an emotional and thrilling story within a story! Ted's approach allows you to see faith in a whole new light."

— MAC POWELL,
Third Day

"Ted Dekker paints a picture that will create a longing in each of us to be with our heavenly father."

— DEBBIE DIEDERICH, National Director,
30 Hour Famine, World Vision

"*The Martyr's Song* drives home the realities of standing for your faith in a world where it isn't always an easy decision."

— MIKE YODER,
Director of Church Programs,
World Vision

"I can think of no better way to say it than: this is Deeper Magic. High praise indeed, for those who recognize the reference. For everyone else, I'll just say: Highly Recommended."

— *Christianfictionreview.com*

"Everything a Book Could Hope to Achieve . . . a cross between Peretti and The Stand."

— *Religionexplorer.com*

SHOWDOWN

Other Books by Ted Dekker

House
(with Frank Peretti)

The Martyr's Song

Obsessed

Black

Red

White

Thr3e

Blink

Heaven's Wager

When Heaven Weeps

Thunder of Heaven

With Bill Bright:

Blessed Child

A Man Called Blessed

Nonfiction:

The Slumber of Christianity

SHOWDOWN

TED DEKKER

A Division of Thomas Nelson Publishers
Since 1798

visit us at www.westbowpress.com

Published in Nashville, Tennessee, by WestBow Press, a division of Thomas Nelson, Inc. and in association with Creative Trust, Inc., Literary Division, 2105 Elliston Place, Nashville, TN 37203.

WestBow Press books may be purchased in bulk for educational, business, fund-raising, or sales promotional use. For information, please e-mail SpecialMarkets@ThomasNelson.com.

Publisher's Note: This novel is a work of fiction. Names, characters, places, and incidents are either products of the author's imagination or used fictitiously. All characters are fictional, and any similarity to people living or dead is purely coincidental.

Library of Congress Cataloging-in-Publication Data

Dekker, Ted, 1962–
Showdown / Ted Dekker.
p. cm.
ISBN 13: 978-1-59554-005-8 (HC)
ISBN 10: 1-59554-005-9 (HC)
ISBN 13: 978-1-59554-081-2 (IE)
ISBN 10: 1-59554-081-4 (IE)
ISBN 13: 978-1-59554-222-9 (TP)
ISBN 10: 1-59554-222-1 (TP)
1. Colorado—Fiction. I. Title.
PS3554.E43S56 2006
813'.6—dc22 2005009708

Printed in the United States of America

06 07 08 09 10 RRD 5 4 3

Prologue

"HOW MANY children?" Marsuvees Black asked, examining his fingernails. Strange behavior for a man interviewing for such a lofty position.

"Thirty-seven," David said. "And they may be only thirteen or fourteen years old, but I wouldn't call them children. They are students, yes, but most of them already have the intelligence of a postgraduate. Believe me, you've never met anyone like them."

Black settled back in the tall leather chair and pressed his thumbs and fingers together to form a triangle. He sighed. The monk from the Nevada desert was a strange one, to be sure. But David Abraham, director of the monastery's project, had to admit that genius was often accompanied by eccentric behavior.

"Thirty-seven special children who could one day change humanity's understanding of the world," Black said. "I think I could pull myself from my desert solitude for such a noble task. Wouldn't you agree? God knows I've been in solitude for three years now."

"You'll have to take that up with God," David said. "With or without you, our project will one day change the world. I can guarantee you that."

"Then why do you need me? You're aware of my"—he hesitated—"that I'm not exactly your typical monk."

"Naturally. I would say you're hardly a monk at all. You've spent a few years atoning for rather gratuitous sins, and for that I think you possess a unique appreciation for our struggle with evil."

"What makes you think I've beaten my demons?"

"Have you?"

"Do we ever?"

"Yes, we do," David said.

"If any man has truly beaten his demons, I have. But the struggle isn't over. There are new battles every day. I don't know why you need a conflicted man like me."

David thought a moment. "I don't need you. But God might. I think he does."

Black raised an eyebrow. "No one knows, you say? No one at all?"

"Only the few who must."

"And the project is sponsored by Harvard University?"

"That is correct."

David had spent months narrowing his search for the right teacher to fill the vacant post. Marsuvees Black brought certain risks, but the job was his if he chose to take the vow of secrecy and sequester himself in the Colorado mountains with them for the next four years.

The monk stared at his fingernail again. Scratched at it. A soft smile crossed his face.

"I'll let you know," he said.

Chapter One

PARADISE, COLORADO

One year later
Wednesday

THE SOUND of boots crunching into gravel carried across the blacktop while the man who wore them was still a shimmering black figure approaching the sign that read *Welcome to Paradise, Colorado. Population 450.*

Cecil Marshal shifted his seat on the town's only public bench, shaded from the hot midsummer sun by the town's only drinking establishment, and measured the stranger strutting along the road's shoulder like some kind of black-caped superhero. It wasn't just the man's black broad-brimmed hat, or his dark trench coat whipped about by a warm afternoon breeze, but the way he carried himself that made Cecil think, *Jiminy Cricket, Zorro's a-coming.*

The town sat in a small valley with forested mountains that butted up against the buildings on all four sides. One road in and the same road out. The road in descended into the valley around a curve half a mile behind the stranger. The road out was a "snaker" that took to the back country, headed north.

Paradise was a typical small mountain town, the kind with one of most things and none of many things.

One convenience store/gas station/video store/grocery store. One bar/restaurant. One old theater that had closed its doors long ago. One church. One mechanic—Paul Bitters, who fixed broken tractors and cars in his barn a mile north of town. One of a few other establishments that hardly counted as establishments.

No hospital. No arcade. No real grocery store other than the convenience store—everyone shopped in Delta, twenty miles west. No police station or bowling alley or car dealer or bike shop or choice of cuisine . . .

The only thing there was more than none or one of was hairdressers. There were three hairdressers, one on Main Street and two who worked out of their homes, which didn't really count.

"Looks lost," Johnny Drake said.

Cecil turned to the blond boy beside him. Johnny slouched back, legs dangling off the bench, watching the stranger.

His mother, Sally Drake, had come to town after being abandoned by some worthless husband when Johnny was a baby, thirteen years earlier. Sally's father, Dillon Drake, had passed away, leaving her the house that she and Johnny now lived in.

She'd decided to stay in Paradise for the house, after unsuccessfully trying to sell it. The decision was mighty courageous, considering the scandal Sally suffered shortly after her arrival. The thought of it still made Cecil angry. As far as he was concerned, the town hadn't found its soul since. They were a sick lot, these Paradise folk. If he could speak, he would stand up in that monstrosity they called a church and say so.

But Cecil couldn't speak. He was a mute. Had been since his birth, eighty-one years ago.

Johnny watched the stranger and rolled a large red marble between his fingers. He was born with a crooked leg, which was one thing that had bonded him to Cecil. The Children's Hospital in Denver corrected his leg surgically, and even though he still limped now and then, he was pretty much an ordinary boy now.

No, not ordinary. Extraordinary. A bona fide genius, they would all see that soon enough. Cecil loved the boy as his own. It was probably a good thing Johnny didn't know about the mess that had followed his birth.

Cecil turned back to the stranger, who'd left the graveled shoulder and now clacked down the middle of the road in black, steel-toed cowboy boots like a freshly shoed quarter horse. Black boots, black pants, black trench coat, black hat, white shirt. A real city slicker. On foot, three miles from the nearest highway. *I'll bet he's sporting a black mustache to boot.*

Cecil dropped his eyes to the leather-bound copy of *Moby Dick* in his lap. Today he would give Johnny the book that had filled his world with wonder when he was fourteen.

He looked at the boy. Kid was growing up fast. The sweetest, biggest-hearted boy any man could ever want for a son.

Johnny suddenly gasped. He had those big light brown eyes fixed in the direction of the city slicker, and his mouth lay open as if he'd swallowed a fly.

Cecil lifted his head and followed the boy's eyes. The black-cloaked stranger strutted down Main Street's yellow dashes now, arms swinging under the folds of a calf-length duster, silver-tipped boots stabbing the air with each step. His head turned to face Cecil and Johnny.

The brief thought that Zorro might be wearing a disguise—a Halloween mask of a skull—flashed through Cecil's mind. But this was no mask. The head jutting from the stranger's white shirt was all bone. Not a lick of skin or flesh covered the bleached jaw. It smiled at them with a wide set of pearl teeth. Two eyes stared directly at Cecil, suspended in their deep bone sockets, like the eyes down at the butcher shop in Junction: too big, too round, and never blinking.

Cecil's pulse spiked. The ghostly apparition strode on, right up the middle of the street as if it owned Paradise, like a cocky gunslinger. And then the stranger veered from his course and headed directly toward them.

Cecil felt his book drop. His hands shook in his lap like the stranger's eyes, shaking in their sockets with each step, above a grinning face full of teeth. Cecil scanned the man's body, searched for the long bony fingers. There, at the end of long black sleeves, dangling limp, the stranger's hands swung to his gait.

Flesh. Strong, bronzed, fleshy hands, curving gently with a gold ring flashing in the sun. Cecil jerked his eyes back to the stranger's face and felt an ice-cold bucket of relief cascade over his head.

The face staring at him smiled gently with a full set of lips, parted slightly to reveal white teeth. A tanned nose, small and sharp but no doubt stiff with cartilage like any other nose. A thick set of eyebrows curved above the man's glinting eyes—jet-black like the color of his shoulder-length hair.

The stranger was twenty feet from them now. Cecil clamped his mouth shut and swallowed the pooled saliva. *Did I see what I just thought I saw?* He glanced down at young Johnny. The boy still gaped. Yep, he'd seen it too.

Cecil remembered the book. He bent over and scanned the dusty boards at his feet and spotted it under the bench. He reached way down so his rump raised off the bench, steadied his tipping torso with his left hand on the boardwalk, and swung his right arm under the seat. His fingers touched the book. He clasped it with bony fingers, jerked it to safety, and shoved himself up.

When his head cleared the bench, the stranger stopped in front of them. Cecil mostly saw the black pants. A zipper and two pockets. *A crotch. A polyester crotch.* He hesitated a brief moment and lifted his head.

For a moment the man just stood there, arms hanging loosely, long hair lifting from his shoulders in the breeze, black eyes staring directly into Cecil's, lips drawn tight as if to say, *Get a grip, old fool. Don't you know who I am?*

He towered, over six foot, dressed in the spotless getup with silver flashing on his boots and around his belt like one of those country-western singers on cable. Cecil tried to imagine the square chin and high cheekbones bared of flesh, stripped dry like a skull in the desert.

He couldn't.

The stranger's eyes shifted to the boy. "Hello, my friend. Mighty fine town you have here. Can you tell me where I would find the man in charge?"

Johnny's Adam's apple bobbed. But he didn't answer. The man waited, eyebrows raised like he expected a quick answer. But Johnny wasn't answering.

The man turned back to Cecil. "How about you, old man? Can you tell me who's in charge here? The mayor? Chief of police?"

"He . . . he can't speak," Johnny said.

"That right? Well, you obviously can. You may not be much to look at, but your mouth works. So speak up."

Johnny hesitated. "A . . . about what?"

The man casually slipped his right hand into the pocket of his slacks and moved his fingers as if he were playing with coins. "About fixin' things around here."

Move on, stranger. You're no good. Just move on and find some other town. He should tell the stranger that. He should stand right up and point to the edge of town and tell the man where he should take his bones.

But Cecil didn't stand up and say anything. Couldn't. Besides, his throat was still in knots, which made it difficult to breathe much less stand up and play marshal.

"Yordon?" Johnny said.

The man in black pulled his hand from his pocket and stared at it. A translucent gel of some kind smothered his fingers, a fact that seemed to distract him for a moment. His eyes shifted to Johnny.

"Yordon?" The man began to lick the gel from his hand. "And who's Yordon?" He sucked at his fingers, cleaning them. "Now you're mute, boy? Speak up."

"The father?"

The man ran his wet fingers under his nose and drew a long breath through his nostrils. "You have to love the sweet smell of truth. Care for a sniff?"

He lowered his hand and ran it under Johnny's nose. The boy jerked away, and the man swept his hand in front of Cecil's face. Smelled musty, like dirty socks. Cecil pulled back.

"What did I tell you?" the man said, grinning. "This stuff will make you see the world in a whole new way, guaranteed."

Eyes back on Johnny. "Who else?"

Johnny stared at him.

"I said *who else*? Besides the father."

Johnny glanced at the bar, thirty yards to their right. "Maybe Steve?"

"Steve. That's the owner of the bar?" The man studied Smither's Saloon.

Cecil looked at the establishment's flaking white frontage. It needed a few coats of paint, but then so did half the buildings in Paradise. A plaque hung at an odd angle behind the swinging screen door. Faded red letters spelled *Open*. A dead neon Budweiser sign hung in one of the saloon's three windows.

He looked back at the stranger, who still faced the bar.

But the man's eyes weren't looking at the saloon; they were twisted down, fixed on Cecil. Crooked smile.

He cocked his arm up to his shoulder as if it were spring-loaded and formed a prong with two fingers, like a cobra poised to strike. Slowly, he brought the hand toward Cecil and then stopped, a foot from his face.

What on earth was the man doing? What did he think—

The stranger moved his hand closer, closer. Cecil's vision blurred and he instinctively clamped his eyes shut. Hot and cold flashes ripped up and down his spine like passing freight trains. He wanted to scream. He wanted to yell for help. *Help me, boy! Can't you see what he's doing? Help me, for heaven's sake!*

But he could do nothing more than open his mouth wide and suck in air, making little gasping sounds—*hach, hach*—like a plunger working in a toilet.

A long second crawled by. Then two. Cecil stopped sucking air and jerked his eyes open.

Pink filled his vision—the fuzzy pink of two fingers hovering like a wishbone an inch from his eyes. The fingers rushed at him. Cecil didn't have the time to close his lids this time. The man's pink pointers jabbed straight into his eye sockets.

Red-hot fire exploded in his skull. He saw an image of a cowboy branding a calf's hide with a burning iron. Only this was no calf's hide. This was eyeballs. *His* eyeballs.

Cecil's mouth strained wide in a muted scream.

The fingers dug right to the back of his sockets, wiggled deep. Waves of nausea washed through Cecil's gut. He thought he was going to throw up.

Then he could see he wasn't throwing up, because he could see everything. From a vantage point ten feet above the bench he saw it all. He saw Johnny cowering in horror at the far end of the short bench. He saw the black cowboy hat almost hiding the stranger's excited black eyes.

The man planted his feet wide, grinning with glee, right arm extended toward Cecil's face, fingers plugged into his eye sockets like an electric cord as if to say, *Here, you old bat, let me juice you up a little.*

Cecil's head tilted back with those two bloody prongs quivering above his nose. His whole body shook on the bench.

Pain swept to the ends of his bones and then was gone, as if it had leaked right out his heels. *Maybe that's what happens when you die. Maybe that's why I'm floating up here.*

The stranger's arm jerked back, and Cecil saw his eyeballs tear free from their sockets, cupped in the stranger's fingers. A loud, wet sucking sound filled the afternoon air. Little Johnny threw his arms over his head.

With his left hand, the stranger reached for his own face. Jabbed at his eyes. Plucked out his own black eyeballs.

Now he held a set of round, marblelike organs in each hand, a blue pair and a black pair. From above, Cecil caught a quick glimpse of the stranger's empty sockets, black holes drilled into his skull.

They weren't bleeding.

His own, on the other hand, began to ooze thick red streams down his cheeks. The stranger chuckled once and slapped the two black-marble eyes into Cecil's sockets in one smooth motion, as if plucking and replacing eyeballs was an art long ago perfected by his kind. He flung Cecil's blue eyes into his own skull and then wiped the blood running down the old man's cheeks with his palms. The bleeding stopped, but his eyelids had flapped closed, so Cecil couldn't see what his new eyes looked like.

The man wiped his own eyes as if brushing away tears and adjusted his collar. "Now I have their eyes," he mumbled. He turned to his left and strode toward Steve Smither's saloon.

The black-clad stranger had taken three steps when he stopped and turned back to Johnny, who was still fixed in shock. For one horrifying moment Cecil believed the stranger was considering another victim.

"You ever see a trick like that, boy?"

Johnny couldn't have answered if he'd wanted to.

The stranger winked, spun on his heels, and walked toward the saloon.

The pain was back. It washed over Cecil's cranium and spread like a fire, first through his eyes and then directly down his back.

Oh, God Almighty, help me!

Cecil's world began to spin in crazy circles. From somewhere in the dark he heard a *thump* echo through his mind. *My book*, he thought. *I've dropped my book again.*

JOHNNY CRINGED in horror. He gaped at the stranger, who appeared frozen on the steps to Smither's Saloon. Everything had stopped. Everything except for his heart, which was crashing in his ears.

The saloon door slammed.

He tore himself from the bench, tripped on a rock, and sprawled to the dirt. Pain knifed into his palm. He scrambled to his feet and spun. The old man was slumped on the bench, eyes closed, mouth open.

"Cecil?" Johnny whispered. Nothing. A little louder. "Cecil!"

He stepped forward cautiously, put a hand on Cecil's knee, and shook it. Still nothing.

Johnny lifted a trembling thumb to the old man's left eye and pulled up the eyelid. Cecil's blue eyes, not the stranger's black eyes. And there was no blood.

He released the eyelid and stood back. It occurred to him that Cecil's chest wasn't moving. He leaned forward and put his ear against his shirt. No heartbeat.

He bolted, nearly toppling again, and ran for home, ignoring the pain in his leg.

CHAPTER TWO

PARADISE

Wednesday

STEVE SMITHER stood behind his cherry bar and polished a tall Budweiser glass. Paula Smither, his wife, sat at the end of the bar, next to Katie Bowers and the minister's secretary, Nancy. Behind the women, Chris Ingles and his friend Mark had herded six others into a poker game. Waylon Jennings's mournful baritone leaked out from the old jukebox. But it wasn't the poker or the beer or the music that had brought the crowd today.

It was the fact that the town's one and only mayor/marshal, Frank Marsh, had run off with his "secretary" three days ago.

Katie Bowers pulled a string of gum from her mouth, balled it into a wad, and dropped it into the ashtray. She lifted her beer and glared at Steve. Strange how a pretty valley girl like Katie, who wore her makeup loud and talked even louder, could be so unattractive.

Katie set her bottle down. "Lighten up, Paula. It's not like we haven't been here before."

"That was different," Paula shot back.

"Was it?" Katie glanced at Steve. "Be a doll and give us some peanuts."

"She's right, that was different," he said, reaching under the counter for the Planters tin. The air had thickened with the last exchange.

Katie's husband, Claude Bowers, spoke without looking at his wife. "Go easy, Katie. It's not like *nothing* happened here." The huge Swede sat at the bar, running his forefinger around the rim of his mug.

"Oh, lighten up. I'm not actually endorsing what he did. I'm just saying that it's not that big a deal, and I think most of us agree. Last I heard, 50 percent of marriages in this country end in divorce. So that's the world we live in. We might as well get used to it." She took another sip of her beer and dipped her hand into the peanut bowl.

Steve caught his wife's eyes and winked. She might not be as slender as Katie, or have her magazine looks, but to him Paula was the prettier woman by far. They met in high school, two immigrants trying to make their way in a country insensitive to both of them. The Colorado mountains proved to be the perfect refuge for their wild romance.

"Frank didn't do anything right by Cynthia," Steve said.

That silenced them for a moment.

"Well, as far as I'm concerned, it takes two," Katie said. "I doubt Cynthia's totally innocent in all this. What goes around, comes around."

Paula stared Katie down. "How can you say that? Cynthia's only crime is that she's twenty years older than that bimbo Frank ran off with. And what about little Bobby? He's seven, for heaven's sake! What did he do to deserve this?"

"What did Johnny Drake do to deserve the scandal his mother caused?"

Steve glanced at Nancy and rolled his eyes. "What's Stanley saying about this?"

"Yeah," Katie said with a twinkle in her eye. "What's good old Stanley say about all this?"

Nancy shrugged, making her heavyset body jiggle. "Not much. Life can be rough."

Steve could have told them that much. It was a stupid question, all things considered.

"All I'm saying is we shouldn't get our panties in a wad as if this thing's the black plague sent by God to punish our little village," Katie said.

Chris and Mark both broke into a chuckle.

Steve walked over to Paula and kissed her on the forehead. "It'll be okay," he said softly. Their eyes met and Paula softened. She always defended victims and underdogs, regardless of the cause.

The screen door creaked open and then slammed shut.

Steve turned, grateful for the interruption. A stranger stood at the door, eyeing the room.

"Afternoon," Steve said.

The stranger was dressed in a crisp black getup that looked like it had come off a Macy's rack only this morning. Clean-cut. A bit like Johnny Cash. Waylon Jennings ended his song on a sad note, and the jukebox hissed silently.

The man removed his hat and shed his coat. What was he doing wearing a coat in the middle of summer anyway? And a black coat at that.

The man threw his coat over a chair and stepped up to the bar. Strong, sharp, tanned face. "You wouldn't happen to have a drink in this place, would you?"

"Last time I checked," Steve said with a grin.

The stranger slid onto a stool two down from Claude and smiled warmly. "Good. Soda water will be fine."

Steve dug a bottle from the ice chest, popped its cap under the bar, and slid it to the man. "One dollar," he said.

The others stared at the stranger, and although the poker game continued, Steve doubted the players were as fixed on their cards as a moment ago. It wasn't every day that a character like this walked into town.

A pool ball clicked across the room. The stranger tossed a silver dollar onto the counter. "So. This is Paradise." He shoved a hand toward Steve. "Name's Black," he said. "Marsuvees Black. You can call me Preacher if you want."

Steve took the hand. A preacher, huh? Figured. A preacher named Black dressed like an urban cowboy. A cowboy with blue eyes rimmed in red as if they hadn't slept in a while.

"Smither. Steve Smither. So where you headed, Preacher?"

The preacher took a sip of the water and followed it with a satisfied *aaahh.*

"Well, I'm headed here, Steve. Right here to Paradise, Colorado." He set the bottle on the bar. "Funny thing happened to me this afternoon."

Black looked at Paula and Katie for a moment and then shifted his gaze to the poker players, who ignored the cards for the moment and returned his stare.

"I was coasting down the highway with my window rolled down, enjoying the mountain air, thinking how blessed I was to have a life filled with hope and grace when, *pow*, the engine bangs in front of me and the front wheels lock up solid. By the time I get Mr. Buick over to the shoulder, she's smokin' like hell's gateway. Motor was gone."

The preacher took another swig from the bottle of soda and swallowed hard. The room listened. No one bothered to restart the jukebox.

"Soon as I climbed out, I knew it was God," Black said.

Steve felt a burning in his ear at the word. Not that there was anything unusual about the word *God* in Paradise. Practically the whole town packed the Episcopal church every Sunday. But the way the theatrical man *said* the word sent waves of heat through Steve's ears. Formal and hollow, like it came from a deep drum. *Gauuwwdd.*

"God?" Steve said.

The preacher nodded. "God. God was saying something. And the second I saw the sign that my '78 Buick had nearly run over, I knew what he was saying."

Black lifted the bottle to his lips again. Steve glanced at Claude and smiled one of those can-you-believe-this-guy smiles. "And what was that?"

"The sign said, *Paradise 2 Miles*. And then the voice popped in my head. *Go 2 Paradise*, it said." Black drew a two in the air as he spoke. "Bring grace and hope to the lost town of Paradise."

Steve picked up another glass and rubbed it with the towel at his waist. Grace and hope. Paradise had enough religion for a town twenty times its size. The church already dominated the community's social life.

The man named Marsuvees Black drilled Steve with a blue stare. "But there was more," he said.

Steve felt his gut tighten at the look and stopped rubbing the glass.

"God said he'd give us a sign." Black reached over to the peanut bowl without removing his eyes from Steve and brought a nut to his lips.

"A sign?"

"A sign. A wart. A man with a wart. Said there's something ugly hidden under this town's skin. Said I was to bring grace and hope with a capital *G* and a capital *H*."

Steve looked at the others. They were no longer smiling, which was odd, because he figured Chris at least would be snickering. But there was something in Black's voice. Something like Freon, chilling to the bone. Paula and Katie sat wide-eyed now. Claude fidgeted. By the pool table, Case Donner leaned on his stick and stared at Chris.

Black looked at the poker table. "Any of you have a wart?"

Mark smiled and uttered a nervous chuckle. He shifted his gaze to Chris, wooden next to him.

"No?" The preacher popped another peanut into his mouth and crunched down. "None of you has a wart over there?"

Still no response. Steve felt his heart pick up its pace.

"How about you there?" Marsuvees asked, nodding at Chris. "You sure you don't have a wart behind your right ear?"

Chris opened his mouth slowly, and Steve believed that the man had a wart precisely where the stranger suggested. He turned back to Black, who continued chewing on a peanut.

"No? Well, I know it's there. A redhead with a wart. That would be the sign. Now, if you're not a redhead with a wart, I'll eat my hat and walk right out of here."

Chris sat dumbfounded.

"This is your day," Black said. "Because there's always two sides to a sign. My side and your side. For me to know that God did indeed bring me to Paradise, and for you to know that I was sent." The man stood from his stool and strolled toward Chris.

"Do you mind if I touch it?" Black asked softly.

"Touch it?" Chris stammered.

"Yes, touch it. Do you mind if I touch the wart behind your ear?"

Chris swung his stricken eyes to Steve, but Steve felt just as much surprise. For a while they held their places, frozen in the scene, totally unprepared for this surreal script. All except the preacher. He seemed to know how this play would end.

"It's okay." He placed a gentle hand on Chris's right shoulder and brushed imaginary dandruff from the blue mechanic's shirt that read *Chris* over the left pocket. "I can help you. A sign, remember?" And then he reached for Chris's ear like a magician doing a disappearing coin trick. His fingers brushed the side of Chris's skull, just behind his right ear. Black turned around, walked back to his stool, sat, and popped another peanut into his mouth.

"Now we will see what God meant when he said bring grace and hope to Paradise," Black said. "You ready, Chris?"

The stranger faced the redhead. "Feel your head there, son." Chris made no move.

"Go ahead, feel the wart."

Now Chris raised a hand to his cheek and then let his fingers creep up behind his right ear, keeping his eyes on the preacher. He reached his ear. Felt behind.

His fingers froze.

"It's . . ."

Silence.

"It's what?" Steve asked.

"It's . . . it's gone."

"What do you mean, it's gone?" Steve said.

"I swear. I had a wart here just like he said, and now it's gone!" Chris stared at the preacher with wide eyes.

Steve spun to the preacher, who was now grinning, big pearlies gleaming white. His front teeth gripped a single nut.

The glass in Steve's hand trembled. The brown knob between Black's teeth looked somewhat like a peanut, but he knew it couldn't be a peanut because peanuts did not bleed. And this thing was bleeding a thin trail of red down Black's lower teeth while the preacher sat there with his lips peeled back and his eyes wide, proudly displaying his catch.

To a person they all gaped at the man, slack-jawed.

Then, like a gulping fish, Black sucked the wart into his mouth, crunched twice deliberately, and swallowed hard.

He slowly surveyed the patrons, his eyes sparkling blue. *Face the music,* they were saying. *This is how you do grace and hope. You got a problem with that? Well, suck it up. I'm the real thing, honey.*

And he was, wasn't he? He had to be.

"Am I getting through?" Black scanned the crowd.

"God have mercy," Katie Bowers muttered.

"*God* is right, my sweetness. The rest we'll see about. Now that I have your attention, I'm going to make a demand. With this kind of power comes great responsibility—I'm sure you understand. My responsibility is to make sure that each and every one of you, those here and those not here, attend tonight's meeting."

What meeting?

"Seven o'clock sharp, in the church," Black said. "No excuses, no exceptions."

He snatched his hand up by his shoulder as if to keep everyone seated. He cocked his head to one side, faced the street outside.

"Another sign," he said, listening to the silence. "An old man. A deaf mute. Wasn't going to come to the meeting tonight. Thought I was too pushy."

Black lowered his hand slowly and faced them. "Seems as though he's dead now. Had a heart attack as I spoke."

Nancy gasped.

"You sure about that?" Steve asked. He was surprised he even asked the question, as if this man had the power to heal *and* kill. What kind of spiritual power was that? A moment ago, he thought Black might be the real deal, but this talk about Cecil cast a shadow over that possibility.

Black ignored his question. "This is serious business, my friends. I suggest you get back to your homes and wherever it is you waste away your lives and think hard and long about coming out tonight."

Tricks, tricks. He's manipulating us with tricks. The monotony of Paradise has been interrupted by a traveling trickster.

Black turned and drilled Steve with a stare. "You going to check outside, Steve, or are you going to just sit there thinking I'm nothing but a bag of tricks?"

Steve blinked.

Claude was up already, heading for the door. He shoved it open and stared outside.

"Steve . . ."

The big Swede stood gaping at the street. He faced them. "You'd better have a look. Something's wrong with Cecil."

Chapter Three

THE MONASTERY

Wednesday

DEEP IN a monastery hidden in the mountain canyons not so far from Paradise, Colorado, an orphaned boy named Billy hurried to class, letting his gaze wander over the bas-relief pictographs inscribed in the rough-hewn stone around him. The pictures peered from their graven settings with fixed eyes. He could rarely look directly at the pictographs without it raising gooseflesh, and he wasn't sure why. Now proved no exception.

He pushed a heavy door open and squinted in the sunlight that filled the library. The monastery was laid out like an old wagon wheel, cut in half and buried into a wedge-shaped gap in the cliff so that its spokes ran into the mountain. At the center lay the one room that had a direct view of the sky through the top of the canyon—the hub of this half wheel, though it wasn't quite symmetrical.

A large, reinforced glass canopy bridged the opening—one of the only truly modern things about this otherwise ancient monastery. Sunlight poured into the expansive atrium. The library's wood floors encircled a large lawn where three oak trees and a myriad of shrubs grew. A welcome half-acre of escape from the Gothic halls.

Billy ran through the empty library and shuffled down a stone hallway leading to one of the monastery's many classrooms. He was late for writing class. In fact, he might have missed it. Not that it really mattered. He'd made the rest of his classes this week—what was one small writing class out of twenty-one subjects? There was mathematics, there was history, there was theology, there was geography, there was a whole line of other disciplines, and

Billy excelled in all of them, including writing. One missed class, although highly unusual, wouldn't mar his record.

He ran a hand through loose red curls and stopped to catch his breath before a door near the end of the hall. The soft whisper of voices floated through the oak door. And then a deep one, above the others.

Raul?

Yes, there it was again. Raul, the head overseer, was teaching this evening. A warm flutter ran through Billy's gut. Then again, any of the twelve overseers would have triggered the same response.

His hand trembled slightly as he reached for the door. He could handle this. He would just pull himself together and handle this like he'd handled everything else.

He twisted the knob and stepped into the room.

Raul stood at one end of the room next to a bubbling stone fountain. The other students—thirty-six in all if they were all here—sat at desks in two large semicircles with their backs to Billy, facing the tall, white-bloused overseer. A few glanced Billy's way, but most seemed intent on whatever nugget of truth the teacher had just tossed out.

Raul eyed him. *You're late.* Most overseers had to restrain their pleasure with the students, easy as it was to pound their backs with accolades or lift them from their feet in big bear hugs. But Raul's idea of a compliment was a slight nod.

Billy took a seat behind the others.

"Peace, my dear students, is the gateway to harmony," Raul said, his eyes still on Billy. "It is also the gateway to destruction. War and peace. Darcy, remind us of our first rule in writing."

"Write an extraordinary story that will leave your reader gasping," the pretty brunette said, taking liberty in paraphrasing the rules as they were all encouraged to do.

The four rules of writing were as familiar to the students as milk was to a baby.

1. Write to discover.
2. There is no greater discovery than love.

3. All love comes from the Creator.
4. Write what you will.

The rules reflected the students' purpose in their studies, certainly, but even more so in their lives as a whole. They were often encouraged to substitute the word *live* for the word *write.* Live to discover, as long as discovery leads to a love that comes from the Creator. One could only write what one knew, because to write well one must know well, as the teachers said, and to know well you must live well. None of the students' other classes made much sense without writing, because in this monastery, writing was the mirror of life.

Billy glanced at Darcy and saw that she looked his way. He winked at her. *You leave me gasping.* She smiled and he turned back to Raul, hoping the teacher hadn't caught the exchange.

"That's right," Raul said. "Forget the foolish notion that there are really only a handful of stories to be told. Write new stories and new characters, embarking on grand, unique journeys with twists and turns that will leave the reader wondering."

The overseer paused. "Now does that sound like peace? Twists and turns and gasping? Not really, does it?"

Except for the water's gurgling, the room fell silent. Students who were gazing at the lifelike murals surrounding the room brought their focus back to Raul. Billy felt a small twinge of excitement at the base of his neck.

"How can there be peace unless there is first conflict?" Raul dropped the statement like a small seed into the freshly tilled ground of thirty-seven young minds.

"Hear, hear," one of the students said. "We could use a little more twisting and turning around here."

Several chuckled.

A boy to Billy's left cleared his throat, and a dozen heads turned his way. The blond-haired boy with blue eyes had long ago earned the right to be heard. At thirteen Samuel was perhaps the most accomplished student in the monastery. Besides Billy, of course. They could both discuss most subjects with any teacher on any day and do it well. At one time Billy would have considered Samuel his best friend. Birds of a feather flock together, as the old cliché said. Until a month ago.

"Or how can there be conflict unless there is first peace?" Samuel returned in a light, polite voice. "We've always known that peace precedes conflict, that conflict disturbs the discovery of love, which is the heart of the second rule."

Approval rumbled through the class.

"Very good, Samuel." Raul stroked his chin. "But how can you write about peace or love unless you first subject the reader to ugly conflict? Wouldn't you minimize peace by minimizing conflict?"

"Unless the reader begins with the knowledge of peace. Why should we demonstrate peace through conflict if the reader already knows peace?"

Raul nodded. "But wouldn't you want to heighten the reader's understanding of peace by drawing him into conflict?"

"Conflict can just as easily compromise peace as amplify it," Samuel said.

The two volleyed as if in a tennis match. Though Raul was four times Samuel's elder, the boy was no ordinary thirteen-year-old. Like the rest of them, he had never been beyond the monastery's walls, where the world waited with all of its compromise. They'd been sequestered their whole lives, learning of virtue and love and all that threatened both. The teachers said they had developed the intellects of adults.

"Yes, but such a story can amplify peace, can't it?" Raul said. "It can make one's understanding of peace as vivid as the conflict. That is the point, isn't it?"

"Makes sense to me," Dan, a short Hungarian boy, said.

Billy smiled. He wasn't surprised that Raul's argument made sense to many of the students, whose questions had grown increasingly bold this year thanks to the teachings of Marsuvees Black. It was difficult to tell exactly where Raul stood on the issue, however, because the overseers often taught with questions. He was either secretly laughing or sweating bullets, depending on who he really was under that Socratic mask of his.

"Would you need to place your hand in a fire to understand a cool breeze?" Samuel asked.

"No, but you might appreciate a cool breeze much more after standing in the fire for a day. What is a cool breeze unless there is also heat?"

"And why not avoid the heat altogether? Move to a milder climate, say. Or stay out of the sun. There's no use in exposing yourself to a lot of hot air when you already have the cool truth."

Raul smiled as laughter erupted around the room. He dipped his head in respect. "Yes, of course, Samuel. Well said. Well said, indeed. And I think on that note we will end our session."

The students began to rise and chatter about the discussion.

Billy snatched up his writing book.

"Billy." Raul motioned for him to wait.

As the last student filed out, Raul donned a long brown cloak with a hood. He lifted the hood to cover his head.

"Having interests outside of class gives you no excuse for being late."

He knew? No, not necessarily. The interests Raul spoke of could be an innocent reference to almost anything. Unless Raul was the masked man from the dungeons. Billy couldn't tell by the voice alone—not distorted as it was by the mask down below.

"I'm sorry, sir."

The teacher acknowledged the apology with a nod. But his eyes pierced Billy's conscience.

Billy slipped from the room, shivering. Raul's look had seemed too knowing, as if he meant to say, "I know you've been below, boy. I know that you're going there now. The dungeons will kill you."

Maybe I want to die, Raul. Maybe I just want to die.

THE ROUTE to the dungeons took Billy back past the library into a dark hall lit only by the flaming torch that he carried. He'd been down the hall a hundred times, but he'd entered the staircase only once, not twelve hours ago.

The memory was fresh enough to send a chill through his bones as he approached the forbidden door. He couldn't possibly resist it—not after his first exploration last night. The dungeon was dark and it was evil, but it was also wonderful, something he'd never dreamed of before, much less experienced.

His cryptic and overcautious journey from the classroom to this remote place had taken him at least thirty minutes. No one had seen him, he was sure of it.

Billy looked up and down the hall one last time, twisted the door's corroded handle, and pulled. The hinges squealed in protest. He slipped in, eased the heavy door shut, and stood breathless on the stone landing.

Before him, a winding stone stairway descended into shadows that moved in the torchlight. Billy walked to the edge of the landing, paused to still his heart, and stepped down. One step at a time.

A single question echoed through his skull. Was the monk here?

Billy assumed the masked man was a monk, having narrowed his identity down to three possibilities. If he was right, this person who'd lured him here earlier was either Raul, the head overseer whose class he left not half an hour ago, or the director himself, David Abraham.

Both were the right height. Both had low bass voices. Both spoke with the same accent and used similar verbiage.

Whomever it was, Billy took comfort in knowing that he wasn't the instigator of this dark sin. And he had no illusion that what he was doing was anything less than evil. Thirteen years under the tutelage of a dozen kind and faithful monks had made their intended impression. He did indeed know the difference between good and evil, love and hate, obedience and sin. And this was an irresistibly dark sin.

But he also now knew that he'd been created for this sin. He'd been born into evil, and now evil insisted that he understand it. For thirteen years the monks did their best to shield him from the truth of his nature, but his God-given desire to explore had won the battle.

Never mind that his decision might cost him the war.

The last thought surprised him. He was in a war between good and evil, and what lay ahead was evil, wasn't it? Yes, it had to be. And yet, if Marsuvees Black was right, he was destined to explore it.

Billy descended slowly, aware now of the flame's faint crackle. He eased off the last stair and stepped into the lower level's ten-by-twelve vestibule.

The black door that led into the dungeons was open! He was sure he'd closed—

"Hello, Billy."

He spun with a whoosh of flame. A tall hooded man emerged from the corner shadows, face obscured by the shiny black mask.

The room smelled mossy and wet. Billy felt an urge to run back up the stairs and slam the door shut on whoever hid in the brown cloak. But he couldn't. The tunnels on the other side of the black door called.

Billy swallowed. "Are you Raul?"

"Who I am is of no concern to you. What I offer you, on the other hand, is. I take it you went in last night?"

Billy didn't answer.

"How far did you get?"

"Just inside the door."

"You didn't enter the tunnels?"

"No."

Billy couldn't see the man's eyes, couldn't make any judgment about his emotions. He didn't know what frightened him more, the tunnels or the man.

"I see you found the desk."

It was the only piece of furniture outside the six tunnel entrances. How the man knew he'd spent some time at the desk was beyond him.

"Yes."

Billy saw the extinguished lamp hanging from the sconce beside the masked man. He must have entered through the tunnels, using that torch. But how did he know Billy would be here at this time?

"Today you'll go into the tunnels?"

"I don't know."

"You must. If you weren't meant to enter these tunnels, they wouldn't be available for you, now would they?"

The musty smell seemed to enter Billy's head, prompting him to agree. The tunnels were like a drug, and his desire to enter them had kept him awake all night. He'd fought the urge to come down here since the first time he found the note in his locker urging him to do so, nearly three months ago.

The dungeons contained discoveries wildly beyond any child's imagination, the note said. And the children had been brought to the monastery with those discoveries in mind. It was only a matter of time before each had an opportunity to enter and experience.

Billy turned toward the black doors. "How many tunnels are there?"

"Too many to count."

"How deep do they go?"

No response. Billy faced him. "Why do you want me to go in? And why won't you show yourself to me?"

"I won't show myself to you because this is a secret matter. I chose you from among the other students; you didn't choose me. Let's keep it that way. And I want you to go in because I want you to discover the kind of power you were made for. As I've said, it's why you were brought here in the first place. The only question is whether you have what it takes to fulfill your purpose."

The odor from the open door grew stronger. Billy wasn't sure what power the monk meant, but he'd felt enough last night to make his skin tingle with excitement. For the first time in his life, he had felt himself—truly himself. Could that be evil?

Billy stepped toward the door and peered in. Nothing had changed. Same damp cobblestones, same tall arching walls, same small desk off to the right.

Same six tunnels, gaping black beyond.

"Go deeper, Billy. And remember what I told you about Marsuvees Black."

Marsuvees Black? And what was that?

The tunnels seemed to suck him toward their yawning mouths with a magnetic force.

Oh yes. He remembered what the man had told him about Marsuvees Black. That the teacher was closer to truth than any of the others. That Billy must consider Black's teaching on exploring the furthest reaches of good and evil.

Billy took one last look at the cloaked man and then stepped into the forbidden dungeon. The door closed with a *thunk* behind him.

ALMOST IMMEDIATELY the musty odor went to work on his mind, dimming or accentuating or what, he didn't know, but time seemed to stall. It was a lovely feeling.

After an indiscernible amount of hazy deliberation, Billy decided that of the six primary tunnels he should enter the tunnel to his far right first, maybe because he was right-handed. Or maybe because the torch flamed in his right hand, dispelling more shadows there. He wasn't even sure why it mattered. He only knew that he had to enter one of these tunnels, and he had to do it now, before his chest burst.

Billy approached the tunnel slowly, torch arm extended. The flame's light lapped at the wall's moss-covered stones. Moisture seeped through the rock and dripped unevenly on the cobblestones, sending echoes down the black hall. He swallowed, set his right foot through the entry, and glanced back at the small desk where he'd stopped last night.

Don't be a weasel, Billy.

Billy entered the forbidden tunnel. He crept forward, one short step at a time, scanning the walls with peeled eyes. A cool draft kissed his cheeks. How deep was this thing? *Go deeper, Billy.*

He'd taken about ten steps when he first saw the pink pipe running along the wall to his right. It was roughly four inches in diameter, and it ran for ten feet before tapering to a head.

The pipe moved. Billy yelped and sprang back, striking his elbow on the wall. His cry echoed down the tunnel. The pipe bunched slowly, like an accordion, then stretched out and slid forward, and then paused.

Rubbing his elbow, Billy glanced back and saw not moss but another worm, resting on the opposite wall.

He leapt to safety and waved his light in an arch. No fewer than a dozen worms inched along the tunnel's walls and ceiling, each trailing a thick band of milky mucus. It smelled like old damp socks.

For several long minutes he remained rooted to the floor, quaking, gripping the torch with both hands. But the worms didn't threaten him, and his courage returned.

The gargantuan worms expanded and contracted silently past him, seemingly on a mission to nowhere. Like the worms of hell in the gospel according to Mark. *Worms that do not die. Those worms would grow to this size,* he thought. But they seemed harmless enough.

He walked deeper. Then even deeper. Water dripped incessantly, and the worms slid along moist walls made slimy by their mucus. Beyond thirty feet, the tunnel faded into blackness. Behind him, the same now.

How deep could this tunnel really go? A hundred yards? Five hundred yards? A mile?

Had it been constructed by human hands? It seemed more likely to him that this forbidden tunnel hidden below the monastery where they'd all been raised to love virtue was nothing less than a shaft into the heart of darkness itself.

And he was the lone warrior sent out to defeat that darkness.

But that was rubbish. Even through the fog that clouded his mind, he knew that much. Or at least suspected it.

Billy stopped and breathed deep. The intoxicating smell filled his mind with flowers, so to speak. It squeezed his heart with warmth. He looked at a large worm on his right, slithering through the translucent mucus. It struck him with sudden clarity that the odor was coming from the worms, not the tunnel itself.

A smattering of gel plopped to the ground two feet in front of his shoes. Seemed harmless. He bent down, touched it with his forefinger. Like thick oil or thin Vaseline. He brought it to his nose. His sense of well-being blossomed. Odd.

Billy wiped the stuff on one of the few dry stones at his feet and resumed his push, deeper.

He walked for a short time in numb contentedness until a large iron gate broke the wall on his right. What was this?

He shifted the torch into his left hand and approached it. The gate was made of iron bars, long ago rusted and covered in moss. By his torch's light he could make out a dusty earth floor and the faint outline of furniture beyond.

Billy raised a hand to the iron gate. A sudden scurrying startled him and he withdrew his hand. An obscenely large rat ran from the room, through Billy's spread legs, and down the hall, where it disappeared.

Billy pushed against the bars. The gate opened with a screech. *That was easy. Easy peasy.* He stepped forward on weak legs.

His torch flooded the room with yellow light, revealing three walls filled with antique hangings. Paintings that looked European and old, mostly portraits of historical figures he didn't recognize. Candleholders made of corroded metals and some woods. Masks.

More masks than he could count at the moment. The kind he envisioned at a masquerade ball in Venice, though he'd only seen pictures.

Weapons were mounted on one of the walls. Chains with nasty spiked balls, large pointed mallets, double-edged swords, helmets with slits for eyes.

Billy approached the wall and ran his hand along several of the weapons. Why such simple displays of antiquity pleased him as much as they did, he couldn't guess. Maybe it was the setting. The sludge. But every surface his finger touched seemed to be magical. Surely forces hid deep in every angle, every form, every shape, every color in this room.

Or, at the least, in his imagination, which was being pried wide open.

In one corner stood a skeleton, one of those he'd seen in museum picture books. Beside the skeleton was an open wardrobe filled with costumes, presumably to go with the masks. Long black trench coats and flashy silver belts and broad-brimmed hats. Boots.

Billy looked at the wall of masks again. He was sure the monk had been here.

After some time, Billy left the room and headed deeper.

Another room dawned on his right, this one empty except for some large rusted chests and shelves filled with small bottles. The milky contents of some bottles looked like the worm sludge but could just as easily be dirty water. Fascinating, but there was more, he could feel it.

He walked on. He couldn't walk forever, naturally. He had to find a place to rest. Not that his feet were tired, but his mind was overloaded and groggy with satisfaction.

A third room loomed on his right. Once again he pulled the gate open, at ease now with the squeal it made.

The scene illuminated by the wavering torch brought a warm flutter to his belly. On his right, a bookshelf rose to the stone cavern's ceiling, stacked with scores of books. Directly ahead, two matching chairs flanked a large, dusty Queen Anne sofa. A large boar head glared from the wall above the sofa, its long, dirty tusks jutting from an angry snarl. A wagon-wheel chandelier hovered above an antique desk on his left.

He'd found a study, carved here in the subterranean corridors.

Billy walked to the bookshelf and lifted the torch to reveal the titles. A thin film of dust covered the books, and he ran his finger down one of the spines. *Antonio's Ball.* He pulled the volume out and flipped it open. Old English.

"Huh."

He smiled and blew along the spines. Dust puffed into the air. They were all old titles he'd never heard of before. Except one: *Moby Dick* by Melville. He backed to the center of the room and turned in a circle. Fascinating. Even more than the room of art and theater, this study seemed to glow with mystery and magic.

Why was this place forbidden? Because evil resided here? According to whom? It seemed to him that the director himself would encourage the students to explore these magical halls. What harm was there in a little milky worm sludge?

It occurred to Billy then, standing in the middle of the small study below the monastery's foundation, that he had to bring someone else down here.

Billy turned to the desk and approached its tall, wooden chair. Several dust-covered books lay on one side, similar to the book he found last night on the desk outside the tunnels. That one was blank. Probably journals. The quill and inkwell looked surprisingly fresh.

He set his torch in an iron sconce and sat on the sofa.

This was a place of mold and moss and dripping water and massive worms. It was a heaven of mystery and books and art and . . . well, he couldn't describe it exactly, but he could feel it.

Billy laid his head back and smiled. He could sit here in dumb pleasure for the rest of his life.

ANDREW JACKMAN hurried down the dim hall, panting from the climb up through the monastery's innumerable stairs. Flames licked at the rock walls on both sides, one torch every twenty feet. Parts of the monastery were powered by electricity, but they wasted their precious light in none of the halls. An electric light bulb was far less expensive to keep lit than an oil torch, but that would mean upgrading the monastery, and upgrading wasn't a priority for David. Besides, it increased their risk of exposure.

David Abraham would never risk exposure. The number of people who knew of this mountain's secret could be counted on one page, and all went to great lengths to keep it that way. The fact that the large monastery was carved out of a wedge-shaped canyon no more than twenty meters wide at the top aided them in keeping its existence unnoticed, but even the best camouflage had its flaws. The school could be found, if one knew where to look.

Today the risk of their discovery had grown. No, not only of being found. Worse.

Andrew rounded a corner, hefted his robe with one hand to give his feet more room, and broke into a run.

He always knew that the project could fail, yes, but he'd given a dozen years of his life to the hope that it wouldn't. Now, the entire project teetered on the precipice of failure.

Why? Because one boy had defied them all.

He reached the tall door that led to the director's study and banged hard. "David!"

"Come."

He shoved the handle down and pushed the door in. Light streamed in from the large windows that faced the west, out of the canyon. David Abraham looked up from his large ironwood desk. A ten-by-ten-foot map of the world made of pearl and jade was built into the wall adjacent the long row of floor-to-ceiling bookcases. Leather and clothbound books only. A large crystal chandelier hung over a thick cross section cut from a redwood. Eight leather chairs surrounded it.

"We have a problem," Andrew said.

The director leaned back in his chair and tapped his hand with his pencil. "And what would that be?"

How should he say this? David might be unshakable, but Andrew had little doubt the news would send an earthquake through his bones.

"Billy's entered the dungeons."

David stared at him.

Andrew walked in. "He's down there now."

"How do you know?"

"He entered the staircase two hours ago and he hasn't emerged."

"That doesn't necessarily mean he's entered the tunnels."

"Of course he has; we both know that. We have to put a stop to it! He's not the only one who's been showing curiosity in the dark side lately. I've warned against this! I demand we put a stop to it. Immediately."

David set down his pen. "No."

He was a big man, more than six feet, and powerful. His blond hair rested on broad shoulders, which were covered by a brown hooded cloak. When he wasn't wearing billowing white shirts and black slacks, he favored the common dress of the teachers. It had been his insistence that they wear clothing befitting of a monastery, as he put it. But in Andrew's eyes he looked more like a Viking than a monk. Not that David pretended to be a monk—he was a world-renowned collector of antiquities and a professor of both psychology and history, tenured at Harvard, before he left it all for the project.

"Absolutely not, we can't interfere, you know that."

"But, sir—"

"I said no!" David stood. He glanced out the window at black storm clouds gathering in the valley near the canyon. "We knew this moment would come. Don't overreact."

"We knew? I certainly didn't know! I feared, but it was never a foregone conclusion. This wasn't part of the plan." Andrew was taken aback by the director's lack of outrage. How could the prospect of failure not ruin him?

"The storm clouds always eventually come," David said. "We always knew the children would be tested. The only question is how they will weather the storm."

"Billy's failed already, by going in. The subterranean tunnels will ruin him."

The director stared at him without speaking for a few seconds. His jawline bunched with tightened muscles. "Or give him the kind of power that you and I only dream about."

Project Showdown had been a highly controversial concept from the beginning. Its stated purpose was appealing enough to attract some of the world's best-educated and pious men of faith, but if the less discerning public knew what was happening here in this mountain, they might cry foul. Even David's decision, however reluctantly made, to exclude female teachers and thereby any maternal influence in the monastery would come under fire. But in David's mind, single-mindedness of the male teachers was paramount. It was a monastery after all, not a college. Andrew agreed.

The proposal that Dr. Abraham sent out to a select group of clergy was simple: Harvard University was conducting a closely guarded and somewhat speculative examination of faith and human nature. The study sought to test the limits of mankind's capacity to affect nature through faith. In simple terms, Project Showdown meant to discover the extent to which a man could indeed move mountains (metaphorically or materially) through faith. A showdown of faith and natural laws, so to speak.

Put another way, the experiment was nothing less than an attempt to test the speculation that a noble savage—a child unspoiled by the rampant effects of evil in society, struggling only with the evil within themselves—might be taught skills that the rest of humanity could not learn. Certainly spiritual skills, perhaps even physical skills. If a person had no reason to doubt, and as such possessed unadulterated faith, they surely would be able to wield the power of their faith to humankind's advantage.

There was one problem, of course. Noble savages did not roam the streets of America or any other country in droves. So David Abraham intended to rear the noble savages from birth.

He took possession of this ancient Jesuit monastery hidden deep in the Colorado mountains and spent millions of dollars transforming it into an ideal setting for his study. He then selected thirty-seven orphans, most from disadvantaged parts of Europe, and arranged for them to be brought to the monastery, where they would be raised in community under specific guidelines. A lone child would not do because the children would be required to enter society one day, a prospect that could render them useless unless they had grown up in a functioning, if different, society of their own.

Perhaps the most important element in the study were the teachers. Twelve monks and priests had each agreed to a four-year commitment, but most remained after they were free to go home. The money paid to their families and various charities only partially justified their commitments. Their desire to see the effects of a noble savage's faith was motivation enough for most of them.

For nearly twelve years they carefully taught each child in the ways of truth, virtue, and faith, and they meticulously recorded every move of every child. Other than morning prayers, conducted before breakfast, the faith was stripped of liturgy and focused on simple teachings from both Old and New Testaments. Religious, doctrinal jargon in particular had been abandoned.

Naturally, they faced many challenges—arguments, jealousy, hurt feelings of one kind or another. But without the smothering influence of a world swimming in faithlessness, the children had matured remarkably well. There had been no overt acts of rebellion.

Until now.

Andrew believed David had always kept secrets. He walked with the air of a man plagued by more than the eyes could see. His understated reaction to the news that Billy had broken a cardinal rule made Andrew wonder if it really was news to the director at all. And now David claimed that good could come of this fall from grace. *A power we only dream of.*

David averted his eyes. "We can't rescue him, Andrew. We've poured our lives into him and we've taught him the way of faith and virtue, but he must choose."

"Then the end may be upon us."

David walked to a large bookcase lined with hundreds of clothbound volumes. Two masks rested on one of the shelves, one black and one white, signifying the basic struggle between good and evil faced by every man and woman and child who lived. The director's eyes lingered on the black mask before returning to Andrew. His eyes revealed deep emotion, whether fear or concern or resolve, Andrew couldn't tell.

"It's the power of the children's choice that we're after, isn't it?" David said. "The power that resides deep in those spirits is staggering. But only when it's tested will we see that power."

"They've been tested, a thousand times."

"Tested? Not really. Not the way they will be now."

Andrew paced, hands on hips. David made sense, but not enough to satisfy him. The tunnels had always been a mystery to the teachers, but from what Andrew knew, they were filled with evil. Raw evil. David repeatedly stated that the tunnels would dramatically alter the life of anyone who entered. The dungeons were off-limits to all.

Andrew faced David. "What precisely will Billy face down there? I certainly have the right to know that much."

David studied him, and for a moment Andrew thought he would break. "You'll know soon enough. Know this, the tunnels will open the mind. The heart." He tapped his chest. "The will. This is where the battle resides, and this is where true power waits."

His vague answers were maddening.

"It's rather strange that this occurs a week after the departure of Marsuvees Black."

No response.

The monk from the deserts of Nevada claimed to have lived there in isolation for three years. David preferred clergy that had lived in solitude, he said. They had the character required for this confining assignment.

But Marsuvees Black didn't strike Andrew as a monk who'd spent three years alone. He seemed more like a one-man Vegas show who had finished his penance in the desert and was reclaiming the glory of his previous life. After nine months, he began to act strangely and was given to outbursts and wild discourses on relativism and man's free will. When David reined him in, Marsuvees withdrew almost completely. Then, without warning, he left the monastery.

"Not that I'm accusing him, mind you. I would expect to see him twisting the ear of some poor parish somewhere, not plotting to affect Billy's good sense. But maybe his departure has undermined Billy's confidence in us. Marsuvees was rather outspoken about free will and grace. For all we know, he told Billy to go down there."

The monk's unscheduled departure caused a stir among the staff. Never had a teacher left without fulfilling his four-year commitment. Where he'd gone was of considerable concern, but the project had little contact with the outside world, and information was scarce.

The closest town was a small pit stop called Paradise, which in theory could provide a link to society beyond the electronic communications that the director reserved for himself. But even when the teachers left the monastery for brief reprieves, contact with this town was strictly prohibited. It was simply too close to risk any interaction.

David didn't seem interested in pursing this tangent on Marsuvees Black.

"What if the rebellion spreads?" Andrew asked. "Others have been questioning as well. What if Billy challenges the rules in an open debate?"

No response. The debate was by design the proverbial apple that David had set before them all. If any student was able to challenge the principles that governed the monastery and win the majority support of the other students, all existing rules would be subject to that student's interpretation until another clear majority overturned him or her.

David had ultimately placed the whole project in the hands of children. The rules guided them, but they had authority to determine the rules. If this incident spiraled out of control, the whole monastery could be run by Billy. It would be a disaster.

Then again, Billy *was* the project. He and the other thirty-six students.

"We do have risk," David finally said. "But the others aren't questioning like Billy has been."

"Risk? You don't throw a child in the pit of death and refer to it as risk."

"The pit of death, as you call it, resides *in* them! They were born with it." David stretched his arm out and pointed at the monastery wall. "Do you think Billy wasn't born evil? This study isn't about protecting them from evil, but teaching them as children to overcome it in the way Christ did."

He lowered his arm, face pink from his outburst. "'Yea, though I walk through the valley of the shadow of death, I will fear no evil.' Should we avoid the valley of death? No! We walk through it and conquer it and then turn back and face it without fear. For the joy set before him, Christ endured the cross. That's what we are doing, Andrew. I've given my life to that, not to false piety!"

"You're suggesting that to be genuine conquerors they *must* face the horrors of evil?"

"I'm suggesting that the horrors of sin will only be flushed out of hiding when the power of faith confronts them."

"Should we sin so that grace may abound?" Andrew demanded. "The children already face evil in their own hearts, as you say. I don't see the value in subjecting them to the pit of hell itself. Isn't it better to deal with this in the classroom?"

For a long moment David stared at him. Then he walked to the bookshelf, withdrew a large ancient Bible, and dropped it on a reading table beside the bookcase. He tapped the cover pointedly.

"Tell me why the Gospel writers gave us so much detail about the passion of Christ? Never mind, I'll tell you: so that we wouldn't forget his suffering. How dare a child of God look away from the pain of evil—doing so undermines the grace that conquers that evil. Of course we don't sin for the sake of grace, but neither do we sweep evil under a rug and pretend it doesn't exist. The consequence of evil must be faced by the students if we have any hope of success here."

Andrew knew that the director was right, but he couldn't help throwing out one last sentimental argument. "But they are only children. What if they don't conquer? What if they are conquered?"

"These students have been capable of abstract thought since age ten, sooner in many cases. They know how to question good and evil. *Billy* has chosen the time, not we. And if they are conquered, so be it. It is out of our hands. Now is the time for more prayer, not interference. Our future is in God's hands."

"I agree, but God has given us responsibility for the students. Our hands matter too."

"And our hands are tied!" David said. "I suggest we double the morning prayer times and leave Billy's heart to God."

The finality in his tone silenced Andrew. David strode to his desk, picked up an eight-by-ten photograph of his son, Samuel, who was among those students, and looked at the smiling face.

The room stilled to the sound of their breathing. The connection between David and Samuel had always been a source of profound respect for Andrew. At times like this, he felt oddly compelled to remove his gaze and leave the father to his thoughts, but today he watched. Love, respect, remorse.

No, not remorse. There was no reason for remorse, not in the case of his son.

"Where is Samuel?" David asked, eyes still on the picture.

"I don't know, sir."

David laid the frame down and set a brisk pace toward the door. "If you see him, tell him I'm looking for him."

"Yes, sir."

David left the room.

Chapter Four

PARADISE

Wednesday afternoon

JOHNNY PEERED out the front window, down the street, where half a dozen people gathered around Cecil on the bench.

The kitchen phone clattered into the cradle behind him. "Gotta go," his mother said. "They want me to take him to Junction."

Johnny dropped the curtain.

Sally swept up some papers from the counter and grabbed a light windbreaker. "They say a bad storm is hitting Montrose, headed north. Don't worry, I'll be back by dark."

"You have to listen to me, Mom."

"Stop it, Johnny. This is crazy. You live in those comics and games, and God help me, you can't come in here and tell me you saw someone kill Cecil by poking his eyes out."

"I didn't imagine the stranger. He was real. If I didn't imagine the man, what makes you think I imagined what he did?"

Sally closed her eyes and took a breath. Eyes open. "Cecil had his own eyes, Johnny—I saw them myself. Blue eyes, not black eyes. How could the stranger poke his eyes out if Cecil still has them?"

Good point.

"If I'm right, Cecil had a heart attack." She used a gentle tone now. "I'm sorry, I shouldn't have snapped, but you have to see how crazy this sounds, right?" She plucked the ambulance keys from the hutch. "The mind can do strange things when it's under a lot of stress. I think seeing someone die of a heart attack qualifies, don't you?"

Johnny chewed on his fingernail.

"Right?"

"I guess. Can't someone else take him?"

"No. This is what I'm paid for." She smoothed his hair, then pulled his head against her shoulder. "Come on, Johnny, everything's fine. I know you were close to Cecil. It has to hurt. I'm sorry. We'll all miss him."

He didn't know what to do, so he just stood still.

"You'll be okay," she said, pulling back.

"Sure."

But he wasn't sure. Not at all. The image of the man in black jabbing Cecil in the eyes refused to budge from his mind.

"I'll call you from Junction." Sally ruffled his hair and stepped toward the door. "There's food in the refrigerator. We're out of milk, maybe you could get some from the store for me."

"Okay."

"What did I say?"

"Get milk."

She smiled. "Maybe you should do something to occupy your mind—clean your room."

"Can I come with you?"

She shook her head. "State regs. I'll be back tonight, I promise."

He nodded.

"And you might want to keep the bit about the eyes to yourself."

Sally let the screen door slam and ran across the lawn toward the crowd.

Five minutes later she pulled the red Bronco-turned-ambulance onto Main Street and headed for Junction.

Johnny sighed and retreated to his room to let his nerves settle.

But they didn't settle so quick. Not for an hour. He had to get out.

"I DON'T care what you think, Katie," Paula Smither said, staring down the California blonde with her best angry eyes. "He's a man of God, not some sex object."

"Who said anything about sex? I said he was handsome. There a sin against that?"

They lounged in Katie's Nails and Tan, and honestly Paula didn't know why she subjected herself to Katie's nonstop crap. *Forgive the thought, Reverend.*

She sat in one of the dryer chairs, which was a bit small for her, but Chrissy and Mary had already taken the yellow vinyl guest seats. Katie was pouring a cup of coffee by the sales counter. The town's only official salon was hardly large enough to turn around in, and more gossip than styling went on in it. Most men went to Clipper Dan, the town's local barber. The women mostly went to Martha or Beatrice, who both cut hair out of their homes. Paula wondered how she'd ended up with this crowd.

Katie put the coffeepot down and turned. "Were you born this way?"

"Meaning what?" But Paula knew what Katie meant.

"You live to make everyone else's life miserable? So what if I think the preacher's good-looking?"

"Good-looking? I think the word you used was *hot.*"

"Okay, *hot* then. You didn't think he's hot?"

"Of course not. He's a *preacher*, for heaven's sake!"

"He's a man. Preacher or circus clown, he's a man." Katie faced Chrissy and Mary. "He was hot, trust me."

Chrissy grinned. "Just what we need around here. A hot preacher."

"Fire and brimstone," Mary said. "You ever date a preacher?"

"Not yet," Katie said with a wink.

Katie was digging for a comeback. Paula refused. This was their regular nonsense, and Katie's latest cutting remark stuck in Paula's mind. Born to make everyone else's life miserable?

Not everyone, Katie, just you. Only those who need it.

At least that's what Paula tried to tell herself. But was that how the others saw her? The goody-goody who walked around making everyone else's life miserable? The ugly, fat prude who compensated for her own failures by making sure others were fully aware of theirs?

Was there truth to that?

"Think about it," Katie was saying. "Cecil kicked the bucket this afternoon, and people are more interested in Chris's wart. What does that tell you? You watch, that church will be packed tonight. And they won't be there for Cecil's funeral."

"Hello, ladies."

Paula hadn't heard the door open. There in the frame stood Marsuvees Black, long black trench coat sucked back by the wind.

They stared as one.

He tipped his Stetson hat. "Lovely afternoon." He grinned. "God is merciful and kind and full of hope and grace. Putting four such lovely women on this earth is all the evidence I need."

Katie smiled. "Good afternoon, Preacher." She glided to him and held out her hand. "My name's Katie."

He took the hand, lifted it to his lips, and kissed it gently. "Katie. Such a ravishing name."

"Thank you."

"I assume I'll see you in the church tonight."

"Of course."

Black's eyes moved to Chrissy and Mary. He winked. It wasn't the kind of wink that was necessarily sensual—perhaps just a father-to-son kind of wink. Then again, Paula couldn't be sure.

His eyes settled on her. It was the first time his deep blue eyes had stared into her own, and she found the attention unnerving. Katie's remarks may have been inappropriate, but her friend was right. Black was handsome.

Beautiful. Intoxicating.

She felt completely flustered by his stare and desperately wanted to break off, but he seemed to have a hold on her. The realization only made it worse.

Black stepped past Katie and strode across the room, eyes fixed on Paula. He stopped in front of her and held out his hand.

She started to lift her hand to him before she realized what she was doing, and by then it was too late to stop without looking like a fool. His fingers gently took hers. He bent and kissed them lightly, letting his warm lips rest on her knuckles for a beat more than she thought necessary. When he straightened, she could feel his hot breath on the back of her hand. He hesitated, looking to her fingers, and for a brief moment she thought he was thinking about licking them.

Paula blinked away the thought, horrified that it had passed through her mind.

Black pulled her in with his blue gaze again. "And what is your name, my dear?"

"Paula," she said in a light voice.

"Paula. Paula, Paula." He seemed to be tasting her name. "Such a . . . beautiful name."

Black withdrew his other hand from his pocket, fingers closed in a fist. "Have you ever been anointed with oil, Paula?"

He opened his hand. A gel-like substance filled his palm—oil, she presumed. It smelled odd. Stale and musty. What he thought he was going to do with this smudge he called oil, she wasn't sure, but she wasn't about to be anointed or anything—

Black lifted his hand and applied it to her head, as if smoothing her hair back. "I anoint you with oil. As a sign of my purity to all who see you, a light shall shine from you."

Black removed his hand from her head and said so that none of the others could hear, "You are lovely, dear Paula. Your purity is a light on a hill for all to admire."

For a long moment he held her eyes. Then he walked toward the door. He turned and smiled at all of them.

"Thank you for such a warm welcome. I'm sure we'll be seeing each other tonight, but now I have to gather the flock. Make the rounds, so to speak. Ladies." He tipped his hat again and was gone.

"Paula?" Katie was staring at her head.

She lifted her hand to feel the spot on her head where Black had rubbed his hand.

"Was that bleach?" Mary asked.

Paula's hair was moist. She pulled her fingers away, smelled them. Same musty smell. "What?" she asked absently.

"Your hair's white!" Katie said. "He have bleach in his hand?" She crossed the salon in two steps. "Bleach couldn't do that, not that quick."

Paula faced the mirror behind her. A streak of white hair ran from her forehead back toward her crown, where Marsuvees Black had wiped his anointing.

Then Katie had her hands on Paula's head and was examining her hair up close. "That's no color, Paula. And if it's bleach, it's no bleach I've seen. Anything that strong would've burned your hair."

Paula pushed her away. Her head was tingling.

For a while they all stared at her in silence. She felt oddly satisfied by the boldness of this one white streak where she parted her dark brown hair, slightly to the right. What was it he had said? A light of purity for everyone to see.

It occurred to her that she hated the man. He'd forced this anointing of his on her without consent. And she was quite sure that the streak wouldn't wash out.

Black was trouble, more than any of them could guess.

Then why wasn't she fuming with rage? Why was she just looking at her hair in the mirror, thinking that it looked quite good? And she was the purest of this bunch, that was no secret.

"He's the devil," Paula said.

"Well, he sure has a strange way of showing it," Katie said.

Paula turned and walked toward the door. "He's the devil."

Chapter Five

PARADISE

Wednesday night

THE PARADISE Episcopal Church was packed to the gills by six forty-five Wednesday evening. Stanley Yordon scanned the restless crowd from the door that led to the baptismal. People milled in the aisles, leaned over pews swatting at each other playfully, snapped at children. They had come out of the woodwork, dressed in jeans and muddy boots—some wearing cowboy hats, others packing holsters. Goodness, who did they think this man was? Wyatt Earp?

Some of the community's more influential residents were dressed for church, in coats and ties and dresses and the whole bit. Well, good for them. Showing the house of God a little respect never hurt anyone.

He stared out at his congregation, which had been turned inside out by this preacher who claimed to be sent by God. Marsuvees Black. Claimed God pulled his car off the road and told him to bring grace and hope to Paradise. The problem was, God didn't speak to people like that anymore. Maybe he used to, to Abraham or Moses or the apostle Paul, but not now, and certainly not here in Paradise, Colorado.

In Paradise, God spoke through Sunday services and potluck and bingo. God spoke through community, even communities like this one, which looked like it might split at the seams.

He held out a hand to Blitzer's boy, Matthew. "Whoa, slow down there, son!" The kid ignored him and ran past, then down the far aisle, yelping like a native.

Coming apart at the seams. Thank God he was leaving for a quarterly board meeting in the morning. He could use a break from this bunch.

He stepped toward the platform. This was his church. He didn't care if the pope himself was coming. No one would trash his house. He leapt to the podium and flashed that preacher's smile he'd learned back in seminary. He leaned into the mic.

"Okay." Feedback squealed through the auditorium. He flinched and backed off. Of the two hundred men, women, and children stuffed into the church, fewer than half turned their attention to the podium, feedback and all.

"Is this better? Okay, let's settle down, folks." The clock on the back wall read six fifty-nine. Black planned to arrive at seven. "Seven o'clock sharp, Stan," the preacher had said. "I'll be here and you can bet your pension on that." For starters, no one called him Stan—his name was Stanley. He didn't care if Black didn't know; he hadn't liked the flash in Black's eyes when he said *Stan*, standing there on the church steps like he owned the place.

"Let's have some quiet here." His voice rang across the sanctuary.

Most of the adults complied, hushing at the sound of his deep voice. Nancy once told him his voice was commanding. Like a general's voice. He lifted a hand to the crowd.

"Let's take our seats, friends." A flurry of movement across the room signaled their obedience. Within ten seconds most of the flock faced him attentively, waiting for his next words.

Most, but not all. Small, scattered groups yammered on as if his request meant nothing at all to them. These were the unchurched. Uneducated, unchurched heathens. *You have to either beat them over the head with a tire iron to get their attention, or ignore them entirely.*

How could a man just waltz into town and have these sheep eating out of his hands so easily? Black had supposedly pulled off this miracle of his in Steve's bar, but that wouldn't account for such a crowd, would it? On any other day the seasoned farmers sitting in the pews would scoff at such a tale. But not today. Today they had flocked here to see more. It made no sense.

He glanced down at Chris Ingles. The man had run around town like a plucked goose, showing off that stupid ear of his. Yordon didn't know how it was that Chris had grown and lost a wart, but there had to be some trick to it. The man sat there with an open mouth, like an idiot. *If Chris came to my door looking like that, I might want to check things out too. The man's flipped his lid.*

Stanley Yordon smiled on, showing none of the anger that rose in him. "Okay, people . . ."

The baptismal door on his right swung open, and before he could say another word, the scene before him changed.

For starters, every eye jerked to his right and stared wide, as if an apparition of the Virgin Mary had just lit the wall. And with the shifting of eyes came a sudden and complete silence.

Black had arrived.

Yordon turned his head to the right, aware that his mouth still lay open, readied to deliver its blow to the heathens.

Marsuvees Black stood in the doorway dressed in black. Yordon's tongue dried up. *Goodness gracious, he's the devil.* He shut his mouth and swallowed.

Black's deep blue eyes slowly scanned the crowd. His feet were spread wide, his hands hung loosely like a man ready to draw. When the preacher's eyes reached Yordon, they stopped and stared for a long moment. And then his mouth lifted into a smile—*a preacher smile*, Yordon thought. The man stepped toward the platform.

Yordon cleared his throat, scrambled for words. "Ah . . . thank you," he said.

Feedback screamed through the sanctuary again. He winced. *Ah . . . thank you? Thank you for what? Compose yourself, man.*

"Sorry." He grinned stupidly. "Let's all give Mr. Minister Black a round of applause."

Mr. Minister?

He stepped away from the pulpit and began to clap as Black took the stage, beaming that plastic devil smile of his.

Marsuvees Black stepped up to the pulpit and dismissed him with a nod. Yordon felt one of the guest chairs at the back of his knees. He sat heavily.

The congregation stared. Then someone started with the clapping that spread through the building.

Black absorbed it, spreading his arms like a rock star at the end of a show. A cool wind from the air conditioner lifted thin wisps of black hair off his shoulders.

"Thank you," Black finally said. His bass voice rumbled over the crowd. "Thank you very much." He raised a hand and the sanctuary fell silent.

"Funny thing happened this afternoon," Black said. "I was driving my '83 Buick along the highway, thinking how good it was to be alive on God's beautiful green earth, wondering where I should go, when my engine locked up, right out there by the sign that says, *Paradise 2 Miles*. And then I heard God's voice speak clear and loud. *Go 2 Paradise*, he said." Black drew a two in the air. "*Bring grace and hope to the lost town of Paradise*, he said."

Eighty-three Buick, huh? That's not what Chris Ingles said.

Steve Smither sat on the front row, leaning forward in his seat. His wife, Paula, sat stiff like a board. There was an unattractive white streak in her hair—undoubtedly one of Katie's experiments.

Steve had served as a deacon since Yordon suggested he take the post two years ago. Paula had run the Sunday-school program for—what?—three years now. She had a heart for the children.

Claude Bowers sat down the bench from Steve. Now there was a leader. Big, conservative, and quiet, but when he did speak, people listened. Except for Katie, of course. Funny how he ended up with Katie, who didn't have a conservative bone in her body. Big Claude and beautiful Katie.

Yordon thought all of this on the fly, in the same way all preachers think a thousand thoughts on the fly while looking out at their congregations.

Black lowered his voice a notch and continued. "So here I am, my friends. Here I am. And I assure you not one of you will remain unchanged when we're through here. Not a one."

The preacher let the words ring through the auditorium. At first no one responded. They just stared at him, some skeptical, some eager.

"How do we know what kind of power you really have?" Steve asked. His voice rumbled through the silence.

Black did not respond.

"Or if it's really real?" someone else shouted.

This time a chorus of *that's rights* and *amens* filled the room. Good. As Yordon knew they would, most of his people weren't buying Black's nonsense.

"Shut . . . your worthless traps," Black bit off. Not loudly, but distinctly and with a slight quaver.

The words took the breath out of the room.

"And consider it a warning, because the man of God can only take so much doubt."

Silence.

Black softened. "Chris Ingles, rise."

Chris jumped to his feet.

"Show them your ear."

Ingles jerked his right ear forward and those closest to him strained for a view. "You had a wart behind your ear?" Black asked.

"Yes."

"And now it's gone, isn't that right?"

"That's right."

Black put both hands on the podium and studied the congregation. Chris sat.

"Did I tell you to sit, Chris?" Black's voice was low, deep. Threatening.

Chris stood.

"Stick out your tongue, Chris."

Chris blinked, as if he hadn't heard right.

"Go on, son. Stick out your tongue for everyone to see."

Chris hesitated then thrust his tongue out.

Yordon leaned to his right for a better view.

Gasps filled the pews nearest Chris, who jerked his hand to his mouth and felt his tongue.

"Ahhhh!" Chris jerked his hand away. "Ahhhh!"

"He's got a huge wart on his tongue!" someone blurted. Cries of alarm filled the auditorium.

"Whadth happen?" Chris slurred, and Yordon wondered how large this supposed wart was.

"Shut up! Sit down."

Chris was feeling his tongue again. "What—"

"I said shut up! Sit down!"

Chris dropped to his seat.

"What I give, I can take, see?" Black let that settle in.

Yordon was sure the preacher hadn't actually healed Chris. Now he had his proof. He should be standing about now and confronting Black head-on. But he didn't.

"Do I have your attention?" Black asked.

No one answered.

"I said, *do I have your attention?*"

Dozens of *yeses* came at once.

"Good. Now, when I say that I've come to bring grace and hope, I may mean something altogether different than what you think. My kind of grace and hope is full of life, my friends. A real trip. Not that you have to agree with my definitions of these two most holy words. I'm not here to ram anything down your throats, no sir. But we're on dangerous ground here, and I strongly suggest you pay attention."

Black walked to his right where a pewter goblet that he'd requested sat on the altar. No bread or crackers, just a goblet filled with wine. For communion, he'd said.

Yordon had filled the goblet with grape juice.

"Before we learn how grace and hope will change your lives," Black said, lifting the goblet, "we're going to remember." He held the cup out. "Remember how things were before grace and hope came to town."

He sniffed the contents, paused for a moment, then seemed to accept Yordon's insubordination and walked back to the pulpit.

The man held the cup just below the pulpit. He was wiping his fingers on the edge of the goblet as if . . .

Yordon leaned forward with surprise. If he wasn't mistaken, Black was wiping a gel-like substance into the goblet! What on earth did the man think he was doing? Surely he didn't expect anyone to actually drink . . .

Unless he was poisoning them.

Black plunged his hand into the cup, causing some of the grape juice to spill at his feet. He swirled his fingers around a few times, then extracted his hand and flicked juice from his fingers back into the goblet.

Yordon came to his feet, terrified and outraged at once. "That's enough! No more theatrics." He stepped forward but didn't have the resolve to toss Black aside by the collar, as he fleetingly envisioned.

"I'm going to have to ask you to step down," Yordon said. "I don't know who you think—"

Black brought his hands together with a thunderclap. He lifted his right hand for all to see. There in his palm sat a large red apple.

No goblet.

Yordon groped for his seat.

"Do you remember?" Black asked the congregation, ignoring Yordon. "First there was an apple. The fruit of pleasure. All was good. Do you remember?"

Stony silence.

"Do you remember, Stan?" Black snapped without turning.

"Yes." The question and his own response caught Yordon off guard.

Black tossed the red apple into the air. "And then there came . . ."

When he caught the apple, it wasn't an apple.

It was a brown snake.

"The snake," Black said.

A gasp filled the room. Some shouts of alarm. Black held the three-foot snake by its midsection as the serpent lifted its head, testing the air with a long flickering tongue.

"But we know what happened to the snake, don't we?"

Slick as a magician, Black slid his hand to the reptile's tail and cracked the snake like a whip.

Crack!

The blurred snake became a rigid object roughly two feet in height. A dark wooden cross.

"The snake was defeated."

The congregation was evidently too stunned to react this time. You could stuff an apple up the sleeve. You could hide a snake past the cuff. But not this hefty cross.

"And that defeat gave us the fruit of the vine once again." Black slammed the cross against the pulpit, where it vanished in a horrendous crash. Wobbling on the surface was an apple, which he held up for all to see.

The same red apple he'd started with.

"Do you remember?" Black called out.

With his free hand, he lifted the goblet of grape juice. Yordon hadn't seen it reappear. He held the apple above the goblet and squeezed it. The fruit compressed like a sponge, and juice flowed into the cup.

Black opened a dry hand for all to see—apple gone. He lifted the cup high. "Do this in remembrance."

The congregation responded in an indistinct, astounded chorus. "Drink from this cup, the hope of my gospel." Black paced, goblet extended to all. "Drink, Chris. Drink, my friend. Show them."

Chris hesitated only a brief second before stumbling into the aisle and hurrying to the front. He took the goblet from Black and waited for some kind of encouragement.

"Just a sip. Don't be greedy. There are a lot of thirsty souls in this place."

Chris tilted the cup, sipped, then handed it back to the preacher.

"Go on, show them your tongue."

Yordon didn't have to look to know what had happened. But the cries of approval confirmed his guess. The wart was gone from Chris's tongue.

Chris was feeling his tongue with both sets of fingers.

Black addressed the congregation. "I want all of you to take a sip of this wine in remembrance. If you think for a second that you'll catch something, I can assure you that the only thing you'll catch is God's wrath if you don't drink."

He held the cup out to Ben Holden on the first pew. The man hurried forward, took the goblet.

"Pass it and drink!" Black said, spreading his arms wide. "Drink the living water and embrace hope."

Ben sipped, then passed the cup. It wound its way down the line.

"That's right. Drink, drink, drink, drink, drink."

Stanley Yordon stared at his congregation, struck by his own powerlessness to stop this incredible charade. His earlier wonder at Black's miracles had been replaced by a firm belief that the man was nothing but a bag of tricks after all.

Who would use such obvious gimmicks to impress a crowd? Please. An apple, a serpent, a cross, an apple. A Vegas entertainer could pull that off. He wondered how much Black paid Chris to play along with the wart business.

But watching Claude and Steve and Paula and the rest drink from the goblet, Yordon lacked conviction that he had the power to do anything other than make a fool of himself.

Black was saying something, but Yordon wasn't hearing. A few members let the cup pass by. But far more drank. Out of fear? Out of hope? Out of fear. Mostly fear. It had to be fear.

". . . have the choice to follow my way or his way."

Yordon froze at the last two words: *his way*. Unless Yordon was mistaken, Black had motioned *his* way when he spoke those two words. *His way*. But then he could have been mistaken, because he hadn't actually seen it. Still, a cold sweat replaced the heat under his collar.

"And believe me," Black continued, "many of you will be tempted to go the old way. I don't blame you really. You've been stuck in the same old ruts for so long, you wouldn't know grace or hope if they both smacked you upside the head at the same time."

Someone chuckled in the back.

"Well, let me tell you something, when I say *grace,* I am talking *Grace*, with a capital *G*, not some ambiguous theological term that preachers throw at you to impress the snot out of you. I mean GRACE. Capital G-R-A-C-E. Liberty. Freedom."

Black stepped out from the podium and opened his huge hands wide.

"And when I say *hope*, I mean *HOPE,* like, 'Man, I really hope I can have that. I *want* that.' " He closed both hands into fists. "I *have to* have that." Black's voice swelled to a crescendo. "Hope like, 'Get out of the way, that's *mine!*' hope!"

Black breathed heavily. Yordon stared, at a loss, still not sure what the preacher was driving at, still wondering if the man really had meant *him* when he said *his way*.

"Now, if any of you are looking for that kind of grace and hope, I'm bringing them to you. Grace and hope are here." He stood perfectly still, glaring at two hundred frozen faces. "You follow me and I'll rock your world, baby. I'll show you how to trip. Things will never be the same again."

Yordon scanned the auditorium. The silence seemed to drift on a bit long. He looked over at Black and blinked.

The man was trembling.

Black faced the crowd, slowly scanning it from left to right, trembling from head to toe.

"I want you to think about that. I need the leaders to understand the message for Paradise. I need you to follow me, baby." His voice intensified. "I need you to let go and let God. I need you to drop the sickening let's-play-church act and start slamming!"

Yordon's skin rippled with gooseflesh. *Slamming?*

An image of some rock star peering from a jewel case popped into Yordon's mind. Gene Simmons, right here in his church.

"Paula," Black said slowly, staring at her. "Katie, Nancy, Mary. I really do like those names. Suck up a little grace-juice, ladies."

His eyes shifted to Steve. "You hear me, Steve? And you, Claude. All of you. Trip with me, baby. Breathe deep and let it go where it wants to. If you let me, I'll show you. I'll show you all."

Yordon caught sight of the man's eyes from the side. Bloodshot.

When Black spoke again, his voice was low and biting. "You have a choice to make. When I come to you, you better not run scared. You just choose the real thing and maybe things will work out for you."

Yordon forced his eyes around the room. To a head they were glued on Black.

"You're going to have to decide," Black said, voice swelling. His trembling had subsided. "Are you going to follow me, the man God sent to Paradise with a new message of grace and hope? Hmm? Or are you going to follow *his* way?"

Yordon jerked his head to the pulpit. This time Black left no room for interpretation. This time, standing alone up on the platform, he stabbed his finger at Stanley.

For the first time since Marsuvees Black's entrance, the flock turned its attention back to Yordon. A sea of eyes gazed at him—some quizzical, some glaring, most big and round.

Johnny Drake stood in the foyer behind them all, hiding behind the door frame, staring directly at him. Yordon held his breath and looked back at the pulpit. Black had dropped his finger, thank God. He peeked out at the crowd again. They had returned their stares to the preacher.

"So you listen and you watch and you prepare your heart for a little change. And if you're lucky, you'll live to tell of the day that Paradise found grace and hope."

Black turned and strode from the podium without the slightest acknowledgment of Yordon. He walked off the stage and through the baptismal door. Twenty minutes after it had started, the service was over.

Yordon began to wonder how foolish he looked up there by himself. But they weren't looking at him. Not paying him the least bit of attention. And why should they?

There was a new preacher in town.

"YOU DRINK it?" Johnny asked.

"No," Roland Smither said. "You?"

"Are you kidding?"

They sat in Johnny's room, Johnny still stunned by what they'd both seen with their own eyes at the church half an hour earlier; Roland toggling the controller for Johnny's PlayStation, throwing tricks in Snowboard Madness.

Johnny couldn't quite bring himself to tell his friend about Black walking into town and killing Cecil. He hated the fact that his mother was still gone.

Roland tossed the control on the bed. "He's a fake. I've seen better stuff on magic shows."

"This isn't a show."

"How do you know? David Copperfield could make an elephant disappear on stage, so why couldn't this guy make a snake appear?"

"Could Copperfield grow a wart on someone's tongue?"

"Course he could, if Chris was in on it. Come on, don't be such a sucker."

What could he say? Maybe the eye thing with Cecil was a trick too. But Cecil was dead.

"You ever hear a preacher talk that way? 'Suck up some grace-juice'? This isn't just some magician on the road. You see the way he was shaking?"

The smile faded from Roland's face. "That's part of his gig, man. Lighten up, you're talking like an idiot."

Johnny stood and walked to his window. The leaves whipped by nearly horizontal. Such a strong wind for the middle of summer. "He put something in the drink."

"Course he did," Roland said. "Part of the show. Pretty cool too, if you ask me. He isn't afraid of Yordon, that's for sure."

Johnny faced his friend. "What if I'm right? What if he's dangerous?"

"My dad's got a gun. And before he used it, he'd call the cops." Roland sighed. "You really have to lighten up, Johnny."

The phone on his desk chirped. Johnny crossed the room and snatched it up. "Hello?"

"Hi, Johnny."

Relief swept over him. "Hey, Mom."

"You okay?"

"Well. Actually I don't know . . ."

"What do you mean? Something happen?"

"The preacher freaked everyone out at the service."

"Like what?"

"Like . . ." Running through the string of magic tricks felt stupid. Johnny condensed. "Like turning an apple into a snake. But it was the way he was talking. He threatened the whole town if they didn't listen to him."

"It'll be fine, Johnny. Listen, it's raining cats and dogs here. I wanted to get to the mall but ran out of time. I was hoping I could stay over and pick up some things in the morning."

Dread passed through his gut.

"Johnny? He died from a heart attack, Johnny. Okay? The doctor here all but confirmed it. There's no sign of any trauma to Cecil's eyes—I made sure of that, just for you. He's an illusionist or something, end of story." She paused. "Maybe Roland could spend the night with you."

"Roland's here." He looked at his friend, who'd returned to the video game, and felt some comfort.

"Ask him."

Johnny covered the phone and asked. Roland nodded. "Sure."

"He says he can do that."

"Okay. I'll be home about noon tomorrow. Lock the doors and make sure you get to bed by midnight. You'll be okay, Johnny. There's plenty to eat in the fridge. I'm at the Super Eight in Junction if you need me, okay? I love you, Johnny."

"I love you too."

He hung up the phone and suppressed an urge to cry. *Easy, Johnny. They're right. You're letting your imagination go wild.*

Roland scrambled from the bed. "I'll call my mom."

Five minutes later it was all settled. Roland was spending the night. They raided the refrigerator and hauled Cheez-Its, four Snickers bars, Planters peanuts, and two tall glasses of milk back to Johnny's room.

"Score," Roland said. "We still hanging out with Fred and Peter at the Starlight tomorrow?"

In the afternoon's excitement Johnny had forgotten about their customary summer gathering at the old theater. "I guess."

Roland jerked his head up. "What was that?"

"What was what?"

Roland stood slowly. "Was that an earthquake?"

They waited. Nothing.

Johnny was about to ask his friend to elaborate when the floor under his feet shifted, ever so slightly.

"Whoa!" He jumped onto the bed. "You feel that?"

Roland looked at him. His lips formed a twisted grin. "No. I didn't feel it the first time either. You see what I mean? Now you're feeling things."

Johnny blinked. He could have sworn . . .

Roland laughed and grabbed the peanuts. "You gotta lighten up, man."

It took Johnny an hour to fall asleep after they turned the lights off at midnight. When he finally drifted off, he dreamed of Marsuvees Black.

A nightmare.

THE TOWN of Paradise slipped into a deep slumber.

Before that, and after the service, the Malones went to Steve and Paula's house for coffee. They were divided on Black's theatrics. None of them could say they were real or an illusion, at least not definitively. Neither could they agree on the intent of his harsh talk. But in the end even Paula agreed that the man was captivating. Maybe too captivating, she said. Steve said she was overstating things, which earned him a glare.

They'd all sipped from the communion goblet, which earned a chuckle from Steve in retrospect. What people would do in the heat of religious fervor. No doubt about it, Black could handle a crowd. As far as Steve was concerned, Paradise could use some excitement.

Steve fell asleep easily enough, at about eleven, and drifted through a dreamless night.

The clock read eight when Steve jolted upright in his bed, wide awake, soaked with sweat, breathing heavily. A loud ringing filled his ears, a buzzing with a high-pitched whine that made him shake his head. He blinked in the morning light and gazed about the room, lost for a moment.

Paula was gone.

He swung his legs from the bed, thinking he should throw on a robe.

"Paula?"

No response.

Steve shuffled from the bedroom into the living room.

"Paula!"

Nothing.

She might be in the small garden she'd planted behind the house. Cost twice as much to grow tomatoes as purchase them at this altitude, but she found the hobby relaxing.

He headed for the back door. Morning light streamed through the windows. A beautiful day. He felt as contented as he could remember feeling. It was going to be a good day in Paradise.

Steve grabbed the doorknob and twisted. The air was perfectly calm and the grass was perfectly green and the sky was perfectly blue.

And Paradise was perfectly quiet.

"Paula?"

The garden was deserted. She was probably over talking someone's ear off about Black. Steve paused, thinking through yesterday's events. Had all that really happened? Sure it had. Chris had grown a wart, then lost it, then grown it, then lost it. The apple had become a snake, the snake had become a cross, the cross had become an apple. And more than half the town had tasted the sweet juice from that apple.

Including him.

A nervous excitement fluttered through his gut. Black sure knew how to get the heart moving.

A giggle turned his attention toward the tool shed. He studied the shed. Was that Paula's voice?

A dark hat broke the shed's vertical corner line. A man. But that hadn't been a man's voice giggling.

Steve was about to call out when the laughter came again, shrill this time.

The man stepped backward into Steve's line of sight.

Black.

Steve couldn't see who the preacher was holding behind the shed wall, but Black was turning to face him . . . had turned . . . was staring right at Steve, wearing a grin that Steve couldn't quite interpret.

"Hello, Steve."

Black's low and gravelly voice, hardly more than a whisper, carried clearly in the morning stillness.

"Good morning, Rev—"

"Do you know what I have back here, Steve?" His right arm was still hidden from view.

Paula? Steve's mind began to spin. No, that was ridiculous.

Marsuvees Black withdrew his arm. He gripped a wooden stake, about two feet in length and roughly three inches in diameter.

"Do you know what this is, Steve?" Still grinning. Another giggle behind the shed. Steve barely heard it, having fixed his mind on that stake in Black's hand.

He swallowed. "No."

"This is pleasure on a stick, Steve. This is what you skewer meat with before you eat it. This is what you stick apples on before dipping them in caramel. Can you fathom that, my friend?"

Black touched his lips to the stake's sharp point, kissed it, and sighed.

"This is grace and hope in Paradise," Black said.

Saliva had pooled under Steve's tongue. He swallowed it. The stick looked smooth, lovely, well shaped, beautiful.

But it was just a stick. What was Black's point?

The stake's point is his point, you idiot.

"And do you know what *this* is?" Black asked. He'd reached behind the shed and yanked a woman out by her hair.

Paula.

Black looked into Paula's eyes and jerked her head back. "Do you want your grace-juice, baby?"

She laughed shrilly.

"She's been a naughty wife, Steve."

Black leaned over Paula and kissed her on the lips. She returned his kiss.

"A very naughty wife."

Rage swelled in Steve's chest. He sucked at the still air but couldn't seem to get enough oxygen into his lungs.

"What do we do to naughty wives?" Black demanded. "We stick them like caramel apples, that's what we do."

The reverend whirled Paula around so that her back faced Steve. It occurred to him that Paula's shrill laugh wasn't a laugh anymore. It was a scream. Or was it?

Steve clenched his hands. "Get away from her!" He took a step forward.

Paula threw her head back, cocked it at an odd angle, like a bent paper clip. She laughed hysterically. No scream at all, just this frenzied expression of delight. Her eyes opened and she drilled him with a mocking stare. He could see her neck, white in the sunlight. Smooth. Her hair fell to her shoulders.

The last thread of reason that moored Steve's mind snapped. He felt himself drift into a sea of incoherent fury.

"What do we do, Steve?" Black asked, still grinning.

Steve hesitated, confused by Black's question.

The preacher repeated himself, yelling this time. "What do we do?"

"Stake them?"

His wife's shrill laughter ceased. For a moment Paradise was still again.

Then she howled with horror. It was a scream now for sure. No laughter for Paula. But fact was, she deserved it. He would do . . .

You don't mean that, Steve.

. . . it himself if he was a little closer. Maybe he still could . . .

What on earth are you thinking?

. . . do it, teach her to . . .

Stop this! Stop this right now!

The preacher winked at Steve and thrust the stick forward.

Steve lunged up, gasping. It was dark. A fan swished slowly overhead.

He was in bed?

Rumpled bed sheets covered his legs. He grasped the covers on his left and felt his wife's sleeping form. She grunted. No harm.

Steve looked at the clock. Midnight. Steve exhaled and dropped back to his pillow. A nightmare.

Something was in his right hand. He lifted his arm.

A bloody stake.

MARSUVEES BLACK stood on the cliff overlooking Paradise, boots planted on the rock like two sledgehammers. Most of Paradise had slipped into dreams.

A hot wind blew into his face, but he didn't blink, did not feel the urge to blink. He stood with his arms cocked on his hips, his trench coat flying back in the breeze so that if Katie were to wake and peer up the mountain she might think a huge bat had landed on the cliff. But Katie wasn't waking up, not tonight, not with all that euphoria in her blood.

If they only knew what lay in store for them. A part of him wanted to go down there, wake them all from their slumber, and tell them the truth, all of it. But he had to bide his time. If he rushed things, they might not understand, and that could get nasty.

He had to help them understand their true makeup. He had to help them feel the horror, just enough to understand the truth of who they really were. Too fast and the plan could backfire. Too slow and they might never reach the maturity required to face the truth.

His legs were tired, so he folded them under himself and sat on the rock ledge. Crossed his arms.

It had been a good day. An even better night. They bought the whole thing without hardly a protest. It was hard for Black not to feel pride in what he'd done, but that wasn't the point. Pride could lead to a mistake. When it was all done and he'd set this town free, then he'd grant himself pride.

Someone coughed behind and to his right. Black knew who it was, but he didn't feel the need to acknowledge the man.

A tall figure dressed in a long hooded robe stepped from the shadows and stood beside him. For a minute the sight of the sleeping town seemed to hold them in a trance. The others in the monastery would undoubtedly crawl out of their skins if they knew these two met here, and why.

Then again, depending on how this all turned out, they might shout their praises.

Black could feel the weight of the man's eyes on him now.

"How does it feel?" the man asked.

"Incredible," Black said.

"Tell me what you did. I want to know everything."

"I did what was expected."

"Details."

Black supposed he owed the man at least that much. The telling took fifteen minutes, interrupted occasionally by questions and requests for further elaboration.

When he finished, silence engulfed them. Above, the black clouds boiled, visible even in the night sky like a claw reaching down from the heavens to crush this little victim nestled in the Colorado mountains.

But the clouds didn't tell the whole story. Not even half of it.

"You've done well." A hand settled on Black's shoulder, rested there for a moment, then withdrew.

"It's hard to believe we actually have this much power."

"We aren't the only ones with power," Black said.

"No. But we're ahead now. I think we will succeed."

"Yes, we will."

The wind howled.

"You need to rest."

Black smiled softly in the darkness. "Do I?"

"A little power doesn't make you immortal, now does it?"

"No, I suppose it doesn't."

The man turned and vanished into the black night behind them.

Marsuvees Black stared into the wind, barely breathing. Tomorrow was coming. He needed rest.

Chapter Six

PARADISE

Thursday morning

REVEREND STANLEY Yordon crawled out of bed, surprised to find the little hand cocked past the ten.

Ten? Heavens, it had been years since he slept so late. Even when he drank with the boys, which he rarely did these days, he woke by eight at the latest. And here it was, past ten o'clock Thursday morning, the day after the big service.

The big service. The one in which a stranger had basically told the town to choose between his way or Stanley's way. By the looks of the flock after the meeting, they chose Black's way. They chose a message of so-called grace and hope that sounded more like the gospel according to Hugh Hefner than the gospel according to Luke.

Yordon walked into the bathroom and splashed water on his face. This cowboy preacher had waltzed into town and shown Paradise a party, all right. Forget bingo night, we're having us a real party. What'll you have? Some grace? Some hope? Let's throw in some magic to boot. We can grow and ungrow warts on demand.

They loved the entertainer! He'd have to talk to the bishop about this. Stanley shaved, dressed, ate a slice of dry toast. Hopefully, by the time he returned from Denver on Saturday, this fool would be gone and they could get back to church and the old reliable pig-roast potlucks that never failed to draw a crowd.

Yordon walked outside and immediately noticed the wind. A warm breeze blew down the road, almost hot. Dark clouds boiled overhead—the news had mentioned a coming rain storm, but here there was only wind. Wind and dust.

Main Street was deserted. At least Black wasn't holding a rally.

He walked briskly to the church, skirting a few dust devils as he went. The auditorium was still a mess from the previous night. Visitor cards and hymnals lay strewn about the pews and floor. *Those unchurched* . . . Yordon grunted. Wouldn't know respect if it hit them upside the head.

"Nancy?" He walked into the offices. "Nancy?"

"Here."

"Where?"

"In the kitchen."

He found his secretary with her head stuck in the church refrigerator. Her wide body all but obscured it. "I have to get going," he said, reaching for a coffee mug.

Nancy straightened and looked at him. "Going where?"

"Denver. Bishop Fraiser? Quarterly meeting?"

"Oh."

He poured hot coffee into his cup. "Frankly, it couldn't have come at a better time. With our mayor running off and that preacher coming in, I believe we have us a class-one mess on our hands."

"Come on, Father, the preacher's harmless. It's good for the town to get a little spice now and then."

Some of the coffee missed the cup. "A little spice? That's what you call last night? The man threatened me."

"Please. You can't take that seriously. Do you know what we did with those leftover danishes?"

"What danishes? I'm worried about the church and you're worried about danishes?"

"The danishes from Sunday's potluck. The cherry-apple ones with frosting. There was a whole rack of them right here yesterday."

Yordon sighed. "I'll be back Saturday."

"Oh, here they are!"

Nancy grabbed a tin plate from the top of the refrigerator and dug at the shrink-wrap that covered the old danishes. She pried a gooey pastry out and took a large bite.

"Personally, I think you're overreacting, but you go right on ahead. We'll be here when you get back." She smacked at the danish. "You're back Saturday? Why not tomorrow?"

"I always go for three days."

She shoved the rest of the pastry into her mouth.

Yordon wasn't sure what to think of this. Nancy lost fifty pounds in the last six months, thanks to a no-sugar diet. But here she was, stuffing her face with enough sugar to fuel the church for a week.

He thought about asking her but decided it would do more harm than good.

"I'll call you from Denver."

She nodded and dug out another pastry.

Yordon left the church, walked to a blue Chevy Caprice parked in the church lot, slid behind the driver's wheel, started the engine, and was past the old theater before it occurred to him that he'd forgotten his shaving kit. Never mind, he would pick up the basics at a convenience store.

Honestly, he couldn't get out of town fast enough.

Ten minutes later he approached the highway and slowed the old Caprice to a stop. The road was empty—as quiet as the road leading up to Paradise behind him.

An image popped into his mind. An image of an old Buick—Marsuvees Black's '83 Buick—sitting on the shoulder with its front bumper stuck into a buckled road sign. *Funny thing happened to me this afternoon*, Black had said.

But there was no car.

The sign was there, but no '83 Buick. When a car broke down on this strip of highway, it usually remained on the roadside for at least four or five days before the cops towed it away.

Curious, Yordon climbed out and walked toward the sign. A ringing lodged in his ears, and he whacked the side of his head to no avail. The air was still and cool down here. Amazing how the mountains play with weather. Hot in one valley and cool in the next. Seemed like it should be the other way around though. Hot down here and cool higher up, in Paradise. His boots crunched on the gravel as he rounded the sign.

Go 2 Paradise, Black had said. *Paradise 2 Miles*, drawing that stupid two in the air as if that was how to drive a point home.

Yordon shielded the sun from his eyes and gazed up at the green sign. *Paradise 3 Miles.*

That's what he thought. The sign read three, not two. The ringing in Stanley's ear grew a little louder. He looked down the road again. Three miles instead of two miles, and no car.

The man was a fake. But he already knew that.

He thought about turning the car around and heading back. The town had no mayor, no law enforcement. Only the Episcopal father. Stanley Yordon.

He slid into the Caprice, and with a last look down the deserted highway, he pulled the car into the road, bound for Denver, two hundred some-odd miles east.

JOHNNY AWOKE late Thursday morning, and for a full ten seconds he didn't think about the previous day's events. It was just another summer day after a sleepover.

He sat up. Mom was probably . . .

Mom was gone. Cecil had died. Marsuvees Black had poisoned the town.

He flung the covers off and stumbled into the hall. "Mom?"

But she was still in Junction, shopping—he already knew that. She wouldn't be home until noon at the earliest. And knowing her, it would be closer to late afternoon.

"What's up?" Roland asked, leaning out of the room. "You yelling?"

"Nothing. Just seeing if my mom's back."

Roland turned back into the room, dropped facedown on Johnny's bed. Johnny walked past him and peered out the window. Wind howled. Roland lay as if dead.

"You okay?" Johnny asked.

Roland groaned, pushed himself up on both elbows. "How late did we stay up?"

"Midnight. You want to see what's happening?"

Roland glanced at the clock, rolled off the bed, and grabbed his jeans. "Sheesh, it's ten o'clock! I have to mow. I'll see you at the Starlight later."

"You sure you don't want to see what's up?"

"What do mean, what's up? Nothing's up."

"After what happened last night? Trust me, something's up."

"My mom's going to kill me if I don't mow this morning," Roland said, pulling a worn yellow T-shirt over his head.

"In this wind?"

"Gotta go, trust me. See ya."

Roland left. Except for the wind moaning occasionally through the rafters, the house was quiet.

Too quiet for Johnny's peace of mind.

STEVE SMITHER pulled himself from a groggy sleep late Thursday morning, dressed in blue jeans and a red plaid shirt, and headed out to the kitchen.

Not until he passed the picture window that looked over the back lawn did he remember the dream.

The details fell into his mind. Black, stakes, Paula, *stakes*, shed, *STAKES*, screaming. A gust of wind whipped at the shed—no sign of Black or Paula. He had half a mind to check behind it. For stakes.

Steve swallowed, unnerved by the strong impulse. Then he remembered the stake in his hand. He ran back into the room and scanned the bed, the floor.

No bloody stake. That had been part of the dream too?

He headed back into the living room. Where was Paula?

Maybe he was still in the dream. Or maybe it *hadn't* been a dream.

He took a step toward the back door.

"Steve?"

"Hmm?" Steve stopped and turned toward Paula's voice. His head swam and for a second he thought he might fall, but the dizziness passed, leaving him with a headache.

And a lingering case of grogginess.

Paula leaned against the kitchen door frame, arms crossed. She looked a bit fuzzy to him. A bit loose. Her bathrobe draped over her body, untied, and her hair hung in tangles, straddling that terrible-looking white streak—God only knew why she'd let Katie do that to her.

Looked like a worn-out mutt.

He chided himself for the thought.

"What are you doing?" she asked.

He headed for the front door. "What does it look like I'm doing? The saloon doesn't open by itself."

She let him go without comment.

Steve paused in the wind, noticing it only as a faint distraction from an uncommon drive to check out the shed. Just to be sure. He had a dream, sure, but this feeling wasn't a dream. He had to check out the shed.

Steve rounded the house, approached the shed, and stopped three feet from the corner. His heart was hammering with an almost palpable desire to turn the corner and find the very stakes Black had used in his dream. Maybe even with blood on them. *Why?*

He took a deep breath and stuck his head around the corner.

Nothing.

"For the love of . . ." He clenched his teeth. "I can't believe he'd do this."

Do what, Steve? Who would do what?

What was he thinking? He put his hand on the fence, patted it once, and turned to leave.

Pain shot through his palm. He swore and jerked his hand away from the fence. A splinter the size of his little finger had sliced into the heel of his palm. He stared at it, speechless. Pain throbbed and his hand began to tremble. The thing was in deep, buried at an angle.

Steve dug at it with his fingernails but couldn't get a grip on the wood. He gripped his wrist and held his hand for a better view.

A stake. There was a stake in his palm. For crying—

"Hello, Steve."

Steve spun. Black stood by the shed, smiling warmly. His eyes dropped to Steve's hand, and his smile faded, replaced by a shadow of concern.

"You okay?"

Black moved forward, seemingly intent on examining him. But Steve wasn't sure he wanted the man to examine him.

"Do you mind?" Black asked, searching his eyes. Blue eyes. Comforting eyes. Genuinely concerned. The man looked different today than he had looked yesterday. He looked . . . kind.

Steve turned his hand for Black to inspect.

The man's fingers were warm. "Pretty deep," he said, digging in his pocket. He brought out one of those multipurpose pocketknives with small pliers.

"I think I can get it. Do you mind?"

Steve felt disconnected from the scene, despite the intensity of the pain and the sudden appearance of Black.

"Okay."

Black opened the knife and gently worked at freeing the sliver. The stake. Steve turned his eyes away and let him work.

The moment wasn't awkward, something that surprised him.

"Everything will make sense to you soon, Steve," Black said softly. A burst of pain made Steve flinch. When he looked at his hand, the sliver was gone. Black held it up in the pliers, smiling.

"You see, it hurts coming out, but in the end you wouldn't have it any other way." He let the sliver fall to the grass. "Just like this town. After a bit of pain it will all make sense. My ways are a bit unconventional, but you'll thank me, Steve. The whole town will thank me."

He lifted a hand and tipped his hat.

"Where are you going?" Steve asked.

"I was on my way to speak to the father when I saw you down here. I'm sure he's all messed up about now. It's not every day that someone comes into town and pulls the stunt I did yesterday. I think he deserves an explanation, don't you?"

Black walked away.

Steve wanted an explanation too, but he felt stupid calling out again. *What's that explanation, mister? And why did I dream what I dreamed?*

He was talking before he could stop himself. "What about my dream?" he called out.

Black stopped and turned back. "What dream?"

It was clear by his blank stare the Black really didn't know of any dream.

"Never mind," Steve said.

"Your dreams are your own, Steve." Black tipped his hat again and left.

Steve rubbed his palm with a thumb, relieved that the pain was gone. He stuck his hands into his pockets and headed for the saloon.

His head felt heavy.

STEVE SPENT the first thirty minutes by himself, wandering aimlessly around the bar, setting up shop. Wiping the counters down. Putting out glasses. Setting out peanuts. All without a thought.

His thoughts were elsewhere, on the stakes.

Claude came in about eleven, shirt untucked but buttoned up tight around his neck. He grunted and sat down in his regular spot along the bar. Early for Claude, who often came in for lunch, but never before noon.

"You open today?" Steve asked.

The big Swede didn't seem to hear.

Steve looked out the window and saw that Katie and Mary were angling for the saloon from across the street. Early for them too. It meant that others would see them coming and join them. That's how it always worked. Word spread fast in a small town. The lunch crowd was coming in early today.

"Sure," Claude said.

"Sure what?" Then Steve remembered his question.

"Sure I was open. Closed for lunch. Traffic's dead. Can I have a drink?"

"Lemonade?"

"Actually, I wouldn't mind something stronger if you have it." Claude rubbed his temples. "Head's throbbing."

"Beer?"

"Jack and Coke?"

Odd for a nondrinking man. Steve made the drink and served Claude. His mind drifted again.

The door banged and Katie walked in with Mary. Both ordered drinks. They were as quiet as Claude. Others started wandering in then, each entry punctuated by the slam of his screen door.

In some ways the stupor that clouded Steve's mind felt like the effects of the strong painkiller prescribed to him after some fool tourist's Doberman tried to rip off his hand.

Steve was normally a controlled fellow, ask anyone. But that hadn't stopped him from hauling out his shotgun with his unshredded hand and sending the Doberman to mutt hell with enough buckshot to splatter its head over a ten-foot-square section of the back wall.

Paula walked in. She was dressed for Sunday in a navy blue cotton dress with white piping on the neckline and pockets. Black leather flats. Who was she trying to impress? She sat at the end of the bar, and Steve ignored her.

Two fans swished overhead, and no one bothered turning on the jukebox. Steve stopped whatever he'd been doing, which was already a distant memory, and looked around at the "in" crowd of Paradise, Colorado. Without counting, he'd say about twenty.

The silence grew uncomfortable. Awkward. Downright infuriating.

Steve slammed his fist on the bar. "What's the problem?"

Katie looked up at him, blinking. "What do you think you're doing?"

He wasn't rightly sure, actually. He just didn't like the silence. A person can hide in a cacophony of noise, but everyone stands out in this kind of melancholic silence, and Steve wasn't in the mood to stand out.

"You think he poisoned us?" someone asked.

Katie faced Bob, an older farmer who raised the question. "Right."

Bob looked at one of his fingernails as if deciding whether it needed cleaning.

Once again silence stretched through the bar. A fly buzzed by Steve's ear.

"Could be," Claude said after a while. "We all drank his communion. Could be he poisoned us. I feel . . ." He stopped, either distracted or unsure how he felt.

"Well, if he did poison us, bring it on, medicine man," Katie said. "I feel pretty relaxed."

"Don't be stupid," Paula said. "The man's a devil, not a medicine man."

"You think a devil got up there and turned water into wine?" Katie challenged, coming to life.

"What water into wine?"

"Okay, then an apple into wine. Whatever. You get my point."

"No, Katie, I don't think I do. What is your point?"

"My point is if he wanted to kill us, he'd have done it last night."

They stared at her, uncomprehending. Steve didn't know what she was driving at either. Maybe she'd had a dream like his about a killing.

"Who said anything about killing?" Claude asked. "He's off his rocker maybe. He might be playing us for some reason, but I doubt a killer would be so obvious."

"What in the world are you all talking about?" Katie demanded. "He's no killer. He's a preacher."

"Come to bring grace and hope to Paradise," Bob said, still inspecting his fingernails.

"You're the one who brought up killer, Katie. And frankly it wouldn't surprise me. Either way, he's a devil," Paula said. "No man of God would talk the way he talked. I say we have our way with him before he has his way with us."

"Has his way with you?" Mary asked. "You holding out on us?"

A lone voice spoke out loudly from the rear door. "Paula's right. You should get rid of him or call the cops in Delta."

They turned as one to face Johnny Drake. The boy had come in the back and stood facing them with a fixed face.

"You eighteen, boy?" Steve asked. "Get out."

Paula stood. "Shut up, Steve." She walked toward the boy. "What makes you say that, Johnny?"

Johnny eyed them. "He may not be the devil, but he's not right." He hesitated. "And he's a killer."

Surprisingly, no one jumped on the boy. They were too lethargic to be jumping. Johnny seemed encouraged by this and continued.

"I watched him walk into town yesterday. Me and Cecil were on the bench. I know this may sound crazy, but Black killed Cecil."

Steve wasn't sure what to think about that, except to notice that the notion didn't seem preposterous. On the other hand, he doubted the boy had a clue what he was talking about. Probably dreamed Black had killed Cecil, just like he'd dreamed Black kissed and skewered Paula.

"You saying he actually killed Cecil?" Steve asked. "Or that Cecil died when Black was there, which is what he said."

"I mean he killed him."

"And how was that?"

"He . . ." Johnny shifted on his feet. "He jabbed his fingers into Cecil's eyes. Deep, maybe into his brains. I watched the whole thing. He killed him, and last night he threatened the whole town."

Did I hear that? I can't remember. I remember the stakes, but do I actually remember Black threatening . . .

"I remember it," a soft voice said. The rest of them were staring past Steve. He turned to the front door.

Marsuvees Black stood in the doorway, smiling at them. How'd he get in so quiet?

"It seems that Father Yordon has taken a leave of absence, so I suppose I should explain myself to the rest of you."

The man walked up to the bar. "Smart boy, Johnny. The rest of you should listen to him." He chuckled.

Black's sudden appearance had stunned them all. Steve had no doubt about his earlier judgment; there was something profoundly different about Black today. His eyes, though still blue, seemed a softer smiling blue rather than the drilling blue. His mouth had no mocking twist or angry snarl. He seemed almost earthy.

Black dug into his breast pocket and withdrew two objects, which he held, one in each hand.

"These look familiar?" he asked Johnny.

They were plastic or glass eyeballs, Steve saw. Smeared with paint to look like blood. Black rolled them down the bar toward Paula, who stepped back, repulsed. The eyeballs rolled off the bar and over to Johnny.

"Cecil's eyeballs," Black said gently.

Johnny stared wide-eyed as the balls stopped three feet from his shoes. He looked up. "But . . . that's not what I—"

"You saw what I wanted you to see. You saw me stick my fingers into Cecil's eye sockets and pull those eyes from his face. But those eyes are glass. Go on, pick them up."

Johnny bent, touched, then picked up the eyeballs. "Glass."

"Glass," Black said. "This, on the other hand"—he pulled an apple from his other breast pocket—"is a real apple. The same one you all saw last night. And this"—the preacher tossed the apple into the air, and when it landed in his hand it was a mug of lemonade—"is sleight of hand."

Steve was sure he'd seen an extra movement in there somewhere. "An illusion," he said. "You're a magician?"

"More than a magician. I'm a preacher who uses illusions to make a point, and I don't mind telling you that I've never had a town so wholly swallow my nonsense as this town did yesterday. You, my dear friends, have been like putty in the devil's hands."

They stared.

"But Cecil's dead!" Johnny said.

The glint left Black's eyes. He looked at the bar. "Yes, that was unfortunate." Eyes on Johnny. "Cecil had a heart attack, Johnny. Plain and simple. My trick sent him over the cliff he was already headed for. The only reason I didn't stop to pay him respects and administer rights was because I have been called to this town and I do have a message from God. I couldn't compromise for the sake of one man. I know it sounds crass, but doing anything else would have compromised my mission."

He let the statement rest. No one challenged him.

"And believe me, if you knew what I know about this town, you wouldn't want me to compromise my mission."

He held out a fist, then opened it. There lay a small clear bottle containing a milky translucent substance. "This look familiar? It's aloe vera mixed with a strong hallucinogen called peetock moss, which really isn't a moss at all, but something excreted by a rare worm. It was often used by Indians to call up images of what they thought were spirits."

Black set the four-inch-tall bottle on the bar. *Clunk.* A red ring circled the neck, otherwise there were no markings on the glass.

"It's potent but harmless. Forty-eight hours ago, I introduced quite a bit of this into the town's water supply. That was enough to soften up your susceptibility yesterday. Last night I put more into the communion glass. Most of you saw what I wanted you to see. Do any of you feel groggy?"

They didn't answer.

"The side effects. You've been duped, my friends. And in so doing, I've revealed the depravity of your hearts. Which is important if you know what I know about this town."

"Which is what?" someone asked.

"Which is that something very bad is coming. Without me, you poor folk don't stand a chance. Consider this training."

Steve's mind was still working a bit slow, but if he was catching all of this, Black was claiming to be nothing more than a magician who'd employed some drug called peacock or peetook or something or other, and he'd done it to make a point. Something bad was coming, and Black had a mission to protect the town from whatever that was.

Steve grunted. "Huh. You do this often?"

"On occasion. But not like this. Paradise is special. That's all you need to know. From here you'll have to trust me. Trust me, my friends, or die."

They stared at him, half in dumb wonderment.

"You drugged us?" the Swede asked.

"No, not really. I cleared your minds by feeding them something they wanted. Like feeding the body bread—no different. No lasting effect. No harm. I know it's a bit unorthodox, but it's the only way for the dumb saps in these parts to get a grasp on hope and grace, which is essential for what lies ahead."

"What's that?"

Black eyed Claude. "You're not only dense, you're deaf? I told you, that's it for now. Please try to concentrate when I speak. We don't have enough time to repeat every last thing I say."

A bit of the old Black was back. Frankly, Steve didn't mind.

"So they were tricks, right?" Katie said. "I knew it." She eyed the bottle on the bar and bit her lip. "I knew it."

It occurred to Steve that tricks or not, the stuff in that bottle was the real magic.

"So what's your point?" Paula asked. Her tone was harsh. She cleared her throat. "I mean how does this show us hope and grace? You're saying that you frightened Cecil into a heart attack with a trick, and you don't have a problem with that?"

"Paula, the pure one. That's good, I *want* you to question me. Of course I have a problem with Cecil's heart attack, but there was nothing I could do about it. I do magic, not miracles. Anything could have made that old heart of his stop."

"Still doesn't seem like anything a preacher would do," she said. "Neither does doping up a whole town."

Black studied her for too long, then put both palms on the bar and rubbed the wood gently. "Lovely," he said. "So lovely. Not all is as it seems, my friends. But the things that appear to us in everyday life are so compelling that we have a hard time looking past them to a greater reality. Sometimes it takes a very heavy dose of the other reality to get our attention. Think of me as the sword of truth, dividing bone from marrow."

He looked up and scanned them. "Preachers these days aren't willing to hand out heavy doses of that greater reality. They talk in old clichés that mean nothing to real people with real problems. I use a different language, and believe me, I am ready to dispense a heavy dose of a greater reality. You'll have to choose between your old way and my new way. The old way is to talk . . . all talk and no juice. My way is to show. All juice. Not everything I said yesterday is a sham. I have every intention of rocking your world. I will show you true grace and hope, and it won't look like the world's version of grace and hope. I'll show you a world swimming in the reality of God himself, but you'll have to allow me."

Black drilled Steve with a blue stare. "Let go and let God. Do you want to do that?"

Steve wasn't sure the preacher wanted an answer. But he *did* want to let go and let God, whatever that meant. He nodded.

"You'll have to give up your doubts. You'll have to trust me to remove the sliver that's worked its way under your skin, the stake that's been driven into your heart." Black's eyes shifted to Katie and the others at the end of the bar. "But in the end I will rock your world. Can I do that?"

"Yes," Katie said.

Black looked at the Swede. "Claude? I need agreement."

Claude glanced at his wife. "I guess."

"Then I would like to have dinner with you and your lovely wife tonight."

The preacher was looking at Claude, but Katie answered. "We'd love to have you."

Black faced her and bowed his head. "A wise choice, ma'am." He put his hand on the bottle, hesitated a moment, then slid it down the bar toward her.

"A little more won't hurt you," he said.

Then Marsuvees Black tipped his broad-rimmed hat, turned around, and walked out the door.

For a moment no one moved. Except Johnny. The boy slipped out the back the moment the screen door slammed shut.

"Wow," someone said.

Yeah, wow. Steve's eyes lingered on the bottle. They were all staring at Katie. She took the bottle and held it up to the light. Steve eased down the bar toward her.

Without further hesitation she spun the lid off and set it on the counter. Smelled the contents as if it were perfume.

"Seems harmless."

Katie splashed a little in her beer, swirled the drink around with her finger, and sipped at it.

Ten minutes later they had all tasted Black's concoction, some more than others. Although to say Paula tasted it might be an overstatement. She sniffed it then finally touched her tongue to the inside of the lid.

Tasted like nothing, she said.

But to Steve it tasted like wood.

Like wood stakes.

Chapter Seven

THE MONASTERY

Thursday morning

BILLY STROLLED into the cafeteria for a late breakfast, feeling self-conscious without knowing why. He'd missed the morning prayers, but that was no cause for guilt. He had violated the most sacred of monastery rules by entering the caverns below, but none of his classmates suspected anything.

Besides, if they knew what he knew, they would probably do the same. Marsuvees Black had been right. The impulse was in them for a reason. An animal created to be fed.

He'd spent half the night in the one tunnel, feeding the animal, and in the end it felt more like an hour. Maybe half an hour. He wasn't even sure what he'd done to eat up so much time. He had explored deeper—didn't matter. He could have sat on the couch and been just as happy.

Everything down there was exhilarating. He'd been awake less than an hour, and the thought of going back was already driving him crazy.

Half the kids had finished eating and vacated the cafeteria, but Darcy sat next to Paul at the far table. Billy went through the line, politely wishing the two overseers on serving duty a good morning, and shuffled to the table.

"Morning, Billy," Darcy said, smiling sheepishly. "You sleep well?"

Billy plopped his tray down and arranged his silverware. "Sure."

Paul shoved a piece of meat into his mouth. "Running a little late, are we?"

"Yeah." Billy nibbled on some eggs.

"You've been late a lot."

"Leave him alone," Darcy said. "So he's late now and then. So what?"

"I'm not saying it's a big deal. I'm just making conversation. I never said it was in any way significant. Although now that you mention it, being late repeatedly, as our Billy has been, is indicative of distraction, don't you think?"

The Brit's highfalutin tone irritated Billy. Always had. He ate his eggs without looking up. In writing class they'd memorized a quote from the philosopher Søren Kierkegaard, who'd once described writers as "spies who kept their eyes on suspicious characters, working on espionage, taking notes, observing particulars that everyone else overlooked, scouring the world for clues of meaning." The monastery was brimming with petty spies, because they were all writers.

"Yes, you're probably right," Darcy replied. "But just because a distraction is indicated doesn't mean it actually exists. Either way, his being late isn't necessarily significant."

"Stop it, both of you," Billy said. "You sound like two stuffed shirts from a university book." He raised his head and saw both staring at him with raised eyebrows. "I'm serious. You guys barely know the meaning of puberty, and here you are, discussing the fine points of a student's tardiness. Doesn't that strike you as odd?"

"Not really." Darcy's eyes flashed with mischief.

"It does me. We're too young for so much responsibility. We should be out playing baseball and splashing in the ocean. Not discussing tardiness and speaking like we're graduate students of the English language."

"I don't consider my life here that way," Paul said. "I rather enjoy it."

"Listen to you. *I rather enjoy it,*" Billy mocked, wagging his head. Paul was black and British by birth. Although he'd grown up in the monastery without the accent, he fancied his heritage and practiced it whenever he could. By contrast, Darcy was the perfect Dutch blonde who tended to lift her language only when in Paul's company. They were the perfect pair, black and white, spouting high English.

"You sound like you've eaten a barrel of pickles," Billy said.

Darcy laughed.

"I rather like pickles, actually," Paul returned without missing a beat. "We were just talking about Marsuvees Black before you sat down, Billy. I think his sudden vacancy wasn't planned. What do you think?"

Billy had a spoonful of eggs lifted halfway to his mouth. He stopped, then finished the bite. "I don't know. What's your reasoning?"

"He seemed a bit off at the end there, encouraging the class to reach for the edges and such," Paul said. "To go out and search for the limits. Nothing wrong technically. It was just the look in his eyes when he talked about it. He seemed more interested in pushing us into the darkness than into the light." He turned to Darcy. "You saw it, right?"

"At times, yes. But the desire to explore boundaries is part of the human condition. Maybe it's better to explore them here, in the confines of the monastery, than out there."

"Maybe, within the context of the rules," Paul said.

Billy glanced around the cafeteria and saw that only a handful of students remained. "Please, Paul, don't tell me you never feel like blowing the rules. Take the rules of writing, which mirror all of our other rules. Who decided those particular rules should be the rules of writing anyway? Who erected those walls and said, 'Here, you be a good boy and only write stories that lead to love'?"

Paul looked thrown off. "Why would any writer want to go beyond the four rules?"

"Because they just want to, that's why. Because this little voice in their head keeps whispering that there's more out there than this," Billy said, waving his hand to the ceiling. "Believe me, there is."

The smile left Darcy's face. "Come on, Billy. Don't be like this. You're not making a lot of sense."

The same desire that had propelled Billy to explore the tunnels rose in his chest, urging him to tell. If Darcy could just see what he had seen. Touch what he'd touched.

Only one student remained bent over his meal on the far side of the room.

Billy turned to Darcy and Paul. "I not only think there's more, I *know* there is more." He whispered, looking directly into Darcy's eyes. "I know there's more because I've seen more."

Neither responded to that, so he continued, watching her eyes. "I've been below. I've seen the subterranean levels."

Darcy's mouth opened in shock. She glanced around. Paul sat unmoving, bug-eyed.

"Below?" Darcy asked in a whisper. "You've been to the forbidden levels?"

Billy nodded. "Yes, and they are more wonderful than you could ever imagine. Ever."

"But . . . you can't, Billy! It's forbidden!"

"Why? Have you ever asked that? You have no idea what the lower levels contain. I, on the other hand, do know what they contain, and I'm telling you that they'll expand your mind like nothing else you know."

"But it's prohibited," Paul said.

"By whom?"

"By David. By the overseers."

"And who are they?"

"Who are they? They *built* this place! They're our . . . teachers."

"Yes, but do they run your mind, Paul? Maybe Marsuvees was right. Think about what he's been saying here for the last few months. It's in the fourth rule of writing. There *are* no boundaries. Why? Because each of us makes our own way."

"The rules of writing aren't the only rules we live by," Darcy said.

"Yes, but they do make my point. Consider our writing, for example. We create our *own* stories. Don't you see it? We are *writers*. We choose our own stories. No one forces us to write this plot or that plot. No one insists we do or don't do this or that. It's for *us* to choose! And as long as we have the free will to choose, we have an obligation to explore those choices."

"You stop this talk right now, Billy!" Darcy whispered harshly. "You've lost your senses. Talk like this will get you thrown out of here."

"Talk like this got me to the subterranean levels. And I found the most wonderful halls imaginable there, filled with images and powers that took my breath away and left me shaking."

"But what of the third rule of writing?" Paul asked.

The simpleton was still too shocked to take any of this seriously.

Paul continued. "How can any of this lead to love, or to the Creator? It's all in the third rule, remember? Like Samuel said in class yesterday."

Billy's snarl surprised even him. "Forget Samuel! Samuel's a dope!" He sat back and took a breath. "If you understand that we create our stories, then technically we *do* abide by the third rule because we *are* creators. We discover love by discovering ourselves."

There, he'd said it. He'd repeated the theory that someone left in his locker, encouraging him to descend into the tunnels.

They stared at him, blinking.

"And Raul is right. Stories without proper conflicts are boring. In the real world, the story of life starts with conflict. I could challenge the prevailing rules here and win with my arguments. Maybe I will."

They didn't respond to that. How could they, blinded by denial?

"So when did you go below?" Darcy asked, glancing around nervously.

"Last two nights."

"Two times?"

"I had to, Darcy. The dungeons call. It's as if they know my name and call to me. None of the halls up here speaks to me like the dungeons. None of them calls me."

"Dungeons?"

"Figure of speech. Tunnels. Subterranean halls. I've found a study that contains hundreds of books to be read. I'm telling you, take the enjoyment of reading or writing or eating or anything you do up here, and down there it's ten times better. Try it once and you'll see."

"If you think Paul or I would go down there, you've lost your mind. Proof positive that the 'dungeons,' as you appropriately call them, have rotted your mind."

Billy just grinned.

"What you're doing isn't only prohibited, it sounds nasty, and I for one will have no part in it." Darcy scooted her chair back and stood.

Paul followed her lead. "Sorry, Billy. I do believe she's right."

"Well, don't either of you forget what I said. We have no boundaries, so don't go and flap your jaws about this. I'm entitled to do whatever I choose." He caught Darcy's eye. "I'll be waiting for you."

Billy watched them go, past the tray table toward the entry. *Idiots. Stupid fools.* And yet he had resisted the impulse at first, hadn't he, just like Darcy and Paul were doing now.

A voice spoke behind him. "Good morning, Billy." Billy twisted to face Samuel. The last student eating across the cafeteria while he'd spouted off about Samuel being a dope had been none other than Samuel himself.

Billy turned back to the table and clenched his eyes for a moment, hoping that Samuel hadn't been listening.

"Morning, Samuel."

Samuel stepped around the table and sat down. "You okay, Billy?"

"Sure, Samuel. I'm just fine. And you?"

"I'm good. Are you sure you're okay? You've seemed a bit upset lately."

Upset? And when had he looked upset? Billy's face grew a little hotter. "Well, I haven't been upset."

"You're struggling with something, Billy. It's written all over you. Part of me wants to tell you to snap out of it. Quit licking the floor and stand up." He paused. "But most of me just wants to tell you that we all go through struggles. We can help each other."

"What do you care, Samuel? What difference does it make to you?"

A few seconds passed before the answer came. "Everything each of us does affects the others. None of us lives in a vacuum. We're simply children on a quest to gain the highest forms of wisdom without being compromised in the process. But when one is compromised, the others are compromised. You see that, don't you?"

Billy waved his fork at the blond boy. "Each of us can do whatever he or she wants. You can't take that away."

"You're right. But do you think there aren't consequences to what you say or do?"

"And what would the consequence be if I told you to shut up, Samuel?"

Samuel just looked at him. There was something in his eyes, a look Billy could have identified a week ago, but which now just looked vague. Maybe it was hurt.

Billy thought of the halls below, running with worm gel. He had to get back.

"Just shut up," he said.

Chapter Eight

PARADISE

Thursday afternoon

JOHNNY'S PREDICAMENT had gone from bad to worse.

Now he wasn't sure what he'd seen yesterday. Actually he was sure—he'd seen Black kill Cecil, but he wasn't sure why he'd seen it. Didn't feel right, but it was possible that Black's explanation in the bar was the truth. The others were swallowing it, hook, line, and sinker. Didn't feel right, but that was supposedly Black's point.

Maybe he'd misjudged the man. His ways were strange to be sure, but again, that was his point. He didn't smell right, look right, or talk right. But he did look and talk more normal this morning than he had yesterday.

And all of that was his point.

Johnny's mother still hadn't returned from Junction. No surprise there. She'd be home this afternoon. She hadn't taken any of the stuff Black was handing out. Her exposure, like his own, was limited to whatever the preacher had put in the water supply. She'd be able to tell him what was up.

And maybe Roland and Fred would be straight in the mind. He'd know in a few minutes when they met behind the old theater.

Johnny glanced at the clock. Time to go. He was dressed in a blue Nike T-shirt with a faded brown button-down shirt hanging unbuttoned and tails out over his thin frame. Good to go.

The minute the door slammed shut behind him, he reconsidered taking the trek down Main Street to the Starlight, which loomed two hundred yards off. He'd been so eager to get home from the bar that he hadn't noticed just how odd the town looked.

For starters it was deserted. Not a soul.

Somewhere a screen door was banging in the wind. Wind-blown silt smothered the town in a dull gray-brown haze. Leaves danced by.

Bang, bang, bang. Whose door was that? Across the street stood the church. Closed. No cars in front of Smither's Saloon or All Right Convenience. Didn't mean no one was at either place, just no visitors.

Johnny walked deliberately, ignoring his throbbing leg. Off the sidewalk, under the large maple that shaded their house, down the side of Main Street. He crossed it.

When he reached the middle, at the point Black had turned toward him and Cecil yesterday, he again thought that the alley would have been a better choice. He was alone out here. Stranded. The wind tore at his hair and the dust whipped his pants and he was sure that at any moment something impossible would happen.

Paradise had become the town of impossibilities.

That was yesterday. That was the preacher's point.

Johnny picked up his pace, staring straight ahead, and then ran the last few steps along the old theater's wall. He rounded the back corner and pulled up in front of Roland, Fred Mars, and Peter Bowers, all sitting in a circle, protected from the wind by the large building.

They stared at him as if he'd come out of a snowstorm.

"Hey," he said.

They wore blue jeans and ratty T-shirts, except Fred, who wore a sun-bleached plaid farmer's shirt that looked like it had been found on a rocky riverbank.

"Hey," Roland said.

Johnny walked forward.

"Hey, Johnny," Peter said. The Bowers boy was big, like his father, Claude.

Johnny stopped. There was something out of whack with Fred and Peter. Dark circles under their eyes. Tired faces, as if they hadn't slept a wink last night.

"You gonna sit down?" Fred asked.

"You get any sleep last night, Fred?"

He shrugged. "Sure." But he didn't look so sure.

"What do you think about the preacher?" Fred asked.

Johnny settled to the ground next to Roland.

"I think . . ." Johnny stopped. Actually, he didn't know what to think anymore. "He's pretty weird, that's for sure." No one disagreed.

The mood was gloomy, which was strange because Johnny figured they'd find a way to rip the preacher to shreds with feeble attempts at humor.

"They say Chris was dying before the preacher healed him," Fred said. "Nothing like that's ever happened around here. The preacher's probably pretty close to God. Like Moses. That's what my parents think, anyway."

"Moses?" Peter said. "Moses was a prophet, not some preacher who walked into town growing warts in people's mouths."

"What do you call the plagues?"

"It doesn't matter anyway," Roland said. "Just because someone does something great doesn't make them a great person. Look at Hitler. Everybody liked him in Germany at one time, and look what he did to the Jews."

"What do you mean everybody liked Hitler?" Fred demanded, face red. "Nobody liked Hitler."

"Settle down," Peter said. "What gives, man?"

"If Roland wouldn't be so stupid—"

"I'm not being stupid! I'm just saying that Moses wasn't Hitler. And that maybe this guy isn't Moses either. He could be, I'm just saying he might not be."

Watching Fred, Johnny felt uneasy. He spoke as much to stop their bickering as to fill them in.

"I saw him this morning." They looked at him. "He was in the bar with the others."

Roland pushed. "And?"

"And he was . . . different. He said that he put something in the drinking water to make us all loopy. And that everything he did was just a trick."

"He said that?" Fred's eyes widened. "Why would he do that?"

"Loopy?" Peter Bowers said. He pulled a bottle from his pants. "You mean this?"

It was the bottle that Black had showed them in the bar, only now it was empty. Peter was grinning.

Johnny reached for it. "Where'd you get that?"

"My mom." He snatched it out of Johnny's reach, twirled off the lid, and lifted the bottle to his nose. "She said it was some good stuff."

"Good stuff? She tell you it came from Black?"

"Course she did. Why, does that scare you?" He stuck his tongue into the narrow neck and made a show of trying to lick the inside, but his tongue was too fat for the bottle.

"That's the stuff?" Roland asked.

Peter pulled the bottle off his tongue and licked his lips. "Tastes like toe sludge."

"*Sick!*" Fred grabbed the bottle from Peter's hand and shoved it up to his nose. "Doesn't smell bad. You taste this?"

"Course I did. It tastes like toe sludge."

"Yeah, right." Fred put his finger into the bottle, withdrew some of the residue, and touched it to his tongue. Satisfied it wasn't as disgusting as his friend had insisted, he licked his finger clean.

"Tastes like nothing."

"Let me see," Roland said, reaching for the bottle.

"I wouldn't," Johnny said.

"Come on, Johnny, don't be such a wimp. It's probably just water."

Peter dove for the bottle, but Fred rolled out of his way, laughing. He came to his feet and jumped back, sticking his finger in for another sample.

"Knock it off!" Peter yelled. By the looks of the vein sticking out of his neck, he wasn't too happy. He stood, brushing dust from his shirt. "Give it back."

"What for?"

They faced off, Fred taunting, Peter scowling. But in a flash, that changed. For no apparent reason, both Fred and Peter spun toward the theater's back wall and stared at it wide-eyed.

Their mouths dropped open.

"What?" Roland said, looking at the wall with Johnny. Weathered, once white boards ran vertically in bad need of fresh paint, but nothing seemed out of place.

"Holy . . ." Peter was whispering. He took a step back and Fred followed suit.

"What is it?" Roland demanded again.

Peter's mouth twisted, formed a grin. He stared at the wall. "Wow . . ."

"Wow," Fred echoed.

Johnny scrambled to his feet. *It's the bottle. Black was right, the stuff in the bottle makes people see things. That's what was . . .*

Peter was yelling in terror. He stumbled backward.

Fred screamed, white-faced. He whirled and ran. Straight into Peter. The boys crashed to the ground with grunts and yells. But both were too distracted by whatever they had seen to make anything of the collision. They scrambled to their feet, cast a quick glance at the wall, and ran for the corner, where they disappeared behind the theater.

They weren't screaming anymore. They were just running. The wind swallowed the sound of their feet.

Roland looked at Johnny, then back at the wall. "You see anything?"

"I'm telling you, it was the stuff in that bottle. What did I say? It makes people loopy."

Roland grinned crooked and walked to the wall. He put his hand on the boards. "What do you think they saw?"

Johnny kicked at the bare dirt behind the Starlight. He didn't want to be here and he didn't want to go home alone. Black might be good, Black might be bad, but whatever was happening in this town was officially terrifying.

"The preacher talked about helping people see another reality. Maybe they saw . . ." A thought occurred to him. "Maybe we should leave."

Roland turned back. "What? Like a ghost or something?"

"I don't know. Whatever it was, it wasn't good. I think we should go."

Roland slapped the boards. "There's nothing here, man. That's freaky. What's the world coming to?"

"Good question. You notice anything strange around here today?"

"Yeah, Fred and Peter."

"Not just Fred and Peter. You have any nightmares last night?"

That caught Roland off guard. "What do you mean, nightmares?"

"I mean did you dream about Black?"

"What makes you say that?"

Johnny shrugged. "I did."

"So did I."

"You ever see clouds like that this time of year?" Johnny asked, looking up. Flat clouds hung abnormally low, like someone had painted the sky dark gray just above the town.

Roland's gaze followed Johnny's. "Yeah. Pretty strange."

"There wasn't a cloud in the sky yesterday."

"You really think Black has anything to do with the weather?"

"Have you seen him today?"

"Actually, I did. My mom left her watch on the sink at Nails and Tan and wanted me to get it. Didn't want to talk to Katie. They had an argument yesterday or something. Maybe you didn't hear this, did you? I told Fred and Peter about it before you got here."

"Black was at Nails and Tan? When was this?"

"On my way here." Roland grinned. "He was there all right. He practically had his tongue down Katie's throat. Freaked me out, man."

The revelation stunned Johnny. "He was kissing her?"

"Okay, maybe that's an exaggeration. I couldn't actually see her because his back was to the door, but they were definitely close. Laughing."

"You tell anyone else about this?"

"Just Fred and Peter. I guarantee you my mom would flip."

"And you don't find that just a little bit strange, for a preacher to do that?"

Roland looked at the wall again. "Like you said, he's trying to get people's attention. Look at what just happened to Fred and Peter. The whole thing is pretty freaky, but you have to admit, it's kinda cool."

"Maybe. And maybe not," Johnny said.

"What do you mean, maybe or maybe not? It's either cool or it's not."

"Maybe. But that doesn't mean it's good."

"Has he done anything bad yet?"

Johnny thought about that. Fact was, scaring people to make a point wasn't a bad thing. All preachers did that at times, right? The Bible did that. What do you call God sending a whale to swallow Jonah? Maybe Black was that whale, going to towns to swallow them up so they would change their minds.

"Maybe not," Johnny said. "But we can't tell."

"Well, Peter said Black's gonna be at his house tonight." A thin smile tugged at Roland's lips. "You ever spy?"

"Spy on Black?"

"Come on, you know that half the people around here leave their shades open at night. You just sneak up and look in. You've done it."

"Not for a few years I haven't. And not on Black. What if we get caught?"

"We won't get caught."

"I don't know . . . he's . . ."

"He's Marsuvees Black. Come on, Johnny. He's just a crazy preacher who's messing with people's heads a bit. So we check him out."

Johnny glanced at the sky. Black, black, everything was black. "When?"

Roland shrugged. "Eight? After dark."

"Okay."

Roland grinned. "Cool."

"Cool," Johnny said.

But it didn't feel cool. Nothing about Black felt cool.

Chapter Nine

THE MONASTERY

Thursday afternoon

DARCY SAT in the rear of the class, looking at thirty-six heads covered with blond and brown and black hair. And one covered in red hair. Billy stuck out three rows over on her left, the monastery's cherry.

Billy glanced over with those green eyes of his, and she turned her head back to Raul, who was rambling on about the second rule.

Rambling? Not rambling as in *boring*. Rambling as in *We've heard this a million times, old man. Get on with some good stuff*. In truth, he was speaking eloquently about greatness in purity. On the other hand, it *was* rather boring. It bothered her that she thought so.

She stole a quick look at Billy and saw that he was fidgeting, probably bored out of his skull, waiting for class to end so he could sneak down to the dungeons and play with his ghosts. She was surprised to be thrilled at the idea and turned back to Raul. She pinched the bridge of her nose to concentrate on the overseer's words.

"So, someone tell me why," Raul said. "Why is an adventure which leads to purity so grand? Come on, we've been over this in our sleep."

Tyler raised his hand.

The overseer motioned to the brown-headed Indian boy, the youngest in the class.

"The Creator is pure. Therefore, a life that leads us to purity leads us to the Creator. And no man could possibly find an adventure grander than one that leads to the Creator."

A soft chorus of agreement rippled through the room.

"Yes," Darcy whispered as the approval died down. But her mind was on Billy. Had he also said *yes*, just to be proper?

"Someone else? Yes, Paul?"

Darcy wondered what was running through his head after their talk with Billy at breakfast.

"A path leading to purity will cross enough challenges to make the human head spin." The class chuckled. "It's not only arriving at the conclusion of purity which is so thrilling, but it's the journey to that conclusion. Overcoming the challenges. Each obstacle passed, each challenge met and won. This presents a new level of satisfaction."

Brilliant. Judging by their response, the rest of the class agreed with her assessment. *Brilliant indeed, but old hat, brother. Give me something new.*

The moment she thought it, Darcy knew Billy had gotten to her. Not that she had any intention of actually doing what Billy suggested. Heavens, no. But she wasn't thinking the same, and she wondered why. A little tick had burrowed into her skull, and every time she heard one of the old truths, the insect began to chew on her brain.

She looked at Billy again. He was staring at her, and this time she stared back. He was awfully cute with his auburn hair and green eyes. He was certainly one of the brightest students. Maybe second to Samuel.

Raul was speaking again, but she didn't hear him. Something in Billy's eyes pulled at her. Something that said, *You and I are the same.* And she liked that. It felt good.

Maybe Billy *was* on to something.

She had a responsibility to look after him, didn't she? At the very least she should check up on him. The poor soul was heading for a cliff without the slightest clue.

How did one get to the subterranean levels anyway?

Chapter Ten

PARADISE

Thursday night

AS FAR as Johnny could tell, nothing in Paradise changed that afternoon. Other than the wind, which was blowing harder, and the sky, which was growing darker. He spent the hours in his room, waiting for his mother to return.

Roland hung out for an hour but wanted to go home because, as he put it, his own mother and father were behaving a bit strange, and Johnny was making him nervous with all his talk about Black.

Johnny thumbed the toggle and blasted his way through one of his older PlayStation games, Red Alert IV. He paused the game every fifteen or twenty minutes to check the front window. The streets were empty. Paradise was too far off the beaten track to become a hotbed for tourism, but that didn't keep the odd traveler from braving the mountains to find this fruit-farming community. Maybe the storm discouraged visitors; it was raining hard along the Highway 50 corridor.

Johnny resumed his game and killed a few more bad guys without thinking through the steps. He tried to call his mother on the cell phone but couldn't find her signal. It happened up here, enough to make his mother swear on occasion.

Back to the game.

The front door slammed at six o'clock.

"Mom?"

Johnny ran out to the living room to greet his mother, who held several bulging bags. She was wearing new black jeans with a red and white blouse. Her blonde hair was windblown but she beamed, clearly not bothered by the weather.

"Finally," Johnny exclaimed. "What took you so long? I've been . . ."

He stopped short. Something about his mother's brown eyes scared him more than the horror movie he and Roland rented last weekend. They were . . . distracted. Dull. Not unlike the eyes of the rest in the bar.

"Hello, Johnny. Am I?"

"Are you what?"

"Late?"

"It's . . . it's six o'clock."

"Well, I've been home for an hour. I just stopped in to update the others." She walked past him. "Boy, is it raining down the mountain. Highway 50's a river! I half-expected to find the town washed away." She dropped her bags and faced him. "I tried calling on the cell, but the service is out. The storm's knocked everything out. I'm surprised we still have power."

"Where have you been?"

"I told you, I stayed in Grand Junction to shop."

"But you've been talking to the others?"

Her smile faded. "Well, of course, honey. What's wrong? You look like a ghost."

Johnny swallowed. "Nothing's wrong. It's just that nothing's right around here. The wind, the clouds, the preacher—"

"Of course nothing's normal. We're in the middle of a storm." She walked up to him and ruffled his hair, a habit of hers that he was losing interest in.

"I guess I owe you an apology. They told me about the eyes. I'm sorry for doubting you saw what you thought you saw. I just couldn't imagine anybody actually doing what you claimed the preacher did. I was right about that, but I had no right to dismiss you."

"It's okay." Johnny turned away and sat on the sofa. They'd stolen his thunder. "What did they tell you?"

"You mean Katie? The service, her dreams, the meeting this morning—pretty much everything, I suppose." She opened the refrigerator and studied the contents. "Why? You know something else?"

"So you believe him?"

Sally withdrew a bottle of cranberry juice and flipped open the cupboard for a glass. "Makes sense to me. Sure it's all a bit strange, but this world is half-full of strange people."

They were welcome words. If his mother thought Black was legit, then he probably *was* legit.

"If I'd gone to Junction and the medical examiner told me that Cecil died of trauma to the head or eyes, I would think differently. Actually, it's all a bit exciting, don't you think?"

"Unless he turns out to be a liar," Johnny said.

She poured her drink. "He was a liar. Yesterday, right? Katie said you were in the saloon. You heard him yourself. He did it to make a point."

"And what about this thing that's coming to Paradise? Katie tell you about that?"

"What thing?"

"Black said he's doing all this to help prepare us for something that's coming."

"He said that?" For the first time since she'd entered, a shadow of concern crossed his mother's face. "Hmm. Now that's weird. You hungry?"

His mother had a way of letting the steam out of his concerns. At least she was keeping an open mind.

"Sure. I'm starved."

They made small talk while Sally cooked up some spaghetti and prepared a green salad with tomatoes, Johnny's favorite. For an hour they were the normal small-family unit that Johnny had grown accustomed to since his grandfather's death. His mother was a bit distracted, but he wrote it off to a good shopping day. Funny how buying clothes and shoes could make someone so happy.

As the eight o'clock spying mission approached, his concern made a comeback. He thought about calling Roland and telling him he couldn't go out, but the fact of the matter was, he wanted to find out what Black was up to as much as Roland did. Maybe more.

Sally pushed her plate away. "Boy, that was delicious if I don't say so myself."

She picked up the bottle of oily Italian dressing and eyed it. "The preacher's stuff looks a bit like this. Don't you think?"

The comment caught Johnny off guard. She'd seen the bottle? "What do you mean?"

"Katie had a bottle—"

"You didn't taste it, did you?"

Sally looked up at Johnny, held his eyes. "It was harmless, Johnny." She set the bottle down. "She said it was aloe vera and some kind of mild sedative."

"Mild? It's got half the town seeing things!"

"Well, I haven't seen anything. Besides, I wouldn't mind knowing what all the hoopla's about." Sally stood and took her plate into the kitchen. "It'll be fine, Johnny. Paradise could use a little excitement now and then."

A question ballooned in his mind. Why were the rest so eager to taste Black's concoction while he had no interest? At least not enough interest to give in. They'd supposedly all been exposed to the water. Had he drunk any water in the last couple days? Yes, he had. So then why were they different from him? Maybe they really weren't.

His mother didn't think it was a big deal. So then it probably wasn't.

He looked at the clock—two minutes to eight. He had to meet Roland.

Maybe they were all just questioning things because that's exactly what the preacher wanted them to do. He was thinking pretty hard about things he'd hardly ever thought about, right? Maybe Black was an angel who'd come to save Paradise.

Then who was coming to kill them all?

JOHNNY LOOKED around the old theater and studied the street. He could just see the outline of the Bowerses' house. Like a ghost across the street, barely glowing in the night, shifting behind a thin curtain of blowing dust. The blinds were open.

He pulled his head back.

"Anything?" Roland asked.

"No. Were your parents around this afternoon?"

Roland hesitated. "My mom was. She forgot to make dinner."

"But you didn't see your dad?"

Another hesitation. "He was probably busy. Are we going to do this? I'm getting a headache."

Johnny took a deep breath. "Okay, we see if the preacher's over there. If he is, we watch him and see what he does. If we don't see him, we knock on the door and ask for Peter. That's the plan."

"Sounds good." Roland headed around the corner. He didn't seem bothered by the darkness, so Johnny followed, dismissing the inner voices that suggested caution.

A scrub-oak hedge surrounded the house. The barrier gave them perfect cover up to a height of three feet. They wedged themselves between the hedge and house, and Roland peered into the first dark window. After a moment, he shrugged and motioned them on.

Johnny began to settle. Seemed simple enough.

They crawled three quarters of the way around the house without seeing a single soul. The Bowerses had either left the house or occupied one of three remaining rooms—Claude Bowers's study, the master bedroom, or the main-floor bathroom.

Roland reached the study window and waited for Johnny to squat next to him. "Okay, you go up first this time," Roland whispered.

"Me?" Roland had led thus far.

"Sure. Just go up slow and peek in."

Johnny looked up. Seemed harmless enough, despite the fact that the window glowed faintly.

"You think he's going to poke your eyes out?" Roland asked, wiggling his eyebrows.

Johnny ignored the jab and slowly lifted his head to the window sill. He peered into the study, saw Claude sitting at his desk, and immediately jerked his head down.

"What?" Roland whispered. "They in there?"

"Claude." First contact. Adrenaline coursed through his veins. They hadn't exactly snuck into Fort Knox or anything, but his heart didn't seem to know the difference.

"What's he doing?"

"I don't know."

This time Roland eased up to the sill, held his nose there for a moment and then retreated. "He's . . . he's watching television."

This time both Roland and Johnny eased up to the window.

The room began to flash with blinding white strobes that ignited scenes on a monitor that sat on Claude's desk. Johnny couldn't see the images, but they seemed to mesmerize Claude. His mouth hung open dumbly.

The white strobes yielded to red and blues that lit his face. Johnny could hear music now, the bass thudding low. A music video. An intense music video that had turned Claude into a useless lump of a man.

A bottle of booze slipped from Claude's fingers and fell on the floor with a *thump*. He didn't seem to notice.

Claude blinked. He swallowed and began to chuckle. But he still hadn't moved.

Johnny craned for a better view. He caught a fleeting image of Black's head on the set, flapping back and forth as if on a spring. Then a red image that Johnny couldn't make out.

Claude lunged forward, twisted a knob, and sat back. The music pounded louder. Metal, head-banging music. Claude bent for the fallen bottle on the carpet and chuckled again.

The images popped relentlessly without breaking cadence. Claude took a swig from the bottle, half of which dripped off his chin onto his stomach, and began to giggle.

Johnny felt a tug on his sleeve. "He's not in there. Come on."

He dropped down. "You see that?"

"Lost his marbles. Black's not in there. Come on."

Johnny followed Roland to the next window. Master bedroom.

"Go," Roland whispered.

Johnny pulled himself up and looked through blinds that were closed but not properly, leaving slits he could see through if he pushed his eye flat against the glass.

A figure moved by the mirror above the double dresser. Katie was there, leaning into the mirror.

Johnny shifted for a better view.

"Anything?" Roland whispered.

She was dressed in a red skirt, too short and too tight, unless she was headed for a party. He could see Katie's face in the mirror, chin tilted up as she carefully applied a fresh coat of lipstick. She rubbed her lips together and turned her head for a side view. Maybe she and Claude were going to Delta. To a dance or something.

Roland's face came up next to his. Their breath fogged the glass, and Roland wiped the moisture off with his palm.

Johnny watched Katie fix something at the corner of her mouth. Satisfied, she tilted her head down and smiled into the mirror. She traced her freshly painted lips with a slow tongue.

Katie tried another look, this one with one finger on her cheek and her hip cocked as if to say, *Hey there, stranger*. She shifted into another look, this one tracing her open mouth with her tongue and a single finger along her neckline.

Roland dropped down and Johnny followed.

"You see that?" Roland whispered through his cockeyed smile.

"Well, it is Katie." Johnny glanced back at the office window, still glowing from the lighted computer screen inside. "Pretty weird, though. Both Claude and Katie. I wonder where Black is."

"Basement? We haven't tried the window wells."

"And where's Peter? Maybe we should just knock on the door and ask for Peter."

"Try the next window," Roland said.

Roland edged his way around the corner toward the bathroom window, waited for Johnny to catch up, then rose slowly. Wind howled through the eaves. Light seeped past the blinds, illuminating the hazy dust that filled the air. Johnny shielded his eyes and followed Roland to the windowsill.

The low blind provided only a three-inch gap at the bottom. Something blocked their view—a towel or something that made the window dark. Maybe a closet or . . .

The darkness shifted. He squinted. And then the darkness walked away from the window.

Johnny flinched. He stood there staring at Marsuvees Black's polyester trousers, less than three feet away.

The preacher had been leaning against the window. Right in front of Johnny's face, a pane of glass separating them. Now Black stood at the mirror.

A black, coverless DVD case rested on the white sink. Maybe for the DVD that Claude was watching this very moment in his office.

Johnny couldn't see what Black was doing, because the bottom of the blinds cut the man off at the shoulders. He would have to crouch a little to see Black's face and that meant moving. If he moved, Black might see him.

Roland breathed heavily. The window started to fog. Not good.

Johnny pulled back a fraction to allow circulation between his lips and the glass. Then down a little so that his eyes cleared the blinds.

Black was picking his teeth.

The man's fingernails were long, but well shaped, as if he recently had a manicure. The preacher valued cleanliness. He retracted his lips and studied his large white teeth.

He began rubbing a section of his lower teeth with his tongue. Unsuccessful with a mere tongue, the man's lips attacked his teeth. They moved furiously around his lower jaw. If lips could be double-jointed, the preacher owned a pair.

Still aggravated by something in his teeth, Black went after them with his fingernail. Johnny could see his clean-shaven jaw jutting out toward the mirror as he angled for whatever it was.

Roland had moved down for a better view and was breathing harder. Seeing the man go to work on his teeth was a mesmerizing sight. Not exactly the kind of evidence that revealed anything good or bad about him, but fascinating, nonetheless. The man really was getting worked up about whatever was stuck in his—

Black howled with rage.

The man lost his cool so suddenly that both Johnny and Roland yelped. If not for Black's own howl, he would've heard them for sure.

The preacher grabbed his lower lip with his right hand and yanked it down hard. It peeled cleanly off his jaw as if it were a mask. Long white teeth buried in three inches of pink flesh jutted into a gaping mouth. His lower lip slipped a good four or five inches below his chin.

With his other hand, Black wrenched a single tooth from his jaw and spit angrily into the mirror. A small chunk of white meat stuck to the glass.

The stranger shoved his tooth down into place. He released his lower lip. It snapped up over his teeth, and he rubbed his jaw like a man who'd just been slapped, but no worse for the wear.

Johnny's eyes dried in the wind. And then Black straightened his coat and turned toward the door.

Now, Johnny. Move now, while his back's turned. He dropped to his knees. The jar must have started his stalled heart, because he could hear the blood rushing through his ears now. He was hyperventilating.

Roland was beside him, also on his knees. "You . . . you see that?" He stared up at the window, stupefied.

Johnny tore through the hedge. He ran for the Starlight, across the street, a hundred yards off. His leg was bothering him, but adrenaline pushed him beyond the pain. He ran fast, maybe faster than he had in his life. Thankfully, the streetlight was out.

He broke into the clearing behind the theater and doubled over, wheezing. Roland slid to a stop beside him.

"You see that?" Roland said, panting. "Man, did we really see that?"

Johnny didn't answer.

"We have to tell someone." Roland began to pace.

"We could talk to our parents."

"They'll just say we're seeing things. That's what everyone'll say now."

Johnny hesitated, thinking. "And maybe they're right."

Roland scratched his head. "Man, that looked real. I wonder what Fred and Peter saw."

"Maybe we should go to the cops," Johnny said.

"Cops? In Delta? Now you think it was real?"

"I don't know what to think anymore."

Chapter Eleven

THE MONASTERY

Thursday night

BILLY WAS having a difficult time remembering exactly how many times he'd been to the dungeons in the last couple days. Well, yes, he knew, of course. Three times. Roughly. No, closer to five times. His memory was foggy.

His fascination with the dungeons, on the other hand, was less foggy. Crystal clear, in fact. Like a shaft of light in a pitch-black room, except that the tunnels were actually black, so if you could have a shaft of darkness in a room full of light . . .

Billy left the class in which Paul spouted off as if he owned wisdom itself, and he spent an hour easing his way closer to the east side of the monastery, past the library, to the dark hall. He didn't think he cared whether the others knew what he was up to, but he skirted the students and the teachers with great care anyway.

Raul knew, he thought. He hadn't run into the masked monk again, but upon rather fuzzy reflection, he narrowed the man's identity further. Yesterday he was confident it was either Raul or Marsuvees Black or David Abraham. Now he was quite sure it was either Raul or David Abraham, because the man had spoken about Marsuvees Black as if he was a third party.

The man could have been tricking him, of course. He could be Marsuvees Black, living in the tunnels, driven mad by the worm gel. But why would he wear a mask? He lacked the same motivation as Raul, an active teacher, and David, the director, both of whom would need to conceal their identity to continue their activities.

Simple deduction. The kind of simple deduction Darcy and Paul obviously lacked, at least when it came to considering the tunnels.

Billy took a deep breath, satisfied himself that the coast was clear, stepped into the staircase, grabbed a torch, and ran down the steps with the ease of familiarity. When he stepped up to the blackened doors he was breathing as hard from the excitement of what lay ahead as from the rapid descent.

The dead silence down here was broken only by a faint crackling from the torch. Billy stared at the tunnel doors, and in that moment he didn't care if Darcy or Paul or anybody followed him into the caverns. As long as he could enter himself.

Billy stepped forward and was reaching for the door when the unmistakable sound of a shoe scraping on stone filtered down the stairwell behind him. He jerked his hand back and scanned the room quickly, looking for a place to hide. Nothing.

Feet rounded the staircase. White tennis shoes, the kind students wore. A girl descended into view. Her skirt hung above trembling knees and her eyes were round like saucers.

"Darcy?" His voice echoed around the chamber.

"Billy?" Her voice trembled.

"You . . . you came."

Darcy looked around in dazed wonderment. Billy was too stunned to move. So then he wasn't the only one to come to his senses when presented with the right argument.

"It's . . . it's so gloomy," she said.

She needed encouragement. Billy walked up to her and reached out his hand. This was almost too good to be true. "Don't worry, you'll get used to it."

She took his hand, but her eyes remained on the walls. Throbbing flame light cast an eerie orange hue on the mossy rock walls; the black door seemed to absorb and swallow the light. It *was* rather gloomy.

"Wait till you see the inside."

She looked at him with some astonishment. "I'm not going inside. I just wanted to see what it looks like."

"Okay, but this is not *it*. *It* is through that door." He motioned toward the black doors. "You have to go in there to see *it*."

She shook her head. "No. I can't go in there." She paused. "Aren't you frightened?"

Billy released her hand and walked to the door. When the torch's circle of light moved with him, Darcy followed. He turned to her. "Frightened, Darcy? Tell me, what do you feel like right now?"

"I'm frightened."

"Yes, frightened. But what does frightened *feel* like? Tell me how you feel without using those old words. Say something a writer might write, like *I feel a chill down my spine* or something. Tell me exactly how you *feel*."

She hesitated and glanced at the floor. "I feel . . . awful, Billy. I'm scared."

"Come on, Darcy. Those are the old words. Use the real words. How would you write it? Describe your feeling. *Show* me! What do *awful* and *scared* mean?"

"I think I should go now. This isn't right. This place is . . . it's evil." She took a step backward.

A thought crossed Billy's mind. She had no torch. In fact, she had no torch coming down the stairs, which meant she'd followed the light from his torch.

"It's too dark to go back, Darcy. You wouldn't catch me going up those stairs without a torch to keep whatever's hiding in the dark from stepping out. Will you just tell me what you feel, for Pete's sake? I've got a point to make here."

She looked back at the stairwell. When she turned around, her face was drawn tight and he knew he'd won, for the moment. She stood like a frail doll, dressed in her white cotton blouse and plaid skirt, hugging herself. She looked like she might start crying.

"I'm cold," she said. "My stomach is tied in knots. My legs are trembling, and I want to leave this place. To turn and run up the stairs. But you have the torch. What do you mean 'keep whatever's hiding'? Is there something in the stairwell?"

"Never mind. That's good, Darcy. And I feel like you too. My hands are shaking a little and my heart is beating a hundred miles an hour. See? We're the same here. Only I don't want to run up those stairs because I've been here before. Instead I want to run through that door."

"Well, I don't. Now give me the torch. You can go in there and find another one."

"Oh no, I can't. There aren't any torches in there. Besides, I think you're wrong. I don't think you feel fear at all. When someone tells me their stomach is tied in knots and their knees are knocking, I might guess they were about to step onto a thrilling roller-coaster ride, or maybe meet someone they're in love with. I think that's what you feel, Darcy, only you've never quite felt this way because you've never been *allowed* to ride a roller coaster, and so you're misinterpreting the feelings. You're mistaking something that's good for something that's bad."

Judging by her stare she thought he'd flipped his lid. And maybe he had.

"That's crazy. I'm scared, not thrilled. This isn't a thrill ride I'm feeling—you think I don't know the difference?" She shifted her eyes to the blackened doors.

"Then there is no difference between fear and excitement," Billy said. "Because they both feel the same to me, and they would feel the same to you if you just relaxed a little." He shifted on his feet. "Look, I've been down here several times now. Do I look any worse off? Am I a walking corpse? Do I look dead? I'm more *alive* than I've ever been! I feel like I've just been born into a big incredible world that's dying for me to gobble it up."

"I still don't want to go in. You're trying to lure me and frighten me—you think I can't see what you're doing? What do you take me for?"

"I take you for someone who thinks the way I do. Someone born to know all things well. And here's one thing you don't know so well: if you don't know this"—he motioned to the black door—"you can't even write about it intelligently. That's not trickery. It's common sense."

She stared at the doors. "It's trickery." She shivered and held her arms a little closer to her body. Billy let the silence lengthen.

"I don't have to go in to know what it's like in there. Just tell me what it's like."

"It's new. It's wonderful. There's . . . there's this odor and this salve on the walls . . ." He stopped, thinking his awkward description might deter her. "I can't really describe it."

"Yes, but what does it *feel* like? You made me tell you what I felt, now you tell me."

"Okay. It's dark. Everywhere it's dark. And maybe a little wet. But apart from that the halls are beautiful. They're the most wonderful things I've seen in my entire life. Mysterious, breathtaking. Every nook is packed with a history of its own, Darcy. You take one look at the bones"—he caught himself there; no sense in being too descriptive yet—"at the artifacts there, and you know it fills a hole in your soul."

"Bones? There're bones in there?"

"Not bones really. Just replicas, like carvings or sculptures that could look like bones. But they're wonderful, Darcy. Beautiful. Come in with me and I'll show you."

"There's a reason why this place is prohibited. Have you ever thought about that? The overseers aren't stupid, Billy. If they think it's wrong, then it's wrong."

"Unless they know something we don't. You thought about *that*? I have and it's a fact. They know that whoever enters these halls learns things that can't be learned up there. That's essentially what Marsuvees Black was trying to say before he left. And what's more, I think the director agrees."

"Don't be ridiculous."

"Then who first convinced me to come down here?"

"The director?" she said incredulously.

"Either him or Raul. They know we'll eventually stumble into an evil path too wide to ignore. Unless we face it now, how can we possibly face it later, when it matters more?"

Darcy put one hand on each side of her head, frustrated. "I don't know."

Billy blinked. *I don't know*. Not *yes* but not *no*, which was much better than *no*.

"But you do feel a little excited about the whole thing, don't you?"

"A little maybe."

"Consider this. We are taught to embrace life, right? To read and write and paint and speak and love and to embrace all forms of communication with passion. I mean, the entire purpose of our life here at the monastery is to become exceptional people. Well, I can tell you everything down here is greater than upstairs. Double the pleasure, double the satisfaction, double everything. My exploration down here is mind-numbing. The stories I've read—and I've only had time to read two short ones—were intoxicating. Even my writing takes on a new urgency and meaning." He stopped to catch his breath. "You can pick up a stone in there and find the dead granite in your hands utterly fascinating."

She didn't respond. She was mesmerized, he thought. And so she should be—he excited even himself.

"It's the final step, Darcy. This is what we were meant for. *This!*" He thrust his hand toward the blackened doors.

Billy lowered his arm and stepped toward her. "I'll tell you what. There's one room in there—a room built like a study, full of books and a sofa—very pleasant. Go with me there. Only there. Straight to the study, take a quick look around, and if you don't want to stay, I swear we'll come right back. But you have to at least see if I'm right. See if this isn't really meant for you, or for everyone, for that matter. You *have* to come!"

Darcy stared at the doors. Billy remembered a story they'd studied years ago, a true story in which an executioner had offered his victims the choice between the guillotine or some unknown fate that waited behind an ominous door. Most chose the guillotine. But one chose the door. He walked through, quaking in his boots, terrified, only to discover freedom.

"Just the study," he said. "No more."

She blinked once and then spoke in a thin voice. "I guess."

Billy began to tremble with excitement. "Okay. Okay, give me your hand."

He reached out, and she finally took his hand. He felt her weight leaning away from him, and he gave her a little tug. "I'm right here. I've got the light."

She followed reluctantly.

Billy stepped toward the door, praying under his breath that she wouldn't change her mind at the last second and bolt for the stairs. Shadows shifted on the charred wood, ebbing with the torch's flame. Darcy's breathing deepened at his shoulder, like an old man struggling against black lungs. He raised a hand to the rough cross brace and pushed. The massive doors squealed open. She withdrew at the sound, but he was finished with his reassurances. He wanted in.

Then they were inside and the doors closed behind them with a *thump*. Darcy jerked again and Billy turned around, his mind buzzing with excitement. Her mouth gaped. She tried to speak. At least he thought she tried to speak, but the sound that came out was like a soft groan, so he couldn't know for sure. He tugged at her arm.

"Come on."

He pulled her into the dark shaft on his far right. The sweet musty odor he'd come to love filled his nostrils.

"Billy!"

"Huh?" He stopped and followed her gaze. Yellow light from his torch splashed on the walls, illuminating one of the worms writhing slowly on the stone face.

"It's okay. Just a worm. They're everywhere down here. They don't bite, promise. Come on."

"But—"

"Come on!" He yanked her forward.

Darcy whimpered and then followed willingly enough—she had little choice. He began to jog, past dozens of the long pink worms slithering on the walls, past the two gated rooms he first discovered. Darcy staggered twice, and he yanked her back to her feet. She seemed to follow more willingly as they ran deeper into the tunnel.

And then the gated study loomed ahead to their right. Billy slowed to a walk, panting. He'd left the gate open. Should close it better next time, just in case. Just in case *what*, he didn't know, but just in case anyway.

He released Darcy and shifted the torch to his right hand. It slipped a little in his sweating palm, and he tightened his grip.

"Here it is."

Billy reached for the gate and pulled it open. Darcy bumped his elbow, causing the light to waver in the open study. He felt a surge of anger. Maybe he shouldn't have brought her. She might mess everything up—poke into his stuff and get in his way.

"Careful!" he snapped. They stepped into the small study.

On his right the shelves, stuffed with books, reached the ceiling. Except for a few he'd brushed off and pulled out, the books were still covered by a thin layer of dust.

He looked at the desk on his left. A journal lay on the desk, tilted just so, his pen resting on its cover. He'd filled the first few pages during his more recent visits.

A smile of wonder dawned on Darcy's face. "It's beautiful," she said. That was quick. "It's so beautiful, Billy."

She walked to the bookcase and reached out for a book. "What are these?"

"Classics. Storybooks. Journals. Who knows. I haven't had time to open many of them."

"There're so many."

"And there may be more. It's like a whole new world, Darcy. What did I tell you? Now how does it feel?"

She turned to him. "Stimulating?"

He winked at her, glad she'd come after all. "Yes, stimulating."

They held their gaze for a moment, and Billy thought she was the most beautiful creature he'd seen. His heart began to pick up its pace as he gazed into her eyes.

"Can you smell that?" he asked.

"Yes. It's sweet." She drew a deep breath and grinned.

"I think it comes from the worms."

She looked out at the darkened hall. "Really?"

"From their . . . from the stuff that comes from them. I think it makes everything down here . . . I don't know, maybe magical or something. It's almost like a drug that doubles or triples sensation. Course, I don't know, I'm just guessing."

Billy pulled a plum from his pocket. "See this? Just a plum, right?"

"Right."

"I brought it down to eat. To see if it tastes better here." He grinned and held it up between his thumb and forefinger. "I guarantee you it'll be different. Everything down here is different."

Billy brought the fruit to his lips, winked at Darcy again, and bit deep. Juice flooded his mouth.

The taste wasn't what he'd hoped for. He smacked his lips and let the flavor swirl around his tongue. But that was just it—there was no real flavor. It was bland, similar to nothing.

"Well?" she asked.

"Must be a bad fruit," he said, tossing the plum through the gate. "But everything else down here will knock your socks off. I can guarantee you that."

The failure bothered Billy for a moment. But almost immediately his hazy contentedness returned. The tunnels were working on him now. They certainly were. He was in the tunnels, right? Yes. In the nasty forbidden dungeon, God bless them, thank you very much.

Darcy really was beautiful. He'd never really noticed.

He took her by the hand. "Look at this." He led her to the journal on the desk.

"What is it?"

He touched it. "You can't tell?"

"It looks like a journal." Her voice held more wonder than any journal should engender. She laid a hand on his. "Can I see?"

He didn't respond immediately. He just stood there suspended in the moment with her hand touching his. She looked at him and gently lifted his hand from the book. She opened the cover, keeping her eyes on him. She dropped her gaze to the pages, and he followed her eyes.

"Do you like it?" he asked.

"What is this?"

"Just some doodling."

"I love it," she murmured. "I love it, Billy." She looked up at him, eyes wide. "Can I write?"

"In this book?"

"Are there others?"

"Sure. But maybe we can work on something together." He looked at her and swallowed, knowing that this was exactly what he wanted.

"A collaboration. You think that might be good?"

"I would like that. I would like that very much." And again he thought she must be the most beautiful woman he'd seen, never mind that she was only thirteen. So was he.

She raised a hand to his cheek. "I think you're very kind, Billy." Her fingers pulled his collar back. "You have a rash on your neck. Did you know that?"

The rash had started yesterday, but it wasn't important. What was important was Darcy.

"I think you're very kind too," he said.

She removed her hand. Time drifted by.

She looked at the book. "What kind of story should we write?"

Billy fanned through the pages. "You want to begin now?"

"We're writers aren't we? It's my favorite thing to do. What kind of story?"

Billy thought about that. "A story about discovering everything new. Like the dungeons. Frightful truths and breaking rules." He closed the book. "But there's other stuff to see. Let's explore first."

Darcy walked around the sofa, mesmerized by everything she saw. "I can't believe this place has been here this whole time. It's magical. I love it, Billy. I just love it."

"And I love you, Darcy."

She looked back at him. "You do?"

What was he saying? "I feel like I do."

"Well, I'm not sure I would go that far," she said. "I'm not even sure we should trust our feelings down here."

"But you're glad you came down."

"Yes." She walked toward the gate and peered back down the tunnel. "Yes, I am."

Billy withdrew the torch and walked into the dark hall. "Let's look around."

Chapter Twelve

PARADISE

Friday morning

PAULA SMITHER awoke late in the morning, feeling sluggish, almost dead. Her mind crawled from the gray haze of another world, where it had been trapped for the last—she glanced at the clock—fifteen hours now. Eleven o'clock? What was she thinking sleeping in so late? And for two days in a row.

She slid off the mattress and walked toward the bathroom. What a dream. Wow, what a dream.

It came back to her in little chunks, and she caught her step at an image that flashed through her mind—a scene she didn't think she was capable of imagining. She lifted a hand to her stringy brown hair and ruffled it.

But it had felt so real. Not like a dream at all. More like she'd actually been there with him, letting him touch her face like that.

Amazing. Repulsive. Lovely. She didn't know which. Maybe all three.

There was something wrong with Marsuvees. Something demonic and evil and snakelike. He was finding a way to slither into her mind and whisper things that made her hate him.

Unless, of course, he was really her guiding angel, revealing her true inner self to her false outer self. Purifying her. Cleansing her with the delicious, ugly, brutal, lovely truth.

Which was what? That she wanted to be loved? That she hated herself? That she despised wickedness because she knew that deep inside her bones there was the marrow of wickedness, and the only way to deal with that evil was to draw it out of the bones?

The sword of truth was dividing bone from marrow.

She brought her fingers up to her lips and stroked them gently, the way he had. *If* he had. She turned to the mirror. The woman who stared out at her was short and pudgy. But her hair was long and her complexion shimmered in the glass, smooth and tanned from the summer sun. Her eyes glistened above a small nose. Not too bad really.

Paula looked at her body in profile, draped in one of Steve's old T-shirts. Shapely if you looked just right. At least not huge like Nancy. The one small blessing of giving birth to only one child after three miscarriages.

She moved toward the shower, keeping her eyes on her figure as she walked—no, slinked—across the room, like one of those young models walking down the street in slow motion. Paula's shin slammed into the side of the tiled bath, and she doubled over. She grasped her leg.

"Crap!"

The shock of pain brought her mind out of its lazy spin. *Listen to you, Paula. Using language like that. What's gotten into you?*

Marsuvees, a small voice whispered. *Marsuvees Black.*

She stood up and stared at the mirror again. Another chunk of her dream came to her, the part about meeting the tall preacher in the church basement, right in her own Sunday-school room.

She looked back at her bed—the sheets had been kicked to the floor. It was a dream. Just a dream. Still, she had no business even dreaming things like that. She'd best forget the man altogether, push him right from her mind and pretend she'd never even seen him.

Marsuvees filled in her mind's eye, blue eyes flashing. *Wanna trip like I do, baby?* He licked his lips. She clenched her eyes and shook the vision from her head. What had become of her?

Bone from marrow, that's what had become of her.

Where was Steve? Come to think of it, he hadn't slept in their bed last night, had he? In fact, he hadn't been home for supper either, but he often ate at the bar. He hadn't bothered to call, though. He'd been gone all day, the least he could do was call. She was too preoccupied with her inner dividing of bone and marrow to worry about Steve, but now her mind buzzed with the realization that he hadn't come home. What was going on?

Paula took a quick shower, going through the routines of washing and drying, distracted by the thoughts that peppered her mind.

Steve was gone and she didn't know to where.

Marsuvees was here, in her mind, and he refused to leave.

Her memories of yesterday afternoon were fuzzy. The preacher had come to the bar, she remembered that, but her mind regarded the rest hazily. It was almost as if she'd slept through the afternoon. Maybe she had. Maybe she slept for a full day.

But that couldn't be—she remembered walking through that wind to the church and finding Nancy there, pigging out on Twinkies. Unless *that* had been a dream too. All this nonsense brought on by Black's bland, intoxicating . . . syrup.

Paula slipped into a pink shirt, ran a quick comb through her hair, and walked out into the living room.

"Steve?"

The house was silent.

And where was Roland? Heaven only knew. The boy rarely spent the summer days indoors.

"Steve!" she yelled. She walked past the kitchen to his study, which was really just a place he messed around in. Empty. She checked the rest of the house quickly, now thinking she must be missing some event that the rest of the town was attending, like another meeting at the saloon with Marsuvees. The minister. Not "Marsuvees," but "the minister." *Come on, Paula, get a grip.*

Wanna trip like I do, baby?

She hurried to the front door, opened it, and stepped onto the porch. Dark cumulus clouds hovered low over the town, and a warm wind whipped through the trees, carrying stray leaves and dust through the street.

Summer wind. She loved the wind. Especially when the sun was out like it was now.

She glanced first up and then down Main Street. Deserted. That was odd. Paula walked to the sidewalk. She took three steps toward Nails and Tan and stopped. No, she didn't want to go to the witch's palace.

Katie might think of herself as the one woman in Paradise who really knew about life, but under all that talk she was still nothing more than a small-town girl with a broken tanning bed.

Paula turned and walked toward the church. Leaves flew by. She could barely see the church for all the dust in the air.

Wanna trip like I do, baby?

The base of her brain tingled.

That's the most ridiculous thing I've heard in my life, "wanna trip," like I'm some kind of druggie or something.

Then she heard the first sound of life since waking. A *thump*. Not a wood-against-wood *thump*, as if a branch fell, but a metal-against-wood *thump*. Almost a *crack*. The sound triggered a memory. Her father used to cut the heads off chickens with an ax like that. On a stump. Right through those thin necks in one blow.

She turned to her right. If she wasn't mistaken, the sound had come from behind her own house. She glanced at the church that was still swirling in the thin mask of dust, then veered toward the alley that led behind the house.

The gate to the white picket fence Steve put in last year swung in the wind. She stepped through the opening and headed for the back lawn.

The *thump* came again, closer now, definitely from the backyard, she thought. And then three times in a row—*thump, thump, thump*.

Wind banging something? But it sounded deliberate.

Paula approached the corner of the house and decided at the last minute that a little discretion might be in order. No telling what was happening back there.

Thump!

She stepped up to the gravel that surrounded the house, edged up to the corner, and peered into the backyard. The some-assembly-required shed that had taken Steve three days to assemble stood next to the back fence, its door flapping in the wind. She would have to shut that before the storm came.

An ax head rose past the shed's low roofline and swung back down, out of view.

Thump!

Someone was back there with an ax!

Paula pressed her body against the wall, out of the shed's view. Steve? Sure, it had to be Steve. Who else would be cutting wood behind their shed?

This was ridiculous. She was just going to have to walk over there and find out what he was up to, wasn't she? Paula looked around the corner again, saw that the yard was empty, and stepped out into the open.

Her first two steps were normal, but then she crouched and shuffled quickly to the shed wall without really knowing why she should feel creeped out about Steve chopping wood.

The wind moaned around the shed.

What if he catches me like this? What if Steve stands up and sees me creeping up on him like this? He'll think I'm nuts. But what if it isn't Steve at all? Or Roland? What if it's Marsuvees? She froze at the thought.

That was absurd, of course. No matter how unorthodox his ways, he was a minister of the gospel. Grace and hope. Not some crazy woodsman.

The thought surprised her. Just yesterday, she was quite sure he was the devil. Now she was not only giving him the benefit of the doubt, but defending his sacred mission. Dividing bone from marrow.

She stepped forward, brought her head to the corner, and looked behind the shed.

Steve knelt on the ground with a hatchet raised above his tangled dark hair. He brought the ax down.

Thump.

Paula winced. A long stake rested against the chopping block at his knees, shaved to a sharp point by the ax.

Steve was sharpening a stake. No, not just *a* stake. A dozen stakes. At least twelve of the things leaned against the fence beside him, all pointy sharp. What could he possibly be thinking, turning branches into short fat spears?

The sweaty shirt clinging to his back was the same shirt he'd worn yesterday, only now it was streaked with dried dust. His hair was matted with sweat and speckled with small woodchips.

Thump!

He mumbled something, and for a moment Paula thought he'd seen her. She eased back.

He spoke again. "Shut up . . ." The rest was lost in the wind.

What was he doing, kneeling there like an idiot, whacking at those sticks? She was half-tempted to grab him by the ear. *Get up, you useless good-for-nothing. Get to work and make us some money or something. And where were you last night, anyway?*

You wanna trip like I do, baby?

Paula spun from the shed and ran toward the sidewalk. If the fool wanted to make tent pegs or whatever he was making back there, let him. She had this bone-and-marrow business to attend to.

The street was still empty. Dust swirls danced on the blacktop like a troop of Tasmanian devils. A thin layer of the stuff covered the street and sidewalk. She ran a finger over the top of the mailbox, clearing a swath of dust. She glanced in, saw the box was empty, slammed it shut, and jumped at the *bang*.

Wanna trip, huh? Wanna trip?

Sure, baby, I'll show you how to trip.

Please, Paula, you're downright loose when you want to be.

Did that mean she *wanted* to be loose? Was that what her marrow was telling her?

There was something she was supposed to be doing, but she couldn't remember. Steve was back there making sticks.

"What's the world coming to?" She walked back into the house.

IF A visitor had driven through Paradise that Friday, he might have wondered if it was a deserted Colorado ghost town. So thought Johnny Drake as he stared out the front window.

If the visitor hung around long enough, he might see a stray soul or a dog braving the hot gusting winds, darting from one building to another. But in five minutes of staring, Johnny hadn't seen either. From what he could tell, the shops were closed. Their windowsills were filling with dust, and the streetlight was out. Boiling black clouds kept the valley in a perpetual dusk.

There were no visitors. Not even a lost magpie.

Johnny had awakened late, sat up groggily, and forced his mind to clear. The events of last night crashed through his mind.

Roland had agreed to come by his room when he woke up. But a quick check of his bedroom window showed no Roland.

He pulled on the same shirt he'd worn yesterday and hurried out to the living room. "Mom?"

But she wasn't there. Johnny ran to his mother's room and cracked the door. She was still sleeping under the sheets.

"Mom?"

Sally moaned, made a halfhearted attempt to lift her head, then collapsed back on the pillow.

Johnny stepped in. "Mom, wake up."

"Go."

The way she said it sent a sliver of fear through his chest.

It was Black's poison—had to be.

At a loss, Johnny had come here, to the front window, pulled the curtain back, and stared at the ghost town called Paradise.

A thought occurred to him. The streetlight was out. What about the phones?

Johnny ran to the kitchen and picked up the phone. If they were going to call . . .

No dial tone. Not even a hiss.

He tapped the disconnect twice.

Nothing. The wind had blown over one of the poles or something. Unless it was Black.

Johnny stood in the kitchen, phone in hand, mind numb. Black was either an angel or the devil, and Johnny was completely confused about which. Or why. Or what, if anything, he could do about it. Or if he even *should* do anything about it. He didn't know how to drive, and with the storm blowing . . .

A bang sounded at the back of the house. Roland. He dropped the phone into the cradle and ran to his bedroom.

Roland stood at his window, freckled face pressed against the glass. Johnny hurried to the window, flung it open. His friend looked at him over bags that darkened his eyes.

"Hey."

"You okay?"

"Sure."

Roland climbed inside and looked around. "A bit . . . tired maybe but okay."

Johnny shut the window. "You look sick."

Roland faced him. "Peter came by. You should have seen what *he* looked like."

"Peter? What did he say?"

"He said we had to meet him and Fred at the theater."

"What for?"

"He didn't say. Just said to come."

"I don't know."

"You got a better idea?"

Johnny didn't have a better idea, because he didn't have any ideas.

"When? Now?"

"Sure, now."

Johnny looked at the dark clouds. "Okay," he finally said.

THEY HEADED out into the wind five minutes later. The trees bent under strong gusts, and Johnny had to cover his eyes to keep the dust out. They walked down the alley behind All Right Convenience, toward the Starlight.

They rounded the theater, glad to be out of the wind. "Man, this stuff's really blowing," Roland said.

"So where are Peter and Fred?"

Roland looked around—no sign of them.

"Maybe they already left."

A *thump* sounded on the wind, close.

Johnny spun. "What was that?"

"Something probably blew into the building."

Another thud shook the wall.

"That . . . that came from the far end."

"Or inside," Roland said. His own suggestion dawned on him belatedly and his eyes grew round. He ran to the wall and pressed his ear flat.

"Someone's inside!" He spun around and ran for the corner.

"Where you going?"

"Come on!"

Johnny rounded the corner cautiously. Knee-high grass swayed like a shifting sea. The carcasses of several rusty cars rose from the grass. A dilapidated wooden windmill leaned against the wall, creaking in the wind.

The wind gusted and lifted a board from the wall, then dropped it with a loud *thud.*

Roland strode for the loose siding. He was going in.

Now Johnny was confronted with a decision. On one hand, he knew without a doubt that whatever waited inside the old theater couldn't be good. On the other hand, he couldn't just run from whatever was happening to this town. Particularly not when he had nowhere to run to.

"Hold on."

"They're in there, I heard them."

"Just hold on!" Johnny caught up to him and grabbed his shoulder. "How do you know it's them? You can't just barge in there like you own it."

"I heard music, man. You know anyone else who would be listening to music in the Starlight?"

"Just"—he nudged Roland to one side—"let me take a look."

He gripped the board by the bottom edge and lifted it.

Nothing jumped out at him or bowled him over, and the board was loose enough, so he lifted it higher. The nails had been pulled. Whoever was in there had taken a hammer or a crowbar to the wall to get in.

Together Roland and he shoved the board high, then eased their heads into the dark foot-wide gap.

The first thing Johnny saw were the theater's arching rafters, flickering with white light. Fire? Then he heard the music, pounding from somewhere inside. A wall stood between them and whoever was inside the main hall.

"That's Peter and Fred for sure," Roland said.

"Just stay behind me. And if I run, you run."

"Okay. Lighten up, sheesh."

Johnny squeezed through the opening. Roland followed. The board clunked closed. Protected from the howling wind, he could hear the music loudly now. An eerie, melancholic, thumping rock and roll. Gothic. Evil.

He edged forward—stage door on the right. Carefully, fighting every ounce of good reason, Johnny turned the knob and pulled the door open a crack.

The volume escalated. White light sputtered on the walls inside. No monsters. He pulled the door wider and eased his head through.

Light flashed from a box set on the stage, splashing white across the auditorium in staccato pulses. Three figures jerked in the strobe.

Dancing? More like writhing.

Johnny's heart climbed into his throat.

The auditorium had been ransacked. The place was dirty when he last saw it, two years earlier, but not trashed like this. It took a few seconds for the images to register, because they came at him in flashes of light. The long curtains hanging on the walls were shredded from top to bottom, and the old wooden seats had been torn from their anchors and scattered like a box of spilled jacks. Bottles and cans littered the floor—dozens of them, spilling liquid that sparkled in the light. Someone had spray-painted haphazard lines across the walls and huge Gothic letters on the torn screen.

Screw Hope!

In the middle of it all, the three figures jerked about, like stoned teenagers in a mosh pit.

Roland's head pushed past his arm.

The identity of the largest figure was clear. The bulky body teetering and twitching like a tortured penguin could only belong to Peter's father, Claude Bowers. He faced the flashing box, which Johnny now saw was actually a television set. His hands swayed to the music, creating the strange illusion that his arms were electric cords delivering shocks that convulsed his body.

Ten feet behind and to the left, the second man jerked back and forth like a bebopping bowling pin. He had an ax in his hands, and for one terrifying moment Johnny thought the man might be Roland's father. But then a flash lit the face and Johnny saw Chris Ingles, smiling like a vampire with bulging eyes.

He heard a gasp from Roland. Then he saw what Roland was looking at. The third figure was a boy his size, jumping up and down like a pogo stick.

Peter.

He tugged at Roland's collar, jerked him back through the door.

"You see that?" Roland whispered and stuck his head back in. Johnny hesitated a moment and then took another look.

The whole scene looked like something he might expect from a dream—a nightmare or a scene from an MTV music video—but this wasn't any of those. This was Peter and his father and Chris Ingles in the Starlight Theater in Paradise, Colorado, population 450. Writhing to headbanging music. And by the looks of it, they'd been at it awhile.

The ax man, Chris Ingles, spun and let loose a scream. He jumped from the stage, swung his ax above his head like a tomahawk, and took a swipe at one of the toppled theater seats. The chair cracked and flew across the room. Chris let out another whoop and resumed his lurching dance in front of the stage.

The smaller form—Peter—scooped up a bottle at his feet, cocked his arm back like a pitcher, and hurled the object at the television set. With a loud pop the tube exploded. Just like that, *boom*, and the room fell into darkness and total silence.

A flame from a lighter flickered to life, highlighting Claude Bower's sweaty face. The three stood dumbstruck, arms hanging limp, chests rising and falling.

"Who did that?" Claude asked with a heaving voice.

Peter took a step back.

"You do that, Peter?" Claude spoke as if the boy had just slapped him for no reason. "What . . . what you do that for?"

Johnny could hear his own breathing now. He shut his mouth and drew air through his nose. They should have left already, but Johnny teetered in that awful place between *must* run and *can't* run.

Claude stared at his son through the wavering flame, and for a moment Johnny thought he might actually take after him.

Then he did. He shrieked obscenities and lunged forward.

Peter spun and let out a yelp. He took three steps before his father's hand caught him and together they tumbled to the floor, crushing the lighter's flame under them. The room went black. Piercing shrieks echoed through the theater.

Roland bolted forward. "You sick son of . . ."

Johnny swiped at him, grabbing shirt, then air.

The room was too dark to see Roland running, and Peter's wails covered the sound of his feet.

Now Johnny was faced with another critical decision: to save Roland from sharing Peter's fate or to make a quick escape now, while he could.

He took off after Roland.

Problem was, he couldn't see.

And then he could. Light flared from a rag Chris Ingles had stuffed into a bottle. Johnny heard the sound of swishing liquid.

Johnny pulled up a third of the way down the right aisle. Roland took three more steps, placing him near the front. He slid to a stop.

Claude must have seen the boy, because he froze, fist raised over Peter, head turned toward the auditorium.

The intrusion seemed to disorient Claude. Chris Ingles was a statue—legs spread wide, torch licking the air beside his face, eyes ogling Roland.

Johnny and Roland were rooted in the aisle.

Peter wailed.

Claude released his son and stood up. Peter was still screaming bloody murder. Claude slapped his head with an open hand. "Shut up."

Peter whimpered and then shut up. Out of obedience or unconsciousness, Johnny couldn't tell.

Claude stepped over his son's body. "You guys bring anything?"

What?

"Yeah, we're looking for more stuff," Chris said.

"You have a TV?" Claude asked.

"Yeah, do you have a TV?" Ingles repeated.

Claude looked at Roland. "How about the TV from your dad's bar. You think he'd mind if we borrowed it?"

Roland wasn't responding.

"Listen, you little creep!" Ingles snapped. "He's asking you a question. It's a simple question. Just answer the stupid question, you dope. If you don't tell us, we're going to come down there and slap some sense into you. So shut your trap and just tell us what—"

"Shut up, Chris," Claude said.

Ingles looked at the big Swede. "I was just—"

"I said, shut up!" He was yelling. "Shut up, shut up, shut up!"

Chris looked like he'd been slapped. He swallowed. "Sheesh. I'm trying to get us a TV. If you want—ahhh!" Ingles screamed and jerked his hand from the bottle which had evidently gotten hot enough to burn him. The flame blinked out when the bottle hit the floor.

Darkness.

Johnny ran forward, grabbed Roland by his shirt, and tugged. "Come on," he whispered.

"Get that light back on!" Claude thundered.

"I burned my hand."

"It's dark," Peter said.

Johnny ran for the thin crack of light below the exit door. He slammed into the door. Yanked it open.

Claude yelled behind them. "Hey!"

They rushed through the service hall, crashed through the plank and out of the theater into the wind.

Johnny rounded the corner and pulled up, panting.

Roland looked back the way they'd come. "You see him hit Peter?" A crooked smile nudged his lips.

"You find that funny?"

"What are they doing?"

Good question. Or rather, why were they trashing the theater and going nuts over that television? It was crazy, plain and simple.

"What are we going to do?" Roland asked when Johnny didn't respond.

"I don't know. Maybe we should go get some help."

"How?"

A bang sounded inside the theater. Johnny glanced back. Coast was still clear. He headed for the street.

"Where you going?"

"Home. I have to get my mom up."

Chapter Thirteen

THE MONASTERY

Friday morning

SAMUEL STARED out of his father's study window at the black clouds roiling over the small town far below. "All because of one silly boy," he said.

"Not one silly boy," his father said.

Samuel turned, arms clasped behind his back. "Billy and Darcy. Two."

Dark rings circled his father's eyes, and his flesh seemed to sag around his cheeks. Samuel had never seen his father in such a state. He wanted to run over and hug him.

"Billy's called for a debate."

His father exposed his true concern, something he would guard even from the teachers. But he trusted his son, which made Samuel proud. "You yourself said that you expected it, Father. You told me that a month ago and again, last week, when Marsuvees Black left us. But you were sure that the power we have would all play to our advantage. You still believe that, don't you?"

David stared past him, his gaze distant and aimless. Samuel noticed that they were both standing with hands clasped behind their backs. Like father, like son.

"Yes," David said. "I've staked everything on that belief. You're right, the power in this place has always threatened to wreak havoc. And I've always believed good would prevail—it's why I left the university after your mother's death. But what if I'm wrong? And if I'm right, what will the cost be?"

Samuel walked up to his father and took his hand. When David had taken him for a long walk behind the monastery three days earlier and told him what was happening, without even the teachers' knowledge, Samuel thought his father was playing some sort of game with him. It took a full twenty-four hours for the implications to settle in. Billy had no real idea what he'd done.

But Samuel had the same power. An incredible fact. Then again, all of the children had the same power. And that was a bit frightening.

His father's eyes were glassy. "Can you imagine what would happen if this got out to the world, Samuel?"

"But it won't! We won't let it."

"It's not something we can control. Not now."

"My whole life you've taught me the power of Christ's love to overthrow evil. I know this is difficult for you, Father, but you have to believe what you've taught me."

David looked at his son. "Evil can be very powerful, Samuel."

"And so can love."

The door behind them opened. Samuel held his father's eyes one moment longer, then released his hand. He wasn't used to being the encourager in their relationship, but it felt right now. He was becoming a man, and his father needed him. The realization was both daunting and satisfying.

Two teachers and two students walked into the study. Raul and Andrew ushered the children through the door.

"Hey, Tyler. Hey, Christine."

"Hey, Samuel." They'd both been here before, but a trip to the director's study was an unusual occurrence. Their eyes took in the setting.

David smiled, cloaking all traces of concern. "Thank you for coming. Have a seat, please." He indicated the chairs around the redwood table.

"Thank you, sir," Christine said.

Tyler let Christine sit first. "Thank you, sir."

They grinned at Samuel. Tyler and Christine were both orphans from India and they, like some of the others, had taken to speaking in accents from their mother countries.

"Excuse us for just a moment." David walked toward the adjacent conference room. "Raul, Andrew, please follow me."

They walked into the room and closed the door.

Samuel sat and looked at his friends. Were they strong enough to stand up to Billy? No doubt. His father's concerns were overstated. "You guys eat already?"

"Yes," Tyler said. "Have you guys noticed how quickly they shut down the cafeteria these last two days?"

"No," Christine said. "Two o'clock like always."

"But two sharp?" Tyler snuck a look at the conference-room door and lowered his voice. "The overseers just seem a bit rushed. In fact, I'm not sure they aren't a bit uptight in general. I snapped Christian's boxers in the bathroom this morning, and Andrew happened to be walking by. He told me to grow up. That sound like Andrew to you?"

"Boys," Christine said, rolling her eyes. "How does snapping boxers translate to fun in that lofty mind of yours?"

"It translates as easily as pinning back your hair or painting your nails," Tyler said.

"I paint my nails for beauty. Beauty is intrinsically valuable."

"And I snapped Christian's boxers for humor. Humor's also intrinsically valuable."

Christine thought about that. "Point made."

"I still think the overseers need to lighten up a bit."

"I'll be sure to mention this to the director the moment he steps back in," Christine said with a smirk. "All overseers to ease up on the fun-seekers of our cherished clan."

She turned to Samuel. "So what's this all about?"

The enormity of her ignorance struck him as tragic. This was about the end of all things as they knew it. About the beginning of something either very good or very bad. How could he explain this to two kids who were for the moment preoccupied with snapping shorts and painting nails?

The door opened, saving Samuel from an answer. One look at Andrew and Samuel's gut tightened. The man's face was white. Raul looked concerned as well, but not like Andrew. Perhaps Raul had more faith in Christine than Andrew did.

They crossed the room and sat opposite Christine and Tyler. His father regarded them with unusual gravity.

Christine glanced at Samuel, any trace of a smile now gone. "What's wrong?"

"At least that much is obvious," David said. He drew a deep breath. "Christine, Tyler . . . We are very proud of you both. In fact it's my confidence in you that brings you here. I've watched you both and I see that your character is strong." He smiled.

Christine folded her hands. "Thank you, sir."

Tyler followed her example. "Thank you, sir."

"Good. Then let me tell you what I just told Andrew and Raul. Billy has challenged the school's prevailing rule of love in the first debate of its kind in the history of Project Showdown." He let the statement settle in.

"A debate?" Tyler asked. "Billy's arguing against love? What on earth would make him do that?"

"He and Darcy have entered the forbidden tunnels below the monastery," David said.

"They've what?" Christine demanded. "How could they do that?"

"Oh, it's quite simple, really. There's no lock on the door. Billy was the first to go in. He convinced Darcy to follow. This morning Billy issued his challenge. He'll argue against our assertion that love leads to the Creator and that the discovery of love is the point of our lives. It seems he's found something besides love to satisfy him. The debate will be held tomorrow before all the students. In the end, a two-thirds vote by the students will determine the course we will take. If Billy wins, he will determine what is taught here and who teaches it. He will also establish new rules, which can be overthrown only by a similar challenge and a two-thirds vote."

Christine jumped up. "He's a fool!" She relaxed her fists and sat. "Forgive me, I meant no disrespect, but he's the biggest fool. Not only for entering the tunnels, but for thinking that he can persuade two or three much less two-thirds of us to side with any twisted philosophy he tosses out."

"Why can't we just lock Billy up?" Tyler asked.

Samuel watched his father. Not even the teachers knew the real reason, though what the overseers accepted as truth was compelling enough. What good would it do to create a monastery full of noble savages with the potential to reshape society, and then, having failed, to lock them up? If they ultimately failed, then they would be put back into society to continue with the rest of spoiled humankind.

But if the children survived tests like this one, they would be even stronger in their faith, and their impact on society would be even greater. This is what the teachers believed. And part of it was true.

But only part of it.

Samuel's father finally spoke. "We can't, Tyler. You'll have to trust me on that. No one is forced here. The effects of forcing Billy's hand could be far more devastating than any of us imagines."

Samuel wondered if the two teachers caught his father's insinuation that the stakes were higher than they knew. Andrew stared at him with searching eyes. Raul looked at the bookshelf, expression blank.

"Who will he debate?" Christine asked.

"By rule it has to be a student. I have—"

"What kind of rule is that? Excuse the interruption."

"Not only a student, but one of five that he chooses," David said. "It's a rule that places the ultimate responsibility in any one of the students' hands. We are only as strong as our weakest links, both in life and in here. Billy put five students' names forward. I have chosen you, Christine."

"Me? It should be Samuel!"

"Samuel wasn't an option. It will be you."

Raul cleared his throat. "I must express my objection. I think we're going too fast. Having this debate tomorrow is premature. She needs time to prepare."

"No, no, that's not our call," Andrew responded. "I've looked up the rules. The debate must be held within twenty-four hours." It was odd that even the teachers were foggy on the rules of debate, Samuel thought. Then again, they'd never had to know.

"What on earth for?" Raul demanded. "If the future of the monastery is at hand, we should all tread carefully."

David held up a hand. "We've been treading carefully for twelve years. As it is now, Billy hardly stands a chance. The more time we give him, the stronger his argument will become. Time favors him, not us. The debate will be held tomorrow morning."

"And Billy will debate me?" Christine asked, still unconvinced.

"You know what he's going to argue," Samuel said. "I say throw it back in his face. Make him grovel and cry for mercy."

That earned him a few smiles.

"Oh, you can bet I will. Trying to argue that love has no trajectory, much less one set for our Maker, is like trying to argue that we are nothing more than a sea of slugs, inching aimlessly about in the dark. You're sure this is the basis of his argument?"

"I doubt he'll cast it in those terms," David said. "But in the end all arguments end there. You'll do fine, Christine."

She nodded. "And what happens to Billy when he's defeated?"

"Nothing."

"Nothing? Could he cast another challenge?"

"Not for three days."

"I think it's too soon," Raul said. "They're still children, for heaven's sake. They could drag us all down."

"Then, in the eyes of some, our project will have failed," David said.

"And not in the eyes of others?" Andrew asked.

David didn't respond.

Chapter Fourteen

PARADISE

Friday morning

PAULA WANDERED around her house without really knowing what she was doing. Oh, she did the dishes and made the bed, but she knew there was something else she should be doing. Problem was figuring it out.

It came to her out of nowhere. A blue streak of desire so deep that she gasped right there in her hallway.

Wanna trip, baby?

She left the house and walked up the street toward the church. The streets were still deserted, and the thumping sound was still coming from behind the house. *Get a clue, Steve. Please.*

Wanna trip?

Her pulse quickened and she quickened her pace. Steve could rot in hell for all she cared.

She found the front doors to the church locked. They were never locked. She walked to the side and entered through the office, hoping that Stanley and that fat secretary of his had left for lunch early or something.

Now come on, Paula, you have no right calling people fat. That could be you in twenty years.

But she is fat. Paula walked through the kitchen to the back stairs. *Fat as a cow.*

"Hello, Paula."

Paula gasped, startled. Nancy stood in the back-office doorway holding a large brown grocery bag. She wore a yellow cotton dress that made Paula think of a gunny sack with two holes cut out for those pudgy arms and another for her thick neck. A white substance that must be butter or frosting had dried on Nancy's left cheek.

"Don't scare me like that," Paula said. "Where is everybody?"

Nancy stared at her and held up the bag as though apologetic. "I just had to run to the store." She walked into the office without another word.

Paula breathed a quick sigh of relief and turned down the stairwell. See, now there was another weird thing. Nancy was fat enough as it is. No need to clean out Claude's store.

Wanna trip, huh? Like I do?

Paula stopped halfway down the stairs, her heart in her throat. What was she doing? Where was she going, anyway?

Down to the basement. To divide bone and marrow. Down to her office to trip.

Or at least to check on her Sunday-school room, just to make sure that everything was in order for Sunday service. Never could take the responsibility of teaching the children too seriously, right? Never.

When she landed on the gray carpet and rounded the corner to the all-purpose room, tingles were sweeping through her belly. Goose bumps fanned out at the base of her skull. *You shouldn't be here, Paula.*

Trip, trip, trip. Say it like that, baby. Say it like you mean it.

The room yawned vacant and still. She stepped across it lightly, barely breathing. The door to her office was cracked, but she often left it open. It was her office all right, given to her as the Sunday-school coordinator. The sign on the door said it in brass.

Paula reached the office, ran her sleeve over the brass plate, glanced back to the empty stairwell once, and pushed the door open.

The room was shrouded in darkness. Empty? Of course it was empty. What did she expect? She reached in and flipped the light switch. Four fluorescents stuttered to life.

Her desk sat as she had left it, neat and tidy with her little gray chair shoved under. The room was indeed empty, and an awful sense of disappointment ran through her chest. *Yeah, I'll show you how to trip, you freak show.* Her anger surprised her. *Trip this!* She flicked the air with her tongue.

Now that was forward. She did it again. Goodness, she was a regular sex bomb.

Paula stepped into her office and sighed. What had she come here for again?

A large black body moved to her left and she yelped.

Then she saw the whole of him, and her peripheral vision clouded. He stood there, tall, dressed in the same black trench coat he seemed never to take off, smiling under those sapphire eyes.

"Marsuvees!"

The initial shock fell away, and a cold wave of relief washed down her back. She smiled sheepishly.

He raised his shoulders in a shrug and chuckled. A low, empty chuckle that echoed through the room and bounced around in her skull. Paula felt a stab of fear.

"Paula . . . ha." He ended her name with air, and then clacked his teeth shut, as if taking a small bite out of the air.

Her name came to her like a soothing salve. An image of him standing up at the pulpit, commanding the attention of every last soul in town, ran through her mind.

"Hi." Her voice sounded like a squeak.

"I didn't mean to startle you. I just thought you might come here and . . ." He smiled warmly. "Well, I wanted to show you something."

See? He's so gentle, really. Just like in my dreams.

He looked at her without moving for a long time, until she thought she could feel the heat coming to her from those blue eyes.

"You know the story about the woman caught in adultery?" he asked.

Her heart skipped a beat. "Yes."

He took a step toward her. "You know, now there's a story of grace, Paula. I mean real grace. Don't you think?"

Wanna trip, baby, huh? Wanna, wanna?

"I guess." She took a step backward.

"Do you want to know what the truth of it was, Paula? I'll tell you. The truth of it was that the woman was no worse than the rest of them. They were all the same. All covered by grace. That's the truth of it, Paula. You have any bad thoughts toward anybody lately? Like Steve maybe? Because if you have, you are no better than that woman there in the story."

What was he saying? Of course she knew what he was saying. He was saying that if you think it, you might as well do it. The consequences are the same.

"The consequences are the same, Paula," Marsuvees said. "Either way, you don't get stoned."

She was feeling that tingle in her belly again.

Wanna trip with me? Wanna, baby?

"Yes," she said.

She wasn't sure whom she had said yes to then. Maybe to herself. She had stayed faithful to Steve for fifteen years without so much as looking at another man. Not that there was much to look at around here, but she'd never even had the desire. Now a man sent from God was hitting on her, telling her there was plenty of grace to go around, and Steve was sitting in the backyard losing his mind. Maybe she was losing hers as well.

He'd said that he was here to prepare them to withstand something bad. Something evil that would kill them if they didn't see things his way. He'd come to bring them the sword of truth.

Marsuvees walked toward her.

A wave of heat broke over her crown and cascaded down her shoulders. She could feel tiny beads of sweat popping from the pores on her forehead. It occurred to her that she wasn't wearing any makeup. *If he gets too close, he'll see the pimple on my jaw.* Thank goodness she'd taken a shower.

Wanna trip with me?

"Yes," she said again, and this time she knew she was answering that voice in her head. *Yes, yes, yes!*

No, Paula. No, no, no. This isn't grace and hope.

It's love. Love, love, love.

Love?

Do you want to trip? Do you want love?

Yes.

Marsuvees came within a foot of her and reached a hand to her face. She stood there trembling, wanting his touch unlike she had wanted anything in her memory.

She looked into his eyes, deep, where they became sapphire pools of safety. His hand rose to her cheek and then ever so lightly he touched her, at the corner of her parted lips.

She closed her eyes and let her mind fall.

"Meet me here," he whispered into her ear. She caught a faint whiff of his breath. It smelled sanitized. Like rubbing alcohol.

"After the meeting," he whispered. And then she felt his warm wet tongue on her neck. It ran up her cheek, past her ear, and right up into her hair. She shivered with pleasure and edged forward, wanting to feel his body more than she imagined possible.

"Tomorrow night, precious. Then everything will make sense." He pulled back.

"Yes," she said. His saliva began to dry cool on her cheek.

Tomorrow night?

She opened her eyes.

He was gone.

Gone! Her heart crashed to the ground, as if it had been held in a glass that someone dropped. She hurried to the door and scanned the outer room.

Empty.

Paula walked shakily to her desk and sat down heavily. What was she thinking? Bile rose to her throat and she felt she might throw up, right here on the desk.

Paula set her head in her hands and began to sob. But they really weren't sobs of horror or remorse anymore. They were sobs of self-pity.

She wanted to trip. She really, really did.

CHAPTER FIFTEEN

THE MONASTERY

Friday morning

"YOU'RE PUTTING words in my mouth," Paul cried. "Did I say I *want* to go down?"

"Sure you did," Darcy replied. "Want is part of curiosity. We all know you want. Now it's only a matter of your rights."

He looked confused, Billy thought. But he was caving already. It had been Darcy's idea to pursue the other students so soon. "If *I* went for it, then Paul will go for it. And if Paul goes for it, there's no telling how many we can get."

It had been her idea, but Billy made it his task. They would approach students strategically, beginning with Paul. *Well, swallow this, Paul.*

Darcy pressed. "As you said, Paul—and you're quite correct in saying—you possess full control over what is yours. Such as your will. And your rights. See, and you were prepared for a long drawn out argument. But it's very simple, really. You *do* have the right to do whatever you wish."

"But it's wrong."

"Says who?"

"Says them."

"But it's your right to decide what's right. Right?"

"My right?"

"Yes," Billy said. "And we know what you want. You want to go to the lower levels and have a peek. Like Darcy did. Because you look at Darcy here, and you think she looks quite well for one who's done the forbidden. And now you want to know what it feels like."

Paul's hesitation told Billy that he had his third convert. It took another twenty minutes of discussion, slowly whittling down Paul's increasingly meager objections, to get to the final point.

"So there you have it," Darcy said, grinning.

"So there I have it? Just like that?"

"Just like that. Let's go."

Paul balked. "Go? What do you mean go? Just go?"

"Yes. You exercise your will and you just go. Anything less would be denial of what your heart and your mind are telling you." Darcy stood. "Come on."

Paul stood shakily. "I don't know."

"Of course you don't. How can you know what you haven't tried? Look at me, do I look worse off?"

She scratched her neck, and Billy wondered if Paul noticed her light rash.

"Just a peek?"

"Just a peek."

"Okay, but just a peek."

Billy chuckled and slapped Paul on the back. "Just a peek. Don't worry, this will all be moot tomorrow anyway."

"How's that?"

Billy glanced at Darcy and winked. "I've challenged the monastery rules. No one knows yet, but tomorrow I'll defeat Christine in a debate and open the lower tunnels for all the students."

Paul was back to his bug eyes. "You're serious? Tomorrow?"

"Tomorrow."

"Well, what if you don't win?"

"I will." Billy stood to his feet and brushed off his pants. "You ready?"

"Now?"

"Why not? Just a peek, Paul. That's all you owe yourself. One small peek."

THEY STOOD in the vestibule, facing the huge black doors, three wide-eyed children.

"It's so dark down here," Paul said.

Billy pushed the black doors open.

"Don't be a wuss, Paul. You'll love it. The fear you're feeling is part of the fun. You'll see, I promise."

Billy and Darcy stepped past the door and waved Paul in. "Come on."

He walked toward them as if each step might set off a land mine. Funny how terrified he was. Billy's longing for the study was already mushrooming. *Hurry up, you spineless brat!*

Then Paul's head was in, craning for a view.

"Don't just stand there gawking. Come in!"

Paul stepped all the way in. But his heart remained outside, bouncing around the vestibule like a Super Ball. The thought made Billy chuckle.

He pushed the door closed behind Paul. *Clunk*.

They were in. Paul's words to Darcy rang in Billy's ears. *You went in there?* As if he thought she had tasted death itself.

Open your mouth, Paul boy. How does it taste?

Three thick pink worms writhed slowly under the torch's light on their right. Glistening bands of mucus trailed behind them. Billy could feel Paul trembling beside him.

"Wow . . ."

Darcy giggled. "Yeah, wow. I told you you'd like it." A faint rash had flowered on Darcy's lily-white Dutch neck—the same rash he'd developed. The tunnels had this effect. It was probably some kind of atmospheric thing.

"Wow."

The worms' pungent odor filled Billy's nostrils and made him impatient. He didn't have time for this nonsense.

"Come on." He turned and walked into the far right tunnel, leading the way with the torch. And then he was running toward the study, with Darcy at his side and Paul stumbling behind them, saucer-eyed.

They spent twenty minutes with Paul in the study, putting up with his foolishness. The dark passage sent him around a bend. He literally bounced off the walls of the small study, touching the books and examining the furniture—enough to make Billy wonder if they'd made a mistake in bringing him. Billy wanted to spend their time here exploring or writing, not bouncing around like a lunatic. The distraction was annoying. Infuriating.

"What's this?" Paul asked. "You're writing a story together?"

Billy turned to the desk where Paul held his journal open, reading.

He and Darcy had stayed below deep into the night, exploring and reading and writing. In the end, mostly writing, a continuation of the story he'd begun on his own. Darcy insisted on writing the women in it. "It takes a woman to know a woman's true desires," she said. He chuckled and she lost herself, bent over the book, intoxicated by her own creative power as much as anything else in the dungeon.

"Put the book down. Mind your own business."

"Jiminy Cricket, Billy." Paul dropped the book onto the desk where it landed with a slap. "I was thinking maybe I could write with you, but you've turned into a raging monster."

"We're not saying you can't do things with us," Darcy said. "But you have to take a deep breath and calm down. All your questions are getting a bit annoying."

Paul seemed to shrug off her rebuke. He looked past the gate at the tunnel. "You want to go exploring."

Billy and Darcy exchanged a glance. "We've already explored."

"Well, maybe I'll find another bedroom or something. Or maybe I can try one of the other halls."

Billy faced him, angered by the suggestion without knowing why. His privacy was being trampled, though it had been at his insistence that Paul had come.

"We have only one torch," Darcy said.

"Then come with me."

Billy did want to explore, but the thought of spending any more time with the walking mouth called Paul made him nauseated.

"No, and the torch stays here."

Paul wasn't put off. "Then we'll make another." Without waiting for their approval, he stripped off his shirt.

Billy watched as he tied it into a knot, thrust it onto the end of an old broom handle he'd found in the corner, and turned the old torch upside down over his contraption. Fuel leaked in flaming drips, igniting Paul's shirt. He laughed with delight and jumped aside to avoid a thin line of flame dripping to the floor.

"You won't have long," Billy said. "Maybe half an hour before that thing burns out and leaves you in the dark. Trust me, you don't want to get caught in those tunnels without a light."

Paul left the study without another word.

Billy glared after him and turned to find Darcy staring at him. "What?"

"You have a problem with him suddenly?" she asked.

"He just irritates me suddenly," he said.

"It's the tunnels."

"Yeah, well I hope he runs out of fuel and a bunch of centipedes get to him or something."

"Yeah, wouldn't that be something."

The idea grew on Billy. Maybe, if they were so fortunate, one of the big worms or a big leech or something would suck the blood from his head.

"We should follow him and lock him into a tunnel," Darcy said. "Let him starve."

"What? You have a problem with him suddenly?"

She smiled. "He just irritates me suddenly."

"Touché. What do we do?"

She looked at the desk. "Write?"

Billy sighed and walked to the book. He sat down, picked up his pen, and let his mind fall into the story. The world around him faded. Every word he wrote swallowed his senses entirely, leaving nothing left for distraction. He forgot about Paul; about the monastery; about the study; even about Darcy, until she plopped down beside him, knocking his arm.

He grunted and looked at her. *Oh, it's Darcy.* And then he went back to drawing his pen across the paper.

For a long time the only sounds he heard were sounds of heavy breathing and the scratching of pens. Those and the voices from his story in which he'd lost himself.

Billy filled a page and turned to the next, dabbing his pen in the inkwell as he did. He used red because red was the color of blood and blood brought life. And death.

A scream echoed faintly in his mind and he thought, *The people in my story are screaming.* He pressed his pen more firmly into the paper. The screaming grew louder, and he absently wondered if it was from pleasure or pain, because he couldn't tell by the sound alone. He would have to see their faces. He smiled at that.

The scream ripped through his skull like a blaring siren and he jerked upright. He swung to Darcy and saw her wide eyes. She'd heard it too. As one they spun to the door.

Paul stumbled up to the gate and pulled up, panting. He'd lost his torch. Black streaks ran down his bared chest. He gawked at them with round eyes.

Then, as if a film director had called "cut!" he straightened, grinned, and walked into the study.

Paul stood there in the flickering light, breathing hard and smiling stupidly. Something wet matted his hair and leaked down onto his face.

"Hey," he said.

Billy just stared. He should be writing instead of babysitting this hyperactive punk.

"Where you been?" Darcy asked. Billy heard annoyance in her demand too.

"Around."

Billy felt his mind drifting back to the story he'd been writing, but then he remembered that Paul had come screaming down the hall like a maniac, and he thought maybe it would be interesting to find where the bugger had been. "What did you find?"

"I found some stuff to eat," Paul said, holding out his hand.

Billy and Darcy stepped forward and looked into the outstretched hand. The same gooey substance on his chest filled his palm.

"What is it?" Darcy asked.

"It's like honey," he said, raising his hand to his mouth. He licked at his palm slowly, not bothering to remove his eyes from them as his tongue dipped into the mucus and withdrew back into his mouth. He swallowed and smiled.

"Honey." He held out his hand. "Try some."

Looked familiar, but Billy couldn't place it. He impulsively reached out, rolled his index finger through Paul's open palm, and brought the honey to his lips.

Only it wasn't honey. Tasted like nothing. He swallowed it, wondering where Paul had found the stuff. It didn't taste too bad, really. He reached for another helping as Darcy went for her first.

The room seemed to shift around him. He blinked and stared around. The furniture moved to the dancing flames.

"Wow. It's like a drug." He looked at Darcy who was smiling and nodding like a reflection in a distorted carnival mirror.

He turned back to Paul. "You lost your torch."

"Yeah. Can I write with you guys?"

Billy was too amiable to disagree. He shrugged.

There wasn't enough room for three at the small writing table, so they made Paul move to the coffee table, where he dropped to his haunches and opened one of the journals. They answered his questions about the story but finally told him to shut his mouth and just write something. He frowned in protest. But he did shut his mouth.

An hour passed before Darcy's voice interrupted Billy's stupor.

"The light's dying."

He jerked his head up. The flame was indeed waning. Billy grabbed the torch from the wall.

"Okay, let's go."

He led them back down the hall at a jog. If the flame died, there would be no way to relight it, and he didn't fancy stumbling through pitch-black tunnels.

He glanced at the wall and saw one of the worms throbbing in the light. *Worm hall. We'll call it Worm Hall.* He looked at another oozing that familiar gel.

An image of Paul smiling, holding out an open palm, popped into his mind and he slid to a halt. Paul and Darcy ran past and then pulled up.

"What?" Darcy asked, breathing hard.

Billy brought the flame closer to one of the worms. Its excretions oozed down the wall, a thick mucus reeking of week-old socks. That same odor he'd come to love. But something else tugged at his mind.

"Paul?"

Paul stood smiling at the worm, eyes flashing in the flickering flame. He walked past Billy and scraped his fingers along the wall, through the worm's trail. His hand came away dripping with the mucus. He sniffed his hand, sampled the creamy gel, and stuffed what remained into his right pocket.

He looked up to Billy. "We should take some of this up with us, don't you think?"

For a moment Billy didn't know what to think. On one hand, the mere thought that he had ingested these gargantuan slugs' droppings revolted him. On the other, he felt an odd craving for the taste. And then Darcy walked over to the wall, swiped a wad of goo from the worm's trail, and shoved it into her blouse.

"I suppose it would be okay."

Chapter Sixteen

PARADISE

Friday

FOR THE first time since Marsuvees Black came to town, Johnny began to feel the deadening effects of the poison.

The sluggishness hit him as he ran behind Smither's Saloon and angled for home by way of the back alley. On his right, Katie's Nails and Tan shifted. He pulled up and caught his breath.

The building looked normal, but he could have sworn . . .

The wall on his right shimmered, then returned to its solid state.

Johnny began to run. His head pounded with a dull ache. What was happening to them? Whatever it was, things were getting worse. Why wasn't anyone coming in from Delta? They might still be in some kind of storm, but wouldn't anyone notice that there were no calls or anything coming out of Paradise?

Then again, hardly anything ever came out of Paradise.

He stopped by the back door, settled himself, and looked back toward the alley. Seemed normal enough now. Except for the wind and dust and leaves and the constant dusk, even though it was midday—but at least he was seeing normal.

He pushed into the house and stood stock-still. Howling wind outside, total silence inside.

"Mom?"

He hurried to her room, dreading what he might find.

Sally was still in bed, sheet pulled over her head. He had to make another decision. Either Black was who he claimed to be, a minister of truth sent by God to save Paradise, or he wasn't. If he wasn't . . .

Johnny stared at his mother's prone form and thought about that. If Black wasn't who he claimed to be, then he was the opposite. A liar, a snake, the devil himself maybe.

Whoever he was, the people of Paradise were following him like lambs, either to safer pastures or to the slaughter. But which?

A shaft of pain ran through his head. Johnny pressed a hand against the spot and strode up to his mother's bed. The frustration pent up in his chest boiled over. He tightened both hands into fists and yelled at her.

"Mom!"

Sally groaned.

Again, long-winded this time.

"Mommmm!"

This time she jerked her head up and twisted it around. "What?" Her eyes were round and lost, surrounded by dark circles.

"What are you doing?" she asked.

Looking at her haggard face, Johnny was at a loss for words.

"What do you think you're doing standing at the end of my bed like some crazy bat?"

Bat?

"Get out of here, Johnny!" She thrust her finger at the door. "Get out of my room."

"It's going crazy, Mom. Do you know what time—"

"What's going crazy? You're going crazy, boy. Out!"

Johnny felt trapped. Betrayed. Frantic. He nearly turned and ran.

Nearly.

"Listen to yourself." He stepped forward, not back. "I'm your son and you're yelling at me like I'm a crazy bat! You were dreaming of bats, weren't you? Only it was Black who was the bat, not me." He tapped his chest. "This is Johnny, not a bat. You've been sleeping for over fourteen hours and your eyes are glazed over and you're yelling at me when all I'm trying to do is wake you up because the world is falling down around our ears!"

Sally stared at him, taken aback. Then she turned and dropped on her back, hands on her face. She exhaled forcefully and groaned. "Sorry . . . I don't know what my problem is. I . . ." She stalled.

"I do. It's that stuff Katie gave you yesterday. And I don't think that's all. Black's destroying our town."

"Please, Johnny, not this again."

"Take a look. Just look outside and tell me it's all fine."

She propped herself on her elbows, stared at him with dazed eyes, and finally agreed. "Fine."

Thirty seconds later they stood at the front door peering out into the dust-whipped dusk-at-midday. She'd see it now, Johnny was sure of it.

His head hammered with pain, then settled into a numb buzz. The sky brightened. The wind eased; the dust settled; the sun broke through. For a few inexplicable moments Paradise seemed less in the clutches of a dark storm than weathering a common summer wind. Johnny lost track of time.

A musty scent filled his nose. *Tastes like nothing.* He wouldn't mind tasting that nothing.

"And?" Sally said. "So we have a storm."

Johnny swallowed and his vision cleared. More accurately, he cleared his vision. Or had he? Somewhere in the back of his mind his mother's voice echoed softly.

And . . . So we have a storm.

Not the response he was looking for. But this new mystery swallowed his mind.

He blinked and stared out at the street, relaxing, searching for what he'd just seen. Again the air cleared. Again the wind eased. Again the sky lightened. His concentration faded, but he forced himself to focus.

The facade vanished. Dark clouds hung low overhead.

Was that what his mom was seeing?

This is what his mom was seeing.

They didn't see what he saw! They were somehow blinded to the true nature of the darkness that had settled over Paradise. So then Black's drug not only opened their eyes to things that weren't really happening, but it blinded them from seeing what *was* happening!

Unless all of it really was happening. Worst case.

Or unless Johnny was seeing Paradise as dark and terrible when it really wasn't.

"A little wind never hurt anyone," Sally said, leaving Johnny by the door.

He turned inside. "How dark is it out there? I mean . . . are the clouds black?"

"Dark? It's a windstorm, not a rainstorm."

"But there's clouds in the sky, right?"

"Sure. So what?"

"How many clouds?"

"Johnny, please . . ."

"I just want to know what you're seeing. Because when I look out I see endless low black clouds, worse than I've ever seen."

Her eyebrows met. "You're not serious, right?"

"That's what I see."

"Then you're seeing things again. It's overcast, but not black."

So, he was right.

Then again, who was seeing the sky as it really was, he or his mom?

"Mom, would you do something for me if I begged you to do it? Something that may seem stupid but to me is real important?"

She sat on the couch and leaned her head back. "What?"

"Don't drink any more water. And don't leave the house or touch any more of that stuff Katie's drinking."

She closed her eyes and took a deep breath. But she didn't answer. Johnny thought she might be going back to sleep.

"Mom?"

"What?"

"Did you hear me?"

"Hear what?"

Wind whistled by outside. He closed the door and repeated himself.

"Sure, Johnny. Whatever you say."

Johnny's head began to throb again, but he kept focus.

"Promise me."

Sally's eyes closed and her mouth parted slightly. She was lost to the world.

Fine. Johnny would just make sure she didn't drink any water. They had enough pop and milk to hold them for a couple days if they were careful.

He left his mother sprawled on the couch and went in search of the water main.

THE MUSIC drummed through his mind. That incredible, haunting music that Peter and his father and Chris had been lurching to.

Roland had seen his mother leave the house and make her way in the direction of the church. His father was gone—probably at the bar. That left him alone in the house.

Last night he was frightened by all of Johnny's talk and seeing Black pull his lip off his face. This morning he felt a continuing sense of dread as they headed out in search of Peter. But something had changed in the theater.

He was furious when Claude took after Peter and beat him. But when he got so close to them, and when he heard Claude ask if he'd brought anything, his anger changed to curiosity. So freaky.

Cool freaky.

Peter's father didn't look mean or angry. He just wanted something and he wanted it bad. He looked like a boy asking for an ice-cream cone.

Only it wasn't an ice-cream cone he wanted. He wanted what was on that TV. And Roland had seen what was on that TV. He couldn't really remember the details, but he thought he might want it too.

Roland watched the street for nearly an hour after Johnny headed home, thinking things through, working up his courage. They hadn't come out of the old theater yet. At least not that he'd seen, and he'd only gone for a drink once and to the bathroom once, and even then he'd been watching as best he could.

What they could possibly be doing in there, he had no idea, but he was vacillating between sneaking back to the theater for a look and staying put. His dilemma had cost him three fingernails so far.

The weather was starting to ease up. Less wind, not so dark.

Johnny was right about one thing—that juice of Black's did something to people. It had done something to Fred and Peter, and frankly he wouldn't mind knowing a little more firsthand.

Still no sign of his mom or dad. They were probably out getting juiced up. What if he was the only one out of luck? He thought about going to Johnny's but immediately decided that was the last thing he wanted. No, he wanted to find out exactly—and by that he really did mean precisely, as in *been there, done that*—what Peter was up to.

Roland let his mind drift. Time seemed hazy. Once he looked at his watch and it was one o'clock and the next time it was two, but he was sure a whole hour hadn't gone by.

Three ghosts walked out in the waning dust storm. Three blind mice, wandering from the big building to the small building. One big mouse, one medium-sized mouse, and one—

Roland jerked his eyes wide. Claude, Chris, and Peter had come forth. They seemed to float from the old theater toward his father's saloon.

All alive. All pretty mellow. All walking straight.

Roland lost sight of them as they exited the front window's field of view. He ran to the bathroom and picked them up again. They walked right up the steps, pulled open the saloon door, and disappeared inside.

For a long time Roland just stared at the empty landing. An image of Claude pouncing on Peter skipped through his brain. He swallowed. Freaky, man. Just plain freaky.

He began to pace. His head buzzed. He could/should just go and check it out, of course. But he shouldn't/wouldn't just go and check it out.

Johnny was yelling in one ear telling him to go bury his head under a pillow and not drink the water.

Roland was yelling in his other ear telling him he wasn't Johnny.

Could/should shouldn't/wouldn't freaky. Way freaky.

Another hour passed. He had to go. Could/would. He was missing out.

STEVE SMITHER walked along the back alley toward his saloon, carrying five more sticks under his arm. He'd already taken eight stakes into the saloon and hidden them under the bar. He wasn't sure when he'd taken them there—the hours were running together now like the letters of a foreign alphabet. Like Chinese letters. But he knew it was way past noon now, and he thought it must be Thursday. Or Friday. Maybe even Saturday. No, it couldn't be Saturday.

His dream kept popping in his mind, like a jack-in-the-box. Only it was Black-in-the-box, jumping up to say, *Surprise, Stevie! Oh, I'm sorry, is this your wife?*

Yeah, well, I've got a little surprise for you myself. He smiled wryly. Somewhere out there Paula was probably wondering where he was. But she would find out soon enough, wouldn't she? And then she would thank him.

He reached the saloon, mounted the steps, and dug for his keys. One of the stakes dropped to the ground and he swore. He fumbled in his pocket, pulled the key ring out, and bent for the fallen stake. A muffled bang filtered through the door, and he snapped upright.

What was that?

Someone's in your saloon, Stevie.

He froze there in the wind with one hand holding his keys and the other stretching over five cockeyed sticks ready to fall with the slightest movement. Muted laughter drifted through the door. He fingered through the ten or so keys, found the big brass one, and shoved it into the lock.

He pushed the door open. A loud crash. Howling laughter.

Yes, sirree, some fool was in his saloon. Well, he'd better not be. This saloon was closed, locked, off-limits to all fools, which meant *everybody.*

Another crash sounded, loud now. He glanced about the storeroom, set the stakes carefully on the floor with trembling hands. He reached the inner door and placed his hand on the knob.

Black-in-the-box popped up in his mind. *Not thinking too clearly are you?* It cackled past that plastic smile. *Not too clearly at all. You can't just walk in there unprepared.*

Another laugh peeled through the saloon, a shrill one that reminded Steve of Claude Bowers from down the street. He let go of the handle, shuffled back to where he'd set the stakes, and picked up the largest one. He swung it through the air, pleased at the small *whoosh* it made.

Wanna trip, baby? Here, let me help you trip.

Steve walked back to the door and shoved it open.

The three fools were there in the middle of his saloon, sitting on the only table left standing. Claude Bowers, Chris Ingles, and Peter, Claude's squirt kid. They looked at him with wide grins, like Black-in-the-boxes only without a box. He looked around the saloon.

The tables and chairs had been splintered into a hundred pieces that littered the floor like kindling. The large Coors chandelier over the pool table hung twisted and smashed so that only the white fluorescent housing looked familiar to him. The pool table glistened with a liquid. Maybe vomit. The heat began to rise up his body like an erupting volcano. Dozens of empty bottles stood along the windowsills and in groups around the floor, like bowling pins waiting to be toppled.

Steve felt his eyes bulge, felt the surge of blood in his temples. He looked to the right. The bar had been hacked at with a sharp tool of some kind. A large knife or an ax maybe. The bar stools were gone. Just gone.

Then he realized that they were on the floor, only they were splinters, not stools anymore. The front door had been ripped from its hinges and lay on its side.

"What in the fiery blazes is going on?"

He heard his voice asking the question, but he was thinking, *Where's Black-in-the-box*, because he knew this was really his doing.

Claude and gang were looking at him like he was a ghost who'd walked in on them.

"Hi, Steve," Chris said. "We didn't think you'd mind. Just having a little fun."

Black-in-the-box grinned in his mind. *Have a heart. They're not doing anything you wouldn't do. Let 'em trip, baby.*

"Didn't think I'd mind? What do you mean you didn't think I'd mind?"

Good for you, Stevie. You tell 'em.

"You little stinkin' weasels! How about I have a little fun with you?" He raised the stake in his hand like a bat. "How'd you like that?"

Peter—the little squirt who was picking his jaw with Steve's furniture—had an ax in his hand, and he laid it carefully on the table. *Clunk.*

You think putting that thing down somehow makes all this okay?

"Take it easy, Steve," Chris said. "We'll clean it up. Promise."

"Oh, I know you will, Chris. That's why I'm gonna let you live. If I didn't think you were gonna clean this up, I'd kill you." He lowered the stick and twirled it in his hand. "I'd run this stake right through your heart."

Now that would be a trip.

Chris chuckled. "Yeah. But we're gonna clean it up, right guys?" Neither Claude nor Peter answered and Chris glanced their way. "Right boys?"

"Of course, Chris," Claude answered, but he wore a crooked grin and Steve wasn't sure he liked the look of the fat man's smile.

"How about I give you exactly fifteen minutes to clean it up?" Steve said. "How about I come back in a quarter hour, and if you make this picture perfect I won't run this stake through your hearts?"

"Yeah," Chris said, chuckling nervously. "What's the use of living if you can't have a little fun now and then, right? We all have our kinds of fun, right, Steve? I mean you have yours"—he motioned toward the stick in Steve's hand—"and we have ours. But we'll clean it up. Swear it."

It was then, just as he was thinking that Chris had a point, that Steve remembered the eight stakes he'd hidden under the bar. He scanned the floor, searching for a sign of them. But wood was everywhere, broken into splinters.

A tiny sliver of fresh oak jumped into his vision. The rest of the wood faded into the floor and just that one little piece screamed up at him.

Here I am. And yes, I am one of your sticks. What do you think of that?

A dozen other splinters seemed to materialize. Steve's forehead began to throb. A sickening weight thudded into his gut like a bowl of thick oatmeal.

He jumped over to the bar. Rounded it. They had done it, hadn't they? They'd destroyed his sticks! He ripped the velvet draping away from the back of the bar.

The shelves were empty!

With a horrendous growl, Steve leaped over the bar and faced Chris. Black-in-the-box screamed in the back of his mind. *Do it, Stevie! Do him!*

Steve rushed.

The weasel raised an arm to protect himself. Steve stopped two feet from Chris, raised his stake high above his head, and swung it down with all of his strength.

Crack! Chris's forearm snapped like a twig. The man howled in pain and rolled into a ball. His right arm flopped onto the pool table at an unnatural angle. Steve raised the shaft again and beat down again.

Surprise, Chris! Say hello to my stake!

He brought the stick down again, and again, and again, feeling power rush through him like a drug that filled him with a hot pleasure.

Wanna trip, baby?

He hesitated and brought the stick down one last time. Chris crumpled, draped over the pool table, still.

Steve looked up at Claude and Peter, whose faces seemed carved of soap. He ran a hand along his stick and tried to wipe off the blood.

"Clean this up," he said and walked out the back, into the alley.

What a trip.

A boy stood in the alley, staring at him. He knew this boy. A rascal named Roland. This was his son.

"Beat it, boy."

Roland just stared at him with round eyes.

He almost said "beat it" again, but he decided not to bother. Roland was a big boy and could fend for himself. He probably didn't have the guts not to beat it.

Steve headed into the forest behind the bar. He looked back five paces past the first row of trees.

Roland wasn't beating it after all. He was already at the back door, peering in. Steve chuckled.

What a very major trip.

Chapter Seventeen

PARADISE

Saturday morning

MOM WAS holding her own, Johnny thought, but that wasn't exactly encouraging considering what her own was. His mother had already half-lost it. She wasn't like Claude or Chris, but she wasn't her old self either. And no amount of prodding convinced her to explain herself to him.

She'd spent most of Friday afternoon on the couch, picking through the refrigerator and reading a novel by Dean Koontz. At least Johnny finally convinced her to stay away from the water, a promise she tried to break once only to discover that water no longer flowed into the Drake house. Johnny had found the main and turned it off.

She retired just after seven, and Johnny finally drifted off to sleep around midnight, still battling that throb that kept trying to latch itself onto his head. He'd actually become pretty good about deflecting the distortions when they came.

Why was he able to do this, but not everyone else? The best he could figure was that he had been terrified by Black when the preacher killed Cecil, and the moment put him on guard.

That and the fact that Johnny stayed clear of Black's poison, despite having undoubtedly ingested some in the water.

He awoke at ten o'clock Saturday. The clouds that he either saw or thought he saw were now so dark that he could hardly see across the dust-blown street.

Phone was still dead. He considered climbing into his mother's four-wheel drive and taking a shot at driving out of the valley. Sally had refused to take him out yesterday. Probably a good thing in retrospect, considering her condition. But he'd never driven, and the conditions were anything but decent for a trial run. There were too many cliffs bordering the two-lane road out.

Johnny stood in the kitchen and squinted against another headache. Stars popped to life, then faded. A musty smell drifted by. The tastes-like-nothing taste filled his mouth. He wanted it, sure he did.

But he also hated it.

He grunted and decided then that he couldn't just sit here without a plan. He had to talk to someone sane, at the very least. He had to talk to Roland even if it did mean leaving his mother for a few minutes and braving the dark wind.

Johnny poked his head into his mother's room, satisfied himself that she was still dead to the world, pulled on a hoodie for protection, and headed down the back alley.

The town was dark and windy and dusty and dead. Hot though.

He couldn't shake the possibility that he was actually only seeing this in his mind's eye. If so, then Black was probably a messenger from God after all. But after all he'd seen, Johnny couldn't make that fit.

A lone howl drifted above the wind. Johnny froze. What was that? A loud crash on his left, nearby in the forest. Then a loud grunt.

He began to run, straight toward Roland's house.

When he got there, he quickly came to the awful conclusion that the house was deserted. At least no one was stirring. Roland's shade was open and his bed was made, but no Roland. The lights were off in the whole place. Not a soul to be seen.

Main Street was just as empty.

Buffeted by fresh fear, Johnny sprinted back to his house, ignoring an ache in his weaker leg. Things were worse than yesterday, much worse. Where was everyone? And where was Black?

He had to get home.

Inside, the back door slammed shut behind him. Then again, things were no better in here. He stood alone in the hall for a few moments, soaking in the silence.

He wanted to cry. He was alone, wasn't he? And he had no place to go. Maybe it would be easier to walk over to the saloon and ask them for some of Black's crud. Maybe he should just walk out into the street and scream his surrender to the black sky, let the black angel administer some of his grace and hope.

Johnny checked on his mother again. No movement other than the rise and fall of the sheets with her breathing. No sense in waking her up.

He walked into his room, sat on his bed, and was about to lie down when the one-inch marble he had with him the day Cecil died rolled slowly toward the edge of his dresser.

Johnny blinked at the sight. The red shooter stopped, then rolled back the way it had come. It stopped in its original position.

Johnny's pulse quickened. Had he really seen that? What could have caused a marble to roll like that? No wind in here. No tremors, no tilting. But things rolled on their own sometimes, didn't they? The slightest force could . . .

The marble vanished.

Johnny stood, amazed. The space where the round red marble had sat just a moment ago was empty. Nothing but an oak dresser top.

He ran his hand over the varnished wood grain. He'd seen eyes poked out and an apple turned into a snake. He'd seen warts come and go. He'd even seen Black pull his lip off his face. But this was different.

This was the first time he'd seen something impossible happen without the magician on hand to execute his magic.

Fred and Peter saw something on the old theater wall, but only after they'd taken some of Black's slimy concoction. And he hadn't seen that himself. They'd all seen the clouds darkening overhead and dust blowing along the streets, but Johnny was quite sure that was real.

So what did that make this disappearance of the red marble? Real?

A *thunk* sounded behind him. He spun, but there was nothing he could . . .

He caught his breath. The red shooter sat on the wall, halfway up, near the door frame. Johnny lowered himself to his bed unsteadily. What was going on here? He watched it for a minute, waiting for it to move. The marble just sat there as if stuck to the wall with glue.

Johnny rose and approached the red shooter. Slowly, ever so slowly, he reached out. Touched it. Gripped it between his forefinger and thumb. Pulled it off the wall.

The glass shooter was smooth and weighty, exactly as it always had been. He let it rest in his palm and opened his fingers. The ball trembled and rose from his hand as if suspended on an invisible string.

Incredible! Johnny moved his hand to the right. The marble followed, precisely equaling the movement of his hand. He jerked his hand to the left. Again the marble followed precisely. No lag.

He moved his hand in a quick circle. The red orb followed every move without falling behind even a fraction of a second. A crooked smile formed on his face. This was absolutely . . .

The marble broke form, drifting toward the dresser. Like an unidentified flying object, the orb hovered two feet above the dresser for a long moment, then sunk slowly to the oak surface and touched down in its original resting place without a sound.

Johnny sat hard on the bed. The box springs squeaked. He didn't know what to think, other than it wasn't a trick. Black wasn't up in the attic floating the ball on an invisible string. He wasn't crouched behind the bed using magical magnets that worked on glass. Johnny had touched the marble. Held it in his hand. What he'd just seen had to be real.

The marble did not move.

Johnny just watched.

STEVE SMITHER had spent the night under the saloon's back porch, where he intended to keep an ear tuned to destruction. He awoke close to noon, although he wouldn't have known it by the sky, because the sun was obscured by dark clouds.

He had only four sticks left—Claude and gang destroyed eight, and he ruined one on Chris. He needed more sticks.

Steve walked home, past the shed, looking for any wood that might work.

No wood.

He returned to the saloon and struck out for the forest, gripping one of the sharpened stakes in his left hand. His mind was foggy and he couldn't see too well, but he lurched toward the grove of saplings from which he'd harvested his other stakes.

The leaves were coming off the trees, an early fall in the middle of summer. What a trip.

Steve stumbled into a small clearing and paused, dazed. Had he forgotten something? His destination maybe. No, he was going to the grove of aspens to make some more sticks.

Or he would cut down some little trees and then haul them to his shed where he would make some more sticks. Unless Paula was there—then he would stay out at the grove where she couldn't ask him any questions, like why he was making so many sticks.

He looked down at the stake in his right hand and then at his left hand, hanging there, limp, empty. Of course! He'd forgotten the ax. Stupid, stupid!

Steve lifted his hand and stared at the dried blood on his forearm. Chris's blood. He wondered if he'd killed the man. An image of Chris lying there on the pool table all curled up filled his mind. He grinned and forgot about the ax for the moment.

Beat that man good, hadn't he? Should've beat the other two while he was at it. In fact, it was probably Claude's punk kid who'd found his sticks in the first place. Kids were like that, poking their noses in where they didn't belong.

Maybe they would come back for some more fun and he could have some more of *his* fun. He flexed his fingers around the crusted blood. This time he might stick the sharp end into them. They would sure howl about that!

The thought of making more sticks struck him as senseless. Why make more stakes when he had four perfectly good sticks? He should start learning how to *use* the stakes, shouldn't he? Like graduating from boot camp. It was time to learn how these things worked for real. He could always make more stakes. But learning how to *use* them, now that would be something.

And not just the blunt end either.

Steve stood in the small clearing, swaying on his feet, left hand clamped around a three-foot stake and the other bloody hand palm up by his chest. He looked around at the trees.

Well, I can't just go around poking people for practice. They'd never understand. So then what? What can I stick my stakes into?

A chipmunk scurried across the clearing, and Steve watched it go. Now there was a thought. Course, the critter was a bit small, but it could make for good practice. It could be like a mission: *Pursue and kill all the chipmunks. And any other bigger animals you encounter.*

Yes, sir. Now *bigger* animals might be something. He could jab them good with his stakes. *Jab, jab, jab.*

Steve clenched the stake with both hands and stalked into the forest.

WHILE STEVE was stumbling through the woods, discovering bloodlust, Claude Bowers was down by the Starlight Theater grinning up at the big sign. Beside him stood a badly bruised and bloodied Chris Ingles. Roland, Peter, and Fred stood to one side, watching his every move.

They'd fixed a crude splint to Chris's broken arm, but he'd complained for the last thirty minutes about the pain, and Claude was getting sick of telling him to shut up.

"Take some more of those painkillers and just shut your trap, Chris! Here, drink some of this." He shoved his bottle of Jack Daniels at the man.

"We're gonna ransack this entire town," Claude said, looking at his son with a wide grin. "What do you think of that?" He snatched the bottle back from Chris and took a slug. Chris had almost emptied it, but Peter had another bottle in his pocket, and they knew where Steve kept the rest.

Stevie Smither hadn't seen nothin' yet! They were going to teach that slime bucket what happened to anybody who messed with them.

"Neat," Peter said. A crooked grin twisted his face, and Claude thought maybe he shouldn't have beat him so hard yesterday. His right eye was swollen shut and his lip was still cracked with blood.

But he'd had it coming, smashing the television like that.

"Yeah, neat," Roland said, looking up.

Claude bent to the pile of axes at his feet, snatched up a large splitting ax, and handed his bottle to Peter. "Here, hold this. And don't go drinking it all."

He swaggered up to one of the two wooden posts that supported the sign swaying in the wind thirty feet above. "Ready?" He gripped the ax with both hands. A strong gust of wind hit him and he staggered back a step.

"Do it, Claude!" Chris said, still holding his right arm gingerly.

Claude raised the ax and put every one of his 280 pounds into the swing. The blade buried itself in the post with a loud *smack,* and Peter let out a *whoop.*

"Do it, Dad!"

"Yeah, do it!" Roland mimicked.

Claude tugged at the ax. It budged, but barely. He placed a foot on the pole for leverage. The blade came loose, and he tumbled to his rear end, cursing loudly. Chris howled with laughter.

"Shut up, Chris! I'll come over there and break your other arm!"

That settled him a bit. Chris snickered as Claude struggled to his feet and lined the ax up for another swing.

Smack!

The watching evidently proved too much for Peter. He set the bottles of booze on the ground, snatched up a hatchet. In his eagerness, his right foot knocked Claude's bottle over. The thirsty dust swallowed the amber liquid.

Claude stared at the bottle, ax just raised for a third swing.

Their eyes met—Claude's glaring, Peter's wide. "You'll pay for that," Claude rasped and swung angrily at the pole. *Smack!*

"I'm sorry. I swear. Can't Chris hold the bottles? He's a lame duck anyway."

"Shut up, Peter," Chris said. "Can't you see I'm hurt here? You think I just want to be a lame duck? I can hardly move here, man!"

"Shut up, Chris," Claude said. "Peter's right. Take the bottles."

Peter helped his dad hack at the large pole with his small hatchet. Roland joined him from the opposite side, swinging sporadically between Peter's continuous warnings not to miss and hit him by mistake.

It took the trio ten minutes of palm-blistering chops and nonstop bickering before the mighty sign at the south end of Paradise began to lean toward the street.

"Watch out!" Chris yelled. "It's coming down! It's gonna hit the car!"

Claude's old blue 310 Datsun was parked on the shoulder fifteen feet from the sign. None of them had considered the sign's trajectory. The sound of splintering wood rose above the wind, and the thirty-foot beacon began its descent.

If Claude had parked his Datsun seven feet to the right, the two supporting poles would have straddled the car. Instead, the massive timber smashed onto the sedan's canopy, crushing it into the driver's seat. The huge Starlight sign slammed into the pavement beyond.

Claude raised his ax above his head, spread his legs wide, tilted his head to the black clouds, and let out a roar of approval.

Peter and Roland hopped up and down, ecstatic. Chris instinctively raised his broken arm in victory and then winced with pain. But the accomplishment was too great to be thwarted by a little pain, and he shouted anyway.

The sign's plastic casing lay shattered on the blacktop. The car sat buckled like a fortune cookie. Claude's gang celebrated their first major feat of destruction.

"I'll drink to that!" Chris shouted.

They slammed the bottles of Jack Daniels together in a toast. Unfortunately, Chris's bottle proved to be a bit too brittle for his enthusiasm. It shattered on impact, spilling more amber liquid into the dust.

It was the last bottle, and none of the others were in a sharing mood. He shuffled off toward the saloon for more, cursing.

"What did I tell you?" Claude said, ignoring Chris. "Now was that a trip or was that a trip?"

"That was a trip," Peter answered.

"Yeah, well, we're gonna show this whole town how to trip. We're gonna do this town, boys!"

WHILE CLAUDE was busy plotting the trashing of Paradise by the Starlight Theater, Nancy was taking a screwdriver to the rear door of his store, All Right Convenience.

Nancy shoved the flat end into the keyhole and pried to the left. She'd never actually broken a lock before, and she didn't know what actually made them open other than a key. Perhaps a sledgehammer.

She doubted a screwdriver was the right tool for breaking into the local convenience store. But it was the only tool she could readily find when she finally made the decision to brave the wind for some food.

Her small indiscretion was Claude's fault. If the fat pig would open his doors for business, she wouldn't have to break in, now would she? The front doors had been locked for over forty-eight hours, and she was out of things to eat.

To make matters worse, the father had called and told her he wasn't coming back until Sunday morning, just in time for church. "I've got a message for the people," he'd said. "And I think the impact would be most powerful if I just walked in while they were already assembled for Sunday morning service. It's going to be powerful, Nancy. Powerful."

"Well, I hope people come," she said.

"What do you mean, come? They always come on Sunday."

"I don't know, Father. I haven't seen a soul all day. Are you going to a Sam's Club?"

"Why would I be going to a Sam's Club? What do you mean you haven't seen a soul all day? You mean in the church?"

"If you went by a Sam's Club, you could get me a large pack of those pastries I like so much. The cherry ones with glaze. Maybe a dozen packs, so we have them for church functions when we need them. And no, I don't mean the church. I mean the town. It's pretty quiet around here."

"But nothing's wrong, right? As far as you can tell everything's okay?"

"Yes, Father. It's just fine. Maybe you'd better get a couple dozen of those packs. They're pretty cheap at Sam's, you know?"

"I'm not going to Sam's," he said. "You weigh enough as it is. The last thing you need are glazed pastries."

Now what was he so rankled about? That jab was entirely unnecessary. But one of the advantages of weighing enough was the pressure you could bring to bear on a lock if you leaned on it hard enough.

The screwdriver bent as she brought her 270 pounds to bear. Something snapped, and she plowed into the white door frame, nose first. A warmth immediately ran down her lip.

I've broken the screwdriver. She pulled back, wiped her face, and brought her forearm away bloody. *Goodness.* She reached out to test the doorknob. *I've broken my nose too.*

The handle turned easily in her hand and the door swung away from her. What do you know? She stepped in, went straight to the bathroom, and flipped the lights on. The face staring at her in the mirror looked like an onion. An onion with two raisins for eyes and a red mustache.

The blood flowed freely over her mouth and down her chin. The white blouse she wore was already wet with blood, so she thought that maybe she looked more like a red-breasted robin. Either way, she was intrigued by the fact that the blood did not bother her. *I'm turning into a regular sinner*.

She grabbed some paper towels and wiped the blood from her chin, not bothering with the shirt for the moment. She had just broken into Claude's store, for heaven's sake. Getting out quickly wouldn't be such a stupid idea.

She snatched up some toilet paper and stuffed two little bullets of it into her nostrils. As long as the blood didn't flood her nasal cavities and drown her, she would be fine. The two red spikes sticking out of her nose didn't look too glamorous, but she was here for food, not a beauty contest.

Nancy hustled from the toilet and entered the store. The stocked shelves beckoned in the dim light. She smiled absently and scanned the goodies sitting faithfully in their little shiny wrappers.

So much food, so little time. Saliva began to gather in her jowls and she swallowed.

Nancy grabbed a bag from the counter and filled it with a single sweep of her arm. The paper sack tore and the goodies crashed to the floor. She swore and snatched up a plastic bag.

Nancy filled six of the bags before reluctantly deciding to retreat to the church to sort through her spoil. It had been a good trip.

She exited through the back without closing the door.

A good trip indeed.

WHILE NANCY was robbing Claude blind to feed her food lust, Katie waited impatiently in her beauty salon, fixing her hair, dreaming of a rendezvous with the preacher. No, not the preacher—for her it was Marsuvees. To others he may be *the minister* or *the preacher*, but she had stepped past that point, gaining access to the inner man.

Marsuvees, darling, could you hand me my dress?

She had this effect on most if not all men, of course. They all wanted her. And she never blamed a single one of them. If she'd been born male, she too would choose a woman with her body rather than one of those pudges like Paula.

Now there was a case. Paula. She recalled an image of Claude sitting in the third pew once, ogling Paula as she gave her annual Sunday-school report. She knew he'd been ogling and not just looking because when she elbowed him he jerked his eyes from the woman—guilty as sin. At the time, she thought the whole incident was rather silly.

But sometime between then and now, the memory had soured in her mind like week-old milk. Not that she cared much whether Claude eyed a woman or two now and then. But she just couldn't believe that he found Paula sexy, of all women. She was the Sunday-school coordinator, for goodness' sake, and you couldn't play Sunday-school coordinator and strut your stuff up there while talking about how many kids were participating in the Easter play. Sunday school and sexy didn't mix.

Katie glanced at her watch. One thirty. Marsuvees said he would meet her here at one.

Wanna trip like I do, Katie? Wanna trip with me?

His words burned in her ears. She closed her eyes and leaned against the wall, savoring the heat. The door opened and she jerked off the wall. She softened her look, cocked her head just a tad, and turned to the front.

Paula stood in the door frame, frowning. Katie's heart fell and she dropped the kiss-me look.

"What in blazes are you doing here?" she demanded, surprised at the revulsion that ripped through her throat. The white strip in the pudge's hair looked ridiculous!

"What am I doing here? What are you yelling at me for?"

"I'm not yelling at you. I'm just asking you what you're doing here. Last time I checked this shop did have my name on it. What do you want?"

Katie grabbed a pack of smokes from the counter and lit one up. Paula's response was coming slow. Marsuvees could show up at any moment, and she certainly didn't want Goody Two-shoes standing here looking so prissy when he walked in.

She blew a smoke ring. "So?"

Paula rested a hand on her waist and cocked her hips. "So I'll be leaving, that's what's *so.* Have you seen Marsuvees?"

Marsuvees? Not *the preacher* or *the minister*, but *Marsuvees*?

Katie raised an eyebrow. "Marsuvees? We're calling him Marsuvees now, are we?" She noticed Paula's black skirt and wondered when Miss Pudge had taken up wearing tight, short skirts. Certainly not while planning Sunday-school lessons.

"So what if I am?"

Heat began to warm Katie's face. A sickening heat, the kind that sometimes builds to fury. But there was no way Marsuvees and Paula were anything like her and Marsuvees. Not intimate and close and ready to take things to the moon.

"You're on a first-name basis with the preacher now? I'll bet Steve would be tickled to hear that."

Katie said it casually, with the intent of dousing any misplaced flames licking at Paula's heart, but she felt like jumping over there and sticking her cigarette into the woman's eyes.

Ordinarily the veiled threat would have earned a gasp of feigned disapproval. Maybe an about-face and a grand exit as an encore for good measure.

Ordinarily.

Things weren't so ordinary in Paradise these days.

Paula lowered her head like a cat intent on guarding her territory. "Stuff it, Katie! You think you're such a hot number? I've got news for you, honey. You're not the only one men find attractive around here. Just because Marsuvees has the hots for me doesn't mean you have to play jealous bimbo, you slug!"

Katie felt her jaw fall, as though someone had tied a ten-pound weight to her lower teeth and shoved it from her mouth. She was having difficulty understanding all of Paula's words, but a few were crystal clear.

Like *slug*.

Paula was calling her a slug and claiming to be having something in the works with Marsuvees in the same breath. She was lying through her teeth, of course. Marsuvees would never lay a hand on that squat tub, not when he knew he could have Katie any time he wanted. She'd made that abundantly clear to him.

"In your wildest fantasy. Marsuvees can't keep his eyes off me. And you have the gall to come into *my* shop and talk about *my* man that way? I oughta rip your tongue from your throat, you Neanderthal!"

She wanted nothing more than to do just that, maybe rip that head off while she was at it. She stuffed the cigarette between her lips and sucked hard.

Paula's face was turning beet red, and a thought dawned on Katie. *She means it. She's actually got something going with Black!*

"It may be your shop," Paula said, "but Marsuvees told me to meet him here at one thirty."

"In your dreams!"

"And it ain't the first time we've met, honey doll."

Katie launched herself at Paula, who took the rush head-on. They met in the center of the tiny shop, fingernails extended. Both managed to draw blood on the first pass—Katie from Paula's right shoulder, and Paula from Katie's left cheek. They attacked again, yowling like cats in heat, flailing their arms.

Within the space of thirty seconds both women looked like the victims of gang violence. The last thing Paula did was clamp her bony fist around a lock of Katie's strawberry hair and yank it cleanly from her skull before running, screaming for the door, her prize flying from her hand like a captured flag.

Katie jerked a hand to her head and pulled it down, wet with blood.

"I'll kill you, you witch! I'll kill you if it's the last thing I do!"

She collapsed to the chair and grabbed her pack of smokes.

What a trip.

WHILE KATIE and Paula were fighting, Johnny was watching the marble on his dresser.

Just watching.

Chapter Eighteen

THE MONASTERY

Saturday morning

ACCORDING TO the rules of a debate, the official announcement detailing Billy's debate with Christine could not be made until the same morning. It was simply posted on the announcement board in the breakfast hall:

An Official Debate has been issued
and will be heard at
10:00 a.m. in the main lecture hall.
All students must be present.

The intention was to let the actual debate frame the challenge, rather than a string of endless debates that would surely erupt sooner if the announcement was posted. But it would have been virtually impossible to live in the monastery during the last twenty-four hours and not know what was afoot.

The teachers wore worried looks, and the student's questions about Billy, Darcy, and Paul were answered in oblique terms. Billy and Darcy weren't so guarded, and Friday evening the halls echoed with soft whispers. Samuel huddled with Tyler and Christine, twice in the library and once in Samuel's bedroom, late at night.

By morning, a strange silence had gripped Project Showdown.

Now the students hurried to the Hall of Truth, as they called the main lecture hall, armed with the understanding that something profound was about to alter their lives.

Samuel had questioned his father at length about the rules of debate, and the minute he stepped into the auditorium he saw they were being followed to the letter.

The room sloped like a theater to a large platform, accommodating long wooden pews that faced the stage. A single aisle divided the seating into two sections of fifteen pews each. Behind the stage, long maroon curtains hung from a domed ceiling, where indirect lighting cast a yellow hue throughout the room. Seven golden lamp stands stood on the platform, set in a semicircle behind ten high-back chairs. The overseers had seated themselves in the chairs. Two wood podiums, slightly angled toward each other, waited for the debaters. A single large chair was centered behind the podiums. His father's chair.

Samuel scanned the auditorium and took a deep breath. The monastery was about to see its first debate. More important, his father was about to watch Billy openly refute him in an attempt to undermine his life's aim. And by all Samuel could see, his father wasn't taking it well.

They spent an hour alone in his father's study the previous evening. He could still see his father's drawn face, often looking away, lost in deep thought.

"Don't worry, Father. Once Billy is brought to his senses, everything will change."

His father smiled. "You know, you and Billy used to play together often when you were young. Billy was the mischievous one. He would sneak up behind you and stick a thin blade of grass in your ear and then run away, squealing. You always overtook him, of course; no one could ever run like you. You would end up rolling around laughing on the grass with him."

"I'd forgotten," Samuel said. "You're right. We were always together, weren't we? What happened?"

"Project Showdown happened. It's always been about this moment."

They prayed for God's wisdom and above all the power of Christ to open the eyes of Billy's heart. But they both knew that the choice was Billy's alone.

Most of the children had taken their seats. They wore their customary uniforms—blue shorts and white shirts—most neatly groomed and giving the left side of the auditorium both a wide berth and numerous stares.

Darcy sat on the left, near the back, shifting on her pew. A red rash covered her face. Paul's as well. Stevie sat with them . . .

Stevie had gone down as well? So Billy had found three converts in just over one day. Samuel felt bumps rise on his neck. But the rules were clear—a two-thirds majority was required to prevail. Twenty-four students would have to vote against Christine for Billy's debate to succeed.

Samuel eased into a seat near the back, across the room from Darcy. Murmurs filled the hall. The monks whispered one to the other. Two dusty shafts of light descended from skylights, highlighting the podiums.

The curtain to the stage's left moved, and the room quieted. The heavy maroon cloth parted and his father walked into the light. Samuel's heart jumped at the sight. *That's my father! To them he is the director, but to me he is Father.* He felt like standing up and yelling, *Hey, Billy, that's my father and you'd better do what he says!*

Of course that would be out of order, but Samuel let the pride swell unchecked.

David walked to the center of the platform wearing a long black robe with a white collar, like a schoolmaster might wear at graduation ceremonies. He looked over the children for a moment. Stillness descended on the auditorium. The overseers sat, rigid; the children stared at David, scarcely breathing. Samuel's father had the air of authority that insisted on stillness.

And then his father's voice filled the auditorium. He spoke without a microphone. None was required in the hall. "Good morning, scholars, teachers. Thank you for coming. As you know, we are gathered for a debate."

He measured each of the students as he spoke, showing no visible reaction to the division in the class, but Samuel knew his father's heart was pained.

"This is our first debate. It's the first time a student has openly questioned my authority and rejected the rules. Some of you are wondering why we don't just put these dissidents out. Why not expel them, you ask? That's how it works in the world. When a man commits a crime, he is put away. When a child is disobedient, he is reprimanded. But here, we groom children not to follow the world's systems, but to change the world."

He cleared his throat. "The power each of you wield is beyond your comprehension. Within this room we indeed have the power to turn this world upside down. It's a great dream I have given everything for."

He raised a finger into the air. "But one rule of Project Showdown supersedes even that desire of mine, and that is the rule that you yourselves be given the complete freedom to choose your own ways. And this, my friends, brings us to today's debate."

He paused and scanned the room. "Billy has questioned the integrity of the third rule and will now debate the matter with Christine. You, my young scholars, will decide today whose argument you will follow. Listen carefully. Remember your lessons well. Think of your purpose. Measure all that you hear against the standard of truth you have always known. The future of this monastery is in your hands."

He stepped back and sat in the chair reserved for him.

The curtains on both ends of the stage parted. Billy stepped from the left; Christine from the right. A few coughs disturbed the auditorium. His father crossed his legs and looked at Darcy and the small band of dissidents.

Billy and Christine stepped up onto footstools that allowed them to stand tall behind the podiums. They were dressed in the blue robes they all wore for choir. The debate had no set structure but would not exceed an hour. At the end of the hour, the debaters and all overseers would be ushered from the room, and the students would be left alone to determine their own fate.

Samuel drew a slow breath, and as he did Christine brought her hand up, level with her shoulder. She extended her index finger to Billy.

"Billy," Christine cried shrilly, and some children flinched. "I accuse you of distorting the meaning of the third rule, the foundational rule by which all in the monastery live, the undeniable truth that all love comes from our Creator. I accuse you of heresy, and I challenge you to argue your heresy here, before the assembly, so that we may know what is the truth."

This was the track they had decided on last night. Christine would control the debate from the start by framing the third rule of writing: All love comes from the Creator, which in turn meant it would lead *to* the Creator. Surely the students wouldn't question the necessity of following God's will.

Identifying his will was the question. Was it found in the monastery rules, or was Billy right in forsaking those rules? This was the real issue.

Samuel was proud of Christine already. She was using strong words, worthy of any overseer.

Christine kept her hand outstretched, waiting Billy's response. But he said nothing.

She spoke again, distinctly, biting off each word. "Tell us, Billy, what is the precise meaning of the third rule?" She lowered her arm.

Billy rolled his eyes in exasperation and let his head loll Christine's way. "The third rule, please. You say that, *the third rule*, as if you spoke about the earth's end."

He chuckled. "The precise meaning? Yes, well, that's the whole problem, isn't it? There *is* no precise meaning. Only vague ambiguities that leave a dozen doors wide open for interpretation. And everyone in this room knows it. We've hinged our lives on the ambiguities of another man's word. Even the Bible, on which all of our rules are supposedly based, requires human interpretation, which is subject to ambiguous conclusions." He looked out at the students and grinned. "That's right, my fellow scholars. If you ask me, it's clear that ambiguity does indeed exist in the rules they've been shoving down our throats all these years."

Samuel glanced at a student near him, Sharon, who was listening intently.

"*Ambiguous*," Christine said, smiling. "A clever word. But let's be a little more specific, shall we? Surely you don't expect such intelligent children to fall for your cute phrasing. We need some content. Give us some content that we can weigh and measure. Perhaps you could answer one simple question directly?"

Billy flashed a patronizing grin. Samuel had half a mind to walk up there and smack it from his face.

Christine pressed. "The third rule emphatically states that all love comes from the Creator, leading directly to the implicit assertion that all love *leads* to the Creator. After all, if the Creator is the sole source of love, then how can one show any love which doesn't in turn lead to the Creator? Answer—he can't. I believe even you, Billy, will agree with the face value of this statement. Am I correct?"

Samuel was surprised to see the boy nod. Although he still wore that stupid grin.

"Good. Then we can at least begin in the arms of sanity," Christine said. "Trying to argue that love does not come from the Creator would be rather stupid, unless of course you don't believe in a Creator at all, in which case we would have to educate you by slogging through the preponderance of evidence that long ago settled this small-minded position."

"Sounds boring," Billy said. "And I can assure you I'm not into boring. Of course there is a Creator." Billy winked at his partners in crime.

"Then is it the Creator's character that's in question? Surely you don't—"

"Who is the Creator?" Billy asked.

In that moment, Samuel understood Billy's tack. The whole thing fell into his mind like a finished puzzle, and he knew rough waters lay ahead.

"The Creator is he who created," Christine said.

Billy faced the students. "You see, this is where we see the first point of ambiguity in the rules. Because we all create, don't we? We are all creators. We create meals and drawings and stories and such every day. The question that I posed to myself when this thought first crossed my mind was, *Well now, which creator does the third rule reference?* Hmm? Is it the Creator with a capital *C*, as they are written? Perhaps. Or perhaps not. After all, who first wrote that word with a capital letter? And who decided that it should refer to this creator or that creator?"

"Don't patronize us," Christine said. "We all know that David Abraham set the rules for the monastery. It's *his* project. How simple can you get? Your words will bury you!"

"David Abraham? I don't dispute the fact that the director does indeed run this project. I take to issue, however, our narrow understanding of the meaning of *creator*. We are all creators. We should live and love to discover ourselves as creators."

"Nonsense. That's not the meaning the director intended, and every last student knows it. You're arguing empty semantics. The Creator, with a capital *C*, as written, is God."

"Believe me, more than one of your precious students has been persuaded by virtue of these very semantics. But if you wish for a stronger argument, then consider this. When God, the Creator with a big *C*, created us, he created us as *creators*. And he purposefully gave us the power and resolve to choose what we would create, correct?"

No argument came from Christine.

"Well then, he has given us permission to live and love as creative beings, guided by our own creative power. How can you have a rule that prohibits you from doing something the Creator, with a big *C*, has specifically given you *permission* to do? Can our director overrule God with his rules?"

Billy faced the students. "Are you confused? Of course you're confused. And why? Because the rule is indeed ambiguous!"

Whispers scurried around the room. Samuel followed the argument. Apart from several well-hidden flaws, the argument seemed convincing. But it didn't matter. The concepts were heady enough to cast confusion in even the best minds.

He looked at his father and saw that he sat still, eyes closed. What if the vote swung against them? What if Christine's debate backfired and forced the prevailing doctrine into reclusion?

It would be a disaster! It would be the death of the monastery! Samuel straightened. *We've got to stop this, Father!*

"How does love fit into this?" Christine asked sharply.

The room grew quiet once again.

Christine continued. "The inclusion of love in the third rule trumps any ambiguity that may exist as a result of your semantic twists and turns. The meaning of love is crystal clear. Wouldn't you agree?"

"Is it?" Billy grinned as widely as before. "And what is that meaning, Christine?"

"Love is the purest expression of selflessness. It is the desire to please at the expense of one's own sense of need. It's looking for another to betray their desire so you can fulfill it. And there's your problem, Billy. You've told us today that the identity of the Creator is in question. Ambiguous, you said. We are all creators, you said. And indeed we *are,* in a sense. But we can't be the Creator as expressed in the rules because we can't love like the Creator. All love comes from the Creator, the third rule reads. Surely you don't hold that *all* love comes from any of us."

"I don't know, Christine. I don't think it's so clear. It's in your definition of love that I and the students find confusion."

"The students haven't expressed an opinion yet. Please refrain from begging the question."

Billy ignored the reprimand. "You say love is the purest expression of selflessness. And you assume that the one who made the universe has somehow expressed this form of love and therefore must be the one referred to in the rule, correct?"

"Yes."

"And how is God's act of creation so selfless? You see, I don't think the Creator is so selfless. I think he created the world for his pleasure. In fact, I don't believe the kind of love you speak of—this completely selfless nonsense—even exists."

A rumbling spread through the auditorium.

"That's blasphemy," Christine said.

"You show me a single act on the part of the Creator that doesn't benefit himself, Christine, and I daresay I will recant. I will withdraw every argument. It would indeed win your case. It would trump my entire premise."

"How is it possible for God to do anything that does not benefit pure goodness, which is, in fact, himself?" Christine shot back. "To say he must be selfless would be to demand that he not be God!"

"So then you agree. God cannot be selfless. And neither, my friends, can we." Billy stepped out from behind his podium. "You see, we are bound to be selfish. We are creators who will and must find love, which serves us as creators."

"Nonsense! You're saying that Christ's sacrifice was selfish?"

"I'm saying that, as Paul's epistle tells us, Christ endured the cross for the joy set before him. Sounds like he was at least thinking about what it would gain him, doesn't it?"

He eyed the children, avoiding Samuel. "At the very least it's a reasonable argument that leaves us with some ambiguity. Ambiguity, my friends. It's my only case. It's my whole case. Because in the face of ambiguity comes not only the *permission* to investigate, but the *responsibility* to investigate. To make forays into the unknown with the intent to discover what might lie there, hidden in the dark corners. I suggest to you today that anything less would be inexcusable for children of the great Creator."

Samuel closed his eyes. His face tingled. Christine was losing this debate. And not by such a small margin.

Christine spoke again, but not as confidently. "Investigate, you say? Then you'd best do it slowly and carefully, lest you inadvertently plunge into a hole from which there is no escape."

"Yes, carefully," Billy agreed. "But one cannot dissect a frog without cutting its flesh."

"I would say that there is a difference between God's rights and the rights of those he created," Christine said.

"And I would say he created us in his image, with the desire and right to investigate ambiguities, something that can be done only by getting your hands into both sides of an argument. Even Jesus Christ went into the desert to be tempted. This was how he discovered the true meaning of love." Billy sighed. "Which brings me to my second point. The second rule, that there is no discovery greater than love, is suspect too. The discovery of love may not be the most exciting thing after all. Dissecting the frog is pretty cool too, trust me on that. Since I'm a creator myself, I've altered the rules to allow for a little discovery of fun now and then, or maybe all the time."

The room fell silent. Christine paled. Billy leaned against his podium, grinning. Samuel looked at Darcy and saw that the girl had fallen asleep. Paul was smiling stupidly, scratching his rash. Samuel turned back to the stage. His father was looking directly at him.

"You're misinterpreting!" Christine snapped.

"Then you've made my case for me," Billy returned. "If something can be misinterpreted, then it is subject to interpretation. It is by nature ambiguous. And we, creatures created to create, must interpret. I am only doing what I was created to do."

The hour wasn't up, but the argument seemed to have stalled. Christine glanced around the room and turned to Billy. "In the end you will see, Billy," she said softly, as if the words were intended for Billy only. But the entire room heard them. "Your confusion will be your own undoing. This interpretation will bring a pain you can't imagine."

"That is for me to discover," he said, scratching the sores on his arm. "So far I don't regret one moment."

Christine looked briefly at David and then turned from the podium.

Leaving? She wasn't finished! There must be a way to put Billy back on his heels. Was further argument that pointless?

Taking the cue, Billy turned, walked to the curtains, and disappeared behind them.

That was it then. Samuel watched as first his father and then the line of overseers rose and walked from the room. The Hall of Truth now awaited the students' verdict.

For a moment no one moved. And then Samuel and Darcy stood simultaneously and made their way to the platform. Someone must have woken the sleeper. With a glance at each other they climbed the stage and walked to the opposing podiums.

So it all came to this. A single vote. No argument. No lengthy discussion. The argument had been cast. Only a single statement for each side of the debate remained. Samuel stepped to the side and allowed Darcy to speak first.

The girl raised a hand to her neck and scratched the rash. Darcy seemed oblivious to the fact, and she brought her hand away red with blood. She ran her fingers through matted hair, leaving thin trails of red in her bangs, then stuffed her hands into her pockets.

Darcy's speech was strained. "Hey," she began. "We all know what Billy said is true. Let's face it, we may not like it, but there's plenty of confusion out there. If you want to escape confusion, you should reapply as a horse or something, 'cause all humans have enough brains to be confused. Heck, *I'm* confused. It's why I decided to investigate. Like Billy said."

She broke into a wide grin. "And trust me, it's very cool. I listened to the holy robed ones for twelve years without questioning their rules. Well, now I've earned the right to spend a few days checking out the competition, just to round out my education, if you know what I mean."

She glanced over at Samuel. "Holy-boy here may not want you to vote for Billy, and that's okay, because he's confused too. He just won't admit it. But you owe it to yourselves, to all that is right, to vote for Billy if you're the least bit confused or even suspect there may be some ambiguity in the rules."

She stepped aside.

The students stared at Samuel with blank expressions. He caught an encouraging nod from Tyler and began his rebuttal.

"Hello, my friends. Two simple questions should be considered in all this mess. One, Billy speaks of ambiguity. Did any ambiguity rest with the rules before you heard him speak this morning? Not for me. In fact, I can't think of anything I am so certain of as the third rule. The rules are the basis for everything at the monastery. Without them, we're just orphans from the street. Your vote may return us there—to the streets."

He waited for any sign of approval. None.

"And second, if you want to judge the words of Billy, just look at the product of his words." He lifted an arm to Darcy. "Do you notice anything strange in this girl? Anything wrong or repelling? You'll have to judge for yourselves, but as I see it, whatever's eating at her flesh should remain in the dungeons where it belongs."

He lowered his hand. It was time to vote.

"All those who side with Christine in this matter should follow me, through the curtains to my left," Samuel said. "All those who side with Billy should follow Darcy to your left. Choose carefully." He turned and walked through the curtains.

The back room was empty except for several stacks of chairs against one wall. Samuel lifted his hands and saw that his fingers trembled. He clenched them and pushed his damp bangs from his forehead. He wanted to leave this place—to run and find his father and hug him and tell him it had all worked out after all.

The curtains brushed open behind him and he spun around. "Tyler!" He reached out for him, and they clasped hands. "Thank God!" he breathed. He looked to the curtains anxiously. "What do you think?"

Tyler took a deep breath. "I don't know, Samuel."

The curtains parted again and Marie walked in, followed by Kevin and Brandon. One by one Samuel grabbed them by the shoulders. "Good!

Good!" he said. Then they came in. Three more, in a group. Then two. "Good! Good!" Samuel felt a great weight begin to lift.

Another child walked in, smiling. And another. And then the curtains hung still. "Good," Samuel said, expecting at any second for the long, pleated fabric to move—to part and allow another child to pass.

But it hung still.

He spun around and counted the children with a shaking finger. ". . . ten, eleven."

Eleven!

Himself and Christine. Thirteen! He spun back to the curtains. That left twenty-four, and twenty-four would constitute a binding two-thirds majority. But that couldn't be!

His chest felt tight, suffocating. The musty air made slow passage through his nostrils while he willed the curtain to move. *Just move. Please move. Please just one more and we can pretend that this never happened. Just one!*

But the curtains hung straight, and long seconds crept by like snails along a razor, headed toward certain death.

FIFTEEN OF the twenty-four dissenters agreed to follow Billy, Darcy, and Paul down to the lower levels right then, after the vote was finalized. The rest would quickly follow. Like the rest, they entered the main door with tentative steps, trembling like tiny high-strung dogs.

"Move it, you fools!" Billy snapped at the huddling newcomers. Their eyes bugged white from taut faces. They stopped when he yelled at them, and he realized they were so terrified they couldn't process his request. He adopted a different tack.

"Come on, you guys. Everything will be fine. I promise."

Within ten minutes they were running through the dark passage, intent on their discovery.

The entourage of defectors had been underground for about an hour when one of the boys yanked Billy from the study and insisted that a monk wanted to meet with him. "In that last tunnel," he said breathlessly. "The one on the far end."

A monk? The masked monk had shown himself to this boy?

Billy brought a hand to his chest and scratched the blistering skin under his tunic. The rash was spreading. Something that sounded like an Indian war cry echoed down the dark hallway, and he spun to see a flame round the corner, bent back in the wind, held by a running girl. He stepped aside and she rushed by him, yelping.

Idiots! Behind him six students slouched around his study. If they tore up his library, he would have their necks. He turned up the tunnel toward the main entrance.

He would have to leave them because the boy said the monk wanted to see him. Who did they think he was, some monk's little puppy? And in the first tunnel to boot.

The worms seemed to have multiplied. They were thick on the walls, sliding around like massive hot dogs. They'd come from deeper in the tunnels, presumably attracted to the humans.

He left the study tunnel, as they were now calling it, passed four other large tunnel openings, shifted the flaming torch to his left palm, and stepped into the far hall. He'd stuck his head in here once but was so taken by the study since that he hadn't returned. Maybe he should have come back sooner.

The tunnel bored into the cliff for twenty feet and then veered to the left. Yellow stones the size of his fingernails glittered on the rough walls. Billy wondered if this tunnel might actually be a mining shaft running through a gold vein. A large worm slid across the ceiling, and he passed under it.

He walked down the hall, amazed at the number of gems flashing from the walls. Not just gold nuggets, but gold chains and trinkets buried among the gems. It looked as if the cavern had been a vault for jewels before a huge blast ripped through the place, driving the precious stones and metal into the wall.

"Billy."

He jumped and swung his torch to the left. The monk stood in a darkened doorway, black mask reflecting Billy's wavering light. If he had used a torch to get here, he'd extinguished it.

"I have something to show you, my friend." The tall man seemed unaware of the large worm that slid down the wall two inches from his right arm.

"What?" Billy felt quite confident, all things considered. He really didn't need this man now that he knew the tunnels and had won his debate. He wasn't even sure why the monk—assuming he was a monk—unnerved him.

"You did well," the man said, making no move to show Billy anything.

"Who are you?"

"I am the man who made you."

"And does this man have a name? What do you have to lose now? We've won!"

A pause. "I have more at stake here than the persuasion of a few students. Far more than one little valley or one small country. You'll see soon enough, my little friend."

"Don't call me your little friend. For all I know, you are my enemy."

Something about the man really did frighten Billy. What could he possibly mean by all this talk? Surely he didn't think he could control the students just because they'd come down here. Even if he did, he couldn't take over the world with them or anything so stupid.

"You don't control us," Billy said.

No response.

"So what did you want to show me?"

The man turned and walked into the darkness behind him. Billy hesitated and then followed, staying clear of the worm that started to squirm when the overseer left. The monk pushed through a side door.

A large room opened up before them, lit by a dozen flaming torches mounted about the walls. They stood on a second-story balcony overlooking a long row of towering bookcases and round tables surrounded by chairs.

Billy caught his breath. The discussion out in the dark hall left his mind. The scene made his heart race. The bookshelves were filled with books. Even from his perch up on the balcony Billy could see they were all the same size, like the books in his study.

He swung to his right and dashed for the stairs that led down to the large library. He hurried out to the center of the room and ran a hand along the nearest round table. Amazing. The furniture looked like it had been hewn from mahogany, a thousand years ago before power tools made shaping wood so easy. He touched the spindles on a chair before him. Tiny chisel marks ebbed in the torchlight. And the cases!

He walked to the closest case. At first he thought the shelves were constructed of a blackened hardwood, but one touch and he knew these were made of iron. Black iron.

He stepped to the front of the cases. The books were firmly secured to the shelving by small chains. He gripped the spine of one and pulled, but he couldn't extract it past the links that held it.

Billy scrunched his brow and replaced the book, wondering how he could read books that couldn't be removed from their shelves. Maybe the man had a key. He ran his hand along the rough iron, captivated by the grandeur of the tall cases.

Billy stepped back to the tables and looked up at the balcony where the man overlooked the rail. "You like it?" the monk asked.

"Like it? I love it. Is it for us?"

"It is for them."

"Them?"

"The other children, Billy. So that you may continue in your study without being disturbed."

Billy didn't know if he liked the idea. He gazed about again and imagined a dozen students strewn about this place. Then he imagined the same students running up and down the tunnels, yelling. Maybe the man had a point.

He would make the rest leave the study hall and come here, to the library, so he and Darcy could find some peace.

"When?"

"Tonight. Tell them to eat from the worms."

Yes, of course, the worm sludge. He'd known all along that it held some great significance. "They already are."

"Then have them eat more. And encourage them to write."

"Write?"

"It feeds their minds and keeps them out of trouble. Write your story. All of you."

"It's *my* story."

"You will make it theirs."

"It's bad enough that Paul has—"

"Do it, boy. We need the children occupied. Nothing occupies the mind down here like writing. But even with writing, one requires a focus. Tell them what your story is and have them write. It will keep them quiet."

Chapter Nineteen

PARADISE

Saturday afternoon

THE RED marble didn't budge for two hours, at least not that Johnny had seen, and he'd watched it pretty close. It wasn't that he was still so fascinated by the shooter, but that he was out of alternatives. He should be doing something to fix the predicament they were in, but he was at a loss.

He couldn't phone out. He didn't want to go out. He didn't want to stay in either, but that was all there was to do now. Stay in his room, a ball of frayed nerves, and watch the marble while his head spun through possibilities.

He thought he heard his mother stirring down the hall once, but he couldn't be sure with all the wind banging things against the house. And he wasn't sure he wanted to confront her now.

Black was bad.

Black was good.

Black was a demon from hell who'd come to destroy and kill and do whatever demons do.

Black was an angel sent from heaven to expose the evil in the hearts of Paradise and give them all a message of hope and grace.

No. Black was bad, period. Nothing good could possibly cause any of this, unless of course Paradise was a modern Sodom and Gomorrah and this was all a new kind of fire and brimstone.

Either way, Johnny was a boy caught in the middle, powerless to do anything about Black, regardless of whether he was a demon or an angel or just a psycho preacher who had drugged the town.

"What ya doin'?"

Johnny's eyes jerked away from the marble. Sally stood in the hall, staring at him. She wore one of the new outfits she'd bought in Grand Junction, brown slacks and yellow silky-looking blouse. She'd done her makeup and brushed her hair, even put on a gold necklace and hoop earrings.

"Nothing."

She walked forward, smirking. "Is that so?" Her eyes weren't right. They were glassy and slightly bloodshot.

"Did you drink any more of the water?"

"Don't be silly, Johnny. Why wouldn't I drink the water, hmm? Because you turned it off, that's why. How do you expect me to flush the toilet?"

"You turned it back on?"

"Why not? Tastes just fine to me."

Johnny felt nauseated. If his mother was gone . . .

"Why are you staring at the marble?" she asked, crossing slowly toward the dresser. "Hmm?"

"It . . . I don't know; I think it moved."

Sally picked the red shooter up. "It did, did it?" She turned it around in her fingers. Then she lifted it up, pressed it against her right eye, and faced him.

She looked like a red-eyed dress-up doll.

Sally released the marble and let it fall to the carpet. It landed with a *thump*.

"Looks like a regular marble to me," she said, walking toward the door.

"Where are you going?"

"I have to go," she said.

Johnny scooted to the edge of his bed and dropped his feet to the floor. "Where? Outside?"

She turned around and curtsied. "I have a date, Johnny. You like?"

A date?

"With who?"

Sally winked, then turned and disappeared down the hall.

Johnny sat frozen to his bed. He didn't want to think anymore. The room shifted out of focus for a moment—the water was speaking. Or Black was speaking. Whatever it was, he thought that maybe he should just start listening because he didn't want to be alone anymore.

Black is bad.

Black is not good.

Black is a psycho preacher, not an angel sent from heaven.

And you, Johnny, are not powerless.

Wind howled through the front door. The screen door slammed shut. He knew that there was no way to stop her, but he had to try—he had to do something!

Johnny ran for the hall and had just stepped past his doorway when a loud *plunk* sounded behind him.

He seized up, midstride. He turned back to his bedroom.

The first thing Johnny saw was that the red marble wasn't lying on the floor. The second was that it had embedded itself in the wall above his headboard.

Plunk.

The marble shot out of the wall and came to a halt six inches from his nose.

He jumped back, but the marble jumped with him, staying exactly six inches from his nose. Johnny turned and ran down the hall, too panicked to scream.

He'd only taken four steps before realizing that the marble wasn't behind him. It was zooming through the air, still six inches in front of his nose.

He yelped and instinctively swatted at it like he might swat a bee doggedly pursuing him. Amazingly he made contact, and the ball flew into the wall, then fell to the floor. And lay still.

For one moment.

It returned to the air and came to rest six inches in front of his nose. This time it started to bounce in little one-inch hops.

If the marble was dangerous, wouldn't it have hit him by now? Didn't matter. Johnny couldn't accept this impossibility, bouncing in the air right in front of his nose.

He backed up. The marble hesitated, then bounced forward.

On the other hand, Johnny *had* to accept this impossibility in front of his nose. It was real, it was here, and it was bouncing like a pet, daring him to play.

Play?

Or daring him to hit it again, so that it would have sufficient justification to smash a neat round hole through his forehead.

Why would a marble bounce in front of him? And how?

The marble stopped bouncing. It slowly floated wide, then down the hall. Johnny watched in fascination.

The red shooter came to rest just in front of the rear door. It began to bounce again. He couldn't help thinking that the marble was like a dog, begging him.

The back door opened. Wind howled. The screen door squealed. The marble slid outside.

The screen door remained still in the face of the wind, unaffected by gusts that whipped into the house and down the hall.

The marble began to bounce again.

Johnny felt like he was being led into a decision. The marble seemed to want him to follow.

To what? A trap set by Black? But if Black wanted him, why didn't he just come and get him? Johnny could hardly believe that he was thinking like this. He'd always doubted the supernatural, mostly because his mother didn't believe in it. She hated the church and convinced him over the years that everything the church stood for was nonsense. That included the miraculous—everything from a virgin birth to blind eyes being opened.

So what would she say about floating marbles?

Well, his mother had been wrong. This was no hallucination, no magic trick. That marble bouncing outside their back door was supernatural.

If he didn't follow, then what?

Johnny turned into the short hall that led to his mother's room. He stepped past the wall. Waited.

The marble zoomed into view. And waited.

Johnny took a step toward it and the red sphere moved away, back down the hall and out of view. Johnny stepped out and faced the back door. The marble had taken up its bouncing just outside the house again.

Completely out of alternatives, Johnny walked down the hall and, when the marble flew into the alley, out of the house.

Gusts of hot wind tore at his clothes, but Johnny hardly cared about anything as insignificant as wind. His eyes were on the marble, which now rose a good ten feet into the air where it hovered, oblivious, like Johnny, to the wind.

Then it moved. At an angle. Gaining speed. Over the trees. It streaked out of sight in the direction of the steep slopes that rose to the south.

And it didn't return.

The sky was empty except for black clouds and blowing leaves. The marble was gone. Johnny felt stranded. Maybe even betrayed. He waited a full minute. Nothing. He couldn't just walk up the mountain.

Strange how badly he wanted that marble to return.

Johnny turned back to the door and saw that it was still open. He took a step toward the house. The door slammed shut.

Okay, so maybe he was supposed to go the other way, up the mountain. There was only one way that he knew of—a path that headed up behind the old theater, and that was rarely used because it traversed property owned by some corporation out east who frowned on trespassing. More than one hefty fine had been paid over the years.

Johnny faced the alley, gathered his courage, and struck out against the wind.

Chapter Twenty

THE MONASTERY

Saturday afternoon

TEN OF the eleven teachers were seated around the thick mahogany conference table when David Abraham stepped into the room from his office. Ten. Raul was still missing.

The teachers looked crestfallen by the monumental defeat they'd been handed two hours earlier. A dozen white candles suspended from a golden chandelier lit their faces. Heavy navy blue velvet drapes imported from Spain lined the entire conference room except for the south wall, where a large painting of two children tickling each other's noses with daisies served as a constant reminder of why they'd all given so many years of their lives to Project Showdown.

"Where is Raul?" David asked, crossing to the head of the table.

"He's checking on the students," Andrew said.

As if on cue, Raul walked in, robe swirling. He walked to the table quickly.

"Fifteen more have followed the others into the tunnels," he said. "That makes nineteen below and eighteen above. I can hardly imagine a worse scenario."

Raul reached the table, but didn't sit. He paced, ran an arm across his wet brow, pushing his locks to the side as he did. "I understand this principle of testing them by fire to harden the steel of their wills, but it appears those wills have melted. At least most of them, and I imagine others will follow."

"Sit down, Raul."

The head overseer sat.

"Where is Samuel?" David asked.

"He's retreated to his room. To write, he said."

David nodded. He had always known that this moment would come, and upon reflection his decision to withhold the truth from these good-hearted men seemed right. Certainly necessary.

Now they would learn what he told Samuel four days earlier, when Billy first entered the forbidden places below.

"Evil has conquered the students," Andrew said.

David pulled out his chair and sat. "Has it, Andrew? Our risk has increased, but can there be life without risk? Did God take a risk by creating man with a free will? Did he know of the horrors that would follow?"

"God knew the outcome. We do not," Andrew said.

"True, but allowed evil to test that outcome. Did you all think this day would never come?"

"Don't get me wrong," Raul said. "God allowing evil and us jeopardizing our life's work strike me as two different things. Just because God allowed evil doesn't mean we should. These are children, David! They're contracting a disease down there!"

David looked around the table. "The rest of you feel the same?"

To a man they looked desperate. Several nodded. The rest didn't respond.

Mark Anthony, the forthright monk who'd come to them from a little-known New Mexico monastery, Christ in the Desert, spoke. "Correct me if I'm misunderstanding the situation, but there are only three ways out of our current predicament. One, the children come to their senses on their own, through a second challenge perhaps. Two, the children remain in the tunnels and disintegrate into an unholy mess, perhaps ending in death. Or three, we intervene."

"I think that summarizes it well enough," David said. "Assuming we can stop what has started. And of these outcomes, which conforms to the purpose of this project?"

Raul responded from the far end. "Certainly not death."

"Then what, Raul, is your suggestion?"

The head overseer hesitated. No matter how much they protested, surely none of them would suggest throwing in the towel until every possible alternative had been explored. David was counting on it.

"We cast another challenge immediately," Raul said. "This time Samuel can argue—"

"The rules require us to wait three days."

"Then change the rules!" Andrew said. "It's the rules that have put us here."

"So you're suggesting we pull the plug on the monastery now? Send the children back to the orphanages and count our project as a failure?"

No response. Good. He would build on this position of strength.

"Excuse me for the interruption." Francis Matthew, the quiet priest from Ireland, looked up at David. "But do we know what is causing their disease?"

David eyed the man. "The worms," he said.

"Worms?" Andrew said. "What worms?"

"There are worms in the dungeons. Their excretions seem to have a harmful effect on . . . certain children."

The teachers stared at him, clearly taken aback by this revelation.

"How long have you known about these . . . these worms?" Andrew asked.

David put his elbows on the table and gently pressed his palms together. "Bear with me for a moment. Mark, please remind us why we are here."

The overseer looked around the table, searching for the catch. They all knew why they were here. Why would David ask?

"We are twelve teachers—now eleven—gathered from around the world for this project sponsored by Harvard University. The project's purpose is to examine innocence and the effects of evil upon that innocence. We are sworn to follow strict guidelines in the instruction of thirty-seven children, which you brought to this monastery nearly thirteen years ago. The children have been carefully isolated from influences that might corrupt them. When they are sixteen, they will be reinserted into society, and we will see what effects the children and society have upon each other."

Mark stopped. In a nutshell that was it. Or, more correctly, that was what they all thought.

"And how have they been instructed?"

"They have been instructed in all disciplines. We have carefully taught them to distinguish right from wrong according to a monotheistic worldview that follows the teachings of Christ."

"Good. And what else?"

"I'm not sure how specific you want me to be. You determined from the beginning that we should focus all of their learning through writing. We've taught the children to understand the best of all human experiences and to pen them eloquently. They are arguably the world's finest writers at this age."

"An understatement, wouldn't you say?"

"I would. To a student, they are brilliant writers, regardless of their age."

David nodded slowly. "You've each done a masterful job with admirable dedication. I couldn't have found more loving and honorable men if I'd spent a decade scouring the earth."

They sat in silence. The air felt heavy.

"What I'm about to tell you will come as a shock. When you've heard, I think you'll understand my decision not to tell you sooner."

For twelve years, he'd dreaded this moment. Now that it was upon him, he was eager for it.

"You all know of me as a historian and psychologist. You also know that I was and am an avid collector of antiquities. My collection was well known before I left Harvard University."

"Left Harvard?" Andrew asked. "You're no longer with the university?"

"No, my friend, I am not." He took a deep breath. "In truth, Project Showdown has nothing whatsoever to do with Harvard. Or, for that matter, any other institution. It is funded and run solely by me. The sale of my collection was quite lucrative."

He paused and studied them. They would need a minute to absorb that he'd been feeding them a bald-faced lie for the past thirteen years. They were in shock. Either that or exceptionally even mannered.

He seized on their silence.

"Nearly twenty years ago, an antiquities dealer from Iran sent me a rather large shipment of unspecified and unverified artifacts for a tidy sum. Mostly clay pots, for which I quickly determined I'd overpaid. But there was one item of interest.

"The shipment contained a crate of ancient books, mostly diaries kept by mullahs and such. Among the books was one particularly old leather-bound volume that was unique for two reasons. One, it appeared to be from a time period earlier than its binding would suggest, like finding a steel sword from the bronze age. Two, it contained only one entry. The rest of the book was blank, which I could not make sense of, because the title was *The Stories of History*. I analyzed the single entry and discovered that it was written in a unique kind of charcoal whose use was discontinued long before the kind of paper in the book was ever discovered. Very odd. Do you follow this?"

They stared at him without responding, but these anomalies weren't lost on such scholars.

"For two years the book sat in my study, a mystery to me. Then one day my eldest son, Christopher, when he was five years old, wrote in the book. Yes, he was a very bright boy."

They all knew that his eldest son had been killed in an automobile accident when he was six.

"How he got the book from the shelf I don't know, but he had the book on the desk behind me. It was a secretary I reserved for paying bills and attending personal business. An oak desk. Stained, not painted. But you see, that was a problem, because when I glanced back to see my son with the book, I saw that the desk was red, not a stained oak as it had been only minutes earlier. I was stunned. Here sat a bright red desk in my office, and I had no idea how it got there."

They stared, uncomprehending. And who could comprehend such a thing?

"It was only after I'd circled the desk twice in disbelief that I looked at what Christopher had written. 'The desk is red.' Those were the words on the page written in his distinctive chicken scratch. He'd written 'the desk is red,' and now I was looking at a red desk."

"Surely you aren't suggesting that it had anything to do with his writing," Andrew said.

"Exactly my thoughts. I was inclined to think that my mind was playing tricks on me. That I'd had someone paint the desk red and forgotten about it, and that my son was simply writing what he saw. But my wife assured me that the desk had indeed been stained oak. She thought I'd painted it that hideous color and was outdoing myself by making up some nonsense about forgetting."

"That could have been."

"But it wasn't. It took me three days to accept the fact that my son's writing had somehow changed the desk. You have to understand, I wasn't a religious man at the time. This desk turning red because it was written red was tantamount to words becoming real, something that I wasn't able to accept. I took a chip off the desk and had it analyzed—trust me, my friends, the desk was red. Candy-apple red, to be exact. It was only then that I formed my hypothesis. This book from Iran was a history book with the power to *create* history. The power to create fact. My son had written 'the desk is red,' and so the desk was red."

"Impossible!" Mark said.

David stood and paced at the end of the table. "Impossible? For me, at the time, yes, it was impossible. But for religious men like you, it should be commonplace!"

He leveled his argument with animated gestures now. "Think of it! Holy Scripture is *full* of references to the power of words. A disciple cries, 'Rise up and walk,' and a man rises up and walks. Christ calls to the storm, 'Be still,' and the waves become still."

David strode to the shelf, pulled out the black leather-bound Bible, and thumped it with his knuckles. "Recorded in this book are scores and scores of events that are no less impossible than my desk turning red. Speaking donkeys, writing on the wall, people rising from the dead. These impossibilities, my friends, are the word becoming real. The word becoming flesh. This is the common ground which all such events share."

He set the Bible down. "'In the beginning was the Word . . . and the Word became flesh and dwelt among us.' That which is supernatural becomes natural—this is the incarnation, not only of Christ, but of all supernatural events. Satan reveals himself as what? A dragon, a snake, through an antichrist who is raised from the dead. Now how do those compare to my desk turning red?"

"They have spiritual significance," someone said.

"And so does this, as you will clearly see." Sweat beaded David's face. He took a calming breath.

"Why would God allow such a book to—"

"Why would God allow Hitler his chapter in history? Why would God send a whale to swallow Jonah or turn a woman into a pillar of salt? Surely there were other ways. But I'll leave the particular methods of God to God."

They could hardly argue. No one attempted to.

"What happened to the book?" Andrew asked.

Chapter Twenty-one

PARADISE

Saturday afternoon

IT TOOK Johnny twenty minutes at a steady climb to reach the lookout over Paradise. He'd been up to the large rock slab that jutted out from the mountain a dozen times with Roland and the others—this far and no farther, their parents warned.

From this vantage, the buildings lining Main Street looked like play blocks strung along a nearly obscured street, black beneath the dust. Other than the Starlight Theater and the church, both of which looked too large for the town, the buildings were proportionate and evenly spaced. Behind the town, homes scattered across the valley, and long dirt roads wandered between a couple dozen fruit farms.

Johnny looked at it all through a haze kicked up by the wind. He'd been delayed by a scene of carnage as he left town. Someone had taken an ax to the south side of a building. Claude and company. Other than the toppled theater sign and several busted-up telephone poles, he couldn't see the damage through the dust from this distance.

Above him, the clouds roiled. They seemed to be lower today. The air was thinner up here. His right leg ached.

He faced the mountain. From here, a game trail led to only God knew where. This was it. This was the end of the line, and no red marble.

Which meant that he'd been mistaken. Deceived. Stranded. He scanned the trees for the red orb. Anything to suggest the red orb had been here. Anything at all out of the ordinary.

But the only thing that was clearly out of the ordinary was the fact that he'd come up here because a floating red marble had led him up here.

Johnny faced the valley feeling like an imbecile. Maybe he'd imagined the whole thing after all. Maybe this was what the others were doing down in Paradise right now. Chasing little red marbles around. Or other things that had worked themselves into their minds. Things like Black.

He stared out at the clouds, swamped with desperation. Something bad was happening, and no one could stop it. His vision clouded, then distorted with tears. Black and gray swirled. There was nothing to do. Nothing to see besides a hazy blur and the red sun floating low . . .

Johnny blinked.

It was a red sun floating low on the horizon. It was the red marble, hovering over the cliff ten feet from him. His heart jumped.

The marble streaked past him and he whirled. It stopped momentarily at the trailhead, then plunged into the brush.

He didn't need any more encouragement. He didn't care if he was being led into a trap. A voice in his head urged him to follow that marble, so he did. Branches broke and fell limp as he passed.

He began to run, stumbled once, caught himself, and continued his pursuit up the trail.

He wasn't sure how long he'd been following the marble when the trees ended and he found himself facing a huge canyon. He pulled up, panting.

The canyon yawned before him like a mouth cluttered with broken teeth. Dozens of rock formations cast shadows along the sandy floor. Boulders the size of small cars squatted at the base of a dozen landslides.

Blue sky, not black clouds, arched above him. The sunlight was bright enough to make him squint after four days of dusk. He started forward, elated.

The red marble moved deeper into the canyon.

Johnny followed.

Chapter Twenty-two

THE MONASTERY

Saturday afternoon

"WHAT HAPPENED to the book?" David said. "Yes, that's the question, isn't it? I'll spare you the tedious details, but suffice it to say that I confidentially tested the book in every way I knew how. My first discovery was that the book didn't work for me. Only for Christopher. If I wrote, 'I have a million dollars in my account,' and then checked my bank balance, I had no more than before. But if I told Christopher to write, 'Daddy has a million dollars in his account . . .' Well, you get the point."

"You did that?"

"Did what?"

"Had your son write a million dollars into your account?"

"Wouldn't you?" He winked at Raul. "I reported it as an error, though not for a few days, I'll admit."

Several soft chuckles.

"Why only children?" Matthew asked.

"Belief. I am quite sure that an adult who possesses the faith of a child would also be able to write history."

"Do you still have this book?"

David held up his hand. "Let me finish. I also learned that the dealer who sold me the crate containing the book had a whole cache of them. Blank, every one of them. I immediately acquired all of them."

"How many?"

"One thousand four hundred and forty-three. Which is—"

"So many!"

"—significant. Yes, so many. I had them sent express delivery at considerable expense. I was a mess those days. Every waking moment was consumed by the book. I knew I had in my possession the most powerful tool in history. I could do anything, make anything. My power was mind-boggling. Or I should say, my son's power was mind-boggling. Fortunately he was willing to write whatever I wanted him to write. Then one day, three weeks after Christopher wrote my desk red, he wrote three simple words about our cat in a fit of frustration. 'Snuffles is dead.' And Snuffles was dead."

"Dead?" Andrew said.

"Dead. Right there in the hallway with no apparent cause of death. This terrible side of the books kept me awake that night. And the next. Imagine what one evil man could do with such a weapon. To make matters worse, Christopher was catching on. He played some havoc with his best friend following a heated argument. He broke the boy's arm. The next morning I made a decision to rid the world of the books. I asked Christopher to write a notation which is permanently etched on my mind into the book:

"'The books of histories are hiding deep in a Colorado canyon, in a home consistent with their nature, where they will remain until the day they are meant to be found by those destined to bring love into the world.'"

"Here?" Andrew said.

"You're getting ahead of me." He picked up his pace, eager to tell them the whole truth. "The books vanished, all of them. One year later, my son Christopher was killed, as you know. It crushed me. I spent months trying to convince my wife, Andrea, to conceive—"

"Another child for the books," one of them said.

"No, the books were gone. I simply wanted another child. She did conceive, and Samuel was born into the world. But the pregnancy was difficult, and my wife died giving birth. This you also know."

David slipped into his seat and leaned back.

"What you don't know is the depth of my depression at her death. I took a sabbatical and set out to find the books. I was desperate to bring my wife back, you see. My sorrow clouded my judgment. For a full year I methodically searched every canyon in the Colorado mountains. But I'd written them into hiding until the day they were meant to be found, and I gradually became convinced that I had done so wisely."

"So then you didn't find them. You want the children to find them."

"Patience, Nathan. One night I had a dream. An epiphany that introduced me to God in a way that haunts me still. I was thoroughly convinced that I should raise my son, Samuel, in total innocence, so that if he were to have the books, he would use them only for good. This, I determined, was the reason God had allowed the events in my life."

"I thought—"

"I found the books the next day. Which only confirmed my vision. The books were meant to be found, and meant to be found by me. To be used, not by me, but by Samuel. Or perhaps more than one Samuel."

Understanding dawned on the overseers' faces.

"I found them here, in this monastery hidden from the world. All 1,443 of them. I found 666 of them in the dungeons below, which I promptly sealed. And I found 777 of them in the library above—though I don't believe there is any difference between the books above and those below except in their symbolic placement. You see, the books had found themselves in a place consistent with their nature, exactly as Christopher had written. My friends, we are sitting on more raw power than has been known by any mortal man in all of history."

"They . . . you're saying that the books are here now?" Andrew demanded. "Where?"

David drilled them with a stare. He rose to his feet, crossed the room, and pushed the wall. It gave way under his weight. Slowly a large bookcase rotated into view. Hundreds of books lined the shelves.

Leather-bound books.

David extracted one and brought it to them. He sat down and placed it on the table.

They leaned in as one. Ancient black leather, roughly an inch thick. No title.

"The rest are in the dungeons. To the best of my knowledge they are the source of the worms in the dungeons. It's not the disease on Billy's skin that worries me most, it's the deception brought on by the worms."

"But nothing you, or we, or any adult writes in these books will occur," Nathan said. "Unless they have the belief of a child."

"That is my belief."

"But if the children, these thirty-seven that we've raised, were to write in the books, their words would actually change history?"

"To a point. As I understand it, the books can't force a person's will any more than God can force a person's will. But they can do almost everything else."

Andrew leaped out of his chair, sending it skidding across the stone floor behind him. "The books in the dungeons—Billy's writing in them?"

David lifted a hand. "Please, Andrew, sit."

He did, but slowly, fearfully.

"The answer is yes. I don't think the children are aware of the books' power, but they are writing a story."

It was too much information in too short a time, but David was confident that if he guided them methodically through the meat of his choice, they would come around to seeing the wisdom of it.

"They are writing a story about a town called Paradise."

"Not the town in the valley below us?" Mark said.

"Yes, that Paradise."

"Is . . . What's happening?"

"The town is coming apart at the seams," David said. "Apart from one man who had a heart attack, I don't think there's been any death, but there is certainly a mess brewing in Paradise."

A cacophony of protest filled the room. He let it run until a single question rose above the rest. "How do we know this?"

"I have my ways. Trust me, Paradise is falling under Billy's pen."

"You said he doesn't know the power of his words," Raul said.

"No, but he knows plenty about the town. He can see what's happening in his characters' minds. Although he can't force their wills, this bunch is influenced easily enough."

David decided against telling them about Marsuvees Black at the moment. The fate of their old colleague, though interesting, wouldn't help them understand the overall picture.

"It must be stopped!" Andrew cried. "This has gone too far!"

"And how would you propose we stop it, Andrew?"

"Pull the children out of the dungeons! Burn the books!"

"And risk interfering with the path the books have put us on? We are here *because* of the books; I believe only they will show us the way out. Project Showdown isn't a benign experiment to test the effects of children raised in isolation. It's about life pitted against death. It's about good in conflict with evil on a grand scale. I launched this project knowing full well that one day we would be seated at this table facing this very dilemma. But I'm convinced that it will lead to good, to love entering the world, *otherwise the books would never have been found.*"

He opened the book in front of him and raised his index finger. "But just to be safe, I had Samuel write another entry into Christopher's book, after we found it in the monastery library. Naturally he was too young to know what or why he was writing."

David read. "'As of this date, any word written in this book or any similar book so described'—I'll spare you the tedious description—'that is written by any person not currently residing in the monastery, and/or that does not lead to the discovery of love will be powerless. This rule is irrevocable.' It goes on to describe in detail this summary. I also had Samuel write the names of every student."

They didn't know how to respond.

"I knew from my tests with Christopher that making something irrevocable seems to bind the books. So you see, I have taken every precaution. The books are now limited to only those who were in the monastery on the date that this rule was written. And their power is limited to the discovery of love."

He shut the cover. Samuel had written another entry on that day, but it would only confuse them at this point. God help him if Samuel's final entry ever came into play.

"And if you require other assurances, I will only say that I have other safeguards."

David said this with far more conviction than he felt, and he prayed that his conviction would prove him right. But anything could happen, regardless of Christopher's or Samuel's entries. For all he knew, those destined to bring love to the world, presumably those in this monastery, wouldn't do so for another fifty years, and then only after destroying only God knew what.

"We are on dangerous ground," Andrew said. The others nodded.

"Without question," David said. "But we can no more pretend that the books don't exist than we can pretend evil doesn't exist. We entered dangerous territory the day Adam and Eve ate the apple."

"But even they had a choice," Andrew said. "You're saying that the whole town is following these evil impulses from Billy? That he simply writes and they listen and follow him, correct?"

"Pretty much, yes."

"Are they nothing but sheep?"

"No more than Eve was a sheep in the garden of good and evil. Do you think that if God had put a Jane or a Betsy in the garden, she would have made a different choice? Given the hearts of the people in Paradise and the powerful nature of Billy's writing, the fall from what grace they had is practically wholesale."

For a while no one spoke. The idea of a *story* wreaking so much havoc daunted them.

"We've assisted the children up to this point. I don't see why we can't nudge them now," Daniel said.

"On the contrary, we must let the children find their own way now, because it's what they've chosen. What is the greatest virtue?"

"Love."

"Yes. Love. From the beginning we've agreed that we must give the children the freedom to choose their own way. Should that change now that the stakes appear to be higher? Love can only be found in freedom of choice. And for choice to exist, there must be an alternative to choose. Something as compelling as love. Something that is evil, yes?"

"Yes," Raul said.

"We must allow our students the opportunity to love the truth in the face of alternatives. We've effectively put Paradise in the hands of the children, as intended by whatever force allowed me to find the books in the first place. Nothing we do can reverse that."

Andrew leaned forward again. "But to let them stay in the *dungeons*—"

"Let me tell you something, Andrew. The world *lives* in a dungeon. It's dark and cold and full of the worst, but it's where the world lives. Most well-meaning books do little to illuminate the way. What we're doing here requires a view of the dungeon. Do you understand? It's the only way to bring hope to that dungeon."

"And in the meantime whatever Billy and the others write will continue to bring destruction."

"To a point, yes."

"I still don't think—"

David slammed his palms on the table. "Then stop thinking, Andrew, at least for a moment! You've believed in me this far; you must believe that I've applied enough reason to Project Showdown to cover a week's worth of argument. You must believe me when I say that if we interfere with the children, we may pay a price far more devastating than Billy's writings."

He drew a deep breath. "We must trust in God. Which in this case means trusting in the books that surely he has given us. To betray the books is nothing less than a betrayal of the creative power that God has entrusted us which in turn is a betrayal of the children! We must trust the books to deliver us love in the end."

David couldn't remember being so forceful, but it was the only way he knew to bring them quickly up to speed with a matter that he'd lived with for twelve years.

Andrew broke the silence. "Can the damage be corrected by another student's writing? Samuel and Christine and some of the others could write."

David took a deep breath. "Samuel is writing," he said. "He's been writing for four days now."

Chapter Twenty-three

PARADISE

Saturday afternoon

THE CANYON was deep and long, but the marble moved slowly enough for Johnny to keep up. He could see that the canyon ended ahead, maybe a hundred yards off. When he'd walked half of it, the red marble veered to the left and disappeared behind a towering gray boulder.

Johnny stopped. The sun was high, but the sheer rock rose so high that even now long gloomy shadows filled the canyon. He walked to the boulder and made his way around the stone.

Here, the canyon wall gaped to reveal another, smaller canyon. Johnny stopped and squinted, trying to make sense of the shadows moving across the granite face.

No marble.

The smaller canyon was wedge-shaped, like a teepee. It ended in a wall that rose roughly fifty feet. Nothing but rock.

He walked toward the wall. His mind was evenly divided, one half insisting that he had no business being here, the other calling him forward. He realized he was holding his breath. He exhaled.

He was ten feet from the cliff when something caught his eye. An irregularity on the surface. A straight, vertical line. Like someone had cut into the stone with a saw.

He ran his hand along the crack.

But it wasn't just a crack. It was the edge of a door. He saw the latch a foot lower. Johnny jerked his hand back. He stood frozen for three loud heartbeats, then turned and ran toward the safety of the boulder.

Chapter Twenty-four

THE MONASTERY

Saturday afternoon

SAMUEL HURRIED down the hall, eager to tell his father this plan that filled his mind in the hours since the debate.

He'd been writing in one of the blank books for four days now, carefully and with tempered purpose, but the time for caution had passed. Frankly, he couldn't wait to begin writing again, but this time with a new purpose.

He discovered on the first day that his writing connected with the characters of Paradise in a unique way. This storytelling experience was more enthralling than any he'd experienced. When he wrote into Paradise, he felt like he was really there, with the characters, speaking into their minds and hearing their thoughts. Thus he could extrapolate Billy's actions by reading the minds of the characters that Billy was influencing.

He also learned from these people what was happening in Paradise, at least to the extent that they actually knew what was happening. He could see the town in his imagination almost as clearly as if he were there.

He also experienced unique limitations. Unlike in his other stories, he couldn't force the characters to follow his every whim. He could play a game of wits with them, interjecting thoughts and suggestions, but in the end the characters did what they chose to do.

Samuel had written hundreds, maybe thousands of suggestions into the minds of Paradise's residents, and although each time he felt at least some influence on them, nearly every character he wrote into chose Billy's way. It made him wonder how Billy was able to influence the people so effectively.

Samuel couldn't write more than one character at a time, so he focused on the most responsive character he found—Johnny. There was something unique about the boy, and Samuel was sure it had something to do with the fact that Johnny had seen Black for who he was when he first walked into town.

Oddly enough, Samuel couldn't enter the mind of Marsuvees Black, the monk who betrayed them all. In a way that Samuel couldn't yet understand, Billy and Black were working together. As an active and willing accomplice, the monk's power was stunning. Samuel couldn't tell where Black ended and where Billy's writing began.

Either way, nothing happening in Paradise was a figment of the citizens' imaginations. It was all real. All except the sludge that Black had persuaded them was hallucinogenic, which, although real enough, was nothing more than starchy water. Billy's writing, not a hallucinogenic sludge, had deceived the people of Paradise. Black had merely distracted them long enough for Billy to sink his claws deep into their minds.

But now Samuel had a plan that he was quite sure would take Billy and company by storm. And for that plan to succeed, he needed his own accomplice.

Johnny.

He knocked on his father's office door. After a second attempt returned no response, he walked in. Vacant. But he could hear muffled voices from the conference room next door.

Samuel crossed to the door, knocked, and waited.

"Come."

He walked into a meeting of the overseers, who all wore dazed expressions.

David rose from the table. "Hello, Samuel."

Samuel hurried to him, eager. At the last second, he second-guessed his intention to hug his father and instead took David's arm.

"Hello, Father."

An awkward moment passed.

David glanced at the teachers. "Excuse me." He stepped away with Samuel. "What is it? You have something?"

"I have a plan."

David patted his hand and lowered his voice. "Nothing to them about Marsuvees yet."

Samuel nodded. "Okay."

Turning back to the table, David reassumed his usual volume. "My son has something he wants to share with us." David looked at him. "Go ahead, Samuel."

"Then they know about the writing?" Samuel asked.

"They know," his father said.

"And you know that I've been writing for several days now."

"Yes, they know everything."

Except about Marsuvees Black.

He let go of David's arm. "Among many things I've learned about how the books work is this fact: though I can't make people do things, I can do whatever I want with objects and animals—anything that doesn't have the capacity for moral choice, I would say. Billy's done some very interesting things . . ."

He decided now wasn't the time for details.

"If I were to write, 'The red marble on Johnny's dresser rises into the air and floats,' for example, then that's precisely what happens. But if I write, 'Johnny grabs the marble,' Johnny only has that thought. The decision to grab or not to grab is his. Has my father explained this?"

"Some, but go on," David said. "Hearing it from you is different."

Samuel addressed his father. "The bottom line is, I can't make ordinary people do things, but I doubt the rule applies to unordinary people."

"Unordinary, meaning what?"

"Fictional characters."

A light filled his father's eyes.

"I'm quite sure that I could write a character into existence, and it would have no will of its own."

"Turning an idea into reality," his father said.

"No different than turning an idea of a marble floating into reality when you think about it."

"That could work?" Andrew asked.

"You haven't tried it?" his father asked.

"No. Not without talking to you. But I'm sure it will work."

"So you want to write a fictional character into Paradise."

"Yes. We have three days before we can challenge Billy here. But his mind is in Paradise. If we can defeat him in Paradise, I think he'll fail here."

"Excellent!" David thundered. "Excellent thinking!" He grabbed Samuel by both shoulders. "I knew I could count on you." He beamed at the overseers. "You see?" Back to Samuel. "Have you given any thought to this character?"

"I would like to write a cop," Samuel said. "The law. And not just an ordinary lawman, but a gunslinger who has the skill and power to bring some order to Paradise."

"The law. I like it. I like it."

"Why only one?" one of the teachers asked. "Why not five, or ten?"

"I think prudence would dictate caution," David said. "Assuming this all works, we don't know what will happen to such a character."

"If you write them into existence, then surely you can write them out."

"So it would seem. But we don't know, do we? We can't very well populate the world with fictitious characters."

"The character that I write will have the strength of five," Samuel said. "I've decided to call him Thomas."

"Thomas?" Raul asked, eyebrow arched. "As in Doubting Thomas?"

"No, Thomas, after Thomas Hunter." Samuel looked at the history book. "In honor of the first entry."

David picked up the book and flipped it open. "I told you there was a single entry when I first received this book. It's a very short entry about Thomas Hunter and Monique de Raison—I'm sure you all know their names from the Raison Strain. It appears that this book is tied directly to him."

He faced Samuel. "So, when will your Thomas bring the law to the streets of Paradise?"

"As soon as I can bring Johnny up to speed."

"Johnny?"

Samuel hurried for the door. "He's a boy from Paradise who's going to help me."

"He agreed to this?"

Samuel turned back. "Not yet. But he will soon enough."

He left the teachers staring after him and hurried for the stairs. It was time to meet Johnny.

THE RED marble hadn't shown itself again. Had it come from behind that door?

Johnny waited ten minutes on the far side of the boulder before concluding that the marble was gone for good. At least for now.

He sneaked around the corner and peered at the box end of the smaller canyon. Nothing had changed. The marble had led him here, that much he knew for certain. He couldn't just run home now. Home was where things were going very, very wrong.

He stared at the door's faint outline for a full minute, working up his courage, assuring himself that, even if it was a door, it probably just led to an old mine shaft or something.

He walked up to the latch. Put his hand on it. Rusted metal. He pushed down. It moved with a creaking sound. The door gaped, four inches at first, then Johnny pushed it all the way open.

At first he wasn't sure what he was seeing beyond the door. Shadows. Another cliff wall. No, a man-made wall. Huge stone blocks were stacked in a brick pattern, rising five stories. A large cross topped two massive wooden doors, dead center. Rows of windows broke the building's flat lines. The space between the old rusted door that Johnny had opened and the large wooden doors was a stone courtyard, covered with sand in a scattered pattern.

An old mining operation? Looked more like something built by Indians. Something ancient. Amazing how well hidden it was. He'd never heard a word of this place.

The large door moved. Then stopped. But he was sure he'd seen it move. Johnny would have turned and run, but his legs refused to budge.

The door opened. A boy about his height, with blond hair and clear blue eyes, stepped out. He wore a white short-sleeved button-down shirt and blue shorts. White socks, brown shoes. The boy's hands hung loosely at his sides.

The boy walked halfway across the courtyard and stopped. "Hello, Johnny."

The boy knew his name? Johnny still couldn't move.

"Did you like the marble?"

"I . . . How did you know my name?"

The boy smiled. "That's a long story." He walked forward and held out his hand. "My name is Samuel."

Johnny took the hand. Real flesh, real eyes, real hair. Real boy.

Samuel walked by. "Follow me."

Johnny finally got his legs working. He followed the boy out into the canyon, where Samuel stopped and stared north, in the direction of Paradise.

"What's it like?" Samuel asked.

Johnny stepped to his side and faced the gaping canyon. "What's what like?"

"Life out there. You know, in the real world. Looking at it out here, it seems like a whole different reality."

"You don't come from the real world?"

Samuel looked at him with those bright blue eyes. "Real? Sure. But as you can see, it's pretty isolated up here. Did the marble scare you?"

"At first. You did that. How did you do that?"

"That's part of the story. But it's a wild story. I'm not sure you're ready for it."

"After what I've seen? I can't think of anything that would surprise me. Do you know what's been happening in Paradise?"

"I know some things, but I need to know more, which is why I brought you up here."

Johnny looked back at the hidden door. Still there. And when he turned his head, the boy was still there.

"How did you make the marble move?"

"I wrote it in a book. Not your typical writing book, but a book that makes whatever you write in it happen. Most things, anyway—I can't make people do things they don't want to do."

Johnny didn't know what to say. This was as unbelievable as Black pulling his lip off his chin. He wasn't dreaming, was he?

Samuel grinned. "I told you it was wild. You're not ready for it."

"I am ready," Johnny said, not sure why he would claim any such thing. "It's just . . . I've never heard of anything like it."

"You haven't? You don't go to church then. You ever hear of the Bible?"

"Yeah."

"It's full of stories that are as crazy as this one. And do you know why they sound crazy? Because they break all the rules that nature sets. They're supernatural. Crazy, unless you understand the rules of the supernatural, then they're not crazy at all. Then they're everyday life, and that's what we have here."

"Everyday life?"

"Everyday life."

Johnny recalled the afternoon when Black walked into town. "So men walking around without flesh on their faces, and apples turning into snakes, and marbles floating through the air are just everyday life?"

"They can be. They will be. They are, aren't they? You tell me. You saw it all with your own eyes. I have to rely on my mind."

"So it's all real. Everything happening down there is real?" Johnny asked.

"As real as anything you've ever touched or smelled or tasted or seen or heard."

"Then who is Marsuvees Black? He's the cause of all this, isn't he?"

"Only a small part of the cause," Samuel said. "There's Billy, and mostly there's the people of Paradise. But to answer your question, Black used to be a monk from Nevada. Before that a performer in Las Vegas. He was on the staff here at the monastery before he disappeared last week. He found the books in the dungeon, discovered their power, and decided to wreak a little havoc. My theory."

"So if he's, whatever, dealt with—"

"Then you still have Billy and the people of Paradise. Black's only one man with a few tricks up his sleeve. Maybe that's an understatement, but Marsuvees depends on Billy, because Billy has the books. See, grown-ups can't write in them. But Billy—he can do a lot of damage so long as the people follow his suggestions. We have to get to the people, Johnny."

Johnny pressed his hands against his temples and closed his eyes. "Okay, maybe you're right. Maybe this is too much for me. None of it makes any sense. You're talking about Billy and dungeons and books with supernatural power . . . It's crazy!"

Samuel smiled. "So we're back to that word again." He clasped his hands behind his back and paced slowly. Johnny had never heard a kid talk the way Samuel talked, walking about like a miniature monk. Not that he minded—it gave him more confidence in the boy.

"I need your help, Johnny. That's why you're here. And in order for you to help me, you're going to have to understand what's really happening in Paradise. And why."

Samuel faced him. "But nothing I tell you will make any sense unless you believe in the supernatural. You have to believe that God not only exists but that life is ultimately about an epic battle over the hearts of mankind. Good versus evil, not only as theological constructs or ideas, but as real forces at work wherever they are permitted to work. Do you follow?"

What choice did he have? His whole world had been turned topsy-turvy in four days, and short of a better explanation, the supernatural worked just fine.

"I guess."

"Not good enough."

"I mean yes. How can I not believe after what I've seen?"

"Trust me, seeing has very little to do with believing. Belief is a matter of the heart, not the eyes. Although I will admit, these books make the struggle between good and evil pretty visible in Paradise."

For the first time Johnny began to feel a sense of hope. He wasn't a lost soul in the hell that was swallowing Paradise. He was the person that Samuel had brought up to the mountains with a red marble.

His mind grappled briefly with that image.

But he had to believe. He would believe.

"I believe," he said. "If this isn't a dream—"

"No ifs."

"Okay then. I believe."

"Good. I think you're ready to hear the whole story," Samuel said.

AN HOUR later, Johnny sat on a boulder next to Samuel, stunned. It made sense, of course. Seeing it through Samuel's eyes, it made perfect sense.

All except for where the books had come from in the first place, but Samuel had no answer for that.

Samuel seemed content to let the silence stretch.

"So you want me to tell them all this at the meeting tonight," Johnny finally said. "Tell them that they've been deceived by Black and that a cop is coming to town tomorrow morning to set things straight."

"Exactly. Don't tell them how you know and don't say a word about Billy, but throw the book at Black."

Johnny frowned, nervous already. "And you want me to help this cop. Show him around and report back to you."

"That's it." Samuel grinned. "I need eyes on the ground, not only for Thomas, but for me. Billy's got Marsuvees Black; I have you."

"Sounds like a mismatch," Johnny said.

"Billy's no match for me."

"But I'm not sure how well I stack up against Black."

"Trust me, Johnny. This will work."

"What if this fictional character you write doesn't work? I mean, it's never been done before, so how can you be so sure?"

"Well, we'll just have to see, won't we? I'm open to suggestions."

Johnny couldn't think of any.

"So, it's a deal then?" Samuel stretched out his hand.

Johnny took it. "Okay. It's a deal."

"I'll be with you all the way."

"Could Black hurt me?"

Samuel hesitated. "If we don't stop them, yes. And that's what we're trying to do here. That's why I need you."

"Why me? I mean, why are the rest being led along by Billy so easily while I'm not? I mean, I know I started to believe the lies a few times, but I resisted, right? Why don't the rest?"

"My father says that all of you should have fallen to Black's lies. Eve ate the apple, right? He says that no matter who was in that garden at that time, they would have done the same. All the suffering and evil the world has ever seen wasn't because God made a mistake by putting Eve in there instead of someone else. Everyone would have done the same in her place. Follow?"

"Makes sense. Never thought about it that way. Then why not me?"

"Simple. You and Cecil saw Black for what he was before he started playing tricks. Why Billy let you see him, I don't know, but seeing Black as a bag of bones was enough to put the fear of God in you. Then I came along and began to counter Billy's nonsense. You felt it, but not as convincingly as the rest. And there's still Stanley Yordon. When he gets back, he could turn out to be a friend in all of this."

Johnny looked back into the smaller canyon. It was all amazing. Hardly believable. But he did believe. He really did.

"You want to take a look?" Samuel asked.

"At the monastery?"

"Yes!" Samuel jumped up, excited. "Just inside. I can't take you around, but it won't hurt to look."

"Sure."

Samuel grabbed his hand and pulled him to the gaping door. "The whole monastery is hidden by the cliffs except for a few places, where my father's camouflaged it. The glass on top, the front, some windows and doors. I've never seen, but they say it's hidden from the air."

Johnny looked up at the towering face, then at the large door beneath a huge old cross. "How long has it been here?"

"As long as the books at least—that's almost twenty years."

"Incredible."

Samuel led him to the double doors, poked his head in, then pushed one open. The foyer was dark, but there was enough light to reveal old paintings on stone walls on either side. A thick wooden table sat at the center of the area, shiny with layers of dried resin. Tall stained-glass windows peered in from above. No sign of lights. The stone floor was slick and shiny with wear.

It certainly looked ancient.

"It's huge," Johnny said.

"This? This is nothing. Go to the right and you find the library. Go up one floor and you'll find the cafeteria. The main hall straight ahead leads to the upper levels. The residences and the classrooms."

"And what about the basement?"

Samuel gestured. "Off the main hall to the left. A long series of stairs take you down. Not a place anyone in his right mind would want to go."

"Incredible."

Samuel put an arm around Johnny's shoulder and pulled him around. He walked with him back out. "We're a team, Johnny. You and me. We'll fix this mess for sure."

In some strange ways, Samuel seemed much younger than thirteen. In other ways, like in the way he reasoned, he seemed more like an adult. A strange mixture of innocence and education. Probably because he was isolated in the monastery his whole life.

Johnny faced the boy. "I need something from you."

"Say it."

"It's my mom. She's . . ." He hesitated. "Black's after her."

"You have to remember, we can't make people do things."

"But can you help?"

He looked at the monastery and spoke as much to himself as to Johnny. "I'll talk to Christine and Tyler. They can help." He slapped Johnny on the back. "Good idea. But you have to promise to talk to the whole town."

"I will."

Samuel grinned. "Prophet Johnny."

"Trust me, I don't feel like a prophet."

"I'll help you. Listen for me."

"I'm counting on it."

Chapter Twenty-five

PARADISE

Saturday night

TOTAL DARKNESS slid over Paradise early that night, before seven, which was abnormal this time of year. Clouds clamped down on the town like a blackened steel lid. Johnny looked for his mother when he stumbled into town at last light, but he couldn't find her.

He couldn't find anyone. No surprise.

He ran straight for the church with one thought on his mind: Black. He had to reach the church before Black did, so he could figure things out in his head before he did what he was about to do.

Which was what?

Johnny eased to a walk. Which was confronting Black head-on. Which was telling the whole town that they'd been deceived. Which was that the law was coming in force first thing in the morning.

Which was, having successfully completed his duties as prophet, to get to a safe place until morning.

He had rehearsed a hundred stinging one-liners while descending the mountain. He couldn't remember any at the moment, but they would come to him.

Johnny mounted the stairs, thankful that he'd beat the town to the service, assuming there was a service. If Billy found out what he and Samuel were up to, he might change things up on them.

He slid into the church and crept across the foyer to the auditorium doors. No sound. He nudged the doors open a crack, peered into the sanctuary, and caught his breath.

A sea of still heads faced an empty pulpit. Several dozen candles lined the stage. The sanctuary flickered in the shifting flames, absolutely silent.

Johnny felt his heart skip a beat and then knock into double time, just like that: *boom*, and then nothing, and then *boom-ba boom-ba boom!*

All four-hundred-some residents sat in the pews, motionless, staring as though seated for a séance. He wanted to run from the church, but the scene glued his feet to the carpet. Nobody seemed to notice him. He craned for a better view.

Children sat obediently by their parents, legs hanging from the pews. No twitching here, much less running and screaming through the rows. For a brief moment Johnny wondered if they were all dead, stuck here in rows like trophies, forced to sit while Black force-fed them his twisted version of grace and hope.

He imagined Black standing tall behind the podium, a monk from Vegas doped up on worm sludge. His eyes were gone and his lips opened wide. His white face mouthed the word *hope*, only it came out long and raspy.

Hhouuuppe.

His lower jaw fell from his face and gaped open to a black throat. His tongue wagged like a worm freshly yanked from the garden.

Johnny blinked and the image vanished.

A woman he recognized as Louise Timbers sat directly ahead of him in the last pew. Her blonde hair sat on her head like a twisted bird's nest, complete with pieces of straw and clumps of sand. Streaks of dried mud ran down her neck, disappearing below a blouse torn at the collar to reveal half of her left shoulder. A gash already scabbed over glared rusty red on her white skin.

They didn't all look as bad as Louise, but a lot did. The bad ones were here and there throughout the church, wearing sores like a new fad.

Johnny looked down the aisle where Claude Bowers sat next to Chris Ingles on the front pew. Peter and Fred sat on one side of them. Roland sat on the other. All five looked as if they had just engaged in hand-to-hand combat on a battlefield. Claude sagged in his seat, hands folded between his knees, mouth hanging open, spittle running down his chin.

Steve Smither sat with blood-spattered cheeks. He'd butchered a cow or something and not bothered to clean up. His wife, Paula, sat five rows behind and to his right. Unlike the others, she was cleaned up pretty, smiling at the empty podium. And beside her . . .

Sally. Even from this distance, Johnny could see that his mother was gone.

Johnny began to tremble with fear.

Crinkling paper disturbed the quiet, and Johnny glanced at the sound. Father Yordon's secretary sat at the far left, carefully unwrapping a Twinkie, shifting her eyes to see if anyone had heard that first loud tear. She wore a beard of blood, dried and cracking over her lips and chin.

The door to the church opened and a couple hurried in. The Jacksons, only they hardly looked like the Jacksons. They walked by Johnny without noticing him and entered the sanctuary.

Johnny stood back from the sanctuary doors. Paradise was hell.

But Black hadn't taken the stage yet.

Prophet Johnny.

Now, Johnny. Do it now, before Black comes to feed them his lies.

He had no choice. If someone didn't do something . . .

I'm with you, Johnny.

He took a deep breath and moved toward the door.

Another voice cackled in his mind. *Wanna trip, boy? How about a stake between your toes? Or a new set of eyes?*

His Adam's apple lodged in his throat, and he had to swallow to free it. He entered the sanctuary.

The people were like wooden dolls. The pulpit still stood vacant. The clock on the wall read 6:55.

I'm with you, Johnny.

A rattling chuckle echoed through his mind. Billy? Or Black.

Johnny forced his foot forward and lowered his head. He pushed himself up the aisle.

I can do this—it's just carpet passing under my feet, that's all. The church is really empty and I'm just rehearsing graduation or something. And even if it isn't really empty, the people in the pews aren't really looking at me. People always think people are looking at them when they're not.

Then he reached the platform. He stepped up. The candles glowed bright in long rows—short candles, tall candles, some thin and some fat, all flickering on the platform.

Any minute now someone's going to yank me back by the shoulders. A dizzying weakness washed over him, and for a moment he thought he was falling, but he grabbed the pulpit and held himself upright.

He pulled himself to the podium. Looked up.

He expected to see a thousand black holes staring at him. Instead he saw their eyes, blank, drained, and drooping. But eyes, not holes. They were all there staring at him, as if wondering what *he* was doing there.

Who is this interesting little boy in front of us? Some kid's up at the podium. Isn't that Sally's kid? What's he doing up at the podium?

They looked half-dead, as if they'd all just spent two sleepless days harvesting fruit and hadn't bothered to wash before coming to church. The candles lit their pupils, hundreds of miniature flames flickering in their skulls.

Speak the truth, Johnny. Tell them.

He swallowed and cleared his throat. "Hey." He immediately realized that only those in the first few rows could hear him. He shifted to his left and bent the microphone down.

"Hey"—his voice rang out over the speakers—"has anyone noticed that something strange is happening in Paradise?"

Not a soul moved.

"Has anybody noticed that the town is falling apart? The wind blowing without moving the clouds? The dust piled high like in a desert? People acting strange?"

"Yeah," a voice said.

Johnny looked toward the back. Old Man Peterson stood. The man wasn't like the others. "I've noticed all right," the man croaked. "Someone did some damage all right."

"Shut up, Bo," a woman said from across the auditorium. "Sit down and shut up."

A cackle rippled through the crowd. Old Man Peterson sat.

I believe, Johnny. Shout it from the rooftops.

In that moment, Johnny knew what he had to do. It didn't make any sense to him, and it had nothing to do with Bo or his wife yelling at him to shut up.

It was just for him. He needed strength.

Johnny clenched his eyes shut. "I believe," he said. Then again, "I believe. I believe."

Louder, Johnny.

He felt a dam burst in his chest. "I believe!" He screamed it with all of his might. "I believe. I believe!" His voice reverberated through the room. He opened his eyes. The congregation just stared at him. But it didn't matter now.

"Bo's right," he said loudly. "Paradise is falling apart at the seams, and most of you are too blinded to see it. Wake up!"

"Hello, boy."

Johnny froze. Black's voice, ahead and on the left. He scanned the pews. Marsuvees Black sat next to Steve, arms folded across his chest, grinning at Johnny.

Johnny gripped the podium to steady himself.

Black stood. "You think anyone here cares what a whippersnapper rabble-rouser says?"

Johnny spoke before he lost his nerve. "Say what you want, but you're not a prophet from God with a message of hope and grace. You're a monk from the Nevada desert full of death and destruction."

Black took that in, and Johnny could see him change strategy on the fly, watched a new approach register on his bronzed face. The man stepped up to the platform and smiled sweetly at Johnny. Johnny thought Black might take his hand and pat it condescendingly.

"Death and destruction?" He swept a hand out at the crowd. "Do you see any death and destruction? No, you see a church full of souls who have tasted life and freedom like they've never tasted it before."

Johnny looked down at Claude Bowers sitting like an overstuffed mummy with drooping eyes. A half-empty bottle nestled in his crotch. He didn't look a bit affected by Johnny's accusations. Nor did anyone else.

"I'll tell you what," Black said. "Let's let the people tell us what they think."

Black brought his hands together. A thick finger of blazing white light crackled to life on the ceiling. Johnny watched in amazement as it slowly elongated, reaching down about six feet, as if God himself had stuck his finger through the roof and was now pointing at the congregation.

The people craned their necks in wonder.

Black chuckled. "Belieeeeeve," he said in a low, soft voice. He clapped his hands again.

A thunderclap shook the building from the inside out. The light ballooned and sent a jagged bolt of lightning to the floor. The lightning crashed into the aisle and was gone, leaving smoke from a six-foot hole in the carpet snaking toward a charred ceiling.

Cries of alarm erupted. Those who'd been dozing or even thinking of dozing were now on their feet, shouting in startled terror.

Marsuvees Black lifted both arms wide and pointed his chin to the ceiling. He sang one long note. The note grew and echoed and swallowed the church. The cries were overwhelmed and then silenced altogether. There was just Black on the stage with his one-note solo, inhumanly loud and deeply troubling.

At least for Johnny.

The rest seemed to find it calming.

Black ended abruptly and lowered his head, keeping his hands outstretched. "Do I have your attention? I think I do. Are you right, Johnny? Am I a demon from hell come to kill your old men?"

He snapped his fingers. Yellow flames hissed to life in each hand and licked six inches of air. "Or have I come to lick the fires of hell from your wounds with pleasure and grace, and with hope for more pleasure and grace?"

Black kept his eyes on the congregation and brought both hands to his face. He began to lick the fire with a long pink tongue. Faster, ravenous, sucking his fingers. It reminded Johnny of a dog going after meat. Black jabbed his right hand into his mouth, past the knuckles. The fire hissed out. He did the same with his left hand.

Black sighed with satisfaction, and then motioned to the people with his wet hands. "You tell me. Have I come to kill you, or have I come to heal your wounds?"

"You've come to heal our wounds!" a voice called from Johnny's right. Katie stood. She looked as though she were going to a dance, all made up and pretty except for a few scratches on her face.

She winked at Black. "I don't know about the rest of you, but I've never felt more alive in all my life."

But look at you, Katie! You're dying! Johnny opened his mouth to say it when Steve jumped to his feet.

"We're being set free!" Steve yelled. "We're learning what it means to be alive. Nobody's going to take that from us. No one!"

A dozen excited parishioners stood to their feet with Steve, all speaking at once, shouting out their agreement in a muddled mess of noise.

Sally watched the whole thing with wide eyes. She seemed confused, caught between Black and her own son.

Johnny could hear Peter Bowers's high-pitched voice through the chorus of objections. "What do you know, Johnny, you little spineless wimp. We should chop off your thumbs, boy! Black's cool."

"He's a liar!" Johnny shouted.

The room shut down. They seemed surprised that he was still up there, much less yelling at them.

Johnny forged ahead, as forcefully as he could. "The police are coming in the morning. I mean it; when they come, they'll put this all straight."

"You lie, boy," Black said in a low voice.

"If I'm wrong and they don't come, then string me up, for all I care. Chop off my thumbs, Peter. But I'm not wrong! You'll see. Thomas is coming. I promise you that."

Black looked amused.

Outrage broke out again.

"Silence!" Black shouted. Those standing took their seats.

Black eyed Johnny, still amused. He stepped toward the podium. Johnny stepped back. The man reached into his trench coat, calmly removed a book, and laid it on the pulpit as if it were a Bible.

But this was no Bible. It was a leather-bound book that reminded Johnny of the books that Samuel had described. A book from the monastery, the ones Billy was writing in.

Black rubbed his hands together slowly and lifted his eyes to the people. He seemed to be considering his next move. Johnny knew his. It was time to leave.

But he was momentarily fascinated by Black's disorientation. The news about Thomas had thrown Black for a loop. The man had a weak side after—

Black lifted his arm high and brought it down on the pulpit with a tremendous *crack*. The podium split in two. Black stood, trembling from head to foot. His right hand began to bleed.

"We will only be so tolerant of deceit!" Black said. "Continue down this road and you will end up like Billy."

A few scattered *amens* sounded to Johnny like the whispers of aimless ghosts.

Johnny ran for the door. He leapt off the platform, ran straight down the aisle over the carpet still smoldering from the lightning strike, smacked through the swinging doors, and staggered out into the howling wind. He doubled over there. Swirling dust filled his throat, and he coughed.

Exactly what had Black meant there at the end? Billy? He really didn't want to try to figure that out.

He believed that what Samuel told him was true, and he'd done what Samuel had asked. And that was that.

He believed. The rest did not.

Johnny headed into the wind to find a safe haven until morning.

Chapter Twenty-six

PARADISE

Sunday morning

STANLEY YORDON sped down Highway 50 before sunrise Sunday morning filled with a sense of terrible unease. Not because he feared returning to Paradise—on the contrary, because he had *not* come back sooner. Four days ago the idea of staying in Denver for an extra day seemed inviting, a well-deserved break and, more importantly, some time away.

Time healed wounds, they said. He'd decided to give Paradise a little time. Time to come to their collective senses. Time for Marsuvees Black to move on.

But he tried repeatedly to raise someone in Paradise last night, and no one answered. For all he knew, they were all down at the church swaying to the tunes of Marsuvees Black.

Unable to sleep, he left Denver at two in the morning. It was now five a.m. The drive had given him the time to flesh out the sermon he intended to preach. No mercy this time. Not an ounce. Just the right mixture of authority and compassion, the thundering voice of reprimand, the gentle words of empathy. And in the end they would have to listen.

The air was still and quiet when he drove through Delta. It was blowing hard and hazy twenty miles later when he passed the sign that read *Paradise 3 Miles.*

Someone had erected a barricade across the turnoff to Paradise. A large orange sign leaned against it.

Road Damage. Road Closed Ahead.

Yordon came to a stop. Road damage?

An image of Black drawing that ridiculous two in the air flashed through his mind. He gunned the motor, steered around the barricade, and headed up the road.

No sign of road damage.

The sun was trying to rise, but weather smothered the mountains. Dark clouds socked in Paradise valley like a cork between the mountains. Mountain storms were notorious for coming up fast and furious. But this . . .

He frowned and drove on, cautiously. Thin wisps of sand whirled across the road through his beams. Quite a wind.

His thoughts returned to his meeting with Bishop Fraiser in Denver. The bishop was smiling at him, telling him he'd better start believing what he was teaching if he wanted to hold on to his congregation. And if there were any hidden sins in his heart, he'd best bring them into the light.

"What you do mean?" he asked, wary.

"Secrets, Stanley."

"We all have our secrets."

"Yes, we do. And some secrets are meant to be secrets, while others will eat away at your heart like a cancer. I've seen whole churches crumble over a single indiscretion that was swept under the rug. But the rug can only cover so much, Stanley."

He left the meeting assuring himself that the bishop had spoken in broad, general terms. He'd swept a hundred small indiscretions under the rug in his time, but nothing worthy of the glint in the bishop's eyes when he said "secrets." There was Sally, of course. There was a possibility that some fool said something out of turn about Sally. But that had been fourteen years ago.

Welcome to Paradise, Population . . .

The sign was missing. Wind?

Yordon turned the corner into Paradise and immediately pumped the brake. Blowing dust blasted by, nearly obscuring the small valley. Now *this* was a dust storm. That must be why they'd closed the road. Stanley couldn't recall a wind so heavily concentrated in the valley like this.

He dropped his eyes to the road's yellow lines to guide him in the early-morning light. The road leveled out and ran straight through the town without a bend. By the time Yordon passed the first outlying house, his orientation began to fail him. Following the yellow line made him dizzy.

The theater loomed on his right. He followed its outline. Looked different somehow. He couldn't see worth a darn, but he—

The car slammed into something. A joint-wrenching crash, shattering glass. His head snapped forward and hit the steering wheel. The fact that he'd been creeping along at under ten miles an hour saved him from any serious injury.

Yordon cursed, something he could only do alone in his car. He shoved his door open, climbed out, and staggered around to the hood. The Starlight sign lay smashed on the blacktop. His bumper had hit one of the support poles, buckling the chrome under the car. The pole must have ripped a hose from the radiator, because it whistled with the wind.

Yordon stared unbelieving at the ruined landmark. His eyes followed the poles back to where they had been chopped.

He swore again.

Past the poles, the theater's front wall had been stripped of its siding, slashed to ribbons. As far as he could see, which wasn't terribly far, the buildings had taken a beating. Telephone poles, shattered doors, branches, and an assortment of broken-beyond-recognition appliances littered the place.

He saw the silhouette of the church like a ghost in the wind and wondered about its condition. He turned toward it, squinting through the whipping sand. Leaves blasted by—brown fall leaves in the middle of summer. Yordon began to run.

"Hello?"

No use in this wind. The streets were vacant, but that wasn't surprising considering the storm.

It's more than a storm, Stanley. He fought a surge of panic.

A selfish little thought crossed his mind—conditions like these would undoubtedly keep a few farmers from attending the morning service. But a much bigger voice chased that possibility. *Not a soul, Stanley! Not a single soul will come to hear your pathetic sermon!*

For all he knew, they were all dead.

No, not possible.

To his right the black sky framed Claude's store—a store that should have a large blue sign along the length of the building three feet above the door.

One side of the large sign banged against the wall in the wind. Stubborn fragments of broken glass jutted from wooden window frames like frozen claws. The door was gone.

Yordon felt gooseflesh ripple up his arms. This was not the work of wind. Who could have done this? The telephone pole next to Claude's convenience store lay across the sidewalk. He stepped over it.

Smither's Saloon was even worse off. The collapsed steps left a three-foot rise to the gaping door frame. The town's only bench had been reduced to matchsticks along the gravel walk.

Surely they wouldn't have trashed the church. Yordon was about to plunge ahead when he saw yellow light flicker in the bar's window.

Someone was inside at this hour?

He ran to the saloon, jumped onto the trashed landing, and shoved the dangling door aside. He stepped in and scanned the interior of Smither's Saloon.

A small fire at the center of the room spewed white smoke to the ceiling and for a moment Yordon thought the saloon was ablaze, but then he saw it was a campfire of sorts, fed by broken table legs that formed a teepee over the flames. The bar lay chopped to kindling; the broken glass of a hundred bottles covered the floor. Only one table remained standing. And around the table sat three chairs, sagging under the weight of three figures, sitting like ghosts by the fire.

Yordon stepped over the rubble. Two men and a boy—resembling Claude Bowers, Chris Ingles, and Claude's boy, Peter, respectively—all leaned on the table, clutching bottles of booze, looking at him through drooping eyes. A toppled can of beer fed a pool of liquid that glistened in the flames.

They saw him and then returned their focus on the spilt malt. Dirt matted their hair; ash streaked their faces; something had torn their clothing to shreds. Chris Ingles wore a sling on his right arm.

"Hi, Stanley," Chris said without looking at him.

At first Yordon couldn't find the voice to respond. *Hi, Stanley?* What was he supposed to say? *Oh, hi, Chris. Having a bad day are we? I see you have a nice fire going. Do you mind if I join you?*

What Chris needed was a good palm to the cheek. A thundering crash upside his right ear. *Wake up, boy! What do you think you're doing?*

But Claude was the leader here. Yordon could see it in his face, below all that crud. "Claude, what are you doing?"

The big Swede turned his head and stared at him. The flames' reflection danced in his glassy eyes. "Hi, Stan."

He looked back at the table. Peter glanced his way for a second, took a swig from the bottle in his hand, and turned back to the reflection of flames in the spilt beer.

Yordon walked up to the table and gave it a good shove. "What's wrong with you guys? Wake up, for crying out loud! You're going to burn this place down!"

The amber liquid spilled over their laps as the table tipped. Claude's eyes snapped wide, as if an electrode had just hit the muscle controlling his eyelids, and Yordon immediately knew that he might be in a spot of trouble.

Claude stared at the table, aghast. He stood abruptly, sending his chair flying across the room.

Yordon stepped back.

The others came to their feet as well, gawking in disbelief at the table. "Wha . . . what happened?" Chris stammered.

The stupidity of the question shoved Yordon into an offensive gear. *The best defense is sometimes a good offense. Sometimes, like when your opponent is a drooling fool wondering why his hands are on his arms.*

"What have you done to the town? Look at this place, you've trashed it!"

All three of their stares turned to him. "We didn't do this," Peter said.

"Then who did?"

"Black did it," Peter said. "*He* told us to do it."

Black? How was that possible? How could anyone turn men so quickly?

"He's just a traveling salesman," Yordon said. "He couldn't do this."

"He's a salesman and he's selling a lot." Claude grinned. "You think we care about your lousy church? You should go look at it now. I don't think you're gonna be preaching too much there anymore."

Claude's son snickered.

He could see it in his mind's eye—the pews hacked up like these tables, the carpet peeled back in long maroon strips, the cross blazing on the wall like at one of those KKK meetings.

Yordon launched himself at the three figures, and he knew with his first step that he was about to experience a great deal of pain.

Yordon never actually reached them. Claude's fist reached his forehead first, like a sledgehammer.

Wham!

He collapsed, belly down on the table, his arms draping limply over the edges. Pain swelled through his head.

"He's on our table," Chris said from a great distance.

"What should we do with him?"

"Let's get rid of him," Claude said.

They pulled him from the table and hauled him like a sack of onions. They heaved him into a hole. He crumpled to the floor. A door slammed. A latch was locked.

They've thrown you into a grave.

His brain crawled through the haze.

You belong in a grave, buried with the rest of your indiscretions. Your secrets.

Yordon opened his eyes. A cool, damp breeze ran across his face. The smell of fresh dirt filled his nostrils, the kind of dirt found six feet under. But the space around him wasn't the two-by-seven of a casket, it was more like ten-by-ten. A sliver of light penetrated some boards above him.

They had dropped him in the saloon's root cellar.

He laid his head on the earthen floor and closed his eyes against a throbbing headache. *Dear God, what have I done?*

Chapter Twenty-seven

THE MONASTERY

Sunday morning

BILLY OPENED the ink jar, dabbed the quill into the liquid, and sent his mind to Paradise. Except for the torch that popped and licked at the ancient walls, only his breathing sounded in the chamber. The quill hovered a centimeter above the blank page. Perspiration beaded his forehead and he brought his left wrist across his brow.

The idea of his sweat falling to the page seemed profane, which in turn struck him as ridiculous, considering where he was. He'd written a thousand stories above, where he was taught to write, encouraged to write. But down here, the writing was different. In fact, it was the writing that drew him now more than the worms. The monk was right, the writing attracted them all.

He focused on a minute droplet of red ink glistening on the pen's very tip. He lowered the tip to the page, watching the gap between it and the paper close. His breathing came to a ragged halt.

He swallowed and pressed down. The pen made contact with the paper, and Billy's world seemed to erupt with light, like a strobe in a pitch-dark cell. A tone hummed through his mind.

Hmmmmmm.

As if the pen had struck a tuning fork in his skull.

A window in his mind blew open. He grinned at the thought of the preacher sitting in the root cellar. *Now how do you like your Paradise? What do you think of your little church now?*

The red words on the page before him glistened, and he blew across the paper to speed their drying. He dipped the quill in the ink jar again.

Easy, bringing the preacher to his knees on the cellar floor, cold and damp, shivering in the darkness.

It had been the monk's idea to write a story about Paradise. And why not? He had heard a little of the nearby town, and what he didn't know, the monk told him. Details of the setting, names of characters. A basic plot that suggested a kind of story Billy had never explored before.

A story of evil, loosed.

The story was like nothing he'd ever written, and Billy figured it was because of the worm salve. When he wrote, he actually felt like he was in the story with real characters who had minds of their own, like all really good stories, only much better.

How many times had he written something, paused, realized that the character didn't want to do it that way, written again and again until finally he got it right and the character did things his way?

Or was it the character's way?

This was the most realistic story he could ever imagine.

Billy laid the tip to the paper.

What do you want, Stanley?

I want what I had.

And what did you have, Stan, that you don't have now?

Warmth. A bed. Light.

More, Stan. What do you really want?

Power.

Grace and hope, Stan. How about grace and hope?

Yes, grace and hope.

But Black brought you grace and hope and you rejected him, deep down there in your heart where no one knew.

Maybe I shouldn't have.

Well, if you stand up right now and cry like a baby and beat your head on the wall until it's bloody, I'll give you some power.

Billy chuckled. He brought his free hand to his neck and scratched.

He could fully imagine Stan's situation at this very moment. He could smell the musty dirt and see the darkness. He was inside Stan the man's mind. Of course he was, Stan was his character.

But right now, Stan didn't want to stand up and hit his head against the wall. He was considering it, but this wasn't where the character wanted to go.

Billy wrote again.

Then instead lay there and sulk, you stuffed-up fool.

I am in a very bad way. I'll lay here for a while.

Good enough. Time to move on to another character.

"Darcy?"

The girl beside him didn't turn from her writing. Billy rubbed his fingers into his shirt. The annoying infections were chronic, a rash of systemic boils. He'd tried bandages, but they wouldn't stick to his oily skin. Washing the area only seemed to keep the flesh clean for an hour. Only the worms' ointment held the sores at bay. And then only as long as he managed to avoid scratching, which proved almost impossible.

The other students suffered the same already, in less than a day. The disease overtook them much faster. This as much as the writing would keep them in the dungeons where they could access a ready supply of the ointment.

They ventured upstairs to the dining hall for short raiding trips only, before returning to the great library the monk had shown Billy. There they hunkered down under Paul's supervision. At least his version of supervision, which was really a kind of chaos.

"You've already ruined the tables," Billy observed after Paul and the others occupied the great library for only a few hours.

"We don't like the tables," Paul answered. "They're too wet and slimy."

"They're wet and slimy because you've spread that worm stuff all over them."

"Yes, well, we don't like them anymore."

Billy gave up. "Just don't let any of the others come to my hall. Keep them here."

"Sure. How many worms do you think you have in that tunnel?"

"I don't know. What difference does it make?"

"We have 338 in our hall alone," Paul said. "But I think they all want to be here. With us. What do you think?"

"I think you're wasting your time thinking about these stupid worms instead of writing our story!"

He left Paul standing in the hall just outside the library. That was last night. It was the last time he'd seen him.

Billy looked around the study. Apart from sludge stains all over the carpet and sofa, his study had survived the brats. Now only he and Darcy used the study.

Darcy grunted and brought her fingernails to her neck. Billy watched, revolted, as she scratched a wide swath of skin away, oblivious to any pain or blood. She resumed her writing, smiling. She smeared a large streak of blood along the margin of her page without noticing. She was writing some of the women. Women could be quite engrossing.

Billy closed his eyes and thought about Stanley again. *Stan the man. You should have run, Stan the man. Now you're in the can without a plan.* He bent over the desk and began to write again, this time in more developed prose.

He wrote for an hour, lost in the valley below, his senses dulled to everything but the story that he brought to life in his mind. And then he took a short walk through the hall to stretch.

His mind drifted back to the debate that he'd won so easily. Seemed like a week ago. Technically, if he remembered right, he could now do whatever he wanted upstairs. Funny thing, though, he didn't care about what happened upstairs anymore. As long as they left him alone to write down here, the monkeys upstairs could do whatever they wanted.

Billy padded lightly on the cold stone, warm and dazed. An image of Paul smiling at the entrance of the larger library popped into his mind. *Do you know how many worms you have?*

Billy shoved his hand into his pocket. It was slightly mushy but for the most part empty. Restocking worm gel would be a good idea. He held his torch to the wall and dipped his hand into a thick layer of the ointment.

Billy was stuffing his pockets when it occurred to him that there were no worms within the circle of light cast by his flame. He turned and walked along the wall, expecting a slug to appear in the light. But none did.

Gone?

Billy began to run. Where were they? They couldn't have just *left*! Slug slime still crisscrossed the walls, but it would eventually run out. Maybe even dry up, leaving nothing but crusty trails. He and Darcy needed the worms. He ran a full hundred meters beyond the study, but the walls were vacant.

Near panic now, Billy sprinted for the study. He had to get Darcy! Maybe they should find buckets and fill them with what ointment still clung to the walls. Store it in a cool damp corner, hidden from the others. Yes, they should do at least that. Maybe barricade their tunnel to keep the others out altogether.

Then he and Darcy could write in peace surrounded by buckets of worm gel. Finish their story. But then how would they get out to eat? The moment they left, the others would break in. Better to barricade them in *their* stinking tunnel!

When Billy raced through the entrance to the study, his torch slammed into the arch and flew from his hand in a shower of sparks.

"Darcy!" He retreated quickly to snatch up his torch then jumped back into the study and faced a glassy-eyed Darcy, pen still cocked in her right hand.

"The worms are gone!"

She was overdosed on writing. He leaned forward and yelled again. "You hear me? The worms are gone!"

She blinked and set her pen down. "Worms?"

"Come on, snap out of it. Yes, worms." He snaked his hand through the air in a slithering motion. "The worms on the walls are gone."

She stood, snatched the other torch from the wall, and ran past Billy into the tunnel. He turned and followed, leaving the study dark behind him. Darcy waved her torch about the cavern and followed the orange splash of light with her head.

"Gone?" she asked in a thin voice. "You sure?"

"You see them? They look gone to me."

"You check up that way?" She motioned toward the black hole Billy had just searched.

"Yes."

"Come on!" Darcy ran the opposite way, toward the main entrance, and Billy ran right on her heels. The slapping of their feet echoed down the tunnel. Their flames whooshed over their heads.

Darcy pulled up just before the tunnel ended, and Billy had to swerve to avoid her. His foot hooked under the tail of a massive worm and he found himself diving headlong.

Three distinct thoughts crashed through his mind as his body flew through the air. The first was one of self-preservation, *Heavens, I hope I don't break my neck. Maybe I should curl up and roll when I land.*

In that instant the second thought materialized. The worm had recoiled when his foot struck its soft flesh. It had compressed like an accordion and raised its head into the air. Maybe it would strike at him like a cobra while he lay on the floor with a broken neck.

But the third thought superseded even this danger. His flame washed across the tunnel and Billy thought, *Jiminy Cricket, there's a* boy *dragging that worm!*

Billy landed with a terrible grunt and rolled to his feet. A boy did indeed stand at the worm's opposite end, gripping a rope tied around it. Paul! Paul was dragging one of *their* worms from *their* tunnel! "What are you doing?" Billy demanded. But he knew what worm-boy was doing. Worm-boy was stealing one of their worms.

"Uh, nothing." Paul stepped backward, tugging at the rope. The worm slid easily on its smooth belly.

"What do you mean *nothing*?" Darcy snapped. "That doesn't look like nothing to me. Looks to me like you're dragging a worm. One of *our* worms."

Paul stopped his tugging and stared at them as though he were having difficulty placing their faces. After a moment he resumed his haul of the giant worm. Billy glanced at the ground and saw dozens of long mucus streaks running along the floor. This wasn't the first worm dragged down the corridor recently.

"Wake up, boy! You hear Darcy? What in heaven's name are you doing, dragging our worms out of our tunnel?"

Paul leaned into the rope, ignoring Billy's charge. He trudged down the hall like an ox pulling a heavy sled.

Billy dove for the worm's tail end. His fingers slipped through a thin layer of mucus and dug into the soft body flesh.

The worm slithered on, probably completely unaware of the failed assault. Billy fell to his rear with a grunt. Paul tugged the worm, their last one maybe, through the tunnel's gaping mouth and around the bend toward his own hall.

"Come on," Darcy said, pulling Billy to his feet. "That fool has no right to steal our worms."

Billy felt the throbbing pain of his disturbed boils aching to the bone and grimaced. "You'd think he has enough of his own."

He shoved a hand into his hip pocket, withdrew a palm full of worm salve, and slapped it along the forearm hit hardest by the first fall. "Man, this hurts!"

"Don't worry, Billy. We'll get our worms back. Sooner than he might think too, assuming he still has the ability to think. You see his eyes? That boy's lost it. He's out there in worm land."

"Come on," Billy said. "Let's find some ropes. No way we can haul those slugs without ropes."

"Yeah."

Twenty minutes later Billy and Darcy slipped into the far tunnel, laden with ropes they'd found in the study. They'd formed a plan of sorts, though it amounted to no more than sneak-in-and-steal-our-worms-back. And if any kid gets in the way, smack them on the neck where their sores hurt most.

They each held a torch and tiptoed along the corridor, hugging the right wall. Darcy watched their rear for any scoundrels who might be returning from the upper levels, and Billy took point, scanning the tunnel's face for their first worm.

But when the first worm didn't appear, Billy began to wonder if this tunnel had been cleared as well. Where had that sicko put the worms if not here, in his own tunnel? Of course, there were four other tunnels between them.

The entrance to the big library flickered in the torchlight and Billy drew up. So soon? And not one worm. Not one student, either. They were probably swinging from the chandeliers, ripping the paneling from the walls, and feasting on worm flesh.

He motioned Darcy forward and crept to the doors. With a deep breath he shoved through the doors and stepped into the library's outer hall. Nothing yet—that was good. He felt Darcy's hand on his hip, and he moved down the hall toward the balcony entrance. He reached it, pried the narrow door open, and peered down into the main library.

The flames of twenty torches burned along the walls, filling the room with dancing yellow light. From his position he couldn't see the tables below, but the library's eerie silence struck him as odd.

"Are they in there?" Darcy whispered.

"I can't tell. I don't hear anything." Billy eased out onto the balcony and crawled to the railing on all fours. He waited for Darcy to slide in beside him and then edged his head over the three-foot wall that bordered the upper level.

The first thought that rushed through his mind was that Paul's band of brats were dead. All of them, dead! Slumped on the floor, surrounded by a thick carpet of worms, twisting slowly on the carpet at their feet.

Billy caught his breath. Dead? No, they couldn't be dead! Writing, maybe. Writing in Paul's swimming pool of worms.

"What?" Darcy whispered. "What is it?" She raised her head above the railing.

"Good night! He's brought the worms *here*!" Darcy said, dropping back beside him. He nodded, thinking that his heart was pounding with enough force to be heard from below. His vision grew fuzzy, and he blinked to clear it.

He snaked his head back up and peered down. They'd returned the tables to the floor. Most, if not all, of Paul's students leaned over the circular tables, writing in books, seemingly unconscious of the thick blanket of slugs at their feet.

Paul's lost it. Completely. At least they're writing. How in the world had Paul managed to get the worms down there? More importantly, how would he and Darcy ever get them out?

The door latch behind them opened and Billy flinched. A boy appeared on the balcony, pulling and tugging at a slug, and Billy realized that Paul was just now arriving with their worm. How had they passed him? He must have taken another route, through one of the other tunnels.

He watched with amazement as the boy hauled the creature first to and then over the balcony railing without paying them any mind. The slug slithered over the handrail, writhing in protest, and then fell to the floor fifteen feet below. It landed with a mighty *thump*.

When Billy looked back up at the balcony, Paul was gone. There was no way they could get any of these worms. They would just have to find another supply—possibly in the other tunnels or farther in their own hall.

"Let's get out of here," he whispered and crawled for the door. He squeezed through and led Darcy from the library.

"You see that?" he asked as soon as they cleared the main doors.

"He's really flipped his lid, hasn't he?"

"Completely. At least he has them all writing. We'll find some others."

She nodded. "Yeah."

It took them half an hour to find another batch of worms deep in their own tunnel and drag them near the study. A few minutes later, Billy and Darcy were writing again.

"Billy?" Darcy said after her first few strokes.

"Hmm."

"You ever get the feeling that this story is, I don't know, maybe more than just a story?"

Actually he had. "Why'd you say that?"

"These tunnels. The worms. So many blank books. I know we're all writing these subplots that don't have a lot of meaning by themselves, but they *feel* like they have meaning. Like they're really happening."

"Yeah, well, I hope it is real. In fact, it is real."

"Really? Why?"

"I can't tell the difference, can you? When I'm writing, it's real to me. Real, period—that's what makes it so. That's why I like it. And I can tell you something, the main plot has more than a little meaning. I'm doing some damage." He grinned. "I mean, we're gonna chew them up and spit them out."

"Who?"

"Whoever doesn't follow us. Whoever rejects our version of hope and grace. Whoever Black wants to, that's who."

"And because they're the same as the overseers and Samuel and all those pukes upstairs who don't get it," Darcy snapped. He was surprised at her tone.

Billy nodded. "Yeah."

A moment passed with nothing to say. Then Billy and Darcy leaned over their books and began to write.

CHAPTER TWENTY-EIGHT

PARADISE

Sunday morning

JOHNNY AWOKE late Sunday morning—nearly noon by his alarm clock. Not surprising considering he'd stayed awake 'til three expecting Claude Bowers to beat down his door.

He glanced at the window, half-expecting a grinning face. It took him a few long seconds, squinting his eyes at the blinds to realize that something had changed. For the first time in five days, the sun's rays replaced the perpetual dusk framed in his window.

He jumped off his bed, bounded across the room, and yanked the blinds open. A white sky blinded him. In that one blast of light, the fear fell from his heart like loosed shackles and he could hardly stifle a cry of delight.

Samuel!

Johnny grabbed his three-day-old T-shirt from the bedpost and pulled it over his head with trembling arms. The town had changed.

How much, though?

"Mom?"

He jumped into his jeans, pulled on his shoes, and ran into the hall. "Mom!"

No response. He opened her door. She lay unmoving under the sheets.

"Mom?"

Dead to the world. Still, the sky had changed. That was a start.

Johnny hurried through the living room and out onto the porch. Several clouds still dotted the sky, but they weren't nearly as dark as before. And the wind was only a gentle breeze.

Johnny walked into the street and looked at Paradise with wide eyes. He saw something like the aftermath of a tornado that had touched down, ripped up the town, then vanished. Rows of miniature sand dunes, each about a foot tall, ran like ribbons over Main Street.

He looked south. The business section had been trashed. The Starlight Theater's sign had toppled to the street.

Then Johnny saw the man standing in the middle of the road next to the theater. He straddled a mound of sand, hands on his hips, surveying the damage from the other end of town.

He first thought it was Black, and a streak of terror hit him like lightning. But the man wore a blue uniform, not a black trench coat.

Samuel's cop.

Johnny scanned the town, looking for any other signs of life. Only the cop, standing on the same line that Marsuvees Black himself had first followed into town.

Johnny headed for the uniformed man, praying under his breath that this was Thomas.

This was a fictional character, he knew that, but looking at him now, Johnny had a hard time accepting it. He didn't look fictional. The only thing odd about him was that he didn't seem to notice Johnny.

Johnny stopped twenty feet from him. Still no sign of recognition. The lawman wore mirrored sunglasses. His hair was short and his face was bronzed by the sun.

The cop's legs were spread wide and his hands rested on the butts of two large pistols in hip holsters. His head moved slowly from left to right as he studied the town. Reminded Johnny of that movie *The Terminator*. Samuel had said something about a gunslinger, but the man looked more like a regular cop.

Was this guy really flesh and blood?

"Closer, son."

Johnny's pulse spiked. He hesitated, then walked up to the man. The cop extended his right hand. "Name's Thomas."

He knew it. Johnny stared into the mirrored glasses, at a loss. This wasn't a real man. He was standing in front of Samuel's gunslinger.

"I don't bite," Thomas said. "Not you anyway." He grinned briefly; then his face went stern again. Was that Samuel talking through him?

Johnny took the hand. Felt like regular flesh and blood. "I'm Johnny."

Thomas released his hand and smiled wide. For a moment he looked like someone different altogether. Same flesh and same clothes, but his face . . .

"Isn't this cool?" Thomas said. "I mean who'd have thought this would actually work?" He snapped his fingers and moved his arms and body in a little jive jig. "Cool, baby. Way cool!"

Johnny stepped back, images of the terminator gone.

Thomas caught himself and cleared his throat. He looked at Johnny for a moment, then returned his hands to his hips and straddled the road again.

"Sorry about that. This is all new to me. I have to stay in character. I'm a gunslinger, son. A bona fide blue-suited gunslinger, and don't you forget that." He looked down at Johnny. "You won't tell anybody about that, will you?"

"About what?"

"The, you know . . ." Thomas removed a hand from his hip and twirled it in a tight circle. "The little dance thing. It doesn't fit my image."

Johnny grinned. This was more Samuel's doing than Thomas's. Had to be.

"Not a word," he said.

"Appreciate it. You want to see some of my moves?"

He wanted to dance again?

Thomas's hands blurred. Then they were cocked on either side of his head and there was a gun in each one. "Pretty fast, huh?" The guns began to spin. His arms moved in steady symmetrical patterns, more like a kung fu master than any gunslinger that Johnny had seen. Jet Li with guns. Thomas snapped the guns back into position on either side of his head.

"Wow."

"That's nothing, son."

"So . . . can you do anything you want?"

"Like what?"

"I don't know. Fly?"

"I'm a gunslinger, not a bird. And even if I could fly, it wouldn't be any good to us."

Thomas returned the guns to his holsters. "Now, let's get down to business. Looks like you've had some trouble here. Mind telling me what happened?"

"Did . . . didn't Samuel tell you?"

"Samuel? Never mind anyone named Samuel right now. Just tell me everything."

Johnny led the cop behind the old theater and told him everything, starting with Black walking into town and ending with the meeting last night. Everything except his trip to the monastery. He assumed that Samuel wanted to keep Thomas focused on Paradise, although for all practical purposes, Thomas was Samuel, wasn't he?

Then again, maybe not. This was new territory. Maybe fictional characters could develop a mind of their own.

Thomas listened to every word patiently, intently, giving no sign that he doubted a single detail. He just nodded as if he understood precisely what had happened here in Paradise because he had faced a dozen identical scenarios in his time.

Every now and then he drew his guns and spun them like batons. To keep fresh, he said.

When Johnny finished, the cop took a deep breath and removed his glasses and twirled them. "You're braver than most kids. Gotta hand it to you."

Thomas placed a hand on his shoulder and squeezed gently. "Don't worry, we're going to clean this mess up. Black may have a few tricks, but then so do I."

"Yeah, about that. How does the *we* part work?"

"You just leave that to me. It may be we, but we follow me, *comprende*?"

"*Comprende*."

"Now . . ." The cop withdrew one gun, snapped the safety off, and cocked it up by his right ear. "Where do you suppose we might find these scoundrels?"

Johnny walked to the corner and looked up the street. "I'd start with the saloon. Either there or in the church. But they might still be sleeping in their houses too. A lot of people are sleeping a lot around here."

Thomas nodded at Smither's Saloon. "Saloon?"

"Smither's Saloon."

"Follow me."

THE SALOON'S exterior was trashed nearly beyond recognition. Of three steps that led to the landing, only the top one remained. Johnny stopped ten yards in front of it.

The streets were still bare. This surprised Johnny; he thought that people would start coming out of their homes when they saw the change in the weather.

Then again, Billy had a lot of help now. No telling how much damage they'd inflicted last night. The key now was to keep Thomas's identity hidden from Black. He had to think Thomas was a regular cop, not a fictional something that Samuel had pulled into the mix. If Billy and Black fought fire with fire, that could get nasty.

Thomas took his sunglasses off and stowed them in his pocket. His hazel eyes flashed with mischief.

"When you said that flying wouldn't help us," Johnny said, "it was because what matters here is what people think, right? You have to change their hearts and minds, not just throw them all in jail."

"That's right, son. But a little butt-kicking never hurt anyone."

"But you don't want to be too obvious, right? Black's out there somewhere. We don't want the wrong idea to make it back up the mountain."

He figured talking in code would be acceptable, although there was no one to hear them anyway.

"Unfortunately, yes." Thomas cocked his head and studied the door. "Do you think it would be too obvious if I kicked the door in?"

"Not really. Cops do that all the time in the movies."

Thomas held Johnny in his gaze for a second, then winked. "Goody."

Then he took three long steps, launched himself effortlessly into the air, planted one foot on the top step, and flew for the door.

He hit it with both feet extended. *Crash!* The door popped off its hinges and disappeared into the darkness with Thomas aboard.

Johnny glanced around the town. Not exactly your typical kicking-down-the-door thing, not even in the movies. He hoped Black wasn't watching.

He wouldn't mind getting his hands on one of those books. Course, it might not work for him. He probably didn't have the simple kind of belief that Samuel or the other kids in the monastery had.

Johnny jumped up and peered through the open doorway. Thomas stood on top of the door, like a surfer on his board, gun drawn. It took a second for his eyes to adjust to the dim light, and when they did, he gasped.

The saloon had been gutted by fire. Blackened wood smoldered around the perimeter. The tables, the pool table, the bar—every bit of it lay in ashes, and Johnny wondered why the frame hadn't gone up as well.

"Wow."

They both turned their heads to the sound of a muffled cry somewhere down low.

"You hear that?" Johnny whispered.

"This place have a basement?"

"There's a root cellar."

"Show me."

Johnny picked his way across the room toward the storage room. Heat rose from the charred floor, although he now saw that someone had doused it with water—probably what saved the building.

A blackened lock with a Master logo hung stubbornly on the blistered root-cellar door. "Here it is." Johnny stepped aside.

"Call out to them," Thomas said.

"Just call out?"

"Don't tell them I'm here. Just try to get a response so we know who we're dealing with."

Pretty smart. "Anybody in there?"

"Down here! Help me!" a muffled voice cried. Johnny could swear he'd heard that voice a thousand times.

Thomas cocked an eyebrow.

"I'm not sure," Johnny said.

"Try again."

He did. This time he knew the voice. Knew it because he *had* heard it a thousand times. Stanley Yordon was back in town.

"It's . . . I'm pretty sure it's the preacher."

"Black?"

"No, Father Yordon. He must have come back last night."

Thomas twirled his gun. Caught it snug. He shot without aiming.

The gun boomed and bucked in his hand. Johnny flinched.

When he looked back, the Master lock was gone. It lay twisted and broken on the floor near the back door.

Thomas raised his foot and nudged the burnt door. It creaked inward.

Stanley Yordon bolted from the dark pit. His foot caught on a burnt two-by-four, and he sprawled across the floor with a loud grunt.

Yordon pushed himself up and attempted to brush himself off. Soot streaked the man's face. And his hand . . .

Yordon followed Johnny's stare to his right hand. A single splinter the size of a ball-point ink refill ran out from under his index fingernail.

The man's hand began to tremble and he grabbed it to hold it still. "Oh, dear God!"

Thomas reached out and placed a comforting arm on Yordon's shoulder. "Tell you what, Father." He took Yordon's hand in his own. "I'm going to have to"—before the trembling man knew what was happening, the cop yanked the stick—"pull this out."

Yordon stared at his hand in shock. Then he did a strange thing for someone as uptight and highbrow as he tried to make himself out to be. He rested his head on the cop's shoulder and began to cry in earnest. For a full minute he sobbed into the officer's uniform, and Thomas just patted his back, like a father comforting a baby. No soothing words, thank goodness. That would definitely be out of character.

As soon as Johnny had completed the thought, Thomas said, "That's it, Stanley, just let it all out."

He looked at Johnny and raised a brow.

Johnny shook his head. *No, Thomas, not cool.*

Yordon quieted. He backed away from Thomas, cleared his throat, and lifted his head. "Sorry." He straightened his shirt. "Sorry, I don't know what came over me."

"You want to tell us who threw you in the cellar?" Thomas asked.

"Claude," he answered. "Claude Bowers, his son, Peter, and Chris Ingles."

"They're the ones who gutted the theater," Johnny said.

"Okay. What say we go around this town and round up some crazies," Thomas said with a wink. "It's time to show them who's boss."

Johnny grinned. He was feeling like a kid again.

AFTER SENDING Stanley Yordon home to collect himself, Thomas demanded his partner—that would be Johnny—lead him to the Bowerses' residence.

Claude's door was open, but the top floor was empty. Thomas headed for the basement with Johnny cautiously behind. The cop descended the stairs in silence, peering around the corner. A grin nudged his lips. He stepped into the basement, withdrawing both guns. Legs spread, guns cocked, Thomas faced the dim light beyond.

Johnny eased down the steps and craned his neck around the corner for a view.

Claude, Chris, Peter, and seven or eight other crazies were packed into the stuffy basement. They slouched like strung-out vampires, heads propped up, eyes drooping or closed. If they noticed the cop in the doorway, they didn't show it.

"Rise and shine!" Thomas yelled. "Morning is here."

Like a turtle watching a passing seagull, Claude Bowers turned his head toward the sound. His glassy, bloodshot eyes were only half-open.

The thought processing slowly in that thick head must have registered the sum of the matter, because his eyelids snapped open and he sat up straight.

"Hi, Claude," Thomas said.

The big man's upper lip lifted in a snarl. The others rustled around him, like bats waking from their slumber.

Thomas leveled his revolver at Claude's head. Then he brought it back to his ear quickly, paused, and leveled it again. He repeated this twice. Why, Johnny had no idea.

"Get up, Claude. Drop the bottle and put your hands on your head." Thomas leveled his second gun. "The rest of you too. Hands on your heads."

Most rose slowly to their feet. Two remained slumped in their chairs.

Claude eyed the gun without moving. Johnny watched his chest rise and fall. The man's upper lip glistened with sweat and twitched periodically, as if his circuits might be shorting.

And he wasn't putting his hands on his head. On the contrary, Johnny thought he might throw himself at Thomas and beat him to a pulp. He was twice the cop's size.

Thomas motioned to the two crazies who hadn't responded. "Rise and shine. Up."

Chris kicked his boot into the men's sides. "Get up you lazy vomit bags." A faint smile crossed his lips as the two men groaned. He didn't seem bothered by Thomas's interruption at all. Too wasted to realize what was happening, maybe.

A grunt from the left signaled Claude's charge. He moved quickly for a man his size.

Thomas didn't move. He'd offered half of his back to the Swede by turning to the two men who now struggled to their feet. Johnny watched the scene unfold with a knot in his throat.

Claude thundered forward, a runaway train.

Thomas still didn't seem to notice.

At the last possible instant, just before Claude's lowered head reached Thomas's, the cop dropped to a crouch and threw one leg forward for balance. He lifted his shoulders as Claude's knees struck him, then stood and sent the Swede catapulting headlong over him.

Claude struck the wall like a battering ram. The Swede dropped on the carpet, unconscious. Maybe dead.

Thomas waved his gun at the others, still ignoring Claude. "The first man who lowers his hands gets a bullet in the knee. You all hear that? I want you to nod if you understand me. No need getting your knee blown off just because you're too wasted to hear me."

They all nodded except for the two who'd just stood. "You two understand? You drop your hands and I'll blow your kneecaps off. Nod if you understand."

They nodded.

"Okay, let's all take a little trip together."

Thomas reached down, withdrew a smaller pistol from his boot, and handed it to Johnny. "Stand at the top of the stairs. If any of these men makes a move on me, you pull that trigger. Can you do that?"

Johnny took the revolver carefully, feeling the cold stainless steel in his hands. He'd shot a gun plenty of times, but not like this. Did Thomas really expect him to kill someone? Samuel would never go for that.

"You mean kill them?"

"If you have to."

Samuel would never suggest he kill anyone. Which must mean that Thomas, although inspired and directed by Samuel, could work on his own as well. Did Samuel know this?

Johnny looked at Claude. "What about him?"

Claude's face was turned to one side and his lips were smashed up into his cheeks. Thomas knelt and raised one of Claude's eyelids. He slapped Claude's cheek. The man groaned and moved his arms and legs, then lay still.

"Wake up, Claude," Thomas said. "Get your lard-self off the ground."

The big Swede struggled to his knees, then stood unsteadily.

"Let's go. Up the stairs. Hands high."

Johnny scrambled up the stairwell.

The sun was out, the wind was down, and they were locking up the bad guys. It was going to be a good day.

One by one they plodded past the cop and climbed the stairs. It took five minutes to march them single file to the church, where Thomas ushered them into the kitchen. He and Johnny removed the knives and other sharp instruments from the drawers and backed to the door.

"Try not to kill each other in here. And get some sleep." Thomas locked the door.

"So you think that'll hold them?"

"It's a steel door, it'll hold them," Thomas said.

"Now what?"

"More. We need more."

CHAPTER TWENTY-NINE

THE MONASTERY

Sunday afternoon

SAMUEL SKIPPED down the hall, mouth spread in an open smile, taking in so much air with each breath that he thought he might choke on it. It had been a good day.

He had to tell Christine and Tyler, who were waiting in the library. Everything was going to be okay now. He had written Thomas into Paradise, and he was sure that Paradise held the key to break the power that now gripped the other students' minds. Billy didn't seem to know what to do about Thomas, and Marsuvees Black was evidently frightened off by the presence of a real cop. This had to mean that neither was wise to the fact that Thomas was fictional.

Samuel had shown his father the pages he wrote, and his father walked to the cupboard with a fresh excitement. He pulled out a tall flask, lifted it triumphantly into the air.

"A toast!"

"A bit premature, isn't it?" Andrew said.

"Every good thing is worthy of celebration," his father said, pouring the liquid into crystal glasses. He winked at Samuel.

It had been a good day indeed.

Samuel rounded the corner into the library, heard sudden cries of rage, and stopped.

Billy! Two thoughts collided: *I must help Billy! Thank goodness he's here.* And *Billy! Oh no, not Billy!*

The monastery's main library was appropriately named *The Field of Books.* Scores of bookcases were arranged in a natural setting, complete with a grassy lawn, trees, and flower gardens. High above, a domed ceiling allowed light to flood the lawn.

Samuel walked around the peripheral bookcases and saw seven or eight students by the tall oak tree arguing among themselves. He quickly scanned the library—Christine and Tyler weren't here.

Billy and Darcy yelled and waved accusing arms at a group of six children who stood with slumped shoulders. Only Billy's red hair and scratchy voice identified him clearly. Large red and blue blotches covered the boy's puffy face. His bare arms were lumpy with sores. The disease was so advanced!

Samuel was overcome by an urge to run down the hill and throw his arms around the boy. *Come back, Billy*, he would say. *It's okay, we love you, Billy.*

He leaned against the bookcase as grief swept over him. Tears slipped down his cheeks despite his best effort to hold them back.

He took a deep breath, sniffed, wiped his sleeve across his eyes, and pushed off the bookcase. Well, Thomas had cleaned up Paradise. Now Samuel would clean up Billy.

He was halfway to them when Billy saw him and stopped his arguing midsentence, right arm still outstretched toward one of the boys.

Don't run, Billy. Please don't run.

Billy did not run, maybe could not run. If the sores didn't hamper his movement, the shock at seeing Samuel must have, because he didn't even find the presence of mind to drop his arm.

The others faced Samuel, one by one. Their faces were as disfigured by boils as Billy's. They'd smeared that gel over their entire bodies, including hair and clothes. Darcy stood by Billy's side staring at Samuel, hands on hips.

He came within ten feet of the group and stopped. An odor that reminded him of sewer water wafted through the air, and he shortened his breathing to keep from blanching in front of them.

"Hey, Billy."

The redhead dropped his arm and narrowed his eyes but didn't respond.

"What are you doing here?" Darcy asked.

Samuel wondered if she had assumed leadership of the group. "I live here, remember, Darcy?" He paused. "You guys getting enough to eat?"

It sounded dumb really, pretending nutrition was a matter of concern considering their present condition. Asking whether they had taken a bath lately might be more appropriate. "We have plenty to eat in the cafeteria, you know."

"Shut up, Samuel!" Darcy snapped. "Billy won the debate, not you."

Billy just stood there, lost.

"How about you, Billy? Is there anything I can get for you?" Sure it sounded ridiculous, but he meant it. "Those sores look like they hurt. Maybe we should get you some medical help. I'm sure we have some medicine in the infirmary that would help."

"Shut up, Samuel!" Darcy said again. "Just shut up!"

Billy finally broke his stare and glanced at Darcy. "Yeah, shut up, Samuel."

Samuel nodded and felt pity rising in his throat again. "We miss you, Billy," he said. "I miss you. I wish you would just come back before anything really bad happens."

"Anything really bad?" Billy said. "And what's really bad, Samuel?"

"Lots of things. You don't look so good. The whole project is being threatened. Paradise is having some problems."

"Paradise is having some problems," Darcy mocked, wagging her head. "What do you know about Paradise anyway?"

He shouldn't have brought it up. "Then let's talk about you. You look like you're in a lot of pain."

"Who said anything about pain?" Billy asked. "We have everything we need, and if you were smart you would quit bugging us here and have a look yourself."

"What kind of salve is that, Billy?"

Darcy answered again. "None of your business. This is our worm paste, and it's none of your stinking business what it is, you understand? So quit bugging us!"

"Worm paste? Does it help the pain?"

"No, we're just wearing the stinking stuff 'cause we can't find our coats. Of course it does! So just quit bugging us." The eloquent, polished Darcy he once knew so well had regressed. She was speaking like a seven-year-old brat. But at least she was talking.

"It comes from worms?" Samuel asked.

"It comes from the worms," a young boy said to Samuel's left.

The boy's eyes were nearly swollen shut. Samuel didn't even recognize the student.

"What's your name?"

The boy glanced at Billy and answered. "Bob," he said.

Bob? This was Bob? "Do your sores hurt, Bob?"

"Yes."

"And the salve helps the pain?"

"Yes."

"Do you like the pain, Bob?"

"No."

"Shut up, Samuel," Darcy said.

"Did you have pain like this before you went into the tunnels, Bob?"

The boy didn't answer.

A single, soft sob broke the silence. Samuel spotted the thin girl behind Darcy.

"Shut up, Shannon," Darcy said, but her voice was less demanding.

The young girl tilted her face into her hands and started to cry softly.

Samuel glanced at Billy and saw the boy staring at Shannon with tender eyes. And then another child on Shannon's left began to cry.

Billy lowered his eyes and nudged the grass with his shoe. So, the boy's heart still pumped red blood and swelled with real emotions.

A gentle hand on his shoulder startled Samuel. He turned to find Christine and Tyler standing there, smiling. Samuel acknowledged them with a nod and faced Billy again.

Billy was horribly deformed, bleeding, and covered in a disgusting salve. But Samuel saw a lost, lonely orphan, confused and dejected, mortally wounded and desperately wanting love. Emotion swelled in his chest. He felt his legs moving under him, carrying him to his old friend. He knew it was crazy, but he couldn't stop himself. And to make matters worse, he began to cry.

He reached Billy, completely not caring about the smell and the sores and the salve, and he encircled the boy's body with his arms and held him gently.

Billy froze.

"I'm sorry, Billy," Samuel said. "I'm so sorry."

Christine and Tyler walked behind Billy and gently laid their hands on him. They stood in silence for several seconds.

And then the beautiful, awkward moment ended, and Samuel dropped his arms. Billy stood still for a moment, his head bowed. He nudged the grass with his toe again.

Then he turned and walked away. Darcy hurried to catch up. As a unit the others followed.

Samuel tried to wipe the tears from his eyes, but he couldn't because of the salve on his hands and arms.

"Boy, do they need a bath," Christine said, sniffing her hand.

"And now I suppose we do too," Samuel said. "As soon as possible. I think this stuff messes with the mind."

Samuel watched the students exit the library. A few short days ago they would have been laughing at someone's joke, or talking in urgent tones about a theory raised in class.

But they'd chosen Billy's path. A path to freedom, they claimed, to the discovery of their true selves—to the creator in all of them. Well, they had discovered something all right, but it resembled slavery more than freedom.

"How's Paradise?" Christine asked.

"Good," Samuel said with a sigh. "Paradise is good."

Chapter Thirty

PARADISE

Sunday night

BY THE end of the day Thomas had two dozen troublemakers in custody, including Steve Smither, who had evidently taken to putting the neighbors' pets out of their misery.

Thomas focused exclusively on those that Johnny considered dangerous. There was no way to round up the whole town, and no reason to do so. The plan was to eliminate Black's front guard before confronting him directly the next time he showed up. If there was a next time. If they were lucky, Thomas had already scared him off.

Good plan.

Only one, the owner of the feedlot, Burt Larson, put up any real fight. But Thomas put him on his back quicker than a heartbeat when the rabble-rouser went for a gun under the counter.

By nightfall they had all the instigators secured.

All but Marsuvees Black.

There was no sign of Black anywhere in Paradise. If any of the others had the slightest clue as to his whereabouts, they weren't saying. A search of the business district turned up nothing but empty buildings. Thomas inspected each of the ringleaders' homes and each time came away empty-handed. Marsuvees Black was simply nowhere to be found.

The only real challenge surfaced late that afternoon, after Thomas and Johnny returned to the church. Stanley Yordon, preacher-turned-jailer, met them at the top of the stairs.

"I'm not an expert on the law," he said, "but doesn't someone have to press charges for you to legally hold these prisoners?"

"Press charges? After what they've done, no."

"Well, actually, that could be a problem." Yordon led them into his office and turned around. "I can't seem to find anyone to press charges."

"Like I said, Reverend. No need."

Yordon continued as if he hadn't heard Thomas. "*I* could press charges, but I'm not sure I *should*. Most of the townsfolk are still behind Black." He shook his head. "God knows I'm not. But I have a certain responsibility to keep my people's confidence. I can't just turn against them. What would that do to their faith in me?"

"They kidnapped you," Johnny said. "They destroyed your church."

"They also paid for that church. And when this is over, I'll need their loyalty. I think you'll have to find someone else to press charges. And I hope you do, but I'm afraid I face a conflict of interest here."

"We don't need to press charges," Thomas said. "Is it just me, or am I repeating myself here?"

"All I'm saying is that I don't want to be associated with what you've done here. It wasn't my idea. I've only been doing what you've made me do. And I find it strange that there aren't more policemen here. I'd feel a lot better if there was a stronger law-enforcement presence to take the heat off me, if you catch my meaning."

Thomas pulled out a chair and sat down. "Fine, Stanley. With the phones out, I can't get help here tonight, but we'll bring the cavalry in at first light."

"What about your cruiser? Can't you call on your radio?"

The cop looked at Johnny. "No."

"Why can't you go for help?"

Thomas shifted in the seat. "You check the vehicles lately? Someone went to a lot of trouble putting everything with wheels out of commission. The distributor cap has been smashed on every car in town. Including yours, Stanley."

They'd discovered this universal damage several hours earlier. It had been Billy's doing—had to be. He could write one sentence in his book and the damage would be done. Samuel could fix them all just as easily, now that he knew about it, but Johnny didn't think he wanted to. That, just like bringing real cops into Paradise, could prove disastrous if Billy got smart to it.

"What about your car?" Yordon asked.

Thomas shook his head. "That won't work."

"So you'll spend the night?" Yordon asked.

"If you don't mind. I'd like to keep an eye on the prisoners."

"Sure," Yordon said, but Johnny could swear he detected a hint of reluctance in the man's voice.

Yordon lifted a hand to his lips and wiped the sweat gathered on his upper lip. "Where *is* your car?" he asked, training his eyes on the cop's face.

"I came on foot," the officer replied as though it were not only obvious but common in these parts.

"You say that as if you always walk around the mountains without wheels. What exactly brought you to Paradise?"

"I received a call," the cop said.

"How could you receive a call? The phones have been out for a while. Cell phones are even out."

The tone in Yordon's voice had just changed from inquisitive to demanding, and Johnny felt a bead of sweat pop from his forehead.

"My call didn't come over the phone, Stanley."

"Is that right? Don't tell me God told you to come."

Thomas just looked at the reverend. He was in a corner. Even if he wanted to lie, he would be hard-pressed for an explanation.

Yordon arched a brow. "Did God tell you it was two miles?" He drew the number two in the air.

"What does it matter?" Johnny asked. "He saved this town, didn't he?"

"No, Johnny, I want to hear this out. Sounds an awful lot like Black to me. What was that Black said? *God told me to bring grace and hope to Paradise?* Something like that if my memory serves me. You peddling grace and hope too?"

"You think Thomas is anything like Black? He's nothing like him."

"Doesn't it strike you as odd, Johnny, that our police officer here came into town on foot, just like Black, claims to hear from God, just like Black, even talks a bit like Black. And the only person we haven't rounded up today *is* Black. Don't you find that just a little strange?"

Johnny blinked. "What're you saying? That Thomas is Black?"

"Did I say that?" Yordon still didn't move his eyes, but now he wore a small grin. "Just stated the facts. You draw your own conclusion. Maybe we shouldn't be so hasty."

Was that possible? Actually, Johnny didn't have proof that Samuel had written Thomas into Paradise. What if something had happened to Samuel, and this was another scheme by Billy, like the story about the hallucinogenic sludge? Maybe he'd found out what was up and written Thomas himself.

"I'm not Black," Thomas said. "I'm the law. I'm the law come to set Paradise straight. Help her see the error of her ways. Consider these my commandments." He slipped one of his six-guns from the holster and spun the chamber. "And these bullets my precepts. And if these aren't enough, there's an awful lot more where they come from. Enough firepower to make your head spin clean off. I suggest you pay them some respect, Stanley."

Yordon stood and walked from the room, leaving Johnny and Thomas in the guest chairs without a host.

Thomas turned to Johnny and winked. "You okay?"

"I think so."

"Too obvious?"

"He's wrong, right?"

Thomas stared into his eyes for a long moment. "Believe, Johnny. Trust me, I am as un-Black as they come. Okay?"

"Okay."

"That's good." He sighed, then stood and ruffled Johnny's hair. "Come on, son. Let's get this place locked down for the evening. We have a big day ahead of us tomorrow."

STANLEY YORDON slept in his house, alone. More alone than he'd felt in a long time. He'd lost his stomach for the shepherding game for the time being. He had lost his flock and with it his power.

Now he had these voices about grace and hope—Black's grace and hope—droning relentlessly in his mind. To make matters worse, his sheep had been reduced to blithering idiots who didn't know how to blink much less think. There was nothing worse than a fixed stare, and this insipid bunch had perfected it.

When he finally drifted off, his head filled with the voices. *Time for church, Stan! Wake up, Stan the man. Suck up some grace-juice, Stan.*

Was he really hearing that?

Wake up! Wake, wake, wake!

Yordon's eyes sprang open. He jerked his head toward the door. Marsuvees Black stood tall, alive and in the flesh, not five feet from him.

"Am I your cowboy, Stan? I rather like that name. Endearing I think." Black's voice rasped as if he had a cold. He smelled musty—like a stale, damp dishrag.

Yordon scrambled off the bed. "How . . . how did you get in here?"

"You have a door, don't you, Stan? Everybody has a door. There's always a way in."

"But it was locked."

"Don't be a fool. Your door has never been locked."

"What are you talking about? I swear I locked it just last night."

"Stanley, Stanley. You're babbling about things that are meaningless. Powerless words. It is a bad habit with you. What does it matter how I came in? The fact is, I'm in."

Yordon felt the wall behind him. "So what do you want with me?"

Black wagged a finger. "Wrong question, Stan. I want nothing with a pitiful soul like you. I'm here because *I* can do something for *you*."

Yordon swallowed. Black's thin black hair snaked past his thick neck. He still wore that blasted hat. What did he have to hide up there, a hole? The wind howled past the window behind Yordon—a storm rode on the air again.

"What can you do for me?" he asked.

"I can give you what you want, that's what."

"What?"

"What, what, what? Power! You want power. I've got it. I want to give it to you."

"Power?"

"What's the matter? You can't speak more than one word at a time now?" Black raised his hand in the air and brought them together in a booming clap. "Power!"

Yordon jumped. "You take me for an idiot? Stop patronizing me."

"Now that's more like it," Black said. "Show some spine. You're going to need it."

"Why?"

"You've always wanted to have power over people, Stanley. It's why you went to seminary in the first place. You weren't about to be a lowly butcher like your father, now were you? No, the idea of a hundred or so lost sheep licking at your hands was far more appealing. And in a small town like Paradise even the pagans respect you, don't they?"

Black clasped his hands behind his back and spread his legs. "But we have a problem in Paradise, Yordon. A very bad problem. The people no longer like you. You are powerless. Let's face it, the only power a preacher really possesses over any flock is bound up with their minds."

Black walked to the desk. He picked up a picture of Yordon standing outside the church during his first week. A large sign that hung over the front doors read, *Welcome to Paradise, Father. We Love You.*

"And you know why they don't respect you. No? Then let's not waste time guessing—I'll tell you. They stopped respecting you the first year you were here, when you had your little fling with Sally Drake after she and Johnny came to town. You do remember that, don't you? You impregnated her, and then you forced her to put the boy up for adoption when she refused to terminate the pregnancy. Couldn't have a scandal in the town of Paradise, now could we?"

"How in the world do you know—"

"Shut up, Stan, I haven't finished. They would have forgiven you then; they always do. But your true indiscretion was sweeping the whole thing under the rug. You like secrets, Stan? You turned your back on your son, and on your lover, and on the commandments for which you stand, all to protect your little secret. And guess what? It worked. The town made it their secret. They pretended that you had the right to do what you did. Why? Because they are no better than you."

Yordon wasn't sure whether he was more terrified or outraged. It was that snake, Paula. Who else would make such a big deal out of something so small, so long ago?

"They played your game, Stanley, but they also lost their respect for you. Every time you stand up there and talk eloquently about the Word of God, half of this town is rolling their eyes and the other half is dead asleep. Not a single one of them believes a single word you have to say. Am I close?"

"How dare you accuse me!" Yordon's anger washed away his fear.

"I can give them back to you, Stanley," Black said, moving to the window. "I'll do one better than give them back to you. I'll make you the talk of the town. Their guardian angel. More power than you ever thought possible, right here over your own flock. When I'm through, they'll do anything for you. Anything."

The words ran into his mind like a hot steel rod.

He knew that, didn't he? And Stanley also knew that if Black could turn Claude into a blubbering fool, he could just as easily turn the man into an adoring fool.

"What about Sally? She's never stopped bad-mouthing me."

Black faced him. "I can make Sally suck your toes, my friend."

"What do I have to do?"

Black smiled thinly. "Give me Thomas."

Figured. One weirdo wanted the other. If Thomas really was the cop he professed, maybe he could prove it now. A confrontation between the lawman and the healer.

A burning sensation stung behind his ears, and Yordon wondered if the flames of hell had ignited there at the base of his brain. He stared at Black, knowing that with that stare he was saying yes.

"Why don't you just do it yourself? You seem to have the power."

"Much to my dismay, Thomas has more power over someone like me than he does over you. Amazing but true. That's half of it. The other half is that I want you to do it, my friend. I want to give you your power back."

"And what makes you think that I can give you Thomas?"

"He's here to protect you from me, not kill you. He's asleep at the moment. If he wakes up while you're in there doing your dastardly deed, I'll get his attention and make things easier for you, but you have to deal with him. Follow?"

"How do you know so much about our town? My affair with Sally was over a decade ago."

"Let's just say that I've been in a lot of people's minds lately. Think of it as one of my tricks."

Yordon didn't trust the man, but his risk was minimal. If Black didn't come through, he could just abort. As for the promise of returning his respect and power . . .

"Okay."

Black turned away. "You're a wise fool, Stanley. A very wise fool."

Chapter Thirty-one

THE MONASTERY

Sunday night

EVEN IN Billy's distorted mind, the wholesale transformation of the students in the library tunnel was surprising. The epidemic of boils had become a kind of accelerated leprosy. If not for the worm salve, most of the children would probably be incapacitated. As it was, when slabs of skin tore loose from scratching, they replaced it with the worm gel.

"Worm gel is better than skin anyway," Paul kept saying.

Paul wandered the halls, all six of them, coaxing or dragging worms to the large library. In a show of reluctant good faith, he agreed to haul one worm to Billy's study for every five he hauled to the larger library. Billy had forced his authority with the agreement and reminded Paul of its terms each time he came huffing and puffing into the study, a slug in tow.

Most of the children devoted themselves to writing without complaint. Any grievances invariably centered on either the itching skin disease or the lack of dry writing spots. The itching came with an easy solution: "Get off your lazy butt and get your own gel!" The same advice could be heard given at least a dozen times each hour in precisely those terms. Another dozen in other terms.

But the gel itself gave rise to the second complaint. The more gel the children slapped around, the more of it landed on their books, which wouldn't be such a problem if it didn't cause the pages to stick together and the ink to smear. With so many children writing in the library, the dry nooks and crannies soon became gooey nooks and crannies.

Both Billy and Darcy noticed that everyone seemed happier when they ingested greater volumes of the gel. Together with the help of Paul, they agreed on the dungeon's first law:

To write in the lower levels, one is required to ingest six helpings of gel each day. And by helpings we mean two hands, cupped together, full. And by each day we mean every twenty-four-hour period, just in case there's any confusion.

They called it their first rule of writing. All of the children agreed that it was a good rule. It made things smooth. It helped them write. It kept them out of trouble.

Billy made his way back from the meeting in the sixth tunnel by himself, leaving Darcy to work out some details with Paul. The memory of his little encounter with Samuel earlier today made him sick. The business with Paul's worms and the new rule of writing distracted him for a few hours, but now the thought of Samuel lodged in his mind like a stubborn tick.

He started to jog. His teeth clacked together with every footfall, like cymbals punctuating the pounding of his heart. His muscles burned, and for a brief moment he wondered if some creatures, like ants maybe, were chewing on them. Maybe the boils housed little animals that fed on the worm ointment and burrowed.

He veered to the nearest wall, swiped his hand along a trail of gel, and slapped the salve on his stinging arms.

The fact was, he could hardly even remember what had happened upstairs, but he knew this: that last thing Samuel had done—that touching thing—that ridiculous display of feeling, that wasn't good. Bogus. Bogus, bogus, bogus! And he had stood there like a cornstalk, like a rebuked child afraid to move. Only he hadn't been rebuked by Samuel. Only touched and held. Man, that was disgusting!

You wanna die, boy? A voice rose above the melee in his mind. *You wanna die?*

Yeah, I wanna die. What's it to ya?

The salve wasn't working so well just now. He grunted and attacked his left forearm with an open claw, wincing as a slab of skin stuck to his fingernails.

No, fool! You can't die yet.

No? What's it to ya?

There's a story to write, boy. A story about grace and hope in Paradise. You know about grace and hope, don't you?

The thought of writing awakened Billy's desire. He saw the study looming ahead in the darkness, glowing. Darcy must have forgotten to take her torch.

The outline of a dozen large worms pulsed in the shadows. He stumbled into the study.

The monk stood in the torchlight.

The monk. He'd almost forgotten about the monk and his black mask. This cloak-and-dagger routine no longer impressed Billy. What did the man care if anyone knew who he was?

Billy cleared his throat. "What are you doing here?"

"I've come to clarify a few things for you."

"Be my guest, clarify."

"I'll start with the book you're writing in. They're blank history books discovered by Thomas Hunter. You do remember Thomas Hunter and the Raison Strain."

"He saved the world. Who wouldn't know about him?"

"In these books the word becomes flesh. Literally. Whatever is written in them actually happens. It becomes fact. History, thus the books of history."

Billy nodded. "And?" He knew the man expected him to be stunned by this revelation, but he relished sounding informed. Besides, it hardly surprised him. *Good. I hope you're right.*

"Have you noticed that the characters seem to have a mind of their own?"

"'Course I have."

"You can't force them, but your influence over them is powerful. Your words are flesh in their minds. Thanks to you, the little town has been coming apart at the seams."

"Good. I've only started." The monk's revelation made everything clear. At least as clear as Billy's foggy mind would allow.

Billy could see the man's eyes glistening in the torchlight through the two slits cut in the ceramic mask.

"Do you know about Thomas?"

"You just told me."

"The other Thomas."

"The cop," Billy said. "Yes, I'm working on that problem."

"Do you know he's not a real cop?"

"What do you mean? Of course he's real."

"He's written by Samuel."

It was the first stunning thing the man had said in days.

"Samuel? He's . . . he's writing into Paradise?"

"He's been writing for four days. If the people weren't so predisposed to listen to you, they'd be walking around in robes of white."

"And Thomas, that stupid kung-fu cop—"

"—has changed the balance of power. Aside from Johnny, he's the only real enemy you have down there. You handled Johnny stupidly by showing him Black's true character in the beginning. Now he's a problem. I suggest you handle Thomas with more skill."

"I couldn't resist giving him a scare. And I've handled myself just fine since then, so have some respect." Billy paused, irritated. "I can kill him, right? I mean, I can kill Thomas. If he's not real, then Black won't get into any trouble if the real law shows up."

The monk didn't answer. He clasped his hands behind his back and paced. "Did the students in the library touch the mucus?"

"Touch it? They're covered in it."

"I mean Samuel and his friends, when they touched you in the upper library."

"Yes."

"Well then. It's worth a try."

"The salve will turn them?" Billy asked.

"Soften them."

Billy couldn't imagine Tyler or Christine or Samuel entering the tunnels, salve or no salve. "There's no way they'll agree."

"No? Do they have greater resolve than you?"

"Of course not. They're just slower."

"Well then, it's time you brought them up to speed."

"What about the story?"

"The story is the point. Christine, Tyler, and Samuel are writing into Paradise too. Remove their influence and you'll be free to write your heart's desire. Your writing is far more concentrated than the others', something I'm still trying to understand. They're writing what you've told them to write, but half of it is conflicting mush that does nothing to achieve our primary objective. Yours and Darcy's is more focused and to the point. It's better to eliminate the opposition above and focus your own writing than to devote time to the others down here."

"What about the cop?" Billy asked.

"Go after Samuel and his friends, then write. And when you write, you can be as obvious as you want. You've already let the thread about the gel die—that's good, there's no need to pretend that a little hallucinogenic gel caused the people to see things. Your writing has seduced them already. It's time to go for their throats." He paused.

"I have some specific statements that I want you to write into your book. I'm working on the wording now. We've just begun, my friend. What I have in mind for this world will blow your mind."

He walked to the gate.

"And what about you? Why won't you show me your face?"

The monk turned back. He stared at Billy for a long time, then he casually raised his hand and lifted the mask off his face.

Billy blinked. How was this possible?

"How did you . . ."

"I didn't, Billy. You did."

IN THE wake of the monk's visit, Billy applied himself to his task with a new urgency.

He and Darcy found Christine and Tyler less than an hour later, walking from the dining room. They probably visited the cafeteria three times a day, like they all used to.

"Let me do the talking," he mumbled to Darcy.

"Yeah."

Christine and Tyler stopped talking and slowed when they were still twenty yards off.

"Hey, Billy," Christine said. She was trying to sound natural, but Billy heard the tightness in her throat, as if she had just swallowed a mouse in that dining room of theirs.

"Hey."

The pair stopped ten feet away. "You okay?" Christine asked.

Am I okay? Well now, that's ridiculous. Do I look okay? Of course I'm okay. Of course not.

"I beat you handily in the debate. Did I strike you as not being okay?"

She nodded. "Yes, you did. It was good to see you earlier."

Oh, quit the mushy stuff, like you're the one to be big here.

"Where's Samuel?"

"He's sleeping."

Honestly, Billy was more relieved than disappointed. "We have a problem," he said. "Down below."

Christine tilted her head in interest and waited for him to continue. He shifted on his feet, wishing he were in his study writing instead of up here playing tiddlywinks with Christine.

"We've had, umm . . . an accident. Shannon's sick and can't get out."

He held his breath for a moment and then forced himself to breathe, trying to think how a person would really act in his supposed predicament. Problem was, he didn't really care if Shannon or David or anybody was really sick, and he was having difficulty remembering how it felt to care.

"Shannon is sick? In the forbidden levels?" A spark of concern lit Christine's eyes.

"In the lower levels. They're no longer forbidden, thanks to you."

Christine didn't bat an eye. "Take her to the infirmary, Billy. It's still open."

"That's just it. We're all kind of weak." Christine would never buy this stupid little story. Even now she was probably on the verge of throwing her head back in laughter.

"You're all sick?" If she doubted his story, her face didn't betray her.

"No. We just have a lot to do down there and we don't get much sleep."

Since when did being tired preclude someone from taking a sick friend to the infirmary? He tried to strengthen his reasoning.

"We do things that take a lot of energy, so we could sleep for days, but we never do because there's just too much to do." He fidgeted with his fingers. "I mean, in a matter of speaking. Kind of like being tired only it feels like you're sick a little."

Billy was quite sure he'd just blown the whole thing, mumbling like a fool.

"Okay, take us to the entrance. But bring Shannon out to us there," Christine said.

Tyler stared at her. "We can't go down there!"

"We're not going *in*. We're just showing a little decency here."

"But it's forbidden! No one ever said we can't go down there unless Shannon is sick and needs a lift. They just said don't go down."

"Technically it's not forbidden, although I get your point, it is for us. But Shannon has never been sick down there, has she? How would you like to be Shannon?"

"I don't see why three or four of them can't carry her to the infirmary. She can't weigh more than seventy-five pounds. They climbed up the stairs to get here, didn't they? They can't be that weak."

"They *are* going to carry her, Tyler. To the entrance. Right, Billy? We'll just help her from there. I don't see how that really violates the spirit of any rule."

Billy watched the whole exchange with fascination. Students in the process of justifying.

"How bad is she?" Tyler asked.

It took a second for Billy to realize the question was directed to him. "Shannon? Yes, well . . . not really. She's okay but not for long. In fact she could die at any time. You never really know with sickness."

"Okay, let's go then," Christine said.

Billy did not move. A small voice objected somewhere inside of him. That was too easy, it said. He blinked and realized they were waiting for him. He trudged toward the staircase at the end of the hall.

It took them five minutes to get to the main floor. Both Tyler and Christine followed diligently. One more flight of stairs into the dungeon. From here the steps were stone, and they absorbed the sound of Billy's steps as he plodded down them.

Then they approached the charred black doors, closed like two tombstones, wavering in the torch's shadows. Billy remembered how his heart had pounded when he first saw the doors. Did Christine feel that now? If the doors didn't get to her, one look inside and she would fold. They all did.

He walked to the center of the room and turned around. Christine and Tyler entered with bulging eyes and parted lips, and if he wasn't mistaken, their apparent wavering resulted from weak knees, not the shifting flames.

He had his answer.

Billy glanced at Darcy, walked to the doors, and shoved them open inward. Darcy walked in ahead of him and he followed without looking back. No matter, he would see them soon enough.

The doors closed behind him, and he forgot about Christine and Tyler in favor of the writing ahead of him, down that hall to the right, where Paradise and Thomas and Claude and Steve waited.

"Come on," he said to Darcy, and together they jogged into the mountain.

Chapter Thirty-two

PARADISE

Monday

FOR THE second day in a row, Johnny awoke with a start and bolted up in bed. For the second day in a row, he knew something had changed, but he couldn't place it.

Then he remembered Thomas.

It was barely light. He scrambled out of bed and shuffled through his drawers for a new shirt. Found one with a faded red Indy car and pulled it out. He started to shut the drawer, then remembered his socks and bent for the first pair his hand felt.

His mother's words rang in his head: *Every morning, Johnny, you hear? That doesn't mean every other morning or every week—you change your socks and underwear every morning!*

Behind him, the glass clattered and his mind posed a simple question. *Why is the glass rattling, Johnny?*

Because of the wind, of course.

Wind?

Johnny spun to the window. The wooden sill framed a nearly leafless forest, bowing to the east, backlit by a dark, overcast sky.

Did Thomas know? He had to get to the church! Unless Black stood in the street between his house and the church with his head raised to the sky, laughing. Johnny shuddered and yanked the shirt over his head.

He tore down the hall and shoved his head into his mother's bedroom. Empty.

Johnny ran through the living room and threw open the front door. The street was also empty. Wind blew in angry gusts, whipping sand around the buildings and batting at the few leaves that clung stubbornly to spindly branches. Above Paradise, the sky lay flat and black, a lid clamped over the valley. Worse than he'd seen it.

Johnny swallowed his dread and ran for the church, shielding his eyes from the wind with his hand.

An obscure thought floated lazily through his mind—a memory of walking along the beach in Florida, feeling the sand squish between his toes and giving way when he pushed hard. He realized he'd forgotten to put the socks on.

Johnny reached the railing, climbed the steps as fast as he could, ignoring a pain in his right leg. He pushed the doors open and stepped into the church, breathing hard.

He ran through the sanctuary toward the stairs that led into the basement. Still no sign of anybody.

The stairway descended into darkness, and he wondered briefly if the town was still asleep. It couldn't be much past eight, and the way folks slept around here . . .

But the cop would be awake. As far as he knew, fictional characters didn't even sleep. Unless Samuel slept . . .

Maybe Thomas was down in the basement making coffee, waiting for him—for Johnny, his partner—to show up so they could go flush out Black and hang him.

Johnny crept down the stairs, scarcely making a sound. He landed safely on the basement floor and poked his head around the corner.

The room looked like a black cavern. He let his eyes adjust to darkness. Slowly, familiar forms took shape: the support posts rising to the ceiling every ten feet, a Nerf basketball hoop mounted on the far wall, the white door leading to Paula's office.

The kitchen door stood in the shadows across the room. Johnny imagined a dozen pairs of eyes glowing behind the door like trapped owls. He focused on a faint white smudge that appeared in the middle of the door. It looked like someone had hung a plate there. Maybe Thomas, so that if it moved it would bang. Smart. But it wasn't really hanging, was it? No, it was sitting. On a counter.

And then Johnny knew he wasn't looking at the kitchen door at all. He was staring *into* the kitchen itself, through a wide-open door, at the far counter where a plate leaned against the wall.

The kitchen was empty!

He spun, half-expecting to see Claude on the stairs, glaring down at him. But the stairs were empty too.

He tore up the steps, terrified.

He wanted to scream out. To shout out the cop's name. "Thomas! Thomas, they're gone! Thomaaaaass!" But Thomas was gone too. Maybe being chased by crazies; maybe chasing crazies.

Or maybe he'd already moved them. Maybe other cops had come with a paddy wagon and taken them all to Junction.

Johnny made the snap decision to run out the back, just in case they were waiting for him in the street. He tore past Father Yordon's open office and struck out for the door, gulping at the air like he had just thrust his head through the waves after being submerged for a full minute.

The door pulled open in his hand, and the black sky filled its frame. Johnny leapt through and found himself face to face with a scene that made the image of Black walking into town seem toasty warm by comparison.

The church's back lawn ran seventy-five feet before meeting the forest. Wooden picnic tables sat along the fence, leaving most of the lawn open for children to play. A large oak tree spread its thick arms over a jungle gym to Johnny's right. The congregation had a running debate over the tree. Half wanted to lop the encroaching oak to the ground so they wouldn't have to constantly repair the damage inflicted to the roof; half wanted to preserve the oak for its shade and beauty.

But none of that mattered right now. Right now Johnny's eyes fell on the crazies who stood on the grass where the children normally played.

They stood like a mob of looters caught red-handed, thirty or forty of them, with their hands hanging by their sides.

A dozen miniature sunflower windmills mounted to the fence posts spun madly in the wind. The door behind Johnny slammed shut, but he barely heard it. He stood frozen on the small porch, his arms and feet spread in a defensive crouch.

Claude Bowers and his little gang stood atop the picnic tables. They might have been gathered for a class photo, all wielding hammers and axes and other heavy objects.

A larger group bunched closer to the building. Johnny recognized Katie Bowers, her long strawberry hair flying back from her head. Nancy stood on the edge like a big piggy bank. No one spoke. Only a few even turned their heads toward Johnny. The rest stared past him to his right, where the huge oak reached for the sky.

All of this he saw in a second.

Then Johnny followed their eyes.

Thomas's body hung from a hemp rope wrapped crudely around his neck and tossed over a wide branch above the jungle gym. The body jerked spastically, as though it had dropped just moments before.

The body had been stripped naked except for a white T-shirt, white boxer briefs, and white socks. They'd cut him up with a machete or maybe an ax. His lower lip sagged, swollen to three times its natural size. His eyes were gone, leaving round red sockets staring into the wind.

They'd tied his hands behind his back and hog-tied them to his ankles, so he appeared to be kneeling in the air.

Johnny's chest froze up. His only movement came from his knees—they shook violently.

Steve Smither stood below the spinning body, looking up at Thomas like a third grader beaming at his first-place science project. His hands were bloody.

They were all killers here, but Steve had wrapped the rope around the neck and yanked. And Black had been there breathing in his ear the whole time.

Johnny's heart and lungs still weren't working right, but he turned around and clambered for the door. By some miracle it swung in and he lurched forward. His head felt like a sounding gong, mounted on his shoulders, vibrating. A taunting voice warbled back there somewhere.

Wanna trip like I do? Wanna trip? Wanna wanna trip?

From deep in his gut, fury rose into his chest. He stumbled down the hall and then began to run. By the time Johnny reached the front doors, he was sprinting. A thousand voices were screaming in his head, but he couldn't make them out anymore. He crashed through the doors and tumbled down the concrete steps.

The first sob broke from his throat there, while he was sprawled on the sidewalk at the foot of the church.

Then Johnny Drake leapt to his feet and fled Paradise.

Chapter Thirty-three

THE MONASTERY

Monday

SAMUEL'S PLAN had failed.

Johnny had no clue how the offenders got out of the locked kitchen, or how they managed to overpower Thomas, but they had. That was all that mattered.

Johnny tore up the mountain, cutting his bare feet and scraping his knuckles. He'd believed. At least yesterday he'd believed. Today he wasn't sure about much except that he didn't have too many alternatives left. Even if he could find a way to Delta, he couldn't risk bringing more people into Billy's line of sight. And he couldn't try to outwit Black's next move. After Johnny's performance at the meeting Saturday night, he probably *was* Black's next move.

Fleeing to the monastery was his only choice. Samuel would be there, waiting for him. Maybe he could get his hands on one of those books. Maybe he could give himself some powers.

Johnny reached the large canyon quickly. He raced around the boulder and faced the cliff where the monastery hid.

"Samuel!"

His voice echoed, then drifted off.

"Samuel!"

Nothing. Johnny called the name repeatedly for the next ten minutes without a response. He took a few more minutes to gather himself. Then he walked to the outer door, twisted the rusted handle, and pushed the door open.

The monastery reached for the cliff top. Anything powerful enough to put this huge, ancient monastery here surely had the power to kill Black.

"Samuel?"

He couldn't just stand here forever. For all he knew, Samuel had gone into the tunnels himself. Or been killed.

The awful possibilities mushroomed in his mind. Why else wasn't Samuel coming out? Thomas had been killed because something terrible happened to Samuel. Billy had done something.

Believe, Johnny. Believe.

He strode to the front doors, turned the handle, and walked right in. The massive foyer was empty except for the paintings and doors and table. His heart echoed in his ears.

"And what about the basement?"

Samuel had hesitated. "Off the main hall to the left. A long series of stairs take you down. Not a place anyone in their right mind would want to go."

Johnny located the main hall before he could tell himself any different. The hall was wide, carved from stone and paved with bricks. Indirect sunlight filtered from high above.

Off the main hall to the left.

"Hello?"

Johnny jumped back. A boy stood by a door down the hall, looking at him. His skin was bleeding, and he'd smeared some kind of ointment all over his body. He looked worse than the crazies in Paradise.

"Hello?" the boy said again. "Who are you?"

"Johnny."

"Have you seen Paul?"

"No."

The boy looked back the way he'd come. "One of the worms died."

Johnny knew he was looking at one of the students who'd entered the lower tunnels. The worm salve had done this to him.

"Have you seen Samuel?" Johnny asked.

"No. I think he's with Billy. Do you know where Paul is?"

"I haven't seen him." The boy wasn't lucid. "How do I find Billy?"

"He's in the first tunnel. The one on the right."

Then the boy walked by him, headed off to find Paul.

The boy hadn't tried to kill him. That was promising. Johnny ran for the door and stepped into the darkness beyond.

Now what? He couldn't go down without light. He was about to turn back to search for a light of some kind, when it struck him that the darkness seemed to thin farther down. Maybe just because his eyes were adjusting to the dark.

He put a hand on the rough wall and descended several steps. Then several more. The stairway curved to his left. And, yes, a yellow light filtered up from below.

Johnny went down on his tiptoes. The light came from a torch in a small room outside a large black door.

The door to hell.

He stared at the door and realized that he was making a terrible mistake. Running from Claude on familiar territory was one thing. Knocking down the gates of hell to take on Black was another. He glanced back at the stairs.

If it was true—if Samuel was with Billy—then as far as Johnny knew, he might be the only thing standing between Billy and Paradise. He wasn't at all confident that anything he wrote in a book would happen. He wasn't even sure he could find a book. Or survive Billy. Or survive Samuel, if he'd been lured down.

Johnny's hands trembled, but he forced them to grip the torch, pull it free, and push on the black door. It swung open.

He stepped into an inner room that smelled like a sewer. The walls glistened with a thin coating of the worm gel. The room branched into several tunnels. Johnny veered into the one on his far right.

He stared down the long dark passage. Thick pipes ran along . . .

One of the pipes began to move. He stood rooted in place for a long minute, breathing hard. Worms!

But he couldn't go back. Not now.

"Samuel!"

His voice echoed down the hall.

"Samuel! It's Johnny."

There was water dripping somewhere. His head felt odd—dizzy. A bit numbed.

"Billy!"

No one responded. He took a few steps and stopped again. The slugs throbbed in his torchlight. What was he thinking? He should find Samuel's father first.

"Come on back," a faint voice called.

Billy? It didn't sound like Samuel.

Johnny hesitated, then switched the torch to his left hand, gave the worm a wide berth, and walked down the hall.

He saw light and headed for it, jogging now.

On the right, a gate dawned. Past the gate, a room with a desk and some bookcases. In the room a boy with red hair sat at the desk. Next to the boy sat a girl. Both had pens in their hands. Both were covered with sores and bleeding skin.

Both stared at him absently.

"Well?" the boy asked. No threats. Not yet.

Johnny stepped into the room, barely breathing even though his lungs strained.

"You're Billy?"

"Yeah."

Just that. Just *yeah*. Now what?

"Is . . . is Samuel here?"

"No."

"You're destroying Paradise," Johnny said. "Do you know that?"

The girl next to him answered. "Take a hike, Johnny."

They were just kids—Samuel had told him that—but somehow he'd half-expected monsters. They looked more lost than mean.

"Who are you?" he asked the girl.

"That's Darcy," Billy said. "And like she said, take a hike."

The books they were writing in looked old, fragile. He could see the outline of Billy's writing. Hard to believe it had done so much damage. But he knew a few things about this writing. That it could be resisted, for example. He'd done it a hundred times in the last few days. And whatever smell was trying to make his head spin down here could probably be resisted as well. Johnny set his jaw.

Billy laid his pen down. A grin tugged at his lips. "So tell me, Johnny? How does it feel to be the lone holdout? We'll get you soon enough. You can't hold out forever. Samuel can only do so much. He's put all his eggs into one little fool, and if I'm not mistaken, the little fool has just wandered into the forbidden dungeons. Have you tried our slime yet? Tastes pretty good."

"It's not too late to stop," Johnny said. "You just killed someone. Do you know what they do to murderers?"

"Steve killed him," Billy said. "Not me. And obviously you're a little short on the uptake. Thomas was no more a real person than Black is."

Black?

"What do you mean, Black? He's a teacher from the monastery."

"Sure he is. The one up here is anyway. The monk told me to write a character named Marsuvees Black who would have a little fun with Paradise, so I did. I wrote him just like the real Marsuvees Black. But the real Marsuvees Black is still here. I saw him yesterday. He never left the mountain."

"You're saying that the man I saw walk into town is just like Thomas?"

"Well, not just like Thomas. Personally I think he's way more interesting."

"Thomas was a bore," Darcy said.

"You see?" Billy said. "I was the first one to write a character into Paradise, and unless I'm mistaken, he's kicked some major Thomas butt."

"Forgive me, boys, but this is boring me to tears," Darcy said. "Johnny, please, please, please take a hike. You can talk till you're blue in the face. While you're at it, give us a hug or something. Show a little love. Samuel tried that. It won't work. We're busy, and you rudely interrupted. Now, take a hike."

Their minds were scrambled. Duped. Doped. No different from the people in Paradise. Deceived to the core.

He looked at the shelves packed with black leather-bound books. An idea dropped into his mind.

"Maybe you're right," he said, edging up to the desk. They looked up at him in a stupor. Several pens lay beside Darcy.

"If I joined you now, would you let me share this office with you?"

"Who said anything about joining us?" Darcy said.

"I just did. What would I have to do?"

"Eat the worm gel," Billy said. "But nobody except me and Darcy write in here."

"When this story of Paradise is over, what will you do?" he said, putting his torch in the receptacle by the boar head.

"Over?" They clearly hadn't thought that far.

"Will you go after another town? Where will it end?" Johnny moved closer to the desk. If he reached out his hand, he could touch it.

"Who says it ever ends?"

"Well, maybe I just have a point that you should listen to," Johnny said. He pointed at the gate. "When you see that gate, what does it make you think of?"

They both turned and looked.

Johnny picked up one of the pens, reached over to Darcy's book, and wrote as fast as he could, speaking to cover the scratch of the pen on paper.

"If you look hard enough, you can see someone's face, can't you?"

Johnny was given great powers to destroy Billy . . .

He scratched out *Billy.*

. . . anyone who stood in the way of truth.

"What are you doing?" Darcy shrieked, jumping up. She slapped his hand. The pen drew a long scratch on the page and flew across the room. "He tricked us! He wrote in my book!"

Billy was on his feet, eyes round. "What did he write?"

She read aloud. "*Johnny was given great powers to destroy anyone who stood in the way of truth.* He wrote your name but scratched it out."

Johnny clenched his eyes and tried to think things that might bring out a great power. But his mind was blank.

"Give me that!" Billy said. He grabbed a pen and scrawled words below what Johnny had written.

"There. *Billy was given great powers like Johnny, only to destroy whoever he wants.*"

Darcy pulled the book away and spoke as she wrote. "*And so was Darcy.*"

She slammed the pen down. "You thought we were so stupid? Go ahead, destroy us with your great power."

But Johnny had no great power.

"The books don't work like that, you idiot," Billy said, face flushed. "I'll give you exactly one minute to get out of here, or I'm going to make every last one of the students switch to write one character and one character only. Three guesses who that might be."

"You can't turn me that—"

"Not you. Sally."

"My . . . my mom?"

Billy nodded, grinning now. "She'll join the cop before nightfall, I can promise you that. The clock's ticking, boy. Forty-five seconds."

"You can't do that!" Johnny felt smothered. "She has nothing to do with this!"

"She has everything to do with this. Forty."

"I'd start running," Darcy said. "Save Mama."

"Thirty-five."

Johnny grabbed his torch and bolted. "Leave her out of this. Promise me—"

"Thirty. It's a long climb up those stairs, boy."

JOHNNY RAN. Down the tunnel, through the black door. He took the stairs two at a time, challenged by a spinning head. Into the hall. He made it, he was sure he'd made it.

But knowing Billy . . . How would the boy *know* he'd made it?

"Johnny?"

Johnny spun. Samuel stood by the entrance to the atrium, staring at him.

Johnny hurried away from the door, past Samuel, into the light. He was trembling, a jumbled ball of confusion.

"You've . . . you've been down there!" Samuel said. "You have to wash that smell before—"

"Marsuvees Black is Billy's character," Johnny said.

Samuel blinked. "Black? He's not the real one?"

"As real or not real as Thomas."

"You're sure? How—"

"I was down there, Samuel." Johnny wasn't sure why, but he was yelling. Not that he didn't like Samuel. On the contrary, he was desperate for Samuel to save them.

"I saw Billy. He told me that the teacher you know is the one who convinced Billy to write Black into Paradise."

"Then Marsuvees is still in the dungeons! The real one. And it means that Billy knows he can bring characters to life. He must have known about Thomas!"

"And what's to keep Billy from writing a hundred Blacks into Paradise?"

Samuel recovered from his shock and glanced around the atrium. For a moment Johnny thought the boy might burst into tears.

Samuel ran to Johnny and threw his arms around him. "I'm so sorry, Johnny! I was with my father after we found out what happened to Thomas. Then I knew you were coming, but I couldn't make sense of . . . The lower levels must have cut me off. And you're right, Paradise is in terrible trouble. It's hopeless!"

Johnny felt awkward standing there with Samuel's arms around him. Samuel's surreal blend of innocence and intelligence unnerved him.

"What are you going to do?"

Samuel pulled back. He was trying to be brave, but he couldn't hide a frantic light in his eyes.

"I don't know. I think my father is terrified. It's not only the dungeons, it's the town. This was never supposed to happen!"

"You don't have any ideas?"

"It's falling apart. It's all unraveling. I'm the only one left; the rest of the students are below. The overseers . . ." Samuel lowered his head into his hands.

"Have you thought about using the books to give yourself power?"

"I have the books. What more power do I need? It's hopeless!"

"No, I mean give *yourself* the power to deal with Black. You're the person who believes. You could move mountains, couldn't you?"

Samuel looked at him.

"Then you could go down yourself," Johnny said. "With that power."

"Down where?"

"To Paradise."

SAMUEL RAN all the way to the top floor. He'd washed Johnny off at the well and then sent him back to Paradise to scope things out in hiding. His father was meeting with desperate teachers. He would join them, but not until he was sure.

Ever since Thomas's death, which had awakened him at four in the morning, he'd racked his brain to understand his failure and the remaining alternatives. He'd pieced most of it together, but Johnny had given him the key.

Samuel slipped into his father's study and crossed to the desk. Behind it stood a bookshelf. On the top shelf, David had placed the original Book of History that Christopher and Samuel had written in.

He stood on his father's chair and pulled the black volume down. Set it on the desk. Opened the cover. His father kept a sheaf of loose-leaf paper in the front. It was a journal of sorts, documenting his experience with the book.

He turned to the book's first page. An entry about Thomas Hunter stared up at him. Next page.

Christopher's childish handwriting. Several entries. One about a desk and one about a cat and a dozen others that looked like experimental entries testing the book's limitations.

Next page. The entry about the books going into hiding.

Another page. Here. Two entries in his own, though much younger, handwriting.

The first entry limited the books to the residents of the monastery and clarified the way the books must lead to love. . . . *which is written by any person not currently residing in the monastery at this time, and/or which does not lead to the discovery of love will be powerless. This rule is irrevocable.*

The second entry. He read it quickly.

Samuel settled into his father's chair. He reread the entry. Again. And he knew he'd found the key.

Samuel returned the volume to its place on the upper shelf. He set the chair as he'd found it and left the office.

He could hear Raul's voice at the conference-room door when he laid his hand on the doorknob. He paused and listened, calming his nerves.

"You have to call the authorities, David. The project has failed! Samuel could write ten Thomases into Paradise without a guarantee that Black wouldn't string up every single one of them. It's over!"

"We're beyond the authorities," his father said. "How do you suppose they'll deal with Marsuvees Black? He's beyond the reach of ordinary mortals!"

"Then what?"

"We have to trust the books."

"There's no one left to write in the books! The rest of the children have fallen."

"There is *Samuel* to write in the books!" his father's voice boomed. They were desperate—all of them. Even his father. Especially his father.

Samuel pushed the door open and stepped into the room. Seven of the overseers were gathered around his father. All turned to look at him when the door opened.

He shut the door and faced them. "Marsuvees Black is in the dungeons," he said.

"He's left Paradise?" Andrew asked.

"He never left the monastery. At least not for long. The one in Paradise is Billy's creation, inspired by the real Marsuvees Black."

Raul struck the table with his fist. "I knew it! Billy would never have gone below without being lured down by that monster!"

"You're sure about this, Samuel?" his father asked.

"I'm sure."

"Then we have to stop him!" Raul said. "That could be the key!"

"It's the students who are writing, not Marsuvees," David said. "I'm not sure stopping him a week ago would have helped. Billy made his own choice. He's the one who holds the power."

Raul stood and paced behind his chair. "What was the man thinking? What does he stand to gain by doing this?"

"That should be obvious," Andrew answered. "He found David's journal and learned about the history books' power. God only knows how long he walked these halls with that knowledge before deciding to use the books.

But to do so he needed the children. I argued six months ago that he should be replaced. As I recall, Raul, you stood with David in suggesting that the students were old enough to consider a few alternative ways of thinking."

"Marsuvees never suggested open rebellion!" Raul said. "The children had to start drawing lines for themselves—better here than out there!" He threw his hand toward the window.

"Enough," David said. "This gets us nowhere. We'll deal with Marsuvees later. The students are our concern now. And Paradise."

"But knowing that Marsuvees has been complicit may help us to determine their objective," Raul said. "Where does Billy hope to take this story of his?"

Andrew shook his head slowly. "Can you imagine the power someone like Marsuvees Black would have if he could control the books?"

"You can't control the books," Raul said. "It's the children you have to control. Where's Billy taking this story?"

"I don't think Billy knows," Samuel said, moving to his father's end of the table. "Marsuvees may, but Billy and the others are writing for the thrill of it. If you had any idea how it feels . . ." He looked at them, wondering if they could understand. "The power to do what you want is nearly irresistible," he said. "Pure free will, with the power to back it up. It's like a drug."

Several of them nodded.

"Then you're saying that Billy writes just because he can," Andrew said. "Literally. He has no ambition except to write until the desire for it begins to burn him. If that's the case, his passions will be insatiable. He'll go from destroying things to killing things. People. And when he's done with Paradise, he'll move on. To what town? Or what country? We must stop him!"

Mark Anthony spoke. "As I see it, there is no way to stop him."

No one argued this time, not even David.

"I have a plan."

They all looked at Samuel.

"We have to get to Billy, or you're right, he won't stop. The key to Paradise is Billy. Are we agreed to that?"

"Go on," David said.

"The key to Paradise is Billy, but the key to Billy is Paradise. Or more precisely, the key to Billy is defeating him in Paradise. The only way to change Billy may be from within the story itself. That's why I sent Thomas, but

Thomas failed because his power was limited to skills given to him by me. You're right, for every character that I write into Paradise, Billy can just write another character with the power to outwit or overpower my character."

They watched him.

"But what if I could write another kind of character who has more power than any character Billy can ever write?"

"What do you mean?" Raul said. "You already tried that with Thomas."

Samuel placed his hands on the back of a chair. "Thomas was fictional. A fictional character is once removed. I doubt he can act or feel on his own. But I think I can write a character who has the power to love and to affect love."

"What kind of character?" his father asked.

"Me," Samuel said. "I can write myself into Paradise, and I can give myself a power that not even Billy can overcome."

They stared at him.

David stood. "You?"

Samuel exchanged a long look with his father. "A character based completely on me. A character that is a perfect representation of me in every way."

"I still don't see how that is so different from Thomas," Andrew said.

"Samuel will be a character that will do exactly what I would do, equipped with my feelings because I know myself and am myself," Samuel said. "But he will also be more than me, because I'll give him a special power to blow Black back into the hole he came from." He paused. "A superhero."

"Do we know what happens if such a character is hurt?"

"What do you mean?"

"Could it backfire?" Andrew clarified. "If Marsuvees Black were killed in Paradise, would the real Marsuvees die here?"

Samuel hadn't thought about that. It didn't matter. He looked at his father, who was now staring at him with round eyes.

"We must trust the books, Father. You said it yourself. This story *will* lead to the discovery of love. If I can't affect Paradise this way . . . I'm not sure there *is* another way."

"You realize you're the last student with the power to write love," Raul said. "It is critical that nothing happen to you."

Nausea stirred Samuel's stomach.

"Nothing will."

Chapter Thirty-four

PARADISE

Monday

JOHNNY REVIEWED the simple plan he and Samuel hatched before he left the monastery. Johnny would go to Paradise, take complete stock of the situation, and wait for the Samuel that Samuel would write behind the old theater.

Showdown at noon.

That was it. Johnny wanted more, but Samuel couldn't or didn't want to give him more. Johnny also wanted to wait for Samuel so they could go down together, but as Samuel pointed out, someone needed to make sure that Sally's life wasn't in danger.

Johnny would be the eyes on the ground. Again.

He reached the overlook and pulled up, panting. The sky was dark, very dark. Black was definitely back.

He looked down into Paradise. The first thing he saw was the smoke, boiling to the sky. Not at an angle, whipped by wind, but straight up. That meant no wind. But this wasn't necessarily a good thing. It was more likely a condition that Billy needed to move his story forward.

His eyes followed the smoke down to a huge ring of fire on the ground, twice as wide as Main Street. It took Johnny a second to make out people through the cloud of smoke, but they were present, maybe half the town, standing around in no particular pattern, watching the fire.

Johnny dropped to one knee to give his right leg a rest. He didn't know what they were doing but one thing was clear—Billy's story was changing. Today was a day of firsts. First time for no wind while Black was in town, assuming Black still was in town. First time any of them had gathered outside around a ring of fire. First time they'd killed a man.

Johnny looked past the smoke toward the church. He could see the oak behind. No body. They'd taken the cop down.

A figure ran toward the fire. Too hard to see who. Johnny watched him cross the line of flame, take something from . . .

He saw the black-clad man in the middle of the ring for the first time. Marsuvees Black.

He handed a blazing torch to the runner, who then sprinted to the south. Toward the old theater. Smoke rose from the building twenty seconds later. They were torching the town?

Johnny stood to his feet. Was Samuel catching this?

The old Starlight Theater began to burn quickly. Flames licked at the roof and spread down the east wall. Johnny watched in wonder as the wood blazed with orange flames that rose three times the height of the building.

This was it. They were reducing Paradise to ashes. What was he supposed to do now? He couldn't just go down there and throw water on the fire.

Something on the theater's roof caught his eyes. It was something wrapped up, strapped to the top. Something the size of a body. Something like Thomas.

This was their funeral pyre!

Marsuvees Black was burning the cop's body and doing it with enough overkill to permanently impress the town. *Mess with me and I'll burn you bad. Real bad. Real, real bad.*

In that case, they probably wouldn't burn the rest of the town. Indiscriminate burning would be too simpleminded for Billy. Then again, in his doped-up state, simpleminded might be just his ticket.

Johnny thought about turning around and running back up the mountain, but the only way he could really help Samuel was to stay here and take stock, as planned. It would be awhile before he could meet Samuel at the theater.

Johnny sat down, pulled his knees to his chest, and watched the Starlight burn.

Black was the first to leave, about twenty minutes later. He walked straight to the church, flung open the door, and entered. The people began to disperse then, in small groups, headed back to their homes or to various buildings to do only God knew what.

In the end only one small group remained. Had to be Claude and company. They hauled a car into the middle of Black's ring of fire, which had now smoldered to the east of the still-blazing theater. One of them threw something—a homemade bomb?—at the car. It burst into flames to the delight of several smaller figures in the group. Fred, Peter, Roland, and another kid.

Ten minutes later, they all left.

Johnny finally stood. He couldn't tell the time by the black sky, but if he figured things right—an hour up at daybreak, an hour at the monastery, a half hour to this point, another hour here—it was about midmorning. Samuel would come in two hours. Johnny gave himself a full sixty minutes to reach the town—no need to rush.

He could hear the dying flames crackling when he was still a good fifty yards this side of the meadow behind the old theater.

Then he was there, at the tree line, staring at the charred and burning remains of what used to be the old theater. No sign of anyone.

He hurried around the south edge of town, toward the alley that led to his house. Still no one. And still no wind. The trees were stripped bare of leaves, and the sand was still piled against the buildings. But something felt different.

Johnny stopped fifty feet from the convenience store. It was the sky. The sky wasn't as dark as it had been when he left the overlook.

Samuel?

Johnny felt a burst of courage and headed up the alley, watching left and right like a hawk.

Still not a soul.

He was supposed to be taking stock. There was nothing to take stock of. At least no people. Thank God.

Someone yelled somewhere, and Johnny dove behind someone's house. But it was distant, he quickly realized. Coming from inside a house where an argument had broken out. Maybe from the saloon. He hurried on.

Johnny entered his house from the back, listened for a moment, and sighed with relief. Not that he was safe here, but the familiar hall with its familiar silence was at least a good sign.

He checked his mother's room and found it empty. He donned the socks he'd left behind and found his shoes. Put them on.

Now what? The church? Not a chance. Black was in there.

Johnny stood in the hall for a full five minutes, trying to think things through, but he really didn't know what he could do short of running out into the street and yelling for Black to come and get him.

His vision blurred. The wall moved.

Billy.

Johnny pressed his palms against his temples and focused on an image of Samuel. The wall became still. Someone, maybe Billy himself, was sitting in that damp dungeon below the monastery, trying to break into his mind. He didn't know how it worked, but he knew enough for it to terrify him.

At least he knew how to fight the images that . . .

The house moved under his feet. That was it, he had to get out. Johnny ran down the hall. The walls bent in, the door buckled. He plunged ahead anyway, slammed through the door and out into the alley.

The ground was shaking out here. Not a slight tremor, but a violent vibration that blurred his feet. He cried out in terror, turned south and sprinted.

Whether by Samuel's doing or his own he didn't know, but the world returned to normal after he'd taken three or four steps. Either way, he had to get out of Paradise. He'd seen all he could afford to see.

Johnny reached the tree line south of town and pulled up behind a large aspen, out of the town's sight. He lifted his hands to his face and leaned against the trunk. The ground might not be shaking anymore, but his fingers were.

Johnny eased his seat to the base of the tree. He would wait for Samuel here.

Chapter Thirty-five

PARADISE

Monday afternoon

"JOHNNY."

Samuel's voice cut through the still air, and Johnny jerked upright.

"Samuel?"

"Here." The boy walked from the trees. He was dressed in the same cotton shorts and white button-down shirt he'd worn both times Johnny had seen him. The only difference was his shoes, which were now brown walking boots. He seemed a bit frail, but in every way Johnny could imagine he looked exactly like Samuel.

Johnny scrambled to his feet. "Thank God! Thank God you came."

"Of course I came." Samuel flashed a mischievous grin. "Did you have any doubts?"

He even talked like Samuel. As far as Johnny was concerned, this was Samuel.

Johnny glanced back in the direction of the town. "Did you see?"

"I saw."

"You saw. And you're not worried?"

Samuel winked. "I have a plan, remember? It was your idea."

"Not really. What now?"

"Now we do some damage. To Black, that is."

"Exactly. But how?"

"Do you doubt me?"

Johnny wasn't sure what he doubted or didn't doubt. A week ago he spent most of his time trying to figure out how to spend another lazy summer day.

Now he spent every minute trying to figure out how to survive the chaos. He trusted Samuel, sure. But he'd trusted him with Thomas too.

"They burned Thomas," Johnny said.

"I saw that."

Johnny looked at the boy's arms and hands. "So, what did you do?"

Samuel held out his hands, palms up, and studied them. "You mean what powers do I have in these hands?"

"Did it work?"

"I guess we'll find out."

"So, what are they?"

"Well, it's pretty powerful stuff, I guarantee you that. Would you like to see me throw a few fireballs?"

The idea that fire could actually come out of those white hands was incredible. He reached out and touched Samuel's palms. "You can do that? Sure."

"Actually no, I can't." Samuel lowered his arms. "It'll take a lot more than a few fireballs to deal with Black. Trust me, Johnny, the power I've written into these hands will terrify even Black. Now"—Samuel walked past him—"shall we go give it a try?"

"Hold on."

Samuel walked toward the town as if he hadn't heard Johnny. He was actually going in to confront Black now? It was all moving too fast. They should take a few hours, maybe the night, to plot a careful plan of attack.

"You're just going to walk in there? Hold up!"

Samuel turned back. "Repeat after me, Johnny. *I believe*. Say that with me. *I believe*."

"I do believe. And I believed with Thomas, but—"

"No, Johnny, you believed in a lawman named Thomas. Now I'm asking you to believe in me."

Was there a difference?

"There's a difference," Samuel said.

"Okay then. I believe."

Samuel smiled. "Shout it."

"Now? They'll hear! We can't just waltz in there like this!"

"That's the point. I want them to know you're with me. Scream it out, Johnny. The louder the better."

Johnny glanced past Samuel at the buildings just visible on the other side of the trees. The sound might not carry too far out here in the woods.

"I have a better idea," Samuel said. He turned and walked toward the town again. "Come on, this way."

Johnny hurried to catch him. "What idea?"

"Stay close, Johnny. This way." Samuel picked up his pace. He walked right out into the open and crossed the clearing, headed for Main Street.

Johnny followed quickly, thinking that Samuel had a point about staying close. At least nobody was in the streets. He scanned the buildings. Saloon was clear, convenience store looked deserted, the church . . .

Johnny stopped. Marsuvees Black stood outside the church, leaning against the back corner, watching them.

"Samuel?"

"Keep walking, Johnny."

"He's right—"

"I see him. Keep walking. You're with me. Remember that. You're with me."

Johnny kept walking. The next time he looked up, he saw that Black was smiling.

They walked out into the middle of Main Street, to the center of the smoldering ring of fire, up next to the car that was still sending up black smoke from its tires.

Samuel stopped. "Here, Johnny. Shout it out for the whole town to hear. *I believe.*"

He was committed now. Surprisingly, Johnny wanted to shout it out. Not in defiance, but in self-defense. He prayed that whatever power Samuel had written into himself was more than what Black could throw at them. This was their last hope.

He had no choice but to align himself with that hope.

He gripped his hands into fists. "I believe!" he yelled. "I believe!"

Fire crackled behind them. Samuel stared at Marsuvees Black, who now stood with his feet planted wide, hands on hips.

Billy's character began to chuckle. He grinned wickedly and walked to his left, keeping his eyes on them. The black-clad monk mounted the church steps. Stretched his neck back and around at unnatural angles as if loosening up. Then disappeared through the doors.

"Come on," Samuel said. "This way." He headed for the church.

Watching Samuel strut straight for the gates of hell, Johnny wasn't sure how much he *wanted* to believe anymore.

"Samuel—"

"Stay close, Johnny."

Then again, he wasn't in a position not to believe. He followed, heart in his throat once again.

THE CHURCH had been nearly gutted by fire. Johnny stared over Samuel's shoulder, through the open inner doors, past the pews, to the stage.

To Marsuvees Black, with his hands flat on the charred pulpit, grinning back at them.

Two nights ago Johnny stood on that very stage, confronting Black in front of the whole town. But that was before. Before the church had been burned. Before they'd torched the theater. Before Thomas had been cut open and hung from the tree.

Before Johnny really understood what Billy could do.

Black tilted his head down and stared up from under the rim of his hat. "Welcome to my home, Samuel," he said.

Samuel walked in and stopped just behind the last pew. Johnny kept the boy between him and Black.

"Do you like what I've done to the place?" Black asked.

"If you ask me, it lacks imagination," Samuel said. "I'm more interested in you. First time I've actually seen someone who's stepped out of a book."

"Then pay close attention, my little friend. Your last creation was a bit of a disappointment. But he bled, I'll give you that. Thomas did bleed."

"I'll be sure not to disappoint you again."

"Do you bleed, Samuel?" Black asked, grin still fixed.

Samuel hesitated. Not good.

"Why don't you find out?" he finally said.

"I intend to. But we really should give this town a little show, don't you think?"

"What's wrong with now?"

"They've waited so long that we have to draw it out. Bring the climax to a slow boil. It's what they want, you know. They want blood."

"Now, Marsuvees. Take my blood now."

"I would love to, but—"

"Now!"

Johnny started. He fought a terrible urge to run for his life.

"Say it again, Samuel. Say it to me."

"You're reluctant to show me your power, then?"

Black spread his arms wide and faced the ceiling. "Oh, how I love the sound of begging. Show me your power, Marsuvees. Please show me."

Samuel clasped his hands behind his back. "That's what I thought. You're thinking that I'm trying to goad you, and you know that the man who gives into goading is the weaker one. But you're wrong. I just want to see if you're half as frightening as my friend Johnny here says you are. All I see now is the copy of a failed monk who's found some fancy black clothes."

Black lowered his head. His grin had softened. "Perhaps I should be the one testing your power."

"Perhaps."

"Then show me what you have. Prove yourself. Show me that you are more than a stupid, reckless little boy."

"No," Samuel said.

"No?"

"Not now. Three days have passed since the debate," Samuel said. "I challenge you to a new debate, at nightfall in two hours, in front of the people of this town. This time they, not the students, will be the judge. Win the debate and I am gone. Lose the debate and you are gone."

Black blinked. "You'll have to take that up with Billy."

"You take it up with Billy. You're his creation. I will debate Billy through you. It's my right to demand a debate, the only difference is that you are my opponent and the people are my judge. Don't tell me you're weaker than Billy."

Black came around the podium. "A two-thirds majority—the same as the monastery?"

"Yes."

"I accept," Black said.

"Then I bind you to the terms."

"Bind all you like. I own their hearts."

Samuel was silent for a moment. "You are in their hearts." He slowly lifted his hand, palm out.

Black's eyes widened. He took a step back. Without any further warning, the man in black began to tremble from head to foot. Johnny had never seen a look that resembled the terror that masked his face.

How could that be?

As quickly as the fear swept over Black, it left him. He began to laugh, as if delighted by the horror he'd just experienced.

Samuel stared him down for a long moment, turned, and walked straight for Johnny, who ducked in front of him and exited the sanctuary first, just in case Black had any parting . . . things to throw their way.

The door closed behind them. Johnny whirled to Samuel. "What was that?"

"The beginning of the end, I would say."

"But what did you do to him?"

Samuel stepped past the outer door and looked out at the smoldering remains of the old theater, a hundred yards south.

"I showed Black himself," he said. "Think of me as the human mirror." He winked and walked down the steps. "Seems as though evil loves evil."

"That's it? You're just going to debate him? What about the town?"

"Don't worry, Johnny, I haven't begun to show my power. We're going to save this town, you can count on that."

Chapter Thirty-six

THE MONASTERY

Monday night

RAUL BALANCED the round silver platter in his right hand and carefully lifted the white lace that covered the delicacies he'd arranged for David. He selected the foods himself from a short list of favorites he kept for special occasions. A delicious crab bisque, sliced Hungarian cheese on crackers, and a small pound cake stuffed with vanilla pudding. He arranged them neatly around a tall glass of passion-fruit juice.

David had retired to his bedroom after Samuel left the conference room several hours earlier. Frankly the food seemed like an empty gesture, but Raul knew that the director hadn't eaten since learning this morning that Thomas had died. For that matter, neither had Raul.

He rapped on the tall cherrywood door twice.

"Come in." The voice sounded strained.

Raul stepped into David's chambers and spoke before looking up. "I've brought you food, sir. Some of your favorites, I think." He shut the door and faced the room. "Andrew prepared this crab . . ."

David's bed lay stripped of its sheets, which were strewn to one side of the mattress. One of the pillows leaked goose feathers, which littered the maroon carpet like large snowflakes. A toppled chair lay beside a tray of untouched food Raul had delivered the previous evening. So even last night, when Thomas had taken the town, David was more worried than any of them knew.

David leaned against a window that overlooked the valley, one hand on the sill, the other cocked on his hip. His hair looked like a mop, his face was gaunt and unshaven.

"Sir?" What could he say to this?

"Yes, Raul. What is it?"

"I've brought food."

"So you have said. Put it down."

David stretched his neck as if fighting off a wrenching headache. His eyes remained closed.

"You haven't even touched the other."

"Yes. Please take it, Raul. Take it all. I appreciate the thought, but I'm not hungry."

Raul noted that a drape had been pulled loose.

"How do you expect me to eat while . . ." He trailed off.

"Truly, I can't imagine your anxiousness." Raul set the tray on the bed. "But isn't this our only hope? You seemed quite confident. It's the safest way, all things considered."

David paced in front of the window. "Don't get me wrong, I care for the town, but when it comes to my son, I think of them as butchers."

"There's nothing concrete to suggest that any harm will come to your son. Besides, Samuel's a strong boy. I'm sure he's doing well."

"And what do we really know?" David demanded. "Only what we can see from the overlook. Anything could happen in any one of those buildings without our knowledge."

Samuel had received his father's reluctant yet firm commitment during the meeting not to send anyone else to the town. It was too dangerous not only for them, but for the town itself. They couldn't risk setting Billy off. "Trust the books, Father. And trust me," Samuel had said.

"Trust the books," Raul said. "Isn't that—"

"This from you, who insisted we shut the project down?"

"I was wrong! Anyway, we're beyond that now. We're committed to this course. At this point no matter what happens we can't interfere. There's too much at stake."

David sighed. "I'm afraid, Raul. For the first time I'm really afraid. What if this fails?"

"Then we're in serious trouble."

"We can't lock them in the dungeon; we can't force the books away from them. God only knows what they've written to protect themselves. We can't just kill them all."

"We still have Samuel."

"And what can Samuel do? If this fails . . ."

David turned back to the window and lowered his head. Raul waited a full minute before breaking the silence.

"Sir?"

But David had slipped into his own world and refused to be interrupted. He stood there, his head hung, leaning on the window overlooking Paradise far below.

Raul finally took the old food tray, replaced it with the fresh one, and slipped into the hall.

God help them all.

MARSUVEES BLACK barged through the lower library doors, his black robe flowing behind him like trailing bat wings.

"Are they all here?" he demanded.

Billy stood by Darcy and Paul, just inside, his hands folded behind his back. "Yes," he replied.

The overseer stormed past them and disappeared through the side door leading to the balcony. Billy nodded at the others and followed. He had never seen the man so agitated.

Samuel was up to something, that much he'd discovered when Black had barged into his small study, cursing the worms on the floor.

"Get these slugs out of here! Remove them immediately, you fools!"

At first Billy had thought it was Black, yelling in his ear from Paradise. But then he turned and saw the gaunt overseer.

"Marsuvees?"

"What are you doing down here? Sleeping? For heaven's sake, boy! Don't you know what's going on?"

Darcy came awake beside him and lifted her head. "Marsuvees Black? You look just like what I imagined."

"Wonderful. Are you as dense as Billy?"

"What do you mean?"

"What do you mean? If you would quit eating so much of that sludge, maybe your minds would be able to see beyond your own stinking noses!"

"It was *your* idea that we eat so much sludge," Billy said.

"I didn't say to drug yourselves into a stupor! Your whole story's falling apart around your ears and you don't even see it!"

"Of course I see—"

"Wake up, boy!" Black yelled. "Samuel's undoing your story!"

"No, he's not. I have things under control."

"You do not! I want every single child in the main library in twenty minutes. You have them there, you understand? Everyone!"

That was twenty minutes ago.

Billy edged up to the balcony railing beside Black. The children were all in the library, slouched over the tables below, some asleep with their faces buried in their books, a few still writing. Black scanned the room and evaluated the scene like a general might measure his troops before a battle. Billy counted them quickly. Thirty-two . . . thirty-three? Oh, right. He, Darcy, and Paul. That made thirty-six.

"Wake up!" Black screamed.

Billy jumped, but the writers below hardly noticed. They turned slowly toward the voice. Billy could almost see their minds crawling from the slumber of deep fantasy where words became flesh.

"Wake up!" This time a few jerked up. The rest lifted their faces toward the balcony.

"Look at you, all slobbering over your own puny stories." Now thirty-three sets of eyes focused in on him like bats.

"What are you writing? I'll tell you what you're writing. You're writing meaningless, disjointed pap!"

He stabbed a finger toward the far wall. "They should have been dead by now! Dead! But does even one of you know what is really happening in our lovely town of Paradise?"

No one provided an answer.

"No! You don't. And do you know *how* I know you don't know? Because if you did know, you would stop it. But you aren't stopping it. You're too busy pacifying your own pathetic fantasies with your individual characters."

What could the man possibly be ranting about? They had been writing nonstop. How could he come in here and accuse them of this nonsense? The monk had lost his lid.

"Does anybody know where Samuel is?"

"He's writing," Billy said. "We know that. He's written a character based on himself to debate—"

"He's in Paradise!" Black said, without looking Billy's way.

"The real Samuel?"

"The real Samuel is in Paradise."

Billy blinked. Samuel in Paradise?

"He's in *your* town, waltzing around as if he owns the place!"

"Physically?" Billy asked.

"Physically, your leader wants to know." Black turned and leaned toward Billy. "Yes, physically!" Spittle flew from his mouth.

Marsuvees turned back to the children, who sat up now, paralyzed by his outrage.

"Now, I want you to write into the minds of Paradise like you've never written before, you hear me? I won't permit a single child to leave this library until we have our way with him."

The statement hung in the air like the reverberation of a gong. "No one will move. For any reason. You don't eat, you don't sleep, you don't talk, you don't even breathe more than absolutely necessary. I want every last cell in your measly, mindless brains to narrow on Paradise. You hear me?"

No one moved. "Well, don't just sit there. Give me a nod or something!"

Like a room full of little pistons, their heads bobbed.

Billy felt Black's eyes on him. "What, me? You don't expect *me* to write here, do you?" Impossible! He could never write with these slobs!

"Have I been speaking to the wall? What does *no one* mean to you? No one but the first fool who fell?"

Black looked back at the statues below. "And I want six of you"—he motioned to a table of six to his left—"you there will do. I want you to write, two each into Paula, Sally, and that cursed preacher."

"But, sir," a small boy said, "what would you have us write into them?"

"Have you learned nothing?" Black asked with a quiet, quivering voice. He began to yell. "Write deception! Write wickedness! Write hate! Write murder! Write death! Just write, you blithering idiot!"

Black spun from the railing and stormed from the balcony. The door to the library slammed and the outer tunnel filled with a horrendous scream that bent the children over their books.

"What do we do?" Darcy asked.

"We write," Billy said.

Chapter Thirty-seven

PARADISE

Monday night

THE TOWN of Paradise waited in eerie silence. A red sunset, the first in a week, glowed on the horizon. A string of citizens shuffled soundlessly into the church.

"If there's trouble," Johnny said, "if things don't go like you want, if we get separated or anything—not that I'm saying we will—but if anything happens, we could meet in the forest behind the theater where we met earlier."

Samuel looked at him without answering.

"I'm just saying if, you know? Just in case," Johnny said.

"And if that doesn't work, we can meet at the monastery."

"That's even better. They'll never find us there." Johnny looked up as the last of them straggled into the church. "We should try to get a jump on Black, don't you think?"

Samuel stepped from under the tree north of Main Street. "Follow me." He walked toward the church.

Johnny followed Samuel down the street and up the front steps. He paused in the entryway, expecting Samuel to give him a word of encouragement before walking into the crowded sanctuary—it seemed like a good thing.

But the boy didn't even look back. He walked straight inside and pushed the inner doors wide, like he was shoving saloon doors open for a six-gun showdown.

Johnny hurried to catch Samuel, fixing his eyes on the boy's heels as they touched the carpet. No one moved as they walked by, at least not that he could see from the corner of his eyes.

He imagined Steve sitting on the far side, bloodied as he had been the last time Johnny had tried to talk sense into them. Of course, Johnny didn't have Samuel's power. Claude and his gang would be sitting like zombies, clutching bottles, eyelids drooping.

Samuel stepped up onto the stage and approached the pulpit. Johnny followed him, walked halfway to the podium, and stopped. He raised his head and scanned the room, careful not to look into anyone's eyes.

Claude and gang sat in the first row, gripping bottles as he'd imagined. Crud and dried blood matted most of those present. Some wore it on their hands, as if the blood had come from another body; others below their nostrils, where they'd ignored a bleeding nose; some bore long, scabbed gashes. The blowing dust had stuck to the mess and hardened, so their skin looked like it was peeling. They sat in the pews, arms limp or crossed.

Steve Smither sat on the far left, grinning wickedly. Father Yordon avoided Johnny's eyes. Paula wore a loose halter top. Her hair was twisted like a nest of snakes, and her eyes were glazed over. He couldn't see his mother.

Then he did, near the back, dress torn and dirtied, face puffy. He could hardly recognize her! Johnny felt a tremor shake his bones.

Samuel cleared his throat. "Hello. My name is Samuel, and I've come here tonight to debate Marsuvees Black. You'll decide who wins. Okay?"

No response from the zombies.

"Black isn't here yet, but I'm sure he'll show himself soon enough. It will be a debate of few words, because most of you aren't hearing too well anymore. But you'll be presented with a clear choice and you'll have to decide. Do you understand?"

Still no reaction.

"Without love, everything falls apart," Samuel said. Something had changed in his voice. "Love is what I offer you today."

The words seemed to flow from Samuel's mouth like red-hot lava, smothering the auditorium, including Johnny, who could barely breathe from the sudden tightness in his chest. This was more like it. Samuel would have them wrapped up before Black even arrived.

"Have you forgotten what true love is?" Samuel choked up. He swallowed, and Johnny wanted to cry.

"No." Steve Smither stood, grinning.

"No, no, we do remember."

Four hundred crazies shifted their gazes to the man.

Steve walked toward the stage, hands clasped behind his back. "He's right, you know. We've been deceived. We're a brood of vipers. We're sick with the stench of death. Just like the boy says."

Samuel hadn't said that.

Steve spread his arms and faced the crowd as if he were the preacher now. "This little stranger here who came out of nowhere is right. We are deceived. All of us, blithering fools wrapped in a web of deceit that's strangling us to death."

Steve stepped onto the platform. Johnny took a step backward. The man's eyes were glassy and bloodshot. Samuel stood by the pulpit quietly, eyes fixed on Steve.

"We're all sick, disgusting perverts. Spineless, puny pukes."

Steve crossed toward Samuel, who stood still, expressionless. No relief, no joy, no anger, nothing but sadness. And that small chin tilting up to Steve—those soft lips, those long lashes unblinking.

Do it, Samuel! Tell him! Tell them all. Tell them you come from a monastery and you have enough power to flatten them with a single word! Tell them, Samuel. Tell them now!

Samuel didn't move.

"And what do vipers do, Samuel? Hmm? You're quite an intelligent little runt; you surely know what vipers do, don't you?" He still grinned and then added in a low raspy voice, "You little puke."

Johnny's knees began to tremble. This wasn't the way Steve normally talked, not even close. Someone was talking through him. Billy or Black. Johnny glanced at the crowd. Some of them sat up a little straighter, he thought, but their faces remained blank.

The grin vanished from Steve's face as if someone had cut the strings that lifted it. "Vipers bite, Samuel. You come down into our town and try to mess with our story and see what you get? You get bit, 'cause our worms are snakes too. Did you know that?"

"This is your idea of a debate, Billy?" Samuel said.

"That's right, I am Billy. And if this isn't a debate, what is? We're all down here in the dungeons and you're up there. What does that tell you? It tells you that you're dead meat."

Samuel had expected to confront Black. Why had Billy chosen Steve? "You know the consequences of evil?" Samuel said.

"Love!" Steve cried, spreading his arms. "I think it all leads to—"

Steve gasped and went white. He stared at Samuel in shock. Slowly his face twisted, first with anguish and then with horror. He threw his arms to his face, doubled over, and screamed bloody murder.

The crowd didn't react. Neither did Samuel at first, he let Steve scream and scream. And then he spoke softly, so that only he and Steve could hear.

"Steve, meet Billy. Billy, meet yourself."

Think of me as the human mirror, Samuel had said. He'd just shown Steve and Billy their own souls.

And then he released the man.

Steve's screaming stopped while he was still bent over. For a moment Steve remained frozen, staring at Samuel from a half crouch. Then his eyes flashed. He stood up slowly. His lips curled back, and his whole body began to vibrate.

Johnny couldn't move.

Steve's face flushed and the veins stood out on his neck. His jaws snapped wide in a shriek that nearly brought Johnny to his knees. Beyond Steve a dozen crazies rose to their feet. Steve was screaming words, Johnny realized. "It was my choice! I deserved that much. *My* choice!"

The man paused to catch his breath and then flung out his arm. "Take him! Take him, take him, take him!"

Mumbles and grunts swept through the crowd. A bunch of them climbed over their pews and started for the stage.

Johnny couldn't move his feet. Steve kept screaming, "Take him, take him, take *them*!"

Take *them*?

Samuel calmly lifted one hand to the dissenters who rushed the platform.

"Back," he said.

The power of the word hit the auditorium like a thunderclap. Four hundred people staggered back. If they were seated, their heads bent back as if struck by a gale-force wind. If they were standing, or climbing over a pew, or walking for the stage, they were thrown backward into their pews or on their seats.

Steve had stopped his screaming.

"I love you, Billy. Do you still know that?"

Steve fell to his knees, face drooping in anguish. "I'm sorry, I . . ."

Silence.

Steve's lips twisted to a snarl. He jumped to his feet.

"I hate you! I hate you, Samuel, you sick little puke." He flung his arm out. "Take them! Take him!"

Claude was on one knee, staring like a fool.

A single, unmistakable voice cut across the room. "Stevieeeeeee . . ."

Black stood at the back, head tilted down, blue eyes flashing.

Every head turned.

"Why are you just standing there, Steve? Hmm? I've been so good to you and now you turn on me? Am I wretched or vile? I should slit your gut and let you bleed dry."

Steve stared, eyes wide with confusion. "I didn't say—"

"Do you like our debate, Samuel? I think it's time for the people to vote." Black walked down the aisle, fixated on Samuel. Johnny turned to Samuel in a panic. For the first time he saw fear on the boy's face. Sweat was leaking down his temple and his eyes were wide.

Just two hours ago he'd thrown off Black's attacks easily. Had something changed?

Marsuvees Black stepped up on the stage. "So, you think that throwing around a little love will do the trick, do you? I'll admit, it's a tad fascinating, but ultimately boring."

He jerked his head to face the people.

"Thing is, I have the same power. Do you mind if I show you, Samuel? I'd like to show you my power." He walked to the far edge of the stage, eyes on the congregation. "I think the people would like a little show."

Black cocked his head back like a Pez dispenser. His neck doubled back, nearly at a right angle to his shoulders. For a moment he gave them a side profile of the stunning pose.

Then his whole body turned, upper torso first, followed by hips and legs, like a robot. Black's round dark mouth faced them like a gaping cannon.

The air blurred with a white streak. Straight from Black's open jaw. Then two, then ten, then two dozen white streaks, flying in formation toward Samuel.

Before they had crossed half the pews, the white objects converged into a cohesive unit. Formed a set of razor-sharp teeth. They were too long and too sharp and too white to be Black's teeth, but from the corner of his eye Johnny saw that Black's mouth was bleeding onto his shirt, and he knew that they *were* his teeth.

The jaw came to an abrupt halt two inches from Samuel's nose. It snapped at the air once, paused, then again. *Clack*, pause, *clack*.

The teeth retreated in another sudden flash and snapped back into Black's jaw. He leveled his head.

"And?" Samuel said. "The point is?"

It struck Johnny that this wasn't Black and Samuel as much as it was Billy and Samuel. Two kids, dueling.

The smirk on Black's face faded. He opened his mouth wide, thrust his head forward, and roared at Samuel. His lips stretched as wide as his head and his teeth flashed like a piranha's.

Three things came from Black's throat. A crackling roar that shook the whole building, a heat wave that blasted Samuel, and a black vapor.

The force of the roar bounced off an invisible shield that enveloped Samuel and rushed past Johnny. He could see it because of the black vapor, like a jet stream in a wind tunnel, and he could feel the heat. Without the shield, a person would probably be burned to a crisp, Johnny thought, cringing behind the boy. Samuel was protecting him.

The roar lasted at least ten seconds. And then Black's mouth clamped shut.

For a moment Billy's character stared at Samuel, amazed that he hadn't dislodged a hair, much less damaged him.

Slowly Samuel lifted his right hand, palm out. Something came from that hand. Johnny couldn't see it, but Black could.

His face twisted into an unholy mess of distorted features. For a moment Johnny thought that his face was melting. His lower jaw came loose from its joints and ran a slow circle. Black began to shake so badly that Johnny thought he might come apart.

Instead, he began to laugh.

He grabbed at his face and pulled at his flesh and shrieked with laughter, delighted with himself.

He was seeing himself. Evil loved evil, like Samuel had said.

Black cocked his head back at a right angle, twisted it to face the church, and let his laughter echo over the auditorium.

As one the people began to scream. Their faces contorted in fear. They pulled at their hair, and their eyes rolled back into their heads.

Then they lunged at each other and began tearing at each other's faces.

Samuel faced the people and held both hands out like a mime pushing a wall. "No," he said.

A barely visible shock wave emanated from him. It rippled through the air and through the people, starting at the first pew and picking up speed as it spread to the very back. As the wave struck them, it cut off their screams. They gasped and were thrown back more forcefully than the first time.

They collapsed, groaning and sobbing.

Even though Johnny wasn't in the wave's path, he felt its effect. A warm force cut through his muscles like an electric current that charged him with love and desire for more love. He staggered back and dropped to one knee. Tears flooded his eyes, and he knew that Samuel would win this contest.

Wailing and sorrow and love swallowed the church.

Black recovered and glared at Samuel in a rage.

Samuel lowered his arms and everything changed. Instantly. The power that had come from Samuel vanished.

Claude struggled to his feet, dazed and confused. Then others, like the resurrected dead.

"The choice is theirs," Samuel said.

For an endless moment no one else moved.

Steve stood on the stage, lost to the world. Claude's face settled and he breathed heavily through his nostrils. Chris and Peter waited behind him, blinking and waiting. Katie looked like a rag doll.

A slow smile formed on Black's face. "The choice is theirs," he said. Then he thrust his hand out toward Samuel. "Take him!" he said.

Still no one moved.

Black stretched his mouth wide, like a snake preparing to swallow a goat, and roared again. Again the building's foundations shook.

But this time Samuel didn't stop it. His body shielded Johnny from most of the shock, but the air around him seemed to shake.

Claude was ten feet from the stage when Black's blast hit him. He grunted and rushed forward, eager to reach Samuel now. At least fifty rushed the stage.

Samuel did not resist. He was either caught off guard or had something planned for the last moment.

Black's roar didn't ease up. His thundering mouth gaped, as long and wide as his face.

Claude leaped onto the platform.

"Samuel!" Johnny didn't wait for a reply. He whirled from the podium and ran.

He's just standing there. This isn't possible!

From the corner of his eye, he saw Samuel collapse under Claude's huge body. He disappeared under a sea of flesh.

A handful of crazies were scrambling over the pews to intercept Johnny.

Fists pounded flesh behind him as he dove for the entrance below the red *Baptismal* sign. He reached the brass knob and yanked the door open.

You're leaving Samuel. You can't leave Samuel!

He turned his head back, just enough to stare into the twisted face of Chris Ingles, just strides away. Johnny bolted.

He slammed through the rear door, stumbled out to the back porch, and took a hard left, over the steps. The dark lawn met his feet hard. He rolled over the grass and spun back just in time to see a large object fill his vision. It smashed into his head and knocked him on his back.

He twisted to one side, fighting for breath, but they stood over him now like grim reapers. Then Johnny was screaming. Long vowels that hurt his throat. His mind could barely form thoughts, much less words.

Hands grabbed at his arms and legs and yanked him roughly from the ground. A big hand pounded down on his forehead, and he heard his screams taper off. Another fist hit his head, and his world began to fade.

It hurts, he thought.

And then he didn't think anything for a while.

A little later or much later—he didn't know which—he opened his eyes and it was dark. The musty smell of dishrags filled his nose. He managed to turn on his back. Slowly, like the coming of the tide, he thought some things.

He thought he was alive. He must be alive because his head was throbbing with pain. He thought he shouldn't be alive—he wasn't even sure he wanted to be alive. He thought he might be in the root cellar below Smither's Saloon.

He thought Samuel was . . .

Actually, he didn't know what Samuel was. Maybe Samuel had opened his mouth at the end there and knocked them all over. Maybe Samuel was dead.

Johnny closed his eyes and wished he were dead.

Chapter Thirty-eight

THE MONASTERY

Monday night

BILLY DIPPED his quill into the inkwell, trying to gauge the emotions that ran through him. A drop of sweat fell from his forehead and marked the page by his thumb.

How would he describe this story? Enthralling, exhilarating to be sure. But there was more. The pen clinked against the glass jar of red ink as he withdrew his hand. An unsteady hand did not suit writing. He swallowed to wet his parched throat.

He'd been writing in the balcony for hours, barely aware of time, forgetting the fact that Black had driven him from his study. He'd lost himself in the singular objective of pushing this story to the ending for which it begged. The shaking in his hand had started when he heard Samuel's voice, like an echo in his skull.

"I love you, Billy."

His first instinct had been to search the balcony for the voice. *Samuel has escaped! He's left Paradise and come here to turn me over to David!*

But the voice hadn't spoken from the balcony. It echoed like a church bell in his mind.

He'd stared back at the writing book, hands trembling. The story was speaking back to him now, as if he were actually there in Paradise, not just whispering suggestions to his characters, but participating with them.

The writing no longer focused on Paradise. Samuel had changed that. The boy was trying to destroy the power *behind* Paradise. He had reached past the people in the church down there and was trying to quiet *him!*

But Billy had no intention of being quieted. Paradise was his. His town, his story. No one would throw him out. Not even Samuel and his precious father. *Especially* not Samuel and his father.

And the boy had the audacity to say, *I love you, Billy*, right there, out loud, as if *that* would gain him favor.

Wake up, boy! Things don't revolve around the four rules down here. We make our own rules, and they're not rules of love. *I love you*—please! Love was for stories.

Of course, this was a story. Everything was really a story, penned or thought or acted out at some time by someone.

Billy brought his trembling fingers to the paper. He could do so much on this page! This was the power of storytelling, that he could tell whatever story he chose.

A stray thought hit him. Thomas Hunter found the books in a place called the Black Forest. Billy impulsively wrote a sentence in the bottom margin, as much to break the tension as for any other purpose.

Then the man named Thomas found himself in the Black Forest, where he fell and hit his head and lost his memory.

Ha. He wondered what *that* would do.

Another drop of sweat plopped onto the page. Billy brushed it aside with his little finger and continued writing into Paradise. The tension of the story immediately gripped him again.

Now let us see about your powers, Samuel. What move will you make now in this chess match of ours?

Samuel had given up too early.

The red lines ran jagged from his quivering hand. A nervous hand doesn't suit good writing, Billy thought again, and then lost himself in the story. His story.

Chapter Thirty-nine

PARADISE

Monday night

FOR THE seventh time in a week, Marsuvees Black stepped out of the trees to meet Marsuvees Black, the character that Billy had written into existence based on him. The black trench coat and Stetson hat, the boots and belt were figments of Billy's imagination, taken from costumes he'd seen in one of the dungeon rooms, but otherwise Black looked exactly like Marsuvees. In so many ways, he was him.

In so many ways, he wasn't him.

It was odd how the progression of evil worked. It always went from bad to worse, no matter how much mind he'd ever applied to the matter. And in the progression was a line which, if crossed, offered no retreat. He reached that line seven years ago, while he still worked in Vegas, but he'd turned and run into the desert for solitude and repentance.

This time he'd crossed the line. Now there was no turning back, any fool could see that. The strange thing was, he really didn't have any ambition to rule the world or wipe out the country or even Las Vegas, that beautiful den of iniquity that spoiled his soul to start with.

He'd joined Project Showdown because of its fantastic promise to test good against evil in the most unusual way. David Abraham had essentially created an incubator for good in these children, believing that if properly protected, good would prevail.

His whole life had been a raging battle between good and evil, and as far as he could see, evil, not good, always ended up on top. The pig always returned to its sty; dogs always lapped up their vomit.

But then he'd found the blank books and discovered the inscription that destined them for the purposes of love. After three months of careful deliberation, Marsuvees could not ignore his one and only conclusion: the books had been found by him, as by David, because he was *meant* to use them.

And how? To test good versus evil, naturally. To test the rule of good and evil that had waged eternal war in his own heart. If by their own irrevocable rule the books would lead to the discovery of love, then he would force their hands, so to speak.

He embraced evil with abandon, knowing that in the end he was really embracing love. Isn't that what the rule meant? If by his embrace of evil he could produce love, didn't that make evil itself a kind of good?

Yes! And a good thing too, because in these last two weeks he'd been once again reminded how much he loved evil. How delicious each terrible, wonderful, delightful act really was.

Why did evil always feel so good? Because evil was in fact a kind of love. True or not, he swam in the hope that it was more true than all the nonsense thrown his way over the past forty years.

Marsuvees stared at his fictional counterpart, who stood on the edge of the greenbelt staring at the now-deserted church across town. The charred remains of the old theater smoldered in the waning light off to their left. Marsuvees wasn't sure what Black had done to Samuel after the meeting, but he knew what had to be done now.

He walked toward Black. In all honesty, if his gamble paid off and evil did turn out to be a kind of good, then he was obligated to flex the muscle of evil as much as possible, wasn't he? And he would have no problem doing so.

In the meantime, there was only one thing that stood in his way.

"So you came after all," Black said without turning to him.

"Was there ever a doubt?" Marsuvees said.

"I never needed you," Black said. "I have this under control."

Amazing how perfectly Billy had formed the character. Black had developed his own idiosyncrasies in the last week, but most of him came from Billy. Or more accurately, from Billy's understanding of the monk named Marsuvees Black. Him. The boy was perceptive, rendering him with surprising accuracy—the mischievous grins, the arching eyebrows, the curvature of his fingers, even his accent.

"Didn't need me? You are me," Marsuvees said.

"You mean my flesh?" Black jerked his head around and flashed a searing smile. He lifted his arm, bit deeply, and pulled a chunk of flesh from his hand like a wolf might pull the flesh from a fresh deer kill. He spit the hunk of meat at Marsuvees.

"Have a bite."

Marsuvees sidestepped the flying flesh. The child in Billy had become part of Black. At this very moment, he wasn't sure if Billy had suggested to Black that he bite his own arm, or if Black had done it on his own.

He stepped up beside the character and stared ahead. Dusk was coming fast. By morning this would all be finished.

"You're sure you can do this?" Marsuvees said.

"You're insulting me?" Black asked.

"No, I just want to know. We have a lot riding on it."

"We? I think you're assuming too much."

"Without me, you have nothing. I've made sure of that. Only I have the knowledge required to take this further. And tonight I will extend my own power by having Billy write several far-reaching statements into the books."

Black pulled a book from his pocket and lifted it up. "You mean the books like this one?"

He had one of the blank books?

Black grunted, replaced the book in his pocket, and faced the town.

Marsuvees would take care of the book later. The last thing he needed was this monstrosity running around with a book in his possession.

"When we're finished here, we'll hand the monks in the monastery the same fate and start over," Marsuvees said. "Only this time it won't be a small town sitting conveniently at the bottom of the mountain."

"It's been a real drag working with you," Black said. Billy talking. "I have to be honest, although I had some respect for you in the beginning, I've come to hate you. Maybe it was the mask you insisted on wearing. Maybe it's the fact that you look like . . ." Black faced him, eyeball to eyeball, not a foot away. "Black."

"Just remember who the real flesh is around here," Marsuvees said.

"I'm not sure I like real flesh." There was a glint in his eyes. If Marsuvees didn't know Billy's dependence on him better, he might suspect a foolish streak of murder in there.

Black sniffed. "Do I smell like that?"

"You smell like the sewer that you came . . ."

Black's right hand shot forward. Marsuvees felt the intense pressure before he felt the pain. He looked down, stunned.

Billy's character had thrust his hand through his midsection. The man's black-sleeved arm was buried up to the elbow in Marsuvees' gut.

Pain overtook him like a tsunami. He felt his body start to fold over the arm and it occurred to him that Black had shoved his hand right through his spine. It had to be broken.

Billy had knifed him with Black's arm! Or Black had done it on his own. Marsuvees tried to speak, but his facial nerves were paralyzed, and his head felt like it might explode. He could hear a loud thumping and then splashing. Blood, from the exit wound.

Black jerked his arm free.

Marsuvees buckled. He heard a chuckle.

Then his world went black.

Chapter Forty

THE MONASTERY

Tuesday morning

GASPING FOR breath from the climb, Raul banged on David's door and then barged in without waiting for a response.

The rising sunlight burst through the window across the room. David lay on the bed, raising to his elbows, eyes wide and lost. Raul's banging had obviously aroused him from deep slumber.

"I beg your pardon, sir, but I have news."

David swung his legs to the floor. "News? Well, tell me."

Raul hesitated. How could he say—

"Tell me!"

"I'm afraid it's not so—"

"Just tell me, man!"

Raul paused, terrified to speak. "Samuel has been taken. Or should I say the character that Samuel has written has been taken."

"Taken? What do you mean, *taken*?"

"They have him. I . . . I don't know how. I can't seem to find Samuel in the—"

"Have they hurt him?" David stood.

Raul stepped back. "They used force. They had to restrain him."

David's face washed white with shock. "My . . . my boy would never resist them!" He swallowed. "Did . . . did they hurt him?"

"Pardon me for saying, but he wasn't—"

"He's my son! Samuel didn't write a character. It's him down there!"

Raul stared at the director, aghast. Samuel himself had gone down? "How could . . ."

"It was the only way! He had to go himself. Have they hurt him?" David demanded.

David's erratic behavior earlier now made perfect sense. Raul wanted to fall down and beg David to end this madness, to save his son, to yank Billy from his tunnels and punish him so that he would never forget. But he knew they were past all that.

So, instead he nodded. Once.

For a moment David stood like stone. His face flushed and he began to quiver. His eyes glassed with tears that dripped straight down his cheeks and to the floor.

Then the father threw his hands to his face and wailed. "Oh, my son! Dear Father, have mercy on my son!"

He stepped across the room, blind to his steps, smothering his face with large hands. "No, no, no!"

Raul could hardly bear the sight.

"Jesus, our blessed Savior, have mercy. My son! How could they hurt you? How . . ."

He whirled to Raul, who jerked in fright. David's face twisted into a furious snarl.

"If they hurt a single hair on his body, I'll kill them!" he roared. "You hear me, man? I'll kill them all!"

Raul settled to one knee, waiting for David to collect himself.

David looked through the open door, hesitated, and then bolted past Raul into the outer hall.

"David! You can't . . ."

He leaped to his feet and ran after David. *He's going down there! He's going down to Paradise to rescue Samuel!* He'd seen the look in those inflamed eyes—that desperate love of a father willing to cast his own head on the block for the sake of his son.

But if Samuel couldn't stop them, neither could David. For the first time since Raul had learned the truth about the books, he knew they had to trust their power or suffer even more harm. He was suddenly certain that if David ran into Paradise, they would kill him along with his son.

The tail of David's nightshirt disappeared into the stairwell.

"David!"

Raul flew down the stairs in threes, hand on the rail to keep from tumbling headlong into the stone walls. David was taking the stairs even faster. The slapping of his bare feet echoed up to Raul. Only once did he see David, and then only his heel.

When Raul burst into the atrium, the large doors were already swinging closed.

"David!"

Raul ran for the doors, yanked them open, and sprinted into the canyon. His sandals slipped in the soft sand as he rounded the first corner. The canyon gaped, a dry riverbed littered with large stones. Now a full fifty yards ahead David sprinted, his arms and legs pumping like a world-class athlete.

Surely he didn't intend to run all the way down to Paradise. But wouldn't Raul do the same? What kind of good sense could overcome blind passion for a son?

On the other hand, if David was right about the books, interfering with them might be the undoing of them all! In trying to save his son, David might condemn him.

Raul ran hard, panting through burning lungs, praying that David would come to his senses. There had to be a way, but it wouldn't be up to a man like David, who had no power. Samuel was a strong boy. He had more power than the lot of them. Including Black. Samuel would find a way.

Raul lost sight of David at the canyon's mouth. If David stopped, it would be at the overlook.

Falling more than running, Raul stumbled down to the overlook. He burst from the brush fifteen minutes later and doubled over, gasping. David knelt at the ledge, silhouetted against the overcast sky. The town of Paradise lay like charred sugar cubes two miles beyond him.

"Sir."

Raul approached carefully. David faced the town and rocked back and forth on his knees, wind whipping at his thin cotton shirt. His body shook with sobs, Raul now saw.

A lump rose into his throat. He knelt beside David and placed a gentle hand on his back. "I'm sorry," he said, feeling the words inadequate. Possibly even insensitive. But he said them anyway, over and over.

"I'm sorry, I'm sorry."

Chapter Forty-one

PARADISE

Tuesday morning

JOHNNY AWOKE with the smell of onions and earth in his nostrils. At first he thought his mother had let him sleep late and was out in the kitchen preparing dinner, but then the image of four hundred crazies sitting in church pews filled his mind, and he jerked his head off the cellar's dirt floor.

His temples throbbed and he groaned. He rolled on his back and tried to focus on his dark surroundings. He'd put potatoes in the cellar for Steve on occasion—on the wood shelves lining the walls. Their roots grew like long white tentacles.

"Pretty smart, eh?" Steve had said once when Johnny pointed them out. "They only grow toward the light. Like snakes trying to escape." He'd chuckled and Johnny decided then that he didn't like root cellars with hairy potatoes.

A distant sound drifted into the cellar, something like a whistle at a soccer match.

Johnny rolled toward the wall—the one made of wood with the crack near the top above ground level. He saw it now, tangled with a dozen roots reaching through. If he remembered right, the crazies had thrown him in here at night, but now daylight glowed through the small crack.

The whistle came again. But it sounded more human this time—a high-pitched shriek, the kind made by placing a thumb and a forefinger in your mouth. Johnny never could whistle that way. Who could possibly be whistling out there?

Samuel.

The boy's face filled his mind. That blond head and those blue eyes, smiling softly.

The whistle came again, a little sharper now. But it wasn't a whistle, was it? It didn't have that piercing, harsh quality. Had more of a throat . . .

Johnny caught his breath and snapped to a sitting position. A scream! It was a scream!

The sound reached his ears again, only this time with a word.

"Pleeeeeease!"

It was Samuel's voice. Johnny scrambled to his feet, ignoring the raging headache.

"Samuel?" The name echoed around him. What were they doing to him? "Samuel!"

He tore at the shelves, sweeping potatoes and onions onto the floor. He yanked the spud roots from the crack and pried his right eye to the thin opening.

A large tin garbage can blocked half his view on the right. The alley lay vacant on his left. Fifty yards ahead tall evergreens bent in the wind under a gray sky.

The morning air carried the sound to him again, and Johnny knew they were doing something to Samuel out on the front street. Something that made the small boy scream.

He beat against the boards on both sides of the crack. The planks were rotted nearly clean through.

Dirt drifted into his eyes. He brushed at it, and then in a fit of frustration he threw himself at the slit.

With a *crack* the rotted board caved out and hot wind blasted into the cellar. Johnny jumped back, surprised that he'd broken the board.

A sharp report chased by a shriek rode the wind. Johnny dove at the opening and pulled desperately at the rotting boards. They came away in clumps. He pulled four down and clambered though the opening into the alley.

He jerked his head each way. The alley was empty. He edged along the back wall to the south corner of the saloon, dropped to his knees, and crept between Smither's Saloon and the convenience store, trembling.

Five yards from the end, he eased down on his belly and snaked along the ground. Then Johnny poked his head around the corner and looked out to where the blacktop split the town of Paradise in two.

The whole town had gathered, right out there on the asphalt, kneeling in a large semicircle with their backs to Johnny. Claude Bowers and his son Peter were dressed in the same overalls they'd worn for a week. Paula was there, on the edge closest to Johnny. Crying. Katie knelt ten feet from Paula, glaring at her with contempt, draped in a weasel or bear or some other fur.

Father Yordon knelt on the far side, his head hung low, his hands folded like he was giving a blessing for the gathering. The rest of the people knelt into the wind, facing Steve. The only missing character in this gathering was Black. No sign of Billy's black-clad preacher.

Steve Smither stood in the center of the circle with arms spread. He had a whip in his right hand, and he was gloating at something on the pavement.

From his perspective hugging the dirt, Johnny couldn't see over their heads to see what Steve was looking at. Very slowly, with quivering muscles, Johnny pushed himself to his knees.

They'd stripped Samuel's shirt off. He knelt with his head bowed to the black pavement, facing away from Steve. His shoulders and arms were bleeding. Long streaks of red and blue on his back.

Johnny's vision swam.

Steve lunged forward with the whip. A black streak lashed through the air and cracked just above the boy's back. A thin red gash opened on Samuel's white skin, as if he were a painting and the artist had flipped a red brush over the canvas.

The boy jerked without screaming. Then settled back to his knees. His soft sobs reached Johnny's ears.

Johnny collapsed face down. He started to push himself up and immediately thought better of it. What if they saw him? Would they beat him like they were beating Samuel? Would they strip him and whip him?

Samuel's quiet cry rose into the wind. But not a scream like before. And no crack of the whip. Johnny lifted his head.

Samuel had struggled to his feet. The young boy stood with the wind at his back, his legs spread and slightly bent at the knees. He was calling out in a thin voice.

"Father . . ."

The words sliced into Johnny's heart like a razor.

"Father, please . . . please help me . . ."

Johnny glanced at the mountains. The lookout jutted from the rocky face like a gray shoe far above them. Beyond it . . .

"Father! Fatherrr! Please, Father! Save me!"

Samuel was wailing now.

The frail boy sucked at the air with a dreadful groaning sound and then shrieked again. "Don't let me die! Don't . . ." He was sobbing now, screaming between gasps. "Please, please, I'm just a boy . . ."

Tears streamed from Johnny's eyes. He began to groan softly, and he knew they might hear him, but he didn't care anymore. He wanted to die. A thought forced its way into his mind.

Why didn't Samuel run?

Samuel stood on the road at least five paces from Steve and the rest of them. The Starlight Theater's remains hid the path leading to the mountain behind. The boy had a way of escape. He had to know that he could reach the theater and lose himself in the hills before the mob caught him.

But Samuel did not run.

He stood there and begged the empty sky to save him. In long weeping wails he cried to the wind until Johnny thought his heart would burst.

The people knelt in their semicircle, unmoved. Steve still gloated, Yordon still bobbed his head. Only Paula wept—possibly for Samuel, possibly for herself.

"Whip him, Stevie," Katie said.

The whip flashed. Samuel fell. His body smacked onto the asphalt like a slab of meat. The fall took the wind from him and he twisted in agony. Then his soft groans carried to Johnny again.

"Father, please. Father, please!"

Anguish. Such anguish.

Johnny clenched his eyes and pushed himself back, keeping his belly low. He turned first to his right and then to his left, undecided where to go, only knowing that he had to get away.

Away from where the people watched the boy rolling before them with mild interest, like chicken farmers watching another rooster go under the ax. *Why do they flop like that, honey? Why? I don't know, they all do.*

Then Johnny staggered to his feet, covered his ears against Samuel's wails, and ran for the trees.

Chapter Forty-two

THE MONASTERY

Tuesday morning

RAUL SAT on his haunches ten yards from the edge, rocking back and forth, a monk committed to a mantra. He'd watched David's endless pacing along the lookout for an hour. In the beginning he'd attempted several approaches of consolation.

"Samuel's a strong boy," he said, and David just wept harder, leaning against a lone tree whose roots had found purchase on the rock surface. "Trust God," he said. "He gave us these books. Trust the books, David. In the end, love will prevail." But David just whirled to him.

"He's my son! Every *moment* is the end!"

Raul had changed tactics then. Never mind that a wrong turn now could wreak havoc throughout the earth; the pain of this one moment seemed to supersede any such risk.

"Go down and save him, David! Together, we could."

"You don't understand," David groaned.

"You're his father, man! What else is there to understand? We'll burn the town to the ground!"

"I can't!" David's cry sounded guttural and horrid, and it struck Raul that he was tormenting the man with such absurd statements. If Thomas and Samuel couldn't stop Black, surely a troop of unarmed monks would only walk to their deaths.

But how could a father stand by while his son was brutalized? David would give his life for Samuel without a second thought. There was more here than Raul knew. More than this simple agreement they'd made to trust the books.

"Samuel!" David groaned loudly. "My son, my son, Samuel!" He tore at his hair with both hands and stepped up to the very edge, sobbing. For a terrifying moment, Raul thought he would leap from the cliff. But he just stood there, moaning in the wind for a long time.

"Please tell me that you know what you're doing, sir! Just tell me that there is a way out of this madness."

But David refused to respond. He hadn't spoken since. He only paced from the tree to a large boulder thirty feet away, bursting into tears so often that Raul wondered where the tears could possibly come from.

After an hour, just as a numbness settled in Raul's mind, the first wail reached them from Paradise, like an arrow shot from the valley below. They both jerked their heads toward the sound.

Raul caught his breath. Could it be a bird? Yes, it could . . .

The cry sounded again, and Raul began to tremble. The sound came from Paradise. From Samuel. Samuel was crying out in Paradise.

David threw himself to his knees and gripped his hair with both hands. His mouth stretched in anguish, but only small sounds broke through his swollen throat.

The next cry carried words, surprisingly clear on the morning air: *"Father! Fatherrr! Please, Father! Save me!"*

David fell apart then. He simply fell to his side and lay there on the ground, still clutching his head. The cries came again and again. But the father did nothing, *could* do nothing. He only wept, face twisted and body quaking.

Raul rocked, crying. He had never imagined such pain was possible, that any living soul could endure so much sorrow and manage to keep their organs from hemorrhaging.

For the first time in his memory, he wanted to die. He wanted everything to end.

Chapter Forty-three

PARADISE

Tuesday

JOHNNY TORE into the hills without caring where he was going as long as it was away from the terrifying sounds in Paradise.

But he couldn't escape them. They drifted through the trees, and they filled his mind, pushing him faster and farther.

Maybe he should have gone home instead of running out here. Surely his mother wasn't part of this. He'd been so overcome by the horror on Main Street that he didn't look for her among the others.

Johnny pulled up, his breathing ragged. Something had changed. He looked around, lost. Tall pines leaned in the gusting wind. The sky seemed darker.

What had changed?

Samuel had stopped wailing.

Johnny whipped his head back to the town. Samuel wasn't crying—maybe they'd let him go. He turned back downhill.

Samuel's faint voice was calling to him. Or at least to his memory.

You and I, Johnny. We'll fix this town.

Johnny found his bearings and cut through the trees, toward Smither's Saloon. His mind played back Samuel's voice, soft and sweet.

In the end we will prevail, Johnny.

Prevail, Samuel? Where did you learn words like that? I've got news for you. We're not prevailing here.

He burst through the trees behind the saloon, slid to a stop, and listened carefully over the pounding of his heart. A muffled cry came from his right, in the direction of the church.

He hurried for the back of Katie's Nails and Tan and leaned against the back wall to catch his breath. Laughter drifted over the wind. Lead by Steve's, Johnny thought.

A *smack* and a *grunt*.

Chills broke over Johnny's skull. He eased around the building, slipped under the steps that led to Katie's side entrance, and pried his eyes through the gaps that faced the street.

The mob stood on the church's front lawn and crowded the steps. They had Samuel on the concrete porch in front of the double oak doors. His body sagged between Claude and Chris, who held him by an arm.

Johnny could see his blond head roll to one side, but the people blocked his view of Samuel's body. A man Johnny thought might be Dr. Malone reached out and slapped the boy somewhere on his body.

Johnny withdrew and slumped to his haunches against the wall. Another *thud*, another *grunt*. He buried his head between his knees and began to sob quietly.

He could hear the sounds when his ears weren't covered by his arms. More thudding blows, more helpless cries, and then mostly garbled shouting and laughter. A dozen times Johnny wanted to run, almost did run. But he couldn't move.

The air grew quiet for a while. Maybe now they were letting him go.

Johnny poked his head around the corner and peered through the gap again. He could see Samuel now, from head to foot.

They held Samuel up against the solid oak doors, with his arms spread and his head lolling on his chest. Johnny watched in horror as Roland strolled up casually and slugged Samuel in the stomach with his fist. Samuel grunted, and the boy turned around.

Johnny's friend walked to the circle's edge and stood next to a woman who stared ahead, face whitewashed and barely recognizable, but there, within five paces of Samuel's sagging body. The woman was Johnny's mother. Every muscle in Johnny's body froze at the sight. He knelt under the steps, eyes wide, heart slamming madly, unable to move. His mind insisted that he had to get away.

Mom?

Wanna trip, baby?

Steve Smither stepped into the circle, gripping one of his sharp stakes low like a spear. A grin split his jaw and he braced himself.

The rest of the mob stood perfectly still, expressionless. The wind whipped their hair to the south.

Steve lowered his head and stared at Samuel. Johnny tried to pull away then—he really did. But his muscles . . .

Samuel's eyes suddenly opened, bright and blue, and he stared past the crowd, directly at Johnny.

Steve Smither lunged forward and shoved his stake at the boy's side, up under his rib cage into his chest.

It sounded like a plunger. Samuel gasped and raised to his toes, face white with shock. Blood poured from the wound, over Steve's fists, and to the ground.

Then the boy screamed.

But this time Samuel's scream was different. A blinding white light rushed from his mouth. Johnny watched in amazement as the shaft of light blazed over the heads of the gathered killers. It cut down the middle of the town, over the charred remains of the car that Claude had burned, and smashed into Smither's Saloon.

The building imploded in a ball of dust. But no sound.

Only Samuel's scream, which wasn't stopping.

The beam of light sliced to the right, leveling buildings in the same puff of dust as it touched them. Katie's Nails and Tan vanished. All Right Convenience was vaporized. The old Starlight Theater, already a black skeleton, turned to white powder and settled flat.

In a matter of ten seconds, the whole southern half of the town was leveled.

And then the scream fell silent, and the beam of light disappeared.

Johnny spun his head back to the church.

Samuel slumped over the stake and was still.

He's dead.

A ball of fire exploded in Johnny's head and shot through his nerves in one blinding flash. He slumped to his right side, and his mind went blank.

Chapter Forty-four

THE MONASTERY

Tuesday

BILLY JERKED upright. A pain flashed through his chest, and he lifted his pen from the page, surprised. Did it come from the *killing* of Samuel or the *death* of Samuel?

He reached down to the floor, scooped some worm salve in his palm, and slapped it on his chest.

Of course, the killing and the death were one and the same, weren't they? No, not really. That was the problem—they carried different meanings. Meanings that now began to flash in Billy's mind.

The killing. Yes, the killing came from his pen as it bit angrily into white paper, inflaming sick hearts. *What did you think you were doing, coming to my town, Samuel? You wanna see what happens to stuck-up kids who try to ruin my fun? Wanna see what it feels like to trip? Wanna die? Huh? I'll show you, you puke!*

The whole thing went down perfectly, like a carefully choreographed dance deserving of thundering applause and satisfaction.

But the satisfaction wasn't flowing. Not even dribbling.

Samuel is dead.

Yes, I killed him. Billy began to shake.

The killing had been one thing, but there was the death. And it felt like the death of writing.

Billy lifted his head and peered over the railing at the library below. Thirty-four children sat upright, pens suspended over paper, looking about as if they had just awakened from a long dream. Not a single one continued to write.

Billy's eyes swung to his right, where Darcy stared at him with wide eyes. *The story has ended. We have written the end.*

Then another thought blasted through his mind. Maybe they hadn't ended the story. Maybe not at all.

Maybe *Samuel* had ended the story.

CHAPTER FORTY-FIVE

PARADISE

Tuesday

A LOUD *clink* sounded in his head. Someone had taken a nail and hammer to his skull.

Clink, clink, clink.

Come on, boy, wake up!

Clink, clink, clink.

Try his forehead, Doctor. Clink on his forehead. See if that wakes him.

It slowly occurred to Johnny that the sound wasn't in his head. It was on the wind, like they were building a railroad through Paradise. Trains were coming to Paradise. Maybe they would bring some help. Some more cops to hang on the trees.

Or maybe it was coming from the church. Wasn't there something bad going on at the church?

Johnny opened his eyes and peered through a gap at the bottom of the steps. The town was half gone. Reduced to lumps of dust and ash. Claude and his gang stood where the old theater used to be and kicked dust. But he didn't care about them anymore.

He turned his head to look at the church. The crowd had left. Only Steve remained. He had backed up and was staring at his handiwork.

Samuel was there, stapled to the solid-oak church doors. They had driven two metal stakes through his shoulders and into the wood. Wide trails of blood had flowed down his sides, pooled on the floor at his feet, and run over the concrete steps.

Johnny rolled over, clambered to his feet, and lumbered toward the alley. He gripped the rear corner of the building and vomited.

I think they killed him. Yes, they most definitely killed him.

Johnny wiped his mouth with the back of his hand, turned into the alley, and staggered into the forest.

WANNA TRIP, baby?

He'd tripped, all right. He'd tripped real good.

It was the only thought that passed through Steve's mind as he stared at the boy's dead body on the church door. Something wasn't right about what had happened here, he figured that much, but it was all he figured.

Was he upset? No, not really. The kid had it coming. He had tried to ruin a good thing, and that wasn't part of the plan. Steve wasn't sure what the plan was really, but this kid wasn't in it. Or maybe this was the plan, killing this boy.

He stared at the bloody stake in his right hand. A wave of nausea swept over him. Then passed.

"Quite something, isn't it?"

Steve turned to the voice. Black stood with his hands on his hips, all dressed up in black without a spot of dirt on him. His blue eyes were fixed on the church doors where the boy hung.

"Yeah," Steve said.

Black looked into his eyes and flashed a tempting smile. "Makes you want to do it all over again."

Steve felt his head nod once. "Yeah." There was some truth to that. He might not want to do it again right away, but a faint hint of desire pulled at his heart.

"Yeah," he said again.

"I'm free, baby," Black said, looking back at the boy. "I do believe that I'm free."

"Yeah," Steve said. This time he had no idea what Black was talking about.

"Do you know what we've done here, Steve? Hmm? Do you know how far we've come in seven short days?"

Steve couldn't really remember that far back. He looked at the saloon that he used to own. That whole part of town was gone, but he didn't mind. He had his stakes, didn't he?

Another wave of nausea hit his gut, then passed.

"Well, I've got good news, buddy boy. It's just the beginning."

"It is?"

"Do you know what we have to do now?"

Steve tried to think of an answer but couldn't. "No."

"We have to kill the rest."

"Really?"

"Yes, really. Every one of them. Starting with Johnny. We'll have to find him first. He gave us the slip. But we will, and when we do, we'll do it again."

Steve just stared at him. He didn't know what to think about that. But then maybe he did. If Black said that's what they had to do, then that was what they had to do.

"Yeah," he finally said.

Black chuckled and winked. "That's my boy. Take a break. Celebrate."

"Umm . . . when are we?"

"When are we what? Say it."

"Killing."

"That's better," Black said. "Six hours. We'll start the killing in six hours." He lowered his arms, turned his back, and walked away.

He thrust an arm out toward the dead boy and spoke without looking back. "And get rid of that body. I don't want to see it again."

JOHNNY SAT on an outcropping of rocks just above Paradise and cried. Below him lay the remains of a town that only seven days ago had been his home. Now it was a graveyard.

He had never felt so desperate in his life. He either had to go to Delta or back to the monastery now. The monastery was closer, but with Samuel dead, he didn't know what waited up there. Billy might have killed them all. Delta was farther, and he would have to walk.

The fact that his mother was still down in Paradise prevented him from taking either option. He didn't know what to do, so he just hugged his legs to his chest and cried.

Then he lay down on his side, curled up in a ball, and tried to lose himself in a safe corner of his mind. If there was one left.

Chapter Forty-six

THE MONASTERY

Tuesday afternoon

RAUL HEARD the rap on his door. It sounded like a woodpecker searching for entrance to his skull. He looked up from the chair in which he'd collapsed, exhausted. According to the clock on the wall it was three in the afternoon.

Samuel's wails came back to him. Unless it had all been a nightmare. No . . . no, it had actually happened. The world had come to an end. At least Samuel's world had come to an end. And David had been sentenced to a life of regret.

"Yes, one moment, please." He stood and took a deep breath, straightening his shirt.

The books had failed. Which meant that the project had failed. And worse, much worse, Billy was still in the dungeons with the books at his fingertips. Somehow, no matter what the cost, the monks had to destroy the monastery and, if necessary, the children.

The overseers had met without David late morning and agreed. They would wait until morning, but then they would do whatever they could to wipe out what they'd created here.

The books were limited to the monastery and the children in the monastery. If they could destroy this place, they could remove the threat. That's where they would begin.

"Come."

The door opened and Andrew stood in the frame. "I'm sorry, Raul, but it's urgent. David insists we come immediately."

"David? Now?"

"Right away, in his study."

Andrew hurried away.

What could he possibly offer David now? No words would suffice; no gesture could comfort him in the wake of his son's death. In fact, their decision to destroy David's life work would surely make things worse.

Raul left his room and climbed the stairs, fighting off stark images that lingered. After the wails ceased, David lay on the stone slab overlooking Paradise for another hour, like a dead man. Twice Raul knelt over him to check his breathing. But David grunted him away.

Black clouds pressed low over the town below. The day was the darkest in Raul's memory, both physically and spiritually.

David finally pushed himself to his feet, looked about, dazed, and returned to the monastery.

Raul had followed him. David showed no further signs of remorse. He simply slogged his way up the mountain, up through the monastery, and to his chambers, where he closed the door.

And now David wished to see Andrew and him.

Raul followed Andrew into the study, closed the door, and faced David. Unlike David's bedroom, everything here was in perfect order, including David. Gone were the bedclothes. He wore his long stately black robe customary for formal visits. His hair was neatly groomed and the stubble had been shaved from his chin.

Had the man gone mad? Or was he simply suffering an utter denial of all that had just happened?

Andrew stood behind one of the guest chairs in front of David's desk.

"Good afternoon, sir." Raul dipped his head.

"Please, have a seat." He motioned to the chairs.

They sat.

David had withdrawn the first history book—the one he showed them three days earlier for the first time. Raul shifted his gaze from the book to David's eyes and found them locked on his.

"You're wondering if I've lost my mind. Perhaps I have. I lost my son Christopher. Then my wife. Now Samuel. I'm within my rights."

Raul glanced at Andrew.

"But I don't believe I have. I believe I have been drawn into the raw creative power of free will. I believe I have been tested and have proven myself worthy of that power."

"Samuel is dead," Raul said. It sounded crass, and he immediately regretted having said it. But it was also true.

"He is," David said. "And why is he dead? Because of the books. Because of the power behind the books. Because the evil in the children's minds was too strong for them to ignore and resist. But isn't that the course we expected of spoiled minds?"

"At some level," Andrew said. "But surely you didn't expect this. Even with the books, this was never the point."

"No, I didn't expect this. But I knew it was a possibility, even from the beginning."

"And yet you went through with it?"

"I didn't truly believe it could happen at first—"

"And when did you suspect?" Raul demanded, frustrated at David's dismissive tone.

The director put his hand on the book and stared at its cover. "I suspected several months ago, when Marsuvees Black found this book. I was nearly sure of it when Samuel insisted that he should go to Paradise."

"That was only yesterday," Andrew said. "Then why didn't you stop him from going?"

David struck the desk with an open palm. "Because it was the only way!"

He glared at Raul. "The project was failing! This reckless notion of mine to unleash the power of the books for good had gone amuck. You so eloquently pointed that out on a dozen occasions."

"Then why—"

"Do you have any idea what kind of monster we may have unleashed here?"

The man was confessing, Raul thought. He had insisted that only love would result, because no history could be written in the books unless it led ultimately to love. Now he would admit his mistake.

David took a calming breath. Beads of sweat rose on his forehead. "As you know, I had Samuel write a new rule into the books seven years ago limiting the book's power to only those in the monastery and reaffirming the requirement that they lead to the discovery of love."

"We know this," Andrew said.

"Assuming these rules you've written actually work," Raul said.

"I think the fact that this monastery exists, created by the books themselves, proves the books' power," David said. "I assume you don't dispute that much."

Raul couldn't. "No, not that much."

"Good. Then assume with me please, for my sake, that the rules do work. Assume that this will lead to the discovery of love. For me."

"Of course."

"Good. Then we believe that love will eventually win the day. But when? The fact of the matter is I saw no way to curb the amount of destruction the books would allow before love finally won the day."

"The rule you had Samuel write made the outcome certain, but not the path to that outcome," Andrew said.

"Exactly. I could foresee inadvertently unleashing terrible horrors on the world that might only turn to good far down the road. I couldn't risk that."

"Yet you did," Raul said.

David took a deep breath.

"You didn't? Then what . . ."

Chapter Forty-seven

PARADISE

Tuesday afternoon

THE AFTERNOON was dark. Darker than any Steve could remember. Then again, that could be his mind.

He walked out into the street and headed for the church. Black had said six hours. He didn't know if six hours had come and gone, but best he could figure, it was something like that.

He'd spent the hours making twelve new stakes. One for Katie, one for Yordon, one for Claude, and one for Paula maybe. Then the rest for some of the others, yet unnamed. He could hardly remember their names.

For Johnny he would use the same stake he'd used for the kid.

Maybe he could use all of these more than once.

He would need one for himself. Eventually it would come to that, wouldn't it? Sure, why not. Kill 'em all—that meant him too. Or maybe he could kill Black.

Not with a stake, he couldn't. Black ate stakes for breakfast.

Steve stopped beside the still-smoldering car in the middle of town. Speaking of his maker, where was Black? No sign of him anywhere he could see.

He'd pulled the boy's body off the church doors and hauled it outside of town limits, about a hundred yards west of the old theater. Dumped it in the dry creek bed there. He started to pile rocks on it, but gave up after a few minutes because his time would be better spent making those stakes.

Steve looked at the bloodstained stake in his hand. The red had dried to black. He looked around. Where was Black?

Chapter Forty-eight

THE MONASTERY

Tuesday afternoon

"I HAD Samuel write a *second* entry into the books," David said.

"Two entries? You made no mention—"

"You weren't ready for it. Now you are."

David turned the book on his desk and slid it toward them.

Raul and Andrew leaned forward. Samuel's familiar handwriting stared up at them. Raul scanned the entry at the top of the page. This was the one David had revealed earlier in the week, limiting the book's power to the children.

"I am as skeptical as both of you. I had to have my insurance."

There was a paragraph break, Raul saw. Then another sentence.

If a writer unleashes death on the path to love, the evil may be reversed by the display of a commensurate love fitting with the nature of these books. At that time, the writer who has unleashed death will no longer be able to write in these books. This rule is irrevocable.

Raul's head buzzed with the new revelation.

"Samuel *knew* this?"

"He was in my office, reading from this book just before announcing his intention to go to Paradise," David said. "He knew."

"You're saying that his death was . . ." Andrew sat back.

"There is no greater love than to lay down your life for a friend," David said. "It wasn't what I had in mind when I asked him to write it, but I now realize that what has happened is precisely within the nature of these books. Billy unleashed death, and Samuel gave his life willingly, my friends."

To think that Samuel had entered the town in full knowledge that his death might be the only way to turn the tide . . .

"Then the tide has been turned?" he asked, shifting forward in his chair. "And Billy's now powerless?"

"Billy should be." Tears moistened David's eyes now. He looked like he would burst out in tears all over again. But he fought back the emotion. "Has anything happened since Samuel's death?"

"Not that we know."

David frowned. "The story is over. Samuel ended it. I have nothing left but to trust the books given to us by God."

For the first time, Raul began to see through David's eyes. He'd sacrificed his own son for the sake of the town. For the children here. But there was something strange about David's demeanor. Regardless of any victory, David should be torn in two over his son's death.

With the thought came a question that lodged itself in Raul's mind and refused to go. How could any father this side of heaven give up his son, regardless of what good it might bring? What kind of man would do that?

"Forgive me, David, but you knew Samuel could die. How—"

"How could I send my son down to those butchers?" David's eyes flashed. He took a breath. "Because I am Samuel's only hope. His life rests in my hands."

"How can you say that? You *didn't* save him."

"The books could still bring him back."

"How? There's no one left to write in them. The books can no longer work for any of the children below, you said so yourself. The rule is irrevocable. The books are limited."

"To those in the monastery with the faith of a child," David said. "That doesn't mean only the children. If you or I were to have this kind of faith, then we could write in the books. Preventing Samuel from going would have completely undermined my own faith. I had to let him go to prove my own faith."

Raul stood abruptly. "It's why you had to let them kill him!" He saw the reasoning clearly. "It was the only way you could save both him *and* the other students!"

The hours of torment leading up to Samuel's death had new meaning now. David had known! He was in essence proving his faith in God by trusting the Word of the book. David had become Abraham, whose faith was tested by offering up his son, Isaac!

Only in this case, the son really had been killed.

Unless by proving his faith, David now had a power the children no longer had. The power to write in the books with power!

"Have you tried?" Raul demanded.

"No."

"What are you waiting for? Write!" He was forgetting his manners. "Forgive me, but you must write."

"I am waiting for the right moment. My whole world comes down to this moment, Raul. It can't be wasted in haste. Either I have been right, or I have been wrong. I'm not sure I want to face the moment of truth."

Raul pushed the history book toward David with a trembling hand. "The moment has arrived."

David stared at Andrew, then at Raul for a long moment. He winked. "So it has."

He hesitated a full ten seconds, then withdrew a quill from its receptacle and touched the tip to his tongue. "I believe, Raul, I really do. God help my unbelief."

He dipped the quill in a jar of ink and brought it to the page. For a while the pen hovered.

Then David withdrew it. What was he doing?

He sighed, and a tear fell from his cheek onto the page. "What if—"

"The books peer into the heart, David," Raul said. "You have given your heart in its entirety to this matter. It *will* work. If I had demonstrated even half the virtue that you have in these last days, I would rip the pen from your fingers and write it myself. Write!"

David nodded and gathered himself. He dipped the pen again for good measure, then lowered it to the page.

He wrote quickly. Several long sentences.

The scratching nearly drove Raul mad with anticipation. He couldn't see what David was writing and leaning closer for a look didn't seem appropriate, so he sat back down, lowered his head, and waited.

The sound stopped.

Raul looked up. David glanced at him, then blew on the page. He replaced the quill.

Closed the book.

David sat back, folded his hands, and stared at the book.

Raul wanted to ask him what he wrote, but this too seemed inappropriate.

But after watching David in silence for a full minute, he couldn't help himself.

"What did you write?"

David refused to remove his eyes from the book. His fingers trembled. "I wrote Samuel, my son, whom I love more than life itself, back to life."

Raul swallowed and exchanged a glance with Andrew. "What else?"

"I wrote the healing of Paradise and the full physical recovery of all our students."

Good. This was good. But there was more, he could see it in David's eyes. "And?"

"And then I wrote that all of the Books of History would vanish, never again to be found by any living soul. For any reason."

Raul's eyes fell to the book on the desk. There was no way to know if Samuel was walking around Paradise at this very moment. There was no way to know immediately if that the town would be healed of her wounds, or if the children would be restored.

But the books vanishing into hiding—such a vanishing would include this one.

It sat on the desk, a black lump of leather and paper, defiant.

Vanish! Be gone! Say to this mountain be thou removed and it shall be removed. Yet this small mountain either hadn't heard the teaching or wasn't listening. The book would not bow to David's will.

The plan had failed?

CHAPTER FORTY-NINE

PARADISE

Tuesday afternoon

THE SOUND of the man's boots crunching on the gravel from behind him was the first sign that Black had arrived.

Steve stifled a shiver of pleasure and fear and let Black come. He wanted to wait and not turn because he thought that showed some backbone, but his determination failed him. He turned.

Black strode with confidence, trench coat swirling around his polyester pants, hat pulled down low over his eyes. He wasn't looking at Steve, but at the far edge of town, in the direction of the dry creek where he'd dumped the kid.

Then he turned his head and glared at Steve with bloodshot eyes. "I told you to get *rid* of his body. Did I tell you to dump him on the edge of town for the first tourist to find? Did I tell you to roll a stone or two against him and call it good?"

Black stopped three feet from him, rolled his head so that his neck cracked, and then swung an open hand at Steve's face. His palm struck Steve's cheek with a loud smack that sent him reeling onto his rump. His head throbbed with pain.

"I . . . I . . ."

Black kicked his boot into Steve's gut. His whole body jerked off the ground, flew several feet, and landed hard.

He still had his stake in his right hand though.

"Stand up."

Steve struggled to his feet.

Black hit him again, this time with a fist to his left shoulder. It popped loudly and dangled at an odd angle, dislocated. Pain flared down Steve's arm. Why was Black doing this? Wasn't he his right-hand man?

"Do you think you'll still be able to kill without eyes, Steve?"

"My eyes?"

"I have a thing for eyes," Black said.

Chapter Fifty

THE MONASTERY

Tuesday afternoon

THE SECONDS passed, one by agonizing one. And with each tick, Raul felt his heart sink. Deeper and deeper. He could hardly imagine the despondency ravaging David's heart now.

Andrew looked on in silence.

David suddenly slammed both fists on the desk, one on either side of the book. It bounced slightly, then rested still. Lifeless.

David's jaw was fixed and his eyes glassy. He stood and strode toward the window, face flushed. He wore his failure on his entire body.

He stifled a sob, then brought his fist to his mouth to control any outburst.

Raul rose and approached David. For the second time in this day he wondered if he wouldn't prefer death to the pain of such great sorrow.

"You have to be patient—"

"I am finished being patient!" David cried, spinning. "I have nothing left to give. I would rather die now than live without my son!"

"You would fall on your sword rather than lead us—"

David's eyes went wide. "What did you do with it?"

"Your sword. A figure of speech—"

"Not the sword, the book!" He was staring over Raul's shoulder.

Raul whirled.

The book was gone!

He glanced at the floor, thinking it might have fallen. "I . . . I didn't touch it," he stammered.

"It's gone!" Andrew cried.

They stood like three schoolchildren, transfixed by the sight of the empty desk.

"It's gone," David said.

Raul ran to the desk. Placed his hand on the spot where the book had laid. "It's gone. The book is—"

The door swung open to Raul's left. There in the door frame stood a boy.

It was Billy.

He was covered in blood and sores, and the rotting gel of worms covered what was left of his flesh. He looked utterly lost.

The boy's arms hung limp, and in his right hand he held a pen.

Raul looked at the boy's face. Only then did he see that Billy was crying. Tears streamed down his cheeks.

His shoulders began to shake with sobs. The pen slipped from his fingers and fell to the floor.

Chapter Fifty-one

PARADISE

Tuesday afternoon

MARSUVEES BLACK cocked two fingers like a rattler's fangs and gripped Steve's dislocated shoulder with his other hand, ready to take his eyes.

Oddly enough, Steve didn't wince. He felt the pain in his shoulder all right. He thought he might pass out from it. He heard the crunching of his bones. But he saw the bright lights in Black's eyes and knew the man was finding fascination and pleasure in this violence, and for some reason that made it all okay.

"I don't need you, Steve, any more than I needed the monk. I can use Claude or Chris. I can use Paula."

Nausea again. This time it didn't pass. It welled up through his chest and stung his eyes. He was going to throw up.

But he didn't. The feeling was worse than the pain in his shoulder. Tears filled his eyes. For the first time since Black had come into town, Steve wanted to die.

"I'll kill them all," Steve said. "I swear, I'll . . ."

His ears began to ring. Black jerked his head up and looked at the sky. Steve followed his stare.

At first he couldn't see that anything had happened. Then he squinted and he saw it. The sun was out. And the black clouds were moving.

Boiling, rolling, flying up and back and away, as if a huge vacuum cleaner was sucking them into deep space. Behind it all was blue sky.

And a brilliant afternoon sun.

Black still had his hand on Steve's shoulder. He twisted his head toward the entrance to town. Nothing there. What was happening?

It was hot. Hazy hot. Midafternoon-on-a-hot-summer-day hot. And so bright.

But nothing else.

Black's face beaded with sweat. Steve followed his gaze again. Nothing but shimmering heat above the flattened buildings. What was happening?

And then Steve saw a distortion in the haze. Something was moving toward them, walking down the middle of Main Street in the distance. A small figure obscured by the heat.

The boy?

Black's hand began to tremble on his shoulder. His arm twitched. Two fingers still raised to strike.

As for Steve, the nausea had passed. Beyond that he didn't know what to feel.

The boy walked toward the edge of town, arms loose at his sides, small and frail, hardly more than an apparition distorted by heat waves. He didn't have a shirt on, and his skin was covered in dried blood, but he was definitely alive. And looking right at them.

Then the child entered Paradise, and the buildings began to rise from the dust.

JOHNNY JUMPED to his feet and stared at the clearing sky. Something was happening! He'd watched Black walk up to Steve and slap him around, but now both of them were still.

Something was happening; he could feel it in the air. Not just the clouds, not just the sun, not just the sudden heat. Something bigger.

He scrambled to the edge of the rocks and strained for a better view. Black still hadn't moved. For a while nothing moved.

And then the old theater began to move.

Johnny crouched, disbelieving what his eyes were seeing. The old theater was rising from the ground, rebuilding itself layer by layer, quicker than he could keep track of, like one of those demolitions he'd seen on the television, only in reverse.

And not just the old theater, but all the buildings around it. Paradise was being rebuilt from the ground up.

Johnny blinked, then blinked again. The Starlight Theater, Smither's Saloon, Claude's convenience store, Katie's Nails and Tan. Houses. How could . . .

He saw the boy then, walking down the middle of Main Street. A snapshot of Marsuvees Black walking into town the same way seven days earlier filled his mind for a second, and then was gone.

This wasn't Black.

This was Samuel!

Johnny tore down the mountain.

STEVE COULDN'T process what was happening around him at first. Things were going backward, rising and flying and moving at impossible angles.

The town was rising from the ashes.

And the small boy was walking straight toward them, right past the buildings as if they weren't rising from the ground miraculously. His eyes were fixed on Steve.

Black cursed once under his breath. He dropped his hand from Steve's shoulder and cursed again, a long string of hushed, vile words punctuated by spittle. His tirade ended midsentence, and in a fit of fury he slugged Steve in the gut, hard enough to break some ribs. Steve gasped and doubled over.

From the corner of his eyes Steve watched as Black grabbed his own coat, spun once, and vanished into the folds of cloth.

Black's clothing collapsed to the ground over his boots. His broad-brimmed hat bounced once, rolled to one side, and came to rest three feet from the pile of clothes.

Steve couldn't breathe. Where had Black gone? What was happening?

But he knew. This boy was happening.

When he managed to stand straight again, he saw two things: he saw that the town was the way it had been a week ago, before any of this had happened, except the leaves were still gone from the trees and sand still dusted the streets. And he saw that the boy had stopped ten feet from him and was staring up at him with soft, round eyes.

He felt dizzy. Hadn't he killed this boy? There was no hole in his side where Steve stuck the stake, but there was caked blood all over. Black had told him to kill the boy and he had done it, done it good.

Others came out of their houses and stared at the town in awe.

Was this a test? Was this how he could keep Black from taking his eyes? Should he take the stake in his hand and kill Samuel again? Maybe that's what Black wanted him to do.

"Look at me, Steve," the boy said.

JOHNNY SPRINTED past the old theater, which now stood in mint condition, or at least in as mint condition as it had been seven days ago, which was pretty tattered but mint, sweet mint, to Johnny.

He ran right into town, briefly glancing at several dozen people who were staring at Samuel and Steve. Claude and Chris stood with Peter and Roland, immobilized by the sudden change. Paula stood on her porch, eyes fixed on Johnny as he ran.

What did I tell you? Huh, what did I tell you?

His eyes searched for his mother. She was standing between their house and the next, watching Samuel.

What did I tell you! Now this, this is the truth. Black was from the pit of hell, but God has sent us a hero. A superhero.

Johnny slid to a stop to the left and behind Samuel.

"Look at me, Steve," Samuel said.

Samuel was naked except for his shorts and shoes. Blood had dried on his body. But Johnny had to hold himself back from throwing his arms around Samuel's chest.

Steve looked at Samuel. His eyes widened and his lips softened. Samuel was showing him love, and Steve wasn't quite sure what to do with it.

What did I tell you all? What did I say? Johnny felt like his chest would explode.

Samuel looked at Johnny. The boy didn't smile; he didn't say anything; he just winked. Then he turned his gaze back to Steve.

The man stood dazed. His hands and clothes were streaked with blood, and he smelled like he'd rolled in a pile of compost. But the glassy look in his eyes faded away, and his mouth opened in dumb wonderment.

"Grace and hope are dead without love, Steve," Samuel said. Just those words. Johnny felt a lump rise into his throat.

"Love, Steve. Do you want me to love you?"

Steve's face wrinkled under the words. He dropped the stake in his right hand. "Yes?" It was more a question than an answer, but that was evidently fine by Samuel.

The air brightened with a white light. A strobe had gone off. A strobe from Samuel.

Johnny gasped and stepped back. White light smothered Steve's face. He threw his hands wide and began to wail.

The light spread out from Samuel in a growing circle. It hit Father Yordon, who'd come out on the church steps. The man staggered under its power. It hit a man who stood under the trees by the church, and the man put a hand on a trunk to steady himself.

Johnny began to cry. He couldn't help it. He just began to shake with sobs.

I believe. I believe.

"You are loved, Steve," Samuel said.

"Oh, God!" Steve groaned. "Oh my God, what have I done?"

Johnny was going to burst. "I believe," he whispered.

"Louder, Johnny," Samuel said. "Say it louder."

Samuel was looking at Steve but speaking to Johnny. He felt unraveled, like a frayed hemp rope. Steve was trembling now, but so was Johnny.

"I believe," Johnny said as loud as his constricted throat would allow him. Then he screamed it at the top of his lungs. "I believe!"

The light hit him with a force that seared his mind, paralyzed his spine, and left him dazed and warm.

Johnny sat hard, dumbstruck. This was love.

Time seemed to slow. He might have been down for only a minute, lost to the world, but it felt like an hour.

The sound of sobbing pulled him back into Paradise. He lifted his head. Steve was on his knees, bawling like a baby. Samuel was holding his head, chin lifted to the sky. Tears streamed down his cheeks. His lips were moving, but Johnny couldn't make out the words.

The sound of wailing smothered him. From the corner of his eyes he saw Claude flat on his belly, shaking with sorrow. Paula was walking toward them, one hand outstretched, weeping.

Father Yordon lay in a ball on the church steps.

Johnny pushed himself to his feet and watched Samuel, straining to catch the boy's words. But he didn't need to strain because Samuel's words suddenly rang out clearly for all of them to hear.

"Father," he sobbed. He drew a breath. "Father, we have done it."

Chapter Fifty-two

THE MONASTERY

Thursday

THE BOOKS were gone. All of them.

Two days had passed since Samuel's death. One and a half days since he'd awakened in the creek bed and walked into Paradise. He'd told the story a hundred times. How he'd been beaten and killed and then left to rot. How his father had brought him back to life and healed Paradise.

"I still can't believe it all happened," Johnny said, staring down at Paradise from the ledge. "How did it feel?" Billy and Darcy looked at Samuel.

The four children had come together for the first time since the story ended. Like the rest of the children in the monastery, Billy and Darcy were healed almost immediately and were eager to renew their acquaintance with the boy who had resisted their writings.

"How did what feel, the dying or the living?" Samuel asked.

Johnny hesitated, unsure he wanted an answer. "Either," he said.

Samuel shuddered. "The dying . . . I'm not sure I can describe how terrible it felt. But I kept telling myself that my father could save me. I had to believe that."

Darcy stared out at the blue sky. She wasn't the same girl Johnny had met in the dungeons. The whole experience seemed to have knocked the wind out of her.

"If you don't mind, can we talk about something more uplifting?" Billy asked. "Considering it was Darcy and I who were responsible."

"Were you?" Samuel asked. "They didn't have to listen to you. Johnny didn't."

Billy shrugged. "And I didn't have to listen to Black. But I did."

Thinking of Billy as his brother was a mighty strange thing. Half brother, actually. Johnny and Billy had different fathers, but they had both been born to Sally, his mother, and that was weird. Samuel's father had taken Billy in as the thirty-seventh orphan when he learned that Stanley Yordon was forcing Sally to put him up for adoption.

In a strange way, Billy's writing had been an act of unwitting vengeance on the town that abandoned him. Maybe it was this wrongdoing that made them so receptive to Billy's writing. Maybe not.

"Where is Black?" Johnny asked.

"You mean the real Black? Dead," Billy said. "My Black killed him."

"In a week the other teachers will be gone too," Samuel said.

"Your father's abandoning the monastery?"

"Burying it. The books are gone, and without the books, there is no project."

"What will you do?"

"My father's going back to Harvard. Andrew and Raul are setting up an orphanage in New Jersey for any of the kids who want to stay with them. Some want to go back to their home countries. You guys decide yet?"

Billy and Darcy shook their heads. Johnny felt sorry for them. All they knew was up in that monastery, about to be buried.

"Maybe you could live with me and my father," Samuel said.

"Maybe."

They sat in silence for a few minutes.

"The thing I can't get out of my mind is Black," Billy said. "The one I wrote."

"Yeah, Black," Darcy agreed.

"Anyone really know what happened to him?"

Samuel pulled the stalk of grass he'd been nibbling on from his mouth. "Hopefully he vanished with the books."

"Hopefully?"

"That's the thing—my dad isn't sure about Black. The books are gone, the monastery is being buried, the town is back to normal, even the people down there are getting back to normal life, right, Johnny?"

"I wouldn't call it normal. They spend a lot of time in the church. Hardly anyone wants to talk about Black, if that's what you mean."

"He's gotta be gone."

"Even if he isn't," Billy said, "I was the one pulling his strings, right? So without the books, he's powerless."

"He had a book," Johnny said. "I saw it on the church podium once."

"A blank book?" Billy asked. "You sure?"

"Looked exactly like the ones you wrote in."

"But it must have disappeared too," Samuel said. "Had to have. Right?"

"Right," Darcy said.

"Then Black's history," Samuel said.

"Probably," Darcy said.

"Probably," Billy agreed.

"And we're not," Johnny said.

They all looked at him. A slow smile formed on Billy's mouth. "Yeah, I guess that's the whole point, isn't it. Black's history and we're not."

"Thanks to Samuel," Darcy said.

"Thanks to Samuel," Billy said.

"Thanks to Samuel," Johnny said.

And then no one said anything for a while.

An Excerpt from
Saint

I SEE DARKNESS. I'm laying spread eagle on my back, ankles and wrists tied tightly to the bedposts so that I can't pull them free.

A woman is crying beside me. I've been kidnapped . . .

My name is Carl.

But there's more that I know about myself, fragments that don't quite make sense. Pieces of a puzzle forced into place. I know that I'm a quarter inch shy of six feet tall and that my physical conditioning has been stretched to its limits. I have a son whom I love more than my own life and a wife named . . . named Kelly, of course, Kelly. How could I hesitate on that one? I'm unconscious or asleep, yes, but how could I ever misplace my wife's name?

I was born in New York and joined the army when I was eighteen. Special Forces at age twenty, Ranger at twenty-one, now twenty-five. My father left home when I was eight and I took care of three younger sisters —Eve, Ashley, Pearl—and my mother, Betty Strople, who was always very proud of me for being such a strong boy. When I was fourteen, I hit Brad Stenko over the head with a two-by-four and called the police when he slapped my mother. I remember his name because his proposal to marry my mother terrified me. I remember things like that. Events and facts cemented into place by pain.

My wife's name is Kelly. See I know that, I really do. And my son's name is Matthew. Matt. Matt and Kelly, right?

I'm a prisoner. A woman is crying beside me.

Carl snapped his eyes wide, stared into the white light above him, and immediately closed his eyes again.

Opening his eyes had been a mistake that could have alerted anyone watching to his awakening. He scrambled for orientation. In that brief moment, eyes wide to the ceiling, his peripheral vision had seen the plain room in which he was held captive. Smudged white walls. A single fluorescent fixture above, a dirty mattress under him.

And the crying woman, strapped down beside him.

Otherwise the room appeared empty. If there was any immediate danger, he hadn't see it. Then it was safe to open his eyes.

Carl opened his eyes again, quickly confirmed his estimation of the room, then glanced down at a thick red nylon string bound around each ankle and tied to two metal bedposts. Beside him, the woman was strapped down in similar manner.

He was dressed in black dungarees pushed up to his knees by whomever had tied them down. No shoes. The woman's left leg had been pulled over his and was strapped to the same post that held his right leg. Her legs had been cut and bruised and the string was tied tightly enough around her ankles to leave marks. She wore a pleated navy blue skirt, torn at the hem, and a white blouse that looked like it had been dragged through a field with her.

This was Kelly. He knew that, and he knew that he cared for Kelly deeply, but he was suddenly unsure why. He blinked, searching his memory for details but his memory remained fractured. Perhaps his captors had used drugs.

The woman whose name was Kelly faced the ceiling, eyes closed. Her tears left streaks down dirty cheeks and into short blonde hair. Small nose, high cheek bones, a bloody nose, and several scratches on her forehead.

I'm strapped to a bed next to a woman named Kelly who's been brutalized. My name is Carl and I should feel panic, but I feel nothing.

The woman suddenly caught her breath, jerked her head to face him, and stared into his soul with wide blue eyes.

In the space of one breath Carl's world changed. Like a boiling heat wave vented from a sauna, emotion swept over him. A terrible wave of empathy laced with a thread of bitterness he couldn't understand. What he did know was that he cared for the woman behind these blue eyes very much.

And then, as quickly as the feeling had come, it fell away.

"Carl . . ." Her face twisted with anguish. Fresh tears flooded her eyes and ran down her left cheek.

"Kelly?"

She began to speak in a frantic whisper. "We have to get out of here! They're going to kill us." Her eyes darted toward the door. "We have to do something before he comes back. He's going to kill . . ." Her voice choked on emotion.

Carl's mind refused to clear. He knew who she was, who he was, why he cared for her, but he couldn't readily access that knowledge. Worse, he didn't seem capable of actually feeling, not for more than a few seconds.

"Who . . . Who are you?"

She blinked, as if she wasn't sure she'd heard him right. "What did they do to you?"

He didn't know. They'd hurt him, he knew that, but he didn't know who *he* was much less who they were.

She spoke urgently through her tears. "I'm your wife! We were on the cruise, at port in Istanbul when they took us. Three days ago. They . . . I think they took Matthew. Don't tell me you can't remember!"

Details that he now remembered rehearsing in his mind before waking flooded him. He was with the army, Special Forces. His training was extensive and dark. They'd been taken by force from a market in Istanbul. Matthew was their son. Kelly was his wife.

Panicked, Carl jerked hard against the restraints. He was rewarded with a squealing metal bed frame, no more.

Another mistake, he thought. Whoever had the resources to kidnap them undoubtedly had the skill to use the right restraints. He was reacting impulsively rather than with calculation. Carl closed his eyes and calmed himself. *Focus, you have to focus.*

"They brought you in here unconscious half an hour ago and gave you a shot," she said hurriedly. "I think . . . I'm pretty sure they want you to kill someone." Her fingers touched the palm of his hand above their heads. Clasped his wrist. "I'm afraid, Carl. I'm so afraid." Crying again.

"Please, Kelly. Slow down."

"Slow down? I've been tied to this bed for three days! I thought you were dead! They took our son and you want me to slow down?"

The room faded and then came back into view. They stared at each other for a few silent seconds. There was something strange about her eyes. He was remembering scant details of their kidnapping, even fewer details of their life together, but her eyes were a window into a world that felt familiar and right.

They had Matthew. Rage began to swell, but he cut it off and was surprised to feel it leave as quickly as it had come. His training was kicking in. He'd been trained not to feel. So then his not feeling was a good thing.

"I need you to tell me what you know."

"I've told you. We were on a cruise—"

"No, everything. Who we are, how we were taken. What's happened since we arrived. Everything."

"What did they do to you?" she asked again.

"I'm okay. I just can't remember—"

"You're bleeding." Her eyes stared at the base of his head. "Your hair . . ."

He felt no pain, no wetness from blood on his neck or in his hair. He lifted his head and twisted it for a look at the mattress under his hair. A fist-sized red blotch stained the cover.

The pain came then, a deep throbbing ache from the base of his skull. He set his head back down and stared at the ceiling. With only a little effort he disconnected himself from the pain.

"Tell me what you remember."

She blinked, still breathing deliberately. "You had a month off from your post in Kuwait and we decided to take a cruise to celebrate our seventh anniversary. Matthew was buying some sugared ginger when a man grabbed him and went into an alley between the tents. You went after him. I saw someone hit you from behind with a metal pipe. Then a rag with some kind of chemical was pushed over my face and I passed out. Today's the first time I've seen you." She closed her eyes. "They tortured me, Carl."

Anger rose, but again he suppressed it. Not now. There would be time for healing later, if they survived.

His head seemed to be clearing from whatever drug they'd given him. More than likely they'd kept him drugged for days and whatever they'd put into his system half an hour ago was waking him up. That would explain his temporary memory loss.

"What nationality are they?"

"Hungarian, I think. The one named Dale is a sickening . . ." She stopped, but the look of hatred in her eyes spoke well enough.

Carl blocked scattered images of whatever Dale might have done to illicit such a reaction from her. Again, that he was able to do this so easily surprised him. Was he so insensitive to his own wife?

No, he was brutally efficient; for her sake he had to be.

Their captors had left their mouths free—if he could find a way to reach their restraints . . .

The door suddenly swung open. A man with short cropped blond hair stepped into the room. Medium height. Knifelike nose and chin. Fiercely eager blue eyes. Khaki cotton pants, black shirt, hairy arms. Dale.

He knew this man.

This was Dale Crompton. This was a man who'd spent some time in the dark spaces of Carl's mind, making himself hated. Kelly had said Hungarian, but she had been talking of someone else because Dale was the Englishman.

The man's right arm hung by his side, hand snug around an Eastern bloc Makarov 9 mm pistol. This detail was brightly lit in Carl's mind where other details remained stubbornly shrouded by darkness. He clearly knew his weapons.

Without any warning or fanfare, Dale rounded the foot of the bed, pressed the barrel of the Makarov against Kelly's left thigh, and pulled the trigger.

The gun bucked with a thunderclap. Kelly arched her back, screamed, and thrashed against her restraints for a moment, then dropped to the mattress in a dead faint.

Carl's mind passed the threshold of whatever training he'd received. His mind cried out for him to feel nothing, to lay uncaring, cold and calculating in the face of brutal manipulation, but his body had already begun its defense of his wife. He snarled and bolted up, oblivious to the pain in his wrists and ankles.

Naturally the movement proved useless. He might as well be a dog on a thick chain, jerked violently back at the end of a sprint for freedom.

He collapsed back on the bed, and gathered himself. Kelly lay still. A single glance told him that the bullet had expended its energy without passing through her leg, which meant it had struck the femur, probably shattering it.

"I hope I have your attention," Dale said. "Her leg will heal. A similar bullet to her head, on the other hand, will produce far more satisfying results. I'd love to kill her. And your son. What is his name, Matthew?"

Carl just stared at him. *Focus. Believe, you must believe in your ability to save them.*

"Pity to destroy such a beautiful woman," Dale said, walking to the window. "Just so you know, I argued to tie your son next to you and keep Kelly for other uses but Kalman overruled me. He says the boy will be useful if you fail us the first time."

The Englishman put the gun on the sill, unlatched the window, and pulled it up. A fresh breeze carried a lone bird's chirping into the room. *It's spring,* Carl thought. *I can smell fresh grass and spring flowers. I can smell fresh blood.*

The Englishman faced him. "A simple and quite lethal device has been surgically implanted at the base of your hypothalamus gland. This explains the bleeding at the back of your head. The device will release chemicals that will destroy your brain within ten seconds of being released, an event that will be triggered by any attempt to remove the device or by a remote signal. Your life is in our hands. Is this clear?"

The revelation struck Carl as perfectly natural. Exactly what he would have expected, knowing what he did, whatever that was.

"Yes."

"Good. Your mission is to kill a man and his wife currently housed in a heavily guarded hotel at the edge of the town directly to our south, three miles distance. Joseph and Mary Fabin will be in their room on the third floor. No one else is to be killed. Only the targets. You have two cartridges in the gun, I suggest you use them wisely. No head shots, we need their faces for television. Do you understand?"

A wave of dizziness swept through Carl. Aside from a slight tick in his right eye, he showed none of it. Beside him, Kelly moaned. How could he ignore his wife's suffering so easily?

Carl eyed the pistol on the sill. "I understand."

"You'll be watched closely. If you make any contact with the authorities, your wife will die. If you step outside the mission parameters I've outlined, she dies. If you haven't returned within sixty minutes, both she and your son will die. Do you understand?"

His mind screamed in protest. He spoke quickly to cover any fear in his eyes. "The name of the hotel?"

"The Andrassy," Dale said. He walked over to Carl, withdrew a knife from his waistband, and laid the sharp edge against the red nylon rope that tied Carl's right leg to the bed frame.

"I'm sure you would like to kill me," Dale said. "This is impossible, of course. But if you try, rest assured that you, your wife, and your son will be dead within the minute."

"Who are the targets?"

"They are the two people who can save your wife and son by dying within the hour." The man cut through the bonds around Carl's other ankle and then casually went to work on the rope at his wrists. "You'll find some shoes and clean clothes outside the window." With a faint pop the last tie yielded to the Englishman's blade.

Kelly whimpered and Carl looked over to see that her eyes were open again. Face white, muted by horror.

For a long moment, lying there freed beside the woman he loved, Carl allowed a terrible fury to roll through his mind. Despite Dale's casual dismissal of him, he knew that he stood at least an even chance of killing him.

A terrible set of emotions collided in his chest. He wanted to touch Kelly and tell her that she would be okay. That he would save her and their son. He wanted to tear the heart out of the man who was now watching them with a disconnected stare, like a robot assigned to a simple task.

He wanted scream. He wanted to cry. He wanted to kill himself.

Instead, he lay still.

Kelly closed her eyes and started to sob softly. He wished she would stop. He wanted to shout at her and demand that she stop this awful display of emotion. Didn't she know that emotion was now their greatest enemy?

"Fifty-eight minutes," Dale said. "It's quite a long run."

Carl slid his feet off the bed, stood, and walked to the window, thinking that he was a monster for being so callous in her moment of horror, never mind that it was for her sake that he steeled himself.

I'm in a nightmare, he thought, reaching for the gun. But the Makarov's cold steel handle felt nothing like a dream. It felt like salvation.

"Carl?"

Kelly's voice shattered any reprieve the gun brought him. Carl was sure that he would spin where he stood, shoot Dale through the forehead, and take his chances with the implant or whatever other means they had of killing him and his family. The only way he knew to deal with such a compelling urge was to shut off his emotions entirely. He clenched his jaw and shoved the gun into his waistband.

"I love you, Carl."

He looked at her, forcing emerging terror back. "It'll be okay," he said. "I'll be back."

He grabbed both sides of the window, thrust his head out to scan the grounds, withdrew, shoved his right leg through the opening, and rolled onto the grass outside. When he came to his feet he was facing south. How did he know this was south? He just did.

He would go south and he would kill.

From the minds of multi-million selling suspense authors Frank Peretti and Ted Dekker comes *House*—an epic supernatural thriller that gives new meaning to the phrase "haunted house."

ALSO AVAILABLE FROM TED DEKKER

THE CIRCLE TRILOGY

Discover more at TedDekker.com

Also Available from Ted Dekker

The Blessed Child Series

Discover more at TedDekker.com